Stud

I

In the opening days of the Great War, on the battlefields of Apres and Ives, I acquired the ability to abandon slumber with the flutter of an eyelid. It was a necessary adaptation, as heavy sleepers were likely to come to greeted by a Dren commando with a trench blade. It's a vestige of my past I'd rather lose, all things considered. Rare is the situation that requires the full range of one's perceptions, and in general the world is improved by being only dimly visible.

Case in point – my room was the sort of place best viewed half asleep or in a drunken stupor. Late autumn light filtered through my dusty window and made the interior, already only a few small steps from squalor, look still less prepossessing. Even by my standards the place was a dump, and my standards are low. A worn dresser and a chipped table set were the only furnishings that accompanied the bed, and a veneer of grime covered the floor and walls. I passed water in the bedpan and threw the waste into the alley below.

Low Town was in full stream, the streets echoing with the screech of fish hags advertising the day's catch to porters carrying crates north into the Old City. At the market a few blocks east merchants sold underweight goods to middlemen for clipped copper, while down Light Street guttersnipes kept drawn-dagger eyes out for an unwary vendor or a blue-blood too far from home. In the corners and the alleys the working boys kept up the same cries as the fish hags, though they spoke lower and charged more. Worn streetwalkers pulling the early shift waved tepid come-ons at passersby, hoping to pad their faded charms into one more day's worth of liquor or choke. The dangerous men were mostly still asleep, their blades sheathed next to the bed. The really dangerous men had been up for hours, and their quills and ledgers were getting hard use.

I grabbed a hand mirror off the floor and held it at arm's length. Under the best of circumstances, perfumed and manicured, I am an ugly man. A lumpen nose dripped below overlarge eyes, a mouth like a knife wound set off-center. Enhancing my natural charms are an accumulation of scars that would shame a masochist, an off-color line running up my cheek from where an artillery shard had come a few inches from laying me out, the torn flesh of my left ear testifying to a street brawl where I'd taken second place.

A vial of pixie's breath winked good morning from the worn wood of my table. I uncorked it and took a whiff. Cloyingly sweet vapors filled my nostrils, followed closely by a familiar buzzing in my ears. I shook the bottle – half empty, it had gone quick. I pulled on my shirt and boots, then grabbed my satchel from beneath the bed and walked downstairs to greet the late morn.

The Staggering Earl was quiet this time of day, and absent a crowd the main room was dominated by the mammoth figure behind the bar, Adolphus the Grand, co-owner and publican. Despite his height – he was a full head taller than my own six feet – his cask-like torso was so wide as to give the impression of corpulence, though a closer examination would reveal the balance of his bulk as muscle. Adolphus had been an ugly man before a

Dren bolt claimed his left eye, but the black cloth he wore across the socket and the scar that tore down his pockmarked cheek hadn't improved things. Between that and his slow stare he seemed a thug and a dullard, and though he was neither of those things this impression tended to keep folk civil in his presence.

He was cleaning the bar and pontificating on the injustices of the day to one of our more sober patrons. It was a popular pastime. I sidled over and took the cleanest seat.

Adolphus was too dedicated to solving the problems of the nation to allow common courtesy to intrude on his monologue, so by way of greeting he offered me a perfunctory nod. 'And no doubt you'd agree with me, having seen what a failure his lordship has been as High Chancellor. Let him go back to stringing up rebels as Executor of the Throne's Justice – at least that was a task he was fit for.'

'I'm not really sure what you're talking about, Adolphus. Everyone knows our leaders are as wise as they are honest. Now is it too late for a plate of eggs?'

He turned his head towards the kitchen and growled, 'Woman! Eggs!' Aside completed, he circled back towards his captive drunk.

'Five years I gave the Crown, five years and my eye.' Adolphus liked to slip his injury into casual conversation, apparently operating under the impression that it was inconspicuous. 'Five years neck deep in shit and filth, five years while the bankers and nobles back home got rich on my blood. A half ochre a month ain't much for five years of that, but it's mine and I'll be damned if I let 'em forget it.' He dropped his rag on the counter and pointed a sausage-sized finger at me in hopes of encouragement. 'It's your half ochre too, my friend. You're awfully quiet for a man forgotten by Queen and country.'

What was there to say? The High Chancellor would do what he wished, and the rantings of a one-eyed ex-pikeman were unlikely to do much to persuade him. I grunted noncommittally. Adeline, as quiet and small as her husband was the opposite, came out of the kitchen and offered me a plate with a tiny smile. I took the first and returned the second. Adolphus kept up his rambling but I ignored him and turned to the eggs. We'd been friends for a decade and a half because I forgave him his garrulousness and he forgave me my taciturnity.

The breath was kicking in. I could feel my nerves getting steadier, my eyesight sharper. I shoveled the baked black bread into my mouth and considered the day's work. I needed to visit my man in the customs office – he'd promised me clean passes a fortnight past but had yet to make good. Beyond that there were the usual rounds to the distributors who bought from me, shady bartenders and small-time dealers, pimps and pushers. Come evening I needed to stop by a party up towards Kor's Heights – I had told Yancey the Rhymer I'd check in before his evening set.

Back on the main stage the drunk found a chance to interrupt Adolphus's torrent of quasi-coherent civic slander. 'You hear anything about the little one?'

The giant and I exchanged unhappy glances. 'The hoax are useless,' Adolphus said, and went back to cleaning. Three days earlier the child of a dock worker had gone missing from an alley outside her house. Since then 'Little Tara' had become something of a cause célèbre for the people of Low Town. The fishermen's guild had put out a reward, the Church of Prachetas had offered a service in her honor, even the guard had set aside their lethargy for a few hours to bang on doors and look down wells. Nothing had been found, and seventy-two hours was a long time for a child to stay lost in the most crowded square mile in the Empire. Śakra willing, the girl was fine, but I wouldn't bet my unpaid half ochre on it.

The reminder of the child provoked the minor miracle of shutting Adolphus's mouth. I finished my breakfast in silence, then pushed my plate aside and rose to my feet. 'Hold any messages – I'll be back after dark.'

Adolphus waved me out.

I exited into the chaos of Low Town at midday and began my walk east towards the docks. Leaning against the wall a block past the Earl, rolling a cigarette and glowering, I spotted all five and a half feet of Kid Mac, pimp and bravo extraordinaire. His dark eyes stared out over faded dueling scars, and as always his clothes were uniformly perfect, from the wide brim of his hat to the silver handle of his rapier. He strung himself up against the bricks with an expression that combined the threat of violence with a rather profound indolence.

In the years since he had come to the neighborhood, Mac had managed to carve out a small territory by virtue of his skill with a blade and the unreserved dedication of his whores, who to a woman were as enamored of him as a mother is her firstborn. I often thought that Mac had the easiest job in Low Town, seeming to consist mostly of ensuring that his streetwalkers didn't kill each other in competition for his attentions, but you wouldn't know it from the scowl etched across his face. We'd been friendly ever since he'd set up shop, passing each other information and the occasional favor.

'Mac.'

'Warden.' He offered me his cigarette.

I lit it with a match from my belt. 'How're the girls?'

He shook some tobacco from his pouch and started on another smoke. 'That lost child has them worked up worse than a clutch of hens. Red Annie kept everyone up half the night weeping, till Euphemia went after her with a switch.'

'They're a sensitive bunch.' I reached into my purse and surreptitiously handed him his shipment. 'Any word on Eddie the Quim?' I asked, referring to a rival of his who had been chased out of Low Town earlier in the week.

'He works a stone's throw from headquarters and doesn't think he needs to pay off the hoax? Eddie's too stupid to live. He won't see the other side of winter – I'd go an argent on it.' Mac finished rolling his cigarette with one hand and slipped the package into his back pocket with the other.

'I wouldn't take it,' I said.

Mac tucked the tab loosely into his sneer. We watched the ebb of traffic from our post. 'You get those passes yet?' he asked.

'Going to see my man today. Should have something for you soon.'

He grunted what might have been assent and I turned to leave.

'You oughta know that Harelip's boys have been peddling east of the canal.' He took a drag and exhaled perfect circles of smoke, one following the other into the clement sky. 'The girls have seen his crew off and on for the last week or so.'

'I heard. Stay slick, Mac.'

He went back to looking menacing.

I spent the rest of the afternoon dropping off product and running errands. My customs officer finally came through with the passes, though at the rate his addiction to pixie's breath was progressing, it might well be the last favor he'd be able to do for me.

It was early evening by the time I was finished, and I stopped off at my favorite street stand for a pot of beef in chili sauce. I still needed to see Yancey before his set – he was performing for some toffee-nosed aristocrats near the Old City, and it would be a walk. I was cutting through an alleyway to save time when I saw something that clipped my progress so abruptly that I nearly toppled over.

The Rhymer would have to wait. Ahead of me was the body of a child, contorted horribly and wrapped in a sheet soaked through with blood.

It seemed I had found Little Tara.

I tossed my dinner into a sewer grate. Suddenly I didn't have much of an appetite.

2

I burned a few seconds taking stock of the situation. The rats of Low Town are an immodest bunch, so the fact that her body was intact suggested that she hadn't been left out long. I crouched down and set a palm on her tiny chest – cold. She'd been dead for some time before being dumped here. Up close I could see the indignities her tormentor had inflicted more clearly, and I shuddered and withdrew, noticing as I did so a strange smell, not the sickly sweet scent of decayed flesh but one abrasive and alchemical, harsh against the back of my throat.

Retreating from the alley to the main street, I flagged down a pair of street urchins idling beneath an awning nearby. Among the lower classes my name carries some small weight, and they presented themselves as if they expected me to draft them into a scheme of some kind, and were excited at the opportunity. I gave the duller-looking of the two a copper and told him to find a guardsman. When he was around the corner I turned to the one who remained.

I keep half the Low Town guard in whores and watered-down beer, so they wouldn't be a problem. But a murder of this sort would demand the attention of an agent, and whomever they sent might be foolish enough to think me a suspect. I needed to get rid of my merchandise.

The boy stared up at me with brown eyes deep-set against pale skin. Like most street children he was a mutt, features of the three Rigun peoples intermixed with any number of foreign races. Even by the standards of the dispossessed he was painfully thin, the rags he wore as clothing insufficient to hide the bony protrusions of his shoulder blades and elbows.

'You know who I am?'

'You're the Warden.'

'You know the Staggering Earl?'

He nodded, his dark eyes wide but unclouded. I thrust my bag towards him.

'Take this there and give it to the cyclops behind the bar. Tell him I said he owes you an argent.'

He reached for it and I dug my fingers in the crook of his neck. 'I know every whore, pickpocket, junkie and street tough in Low Town, and I've marked your face. If my package ain't waiting for me I'm going to come looking for you. Understand?' I tightened my grip.

He didn't flinch. 'I ain't bent.' His voice surprised me with its cool confidence. I had picked the right urchin.

'Off with you then.' I released the bag and he sprinted around the corner.

I went back into the alley and smoked a cigarette while I waited for the hoax to show up. They were longer than I thought they'd be, given the gravity of the situation. It's disturbing to discover your low opinion of law enforcement is still unduly appreciative. Two burned tabs later the first boy returned, a pair of guardsmen in tow.

I knew them vaguely. One was fresh, new to the force six months, but the second I'd been paying off for years. We'd see how much good that would do if things curdled. 'Hello, Wendell.'

I held out my hand. 'Good to see you again, even under these circumstances.'

Wendell shook it vigorously. 'You as well,' he said. 'I had hoped the boy was lying.'

There wasn't much to say to that. Wendell knelt beside the body, his chain coat dragging in the mud. Behind him his younger counterpart was turning the shade of white that prefaces vomiting. Wendell shouted a reproach over his shoulder. 'None of that. You're a damn guardsman – show some spine.' He turned back to the corpse, unsure of his next move. 'Guess I should call for an agent then,' he half asked me.

'Guess so.'

'Run back to headquarters,' Wendell ordered his subordinate, 'and tell them to send for a chill. Tell them to send for two.'

The guard enforce the customs and laws of the city – when they aren't paid to look the other way – but investigating crime is more or less beyond them. If a murderer isn't standing over the corpse with a bloody knife they're not of much use. When there's a crime that matters to someone who counts, an Agent of the Crown is sent, officially deputized to carry out the Throne's Justice. The frost, the cold, the snowmen or the gray devils, call them what you want but bow your head when they pass and answer prompt if they ask you something, 'cause the chill ain't the guard, and the only thing more dangerous than an incompetent constabulary is a competent one. Normally, a dumped body in Low Town doesn't warrant their attention – a fact that does wonders for the murder rate – but this wasn't a drunk drowned in a puddle, or a knifed junkie. They'd send an agent for this.

After a few minutes, a small squad of guardsmen arrived on the scene. A pair of them began cordoning off the area. The remainder stood around looking important. They weren't doing a great job of it, but I didn't have the heart to tell them.

Bored of waiting, or wanting to impress his importance upon the newcomers, Wendell decided to take a stab at police work. 'Probably some heretic,' he said, scratching at his double chins.

9

'Passing through the docks on the way to Kirentown, saw the girl and . . .' He gestured sharply.

'Yeah, I hear there's a lot of that going around.'

His partner chimed in, baby face spouting poison, choked-back bile heavy on his breath. 'Or an Islander. You know how they are.'

Wendell nodded sagely. He did indeed know how they were.

I'd heard that in some of the newer mental wards they set the mad and congenitally stupid to rote tasks, having them sew buttons onto mounds of fabric, the futile labor working as a salve to their broken minds. I wonder sometimes whether the guard is not an extension of this therapy on a far grander scale, an elaborate social program meant to give the low-functioning an illusion of purpose.

But it wouldn't do to spoil it for the inmates. This burst of insight seemed to exhaust Wendell and his second, and they lapsed into silence.

The autumn eve chased the last shreds of daylight across the skyline. The sounds of honest commerce, as much as such a thing exists in Low Town, were replaced with a jittery quiet. In the surrounding tenements someone had a fire going, and the wood smoke almost covered up the state of the body. I rolled a cigarette to block out the rest.

You could sense their arrival before you could see them, the packed Low Town masses scuttling out from their path like flotsam brushed aside by a flood. A few seconds more and you made them out apart from the movement of the crowd. The freeze prided themselves on the uniformity of their costumes, each an interchangeable member of the small army that controlled the city and most of the nation. An ice-gray duster, its upturned collar leading to a matching wide-brimmed hat. A silver-hilted short sword hanging at the belt, both an aesthetic marvel and a perfect instrument of violence. A dusky jewel trapped in a silver frame dangling from the throat – the Crown's Eye, official symbol of their authority. Every inch the personification of order, a clenched fist in a velvet glove.

For all that I would never speak it aloud, for all that it shamed me even to think it, I couldn't lie – I missed that fucking outfit.

Crispin recognized me from about a block away, and his face hardened but his step didn't slow. Five years hadn't done much to alter his appearance. The same highborn face stared at me beneath the fold of his hat, the same upright carriage bore mute witness to a youth spent in the tutelage of dance masters and teachers of etiquette. His brown hair had retreated from its former prominence, but the curve of his nose still trumpeted the long history of his blood to anyone who cared to look. I knew he regretted me being here, just as I regretted him being called.

The other one I didn't recognize – he must have been new. Like Crispin he had the Rouender nose, long and arrogant, but his hair was so blond as to be nearly white. Apart from the platinum mane he seemed the archetypal agent, his blue eyes inquisitorial without being discerning, the body beneath his uniform hard enough to convince you of his menace, assuming you didn't know what to look for.

They stopped at the entrance to the alleyway. Crispin's gaze darted across the scene, resting briefly on the covered corpse before settling on Wendell, who stood stiffly at attention, doing his best impression of a law enforcement official. 'Guardsman,' Crispin said, nodding sharply. The second agent, still unnamed, offered not even that, his arms firmly crossed and something like a smirk on his face. Sufficient attention paid to protocol, Crispin turned towards me. 'You found her?'

'Forty minutes ago, but she'd been here a while before that. She was dumped here after he finished with her.'

Crispin paced a slow circle around the scene. A wooden door led into an abandoned building halfway down the alley. He paused and put his hand against it. 'You think he came through here?'

'Not necessarily. The body was small enough to be concealed – a small crate, maybe an empty cask of ale. At dusk, this street doesn't get much traffic. You could dump it and keep walking.'

'Syndicate business?'

'You know better than that. An unblemished child goes for

five hundred ochre in the pens of Bukhirra. No slaver would be foolish enough to ruin their profit, and if they were they'd know a better way to dispose of the corpse.'

This was too much deference shown to a stranger in a tattered coat for Crispin's second. He sauntered over, flushed with the arrogance that comes from having one's hereditary sense of superiority cemented by the acquisition of public office. 'Who is this man? What was he doing when he found the body?' He sneered at me. I had to admit he knew how to sneer. For all its ubiquity it isn't an expression that just anyone can master.

But I didn't respond to it, and he turned to Wendell. 'Where are his effects? What was the result of your search?'

'Well, sir,' Wendell started, his Low Town accent thickening. 'Seeing as how he called in the body, we figured . . . that's to say . . .' He wiped his nose with the back of his fat hand and coughed out a response. 'He hasn't been searched, sir.'

'Is this what passes for an investigation among the guard? A suspect is found standing beside a murdered child and you converse cordially with him over the corpse? Do your job and search this man!'

Wendell's dull face blushed. He shrugged apologetically and moved to pat me down.

'That won't be necessary, Agent Guiscard,' Crispin interrupted. 'This man is . . . an old associate. He is above suspicion.'

'Only in this matter I assure you. Agent Guiscard, is it? By all means, Agent Guiscard, search me. You can never be too careful. Who's to say I didn't kidnap the child, rape and torture her, dump her body, wait an hour, then call the guard?' Guiscard's face turned a dull shade of red, a strange contrast to his hair. 'Quite a prodigy, aren't we? I guess that set of smarts came standard with your pedigree.' Guiscard balled his fist. I swelled out my grin.

Crispin cut between the two of us and began barking orders. 'None of that. There's work to be done. Agent Guiscard, return to Black House and tell them to send a scryer; if you double-step it there might still be time for him to pick up something. The rest of you set up a perimeter. There's going to be half a hundred citizens here in ten minutes and I don't want them mucking up the crime scene. And for the love of Śakra, one of you find this poor child's parents.'

Guiscard glared at me ineffectually, then stomped off. I shook some leaf out of my pouch and started to roll a smoke. 'New partner's quite a handful. Whose nephew is he?'

Crispin gave a half-smile. 'The Earl of Grenwick's.'

'Good to see nothing's changed.'

'He's not as bad as he looks. You were pushing him.'

'He was easy to push.'

'So were you, once.'

He was probably right about that. Age had mellowed me, or at least I liked to think so. I offered the cigarette to my ex-partner.

'I quit – it was ruining my wind.'

I wedged it between my lips. The years of friendship stretched out awkwardly between us.

'If you discover something, you'll come to me. You won't do anything yourself,' Crispin said, somewhere between an inquiry and a demand.

'I don't solve crimes, Crispin, because I'm not an agent.' I struck a match against the wall and lit my smoke. 'You made sure of that.'

'You made sure of that. I just watched while you fell.'

This had gone on too long. 'There was an odor on the corpse. It might be gone by now but it's worth checking.' I couldn't bring myself to wish him luck.

A crowd of onlookers was forming as I left the cover of the alleyway, the specter of human misery always a popular draw. The wind had picked up. I pulled my coat tight and hurried my steps.

3

Back at the Staggering Earl the weekend trade was in full swing. Adolphus's greeting echoed off the walls as I fought my way through the tight ranks of patrons and took a seat at the bar. He poured a glass of beer and leaned in as he handed it to me. 'The boy arrived with your package. I put it in your room.'

Somehow I had expected the urchin would come through.

Adolphus stood there awkwardly, a look of concern on his mangled face. 'He told me what you found.'

I took a sip of my drink.

'If you want to talk . . .'

'I don't.'

The ale was thick and dark, and I made my way through a half-dozen drafts trying to get the sight of twisted hands and pale, bruised skin out of my head. The crowd surged around me, factory workers finished with their shifts and bravados planning the night's escapades. We were doing the kind of business that reminded me why I was part-owner, but the mass of amiable lowlifes imbibing cheap liquor was poor company for my mood.

I drained my cup and stood up from the counter.

Adolphus waved away a customer and came over. 'You leaving?'

I grunted assent. The look on my face must have betokened violence, because he put one huge paw on my arm as I turned away.

'You need a blade? Or company?'

I shook my head, and he shrugged and returned to chatting up patrons.

I had been saving a visit to Tancred the Harelip since I saw one of his runners moving dreamvine on my territory a half-month prior. Tancred was a small-time operator who had managed to claw his way to minor prominence by an unsavory combination of cheap violence and low cunning, but he wouldn't be able to hold on to it for more than a few seasons. He'd underpay his boys, or try to cheat the guard out of their percentage, or piss off a syndicate and die in an alley with a poniard in his vitals. I hadn't ever seen any great need to hasten his appointment with She Who Waits Behind All Things, but mistakes don't get made in our business. Selling on my territory was sending me a message, and etiquette demanded a response.

Harelip had carved a thin slice of turf west of the canal, near Offbend, and he ran his operations from a dump of a bar called the Bleeding Virgin. He made most of his money from the trades that were too small or ugly for the syndicate boys to touch, moving wyrm and bleeding protection money out of whatever neighboring merchants were pitiful enough to pay. It was a long walk to his shit establishment, but it would give me time to clear my head from the booze. I went upstairs to retrieve a bottle of pixie's breath and started over.

The west end of Low Town was quiet, the merchants gone home and the nightlife pressed south towards the docks, so I walked the dozen blocks to the canal in relative solitude. This late in the evening the Herm Bridge looked ominous instead of just dilapidated, its marble features made indistinct by time and petty vandalism. The ragged hands of stone Daevas curled in supplication to the heavens, their faces worn to wide eyes and gaping mouths. Beneath it the River Andel ran sluggish and slow, carrying the city's waste in a stately procession towards the harbor and out to sea. I continued on, stopping at the entrance of a nondescript building a half-mile west.

Noise from the second floor drifted down to the shadows beneath. I took a hit of breath, then another and another until the bottle was empty and the buzzing was like a crowd of bees swarming around my ears. I dashed it against the wall and took the steps two at a time.

The Bleeding Virgin was the kind of dive that made you want to scrub your skin with lye as soon as you walked out – it made the atmosphere at the Earl look like high tea at the royal court. Torches shed greasy light on the unpalatable interior, a crumbling wooden infrastructure set over a handful of rooms that Harelip rented by the hour, along with a stable of sad-looking whores. These last doubled as servers, the dim illumination sufficient to display a lengthy commitment to their vocation.

I grabbed a spot across from a breach in the wall which served duty as a window and waved down one of the waitresses. 'You know who I am?' I asked. She nodded, dun hair atop a stretched face, crooked eyes dull and unfazed. 'Get me something that hasn't been spit in and tell your boss I'm here.' I flipped her a copper and watched her walk off wearily.

The breath was kicking in hard and I held my fists tight at my sides to keep them from shaking. I glared at the patrons warily and thought about how far one well-placed act of arson would go towards improving the neighborhood.

The server returned a few minutes later with a half-full tankard. 'He'll be out soon,' she said.

The beer was mostly rainwater. I choked it down and tried not to think about the child.

The back door opened and Harelip and two of his boys slid in. Tancred was aptly named – the crevice in his face split his mouth straight through, an aberration which his thick beard did nothing to hide. Beyond that there was little to recommend him one way or the other. Somewhere along the line he had acquired a reputation for being a hard man, though I suspected this was an outgrowth of his deformity.

The two hangers-on looked violent and stupid – the kind of cheap street toughs Tancred liked to keep around. I knew the first – Spider, a squat half-Islander runt with a lazy eye he'd picked up from getting rambunctious around a troop of guardsmen. He used to run with a small-time crew of river rats, busting into cargo barges late at night and making off with whatever they could find. I'd never seen the second, but his pockmarked face and sour odor bespoke ill-breeding as surely as his surroundings and choice of career. I assumed they were both armed, although only Spider's weapon was visible, an ugly-looking dirk that jutted obtrusively from his belt.

They fanned out to cover me. 'Hello, Tancred.' I said. 'What's the good word?'

He sneered at me, or maybe he didn't – the lip made it tough to tell.

'I hear your people have been having trouble with their lode-stones,' I continued.

Now I was pretty confident he was sneering. 'Trouble, Warden? How do you mean?'

'The canal is the line between our two enterprises, Tancred. You know the canal. It's that big ditch to the east of here, filled with water.'

He smiled, the fleshless stretch between his upper lip and nose rendering his rotting gums starkly visible. 'Was that the line?'

'In our business, Tancred, it's important to remember your agreements. If you're having trouble it might be time to look for work more in keeping with your natural talents. You'd make a lovely chorus girl.'

'You've got a sharp mouth,' he growled.

'And you've got a crooked one, but we are as the Creator

formed us. Regardless, I'm not here to debate theology – geography is the interest of the moment. So why don't you go ahead and remind me where our boundary is?'

Harelip took a step backwards, and his boys moved closer. 'Seems to me it might be time to redraw our map. I don't know what you've got going with the syndicates, and I don't care how friendly you are with the guard – you don't have the muscle to hold the land you got. Far as I can tell you're an independent operator, and there ain't no place for an independent operator these days.'

He kept nerving himself into the conflict that was coming, but I could barely hear him through the drone in my ears. Not that the particulars of his monologue much mattered. I hadn't come over here for discussion, and he hadn't rolled out his mob to help him negotiate.

The ringing faded as Tancred completed whatever ultimatum he was making. Spider rested a hand on his weapon. The unnamed thug flicked his tongue off a toothy grin. Somehow they had fallen under the impression that this was going to go easy – I was looking forward to disabusing them.

I finished my last swallow of ale and dropped the tankard with my left hand. Spider watched it shatter on the ground and I lashed out with my fist, breaking his nose back into his face. Before his partner could draw a weapon I wrapped my arms around his shoulders and launched us both through the open window behind him.

For a half-second all I could hear was the rush of the wind and the rapid pulse of my heart. Then we hit the ground, and my hundred-and-eighty-pound frame buried him face up in the mud, a low crack letting me know the fall had broken a few of his ribs. I rolled off him and pulled myself to my feet. The moon was very bright against the dark of the alleyway. I breathed in deep and felt the blood drain from my head. The pockmarked man struggled to right himself and I snapped a boot across his scalp. He groaned and stopped stirring.

Dimly I was aware that the fall had done something to my

ankle, but I was too gone to feel it yet. I would need to finish this quick, before my body had time to wake to the harm I'd done it.

I walked back into the Virgin and saw Spider sprinting down the steps at full speed, blood seeping from his nose, his blade in his hand. He snarled and came at me wildly – foolish, but then Spider was the sort of man who gets rattled by a little pain. I met him halfway and dropped low, setting my shoulder into his knees and sending him hurtling down the stairs. Turning back to finish the job, I saw the white press of bone sticking out from his hand and knew there was no point in further violence. I left him cradling his wrist and shrieking like a newborn.

Back on the second floor most of the patrons were pressed against the walls, waiting to see the outcome. At some point while I was busy below Tancred had grabbed a heavy wooden truncheon, and he rapped it against his outstretched palm. His warped face was twisted into a death mask and there was a long line of notches on the handle of his club, but his eyes were wide and I knew he would go down easy.

I ducked as his cudgel wheezed over my head, then balled my fist into his stomach. Tancred stumbled backwards, gasping for air, waving his bludgeon impotently. On the second swing I caught his wrist and twisted it savagely, pulling him close as he screamed and dropped his weapon. I held his gaze with mine, his ruined lips trembling, then struck him a blow that collapsed his legs under him.

He lay at my feet, weeping piteously. The small crowd of spectators stared back at me, bulbous drunkard noses and mongoloid idiot eyes, a menagerie of inbred grotesques, mouth-breathers and vermin. I had the urge to grab Tancred's cudgel and wade into them, just start clubbing heads, *crack crack crack*, soak the sawdust red. I shook it off, telling myself it was just the breath. It was time to end this, but not too quickly. Theatricality mattered – I wanted these dregs to spread what they were seeing.

I dragged Harelip's limp body toward a nearby table and stretched one arm across the wood. Holding his palm flat with my left hand, I took his small finger firmly in my right. 'What's our boundary?' I asked, snapping his digit.

He screamed but didn't answer.

'What's our boundary?' I continued, breaking the next finger. He was weeping now, gasping for air and barely capable of speech. He'd need to make the attempt. I twisted another finger. 'You've got a whole other hand I haven't touched!' I was laughing and wasn't sure if it was part of the act. 'What's our boundary?'

'The canal!' he shrieked. 'The canal is the boundary!'

The bar was silent but for his wailing. I swiveled my head at the onlookers, savoring the moment, then continued in a voice loud enough to be heard in the first ranks of the audience. 'Your business ends at the canal. Forget again and they'll find you floating in it.' I pulled back his last finger and let him fall to the ground, then turned and walked slowly out the exit. Spider sat slumped against the bottom of the stairs, and he looked away as I passed.

A dozen blocks east the breath wore off and I put my arm against an alley wall and spewed until I could barely breathe, sinking into the muck and grime. I knelt there for a while, waiting for my heartbeat to return to normal. On the way up my leg gave out, and I had to buy a crutch off a fake cripple so I could hobble the rest of the way home.

4

I awoke with a headache that made my swollen ankle feel like a hand-job from a ten-ochre-an-hour hooker. I tried to stand, but my vision swirled and my stomach let me know it was up for a repeat of last night's performance, so I sat back down. Prachetas's cunt, if I never took another whiff of pixie's breath it would be too damn soon.

The sun streaming through my window meant it was past noon. My feeling has always been that if you've missed the morning you might as well go ahead and skip the afternoon as well, but there was work to do. I steadied myself, then pulled on my clothes and walked downstairs.

I took a seat at the counter. Adolphus had forgotten to cover his eye, and the recess in his skull wagged disapproval at me. 'It's too late for eggs. Don't even ask.' I had figured one o'clock was probably past the breakfast rush but wasn't happy to have my suspicions confirmed. 'The boy from last night has been waiting for you to wake up for the past three hours.'

'Is there any coffee at least? And where is my shadow exactly?'

'There is none, and he's in the corner.'

I turned to see the youth from the previous evening uncurl from a wall. He had an odd talent for remaining unnoticed, or maybe my hangover was worse than I'd thought. We looked at each other in silence, some natural reserve keeping him from beginning. 'I didn't idle half the morning away in front of your door,' I said. 'What do you want?'

'A job.'

He was direct at least, and concise – that was something. My head was pounding and I was trying to figure out where my break-fast would come from. 'And what possible use could you be to me?'

'I could do things for you. Like last night.'

'I don't know how often you think I stumble over the corpses of missing children, but last night was kind of a rare occurrence. I don't think I can justify a full-time employee waiting around for it to happen again.' This objection seemed to do little to sway him. 'What is it you think I do exactly?'

He smiled slyly, like he'd done something wrong and was happy to let me know it. 'You run Low Town.'

And what a lovely fiefdom it was. 'The guards might dispute that.'

He snorted. It was worth snorting over.

'I had a long night. I'm not in the mood for this nonsense. Get lost.'

'I can run errands, deliver messages, whatever you need. I know the streets like the back of my hand, I can tussle, and nobody sees me that I don't want to.'

'Look, kid – this is a one-man operation. And if I was to bring on an assistant, my first requirement would be that his balls had dropped.'

The abuse did little to faze him. No doubt he'd heard far worse. 'I came through yesterday, didn't I?'

'Yesterday you walked six blocks and didn't fuck me. I could train a dog to do the same thing, and I wouldn't need to pay him.'

'Give me something else then.'

'I'll give you a beating if you don't scramble,' I said, raising my hand in something meant to resemble a menacing gesture.

To judge by his lack of reaction, he was unimpressed with the threat.

'By the Lost One, you're a tiresome little bastard.' The walk downstairs had reawakened the fierce pain in my ankle, and all this conversation was upsetting my stomach. I fished into my pocket and brought out an argent. 'Run over to the marketplace and get me two blood oranges, a dish of apricots, a ball of twine, a coin purse and a pruning knife. And if I don't get half of it back in change I'll know you're either a cheat or too stupid to haggle a fair price.'

He hurried off with a speed that made me wonder if he would remember everything. Something about the boy made me unlikely to bet against him. I turned back around and waited for breakfast to arrive, but found myself distracted by the scowl atop Adolphus's girth.

'You have something to say?'

'I didn't know you were so desperate for a partner.'

'What did you want me to do, clip him?' I rubbed slow circles into my temple with my middle and forefingers. 'Any news?'

'They're having a funeral for Tara outside the Church of Prachetas in a few hours. Don't suppose you'll attend?'

'You don't suppose correctly. Anything else making the rounds?'

'Word has spread of your encounter with Harelip, if that's what you're asking.'

'It was.'

'Well, it has.'

It was about then that my brain decided the time had come to free itself from its long years of imprisonment, and began a furious if unproductive effort to batter through its casing. From the back Adeline noticed my agony and set a pot of coffee boiling.

I was nursing the second cup, dark and sweet, when the boy returned. He set the bag of goods on the counter and put the change next to it.

'There are seven coppers left,' I said. 'What did you forget?'

'It's all there.' He wasn't quite smiling, but there was a distinct upturn to the thread of his lips. 'I swiped the pruning knife.'

'Congratulations, you're a pickpocket. It's a real exclusive club.' I took an orange from the bag and started to peel it. 'Who'd you get the fruit from, Sarah or Yephet the Islander?'

'The Islander. Sarah's are half-rotten.'

I ate a wedge of orange. 'Did the Islander have his son or daughter helping him today?'

'His daughter. His son hasn't been around for a few weeks.'

'What color shirt was she wearing?'

There was a pause. 'She was wearing a gray smock.' His quarter-grin returned. 'But you wouldn't know if I was right, 'cause you haven't left the bar yet.'

'I'd know if you tried to lie to me.' I finished off the orange and tossed the peel onto the bar, then set two fingers against his chest. 'I'll always know.'

He nodded without taking his eyes off mine.

I scooped the remaining coins into the purse he had bought and held it in front of me enticingly. 'You got a name?'

'The kids call me Wren.'

'Consider this the rest of the week's pay.' I tossed him the bag. 'Spend some of it on getting a new shirt – you look like a bum. Then stop by later in the evening. I might have something for you to do.'

He accepted this development without response or expression, as if it was of little importance one way or the other.

'And quit thieving,' I continued. 'If you work for me, you don't siphon funds from the neighborhood.'

'What does siphon mean?'

'In this context, steal.' I jerked my head towards the exit. 'Off with you.' He headed out the front door, though not with any great hurry. I pulled the second orange from the bag. Adolphus's frown had returned. 'You have something to say?'

He shook his head and began cleaning glasses left over from the night before.

'You're as subtle as a stone. Spit out whatever you're choking on or quit shooting me daggers.'

'You are not a carpenter,' he said.

'Then what the hell am I doing with this pruning knife?' I asked, flourishing the tool. Adolphus's brutish lips kept their curl. 'All right, I'm not a carpenter.'

'And you are not a blacksmith.'

'Nor was there confusion on that account.'

Adolphus set the tankard down with a start, and in his flash of anger I remembered a day at Apres when those massive arms had cracked a Dren skull as easily as you would an egg, blood and brain bubbling out from white bone. 'If you ain't a carpenter, and you ain't a blacksmith, then what the hell are you doing taking on an apprentice?' He spat this last sentence at me, along with a fair bit of, well, spit.

The void where his left eye once sat gave him an unfair advantage, and I broke contact. 'I don't judge you for your trade. But it isn't one a child ought to learn.'

'What's the harm in getting me breakfast?'

Adolphus shrugged, unconvinced.

I finished my second orange and started on the apricots in relative silence.

It's always unsettling when Adolphus is in an ill humor. Partly because it reminds me that if he ever lost his temper it would take half the hoax in the city to bring him down, but mostly because there's just something unpleasant about watching a fat man mope. 'You're in a hell of a mood today,' I began.

The flesh on his face dragged downward, menaced more than usual by age. 'The child,' he said.

It was clear he wasn't talking about the one who had just left. 'It's a sick world, but this isn't the first we've had evidence of it.'

'Who will do right for the child?'

'The guard will look into it.' I could well appreciate what dubious comfort that was.

'The guard couldn't catch pus in a whorehouse.'

'They called in the Crown. Two agents in their prettiest bits of finery. Even sent for scryers. They'll find something.'

'If that child has to rely on the Crown for justice, her soul will never know peace.' He let his one eye linger on mine.

This time I didn't flinch. 'That's not my problem.'

'You will allow her violator to walk free?' The traces of Adolphus's Skythan accent hardened during his frequent moments of melodrama. 'To breathe our air, foul our wells?'

'Is he around here somewhere? Send him over, I'll find something heavy and brain him with it.'

'You could look for him.'

I spat an apricot pit onto the floor. 'Who was it pointing out that I operate on the other side of the law these days?'

'Shrug it off, make jokes, play the fool.' He banged his fist against the counter, setting the heavy wood shaking. 'But I know why you went out last night, and I remember dragging you off the field at Giscan, when everyone had fled and the dead choked the sky.' The planks of the bar settled to equilibrium. 'Don't pretend it doesn't bother you.'

The trouble with old friends is they remember history you'd prefer forgotten. Of course, I didn't have to stick around and reminisce. The last of the apricots disappeared. 'I've got things to look in on. Throw the rest of this junk out, and give the boy supper if he returns.'

The abrupt end of our conflict left Adolphus deflated, his fury spent, his one eye drawn and his face haggard. As I left the tavern he was wiping at the countertop aimlessly, trying not to weep.

5

I started out from the Earl in a sullen mood. I rely on Adolphus for a dose of morning levity and felt ill-equipped without it. Between that and the foul weather, I was starting to wish I'd kept to my original inclination and spent the rest of the afternoon wrapped in bed and burning dreamvine. Thus far the best that could be said for the day was that it was half over.

Last evening's unexpected encounter had diverted my intention to visit the Rhymer – a circumstance I needed to rectify. He'd forgive my absence, likely he'd already heard the reason, but we still needed to speak. This time of day he'd either be working the docks or up at his mother's house. His mom had a tendency to try and set me up with women in her neighborhood, so I decided he was at the wharf and hobbled off in that direction, the pain in my ankle proving as reluctant to dissipate as the one in my skull.

Yancey was probably the most talented musician in Low Town,

and a damn good contact besides. I had met him during my time as an agent – he was part of a clique of Islanders who performed at balls for court officials and aristocrats. I helped him out of a bust once and in return he started to pass me information – little shit, background chatter. He never rolled on anyone. Since then our career trajectories had trended in opposite directions, and these days his skills were in request at some of the most exclusive gatherings in the capital. He still kept his ears open for me, though the uses to which I put his intelligence had changed.

The irony of the situation was not lost on either of us.

I found him a few feet off the west quay, surrounded by a handful of indifferent bystanders, playing a set of Kpanlogo and spouting the rhythmic poetry for which he was named. For all his skill, Yancey was about the worst street performer I'd ever seen. He didn't take requests, he set up in spots unused to traffic, and he was surly to onlookers. Most days he was lucky to make a few coppers, a modest reward indeed for a man of his abilities. Still, he was always cheery when I saw him, and I think he got a kick out of displaying his dizzying abilities to an ungrateful public. He made enough coin playing to the upper crust to make whatever he got busking meaningless anyway.

I rolled a smoke. Yancey hated to be interrupted in the middle of a performance, regardless of the setting. I once had to pull him off a courtier who made the mistake of laughing during his set. He had that unpredictable temper common to small men, the kind of rage that flares up violently before fading away just as quickly.

After a moment he finished his verse, and the tiny audience responded with muted applause. He laughed off their lack of enthusiasm, then looked up at me. 'If it ain't the Warden himself – finally managed a visit to your friend Yancey, I see.' His voice was thick and mellifluous.

'I got caught up in something.'

'I heard.' He shook his head regretfully. 'Bad business. You going to the funeral?'

'No.'

'Well, I am, so help me pack this up.' He began breaking down his set, wrapping each of the tiny hide drums in a collection of cotton sacks. I took the smallest of his pieces and did the same, slipping in his fistful of product as I did so. As a rule, Yancey was apt to injure any man foolish enough to touch his instruments, but he knew what I was up to and let it pass without comment. 'The noblefolk were disappointed you didn't show last night.'

'And their sorrow weighs heavy on my soul.'

'I'm sure you lost sleep. You want to make up for it, you can come by the Duke of Illador's estate Tuesday evening round ten.'

'You know how important the opinion of the peerage is to me. I suppose you'll be expecting your usual cut?'

'Unless you feel like upping it.'

I did not. We continued in silence until the onlookers were out of earshot. 'They say you found her,' Yancey continued.

'They say things.'

'You steady on it?'

'As a top.'

He nodded sympathetically. 'Bad business.' He finished packing up his set in a thick canvas bag, then slung it over his shoulder. 'We'll talk more later. I want to get a decent spot in the square.' He bumped my fist and walked off. 'Stay loose.'

The docks were virtually deserted, the usual mass of workers, merchants and customers long departed for the funeral, like Yancey happy to set aside a few hours of work to take part in a spectacle of public mourning. In their absence a dull quiet had settled over the area, a distinct contrast to the usual bustle of commerce. Making certain no one was watching I reached into my satchel for a hit of breath. My headache eased and the pain in my ankle receded. I watched the gray sky reflect off the water, thinking back to the day I had stood on the docks with five thousand other youths, preparing to board a troop ship to Gallia. My uniform had looked very fine, I'd thought, and my steel helm had glittered in the sun.

I contemplated lighting a joint of dreamvine but decided against it. It's never a good idea to get faded in a maudlin mood

31

– the vine tends to heighten your anxieties instead of blunting them. Solitude was proving an ill fit, and my feet found themselves shuffling north towards the church. It seemed I was attending the funeral after all.

By the time I got there the service had started and the Square of Benevolence was packed so tight you could barely see the dais. I skirted the crowd and snuck into an alleyway off the main plaza, taking a seat on a stack of packing crates. It was too far back to hear what the high priest of Prachetas was saying, but I was confident it was very pretty – you don't get to a point in life where people put gold on your outerwear unless you can say very pretty things at opportune moments. And anyway the wind had picked up, so most of the crowd couldn't hear the speech either. At first they pushed closer, straining their ears to make him out. When that didn't work they got anxious, children pulling at their parents, day laborers shuffling their feet to keep warm.

Sitting on the stage, a respectful ten paces behind the priest, was the girl's mother, recognizable even at this distance by the look on her face. It was one I had seen during the War on the faces of boys who had lost limbs, the look of someone who suffered a wound that should have been mortal but wasn't. It tends to settle like wet plaster, grafting itself permanently to the skin. I suspected this was a mask the poor woman wouldn't ever be able to shed, unless the torment became too much and she put steel to her wrist some cold night.

The priest reached a crescendo, or at least I thought he had. I still couldn't hear anything, but his grandiloquent gestures and the mumbled beatitudes from the crowd seemed to indicate some sort of a climax. I tried to light a cigarette but the wind kept taking my flame, and I exhausted half a dozen matches before giving up. It was that kind of an afternoon.

Then it was over, the oration completed and the invocations offered. The priest held the gilded icon of Prachetas aloft and descended from the dais, the pallbearers following behind with the coffin. Some of the crowd left with the procession. Most did not. It was getting cold after all, and the cemetery was a long walk.

I waited for the crowd to filter out from the square, then pushed myself up from my seat. At some point during the speech I hadn't heard I'd decided to violate my self-imposed exile and return to the Aerie to speak with the Blue Crane.

Fucking funerals. Fucking mother. Fucking kid.

6

The Aerie reigns above Low Town like Śakra the Firstborn over Chinvat. A perfectly straight pillar, dark blue against the gray of the tenements and warehouses, stretching up endlessly. With the exception of the Royal Palace, with its crystalline fortifications and wide thoroughfares, it is the single most extraordinary building in the city. For near on thirty years it has subjugated the skyline, offering glorious contrast to the surrounding slums. It was a comfort, as a youth, to have visible evidence that the remainder of what you saw was not everything there was to see – that some portion of existence prevailed unpolluted by stench and piss.

The hope had proved false, of course, but that was my fault and no one else's. It had been a long time since I'd seen the tower as anything but a reminder of squandered promise, and the foolish hopes of a foolish boy.

They had leveled an entire city block to make room for the Square of Exultation, as the courtyard surrounding the Aerie was called, but no one had minded. This was in the dark times after the great plague, when the population of Low Town had shrunk to a fraction of what it was in years prior. In place of the tenements was built a maze of white stone enclosing the tower itself, intricately complex but barely waist high, allowing anyone willing to look foolish to hop over the walls. As a child I had spent countless hours here playing Rat-in-a-Hole or Bowley Pegs, stalking through the rows of granite or running tip-toe along the fortifications.

The square was likely the only portion of Low Town that the populace had not actively worked to dilapidate. No doubt the Crane's reputation as being among the most skilled practitioners of magic in the nation had some part in cutting down on vandalism, but the truth was that almost to a man the people of Low Town idolized their patron, and would accept no desecration of his monument. To speak ill of the Crane was to call for a beating in any tavern between the docks and the canal, and a shiv to the gut in some of the harder ones. He was our most beloved figure, more highly esteemed than the Queen and the Patriarch combined, his charity funding a half-dozen orphanages and his alms joyfully received by a grateful public.

I stood in front of the house of my oldest friend and lit a cigarette, the wind having died down enough to allow me my petty pleasures. There were very good reasons why I hadn't visited my mentor in five years, and I blew tobacco smoke into the chilly air and piled one atop another, till they loomed over the whim that had carried me this far. I could still call an end to this idiocy, return to the Earl, light some dreamvine and sleep until tomorrow. The mental impression of soft sheets and colored smoke faded as I stepped through the first archway, my feet threading their way forward against my better instincts, instincts that I seemed to be ignoring a lot lately.

I negotiated my way through the maze, half-forgotten memories guiding me right or left. My cigarette went out but I didn't have the energy to relight it, and I stuffed the butt into my coat pocket rather than dirty the Crane's patio.

One last turn and I was facing the entrance, an outline of a door in the sheer azure wall, absent knocker or other obvious means of ingress. Perched on an indentation hammered into the edifice above it sat a gargoyle, white stone like the maze, its maw locked in something closer to a smirk than a grimace. Seconds passed. I was glad no one was around to witness my cowardice. Finally I decided that I hadn't traversed the maze for nothing, and rapped twice on the frame.

'Greetings, young one.' The voice the Crane had created for his watchman was incongruous with its purpose, lighter and friendlier than one would expect from the creature's composition. Its concrete eyes looked me up and down slowly. 'Perhaps not so young these days. The Master has been alerted, and will receive you in the loft. I have standing orders to allow you entry should you ever arrive.'

The crack in the façade widened, stone sliding against stone. Above it the gargoyle's face contorted smugly, no small feat for a creature composed of mineral. 'Although I didn't think I'd ever need to follow them.'

Not for the first time I wondered what in the name of the Firstborn had possessed the Crane to imbue his creation with a sense of sarcasm, there being no great shortage of it among the human race. I stepped into the foyer without responding.

It was small, little more than a platform for the long circular stairway that led skyward. I began the climb to the upper floors, my path illuminated by evenly spaced wall sconces leaking a clear white light. Halfway up I stopped to catch my breath. This had been a lot easier as a child, sprinting up the curving stone with the abandon of someone who was not a hardened tobacco addict. After a rest I continued my ascent, fighting the urge to retreat with every step.

A spacious living room took up most of the top floor of the Aerie. The furniture was neat and functional, making up in clean aesthetic what it lacked in opulence. Two large chairs sat before a narrow fireplace built into the dividing wall that separated this area from Master's private quarters. The décor had remained unaltered since I had first glimpsed the interior, and unbidden memories came to mind of winter afternoons by the fire, and of a childhood best forgotten.

I watched him silhouetted against the great glass window looking south-east over the harbor. From that height the stink and hustle of Low Town evaporate, giving way to the endless ocean in the distance.

He turned slowly and placed his withered hands over mine. I was conscious of my desire to look away. 'It's been too long,' he said.

The years showed. The Crane has always been wizened, his body too thin to support his height, scraggly tufts of white hair sprouting from his head and bony chin. But also he'd always possessed an improbable energy which seemed to make a lie of his age. I could detect little trace of it any longer. His skin was stretched across his frame, thin as paper, and there was a jaundiced tinge to his eyes. At least his costume remained unchanged, an unadorned robe, rich blue like everything else in his citadel.

'My greetings to you, Magister,' I began. 'I appreciate you seeing me without an appointment.'

'Magister? Is that how you greet the man who rubbed unguent on your scraped knees, and made you boiled chocolate to ward off the cold?'

It was clear he wasn't going to make this easy. 'I thought it inappropriate to presume past intimacies.'

His expression soured, and he pulled his arms firm across each other. 'I understand your reticence to return – even as a child you had more pride than half the royal court. But don't suggest that I turned my back on you, or ever would. Even after you left the Crown's service and . . . took up your new vocation.'

'You mean after I was stripped of my rank and started selling drugs on the street?'

He sighed. I could remember him making that same sound when I came to him with a bruised eye from fighting, or he realized I'd stolen whatever new toy I was playing with. 'I spent years trying to break you of that habit.'

'What habit?'

38

'This way you have of taking everything as an insult. It's a sign of low breeding.'

'I am low bred.'

'You could work harder to hide it.' He smiled and I found myself doing the same. 'Regardless, you have returned, and as grateful as I am to see you, I can't help but wonder to what I owe the reappearance of my prodigal son? Unless you reappeared at my doorstep after five years solely to inquire after my health?'

When I was a child the Crane had been my benefactor and protector, doing me what kindnesses the fiercest urchin in Low Town would accept. As an agent I had often turned to him, both for advice and for the assistance his prodigious skill could offer. Yet for all my practice this newest round of supplication choked me on its way out. 'I need your help.'

His face tensed up, a fair reaction to a plea for aid from a man he hadn't spoken to in half a decade, particularly one on the wrong side of the law. 'And what services do you require?'

'I found Little Tara,' I said, 'and I need to know if you'd picked up anything on her from your channels. If there's a divination you think might be helpful, I'd ask you to do that as well, and without alerting Black House or the appropriate ministry.'

I suppose he had assumed I was there for money, or for something illicit. The discovery that I was not evoked the return of his natural demeanor, amiable and slightly mischievous. 'It seems I was confused about the full range of your new duties.'

'I'm not sure I take your meaning,' I said, though of course I did.

'Let me be clearer then. How exactly does finding the murderer of a child fit into your current purview?'

'How does aiding a criminal fall into the purview of a First Sorcerer of the Realm?'

'Hah! First Sorcerer!' He coughed into his hand, a wet and unpleasant sound. 'I haven't been to court since the Queen's Jubilee. I don't even know where my robes are.'

'The ones trimmed with gilded thread, and worth half the docks?'

'Damnable things itched my throat.' The Crane's laughter was forced, and after it was over the late afternoon light fell on an old and tired man. 'I'm sorry, my friend, but I'm not sure there's anything I can offer. Yesterday evening, when I heard of the offense, I ran a message to a contact in the Bureau of Magical Affairs. They say they put a scryer on it but came up with nothing. If they couldn't pick up anything, I don't imagine I'll have any more luck.'

'How is that possible?' I asked. 'Was the scrying blocked?'

'It would take an artist of exceptional ability to completely cover any trace of his presence. There aren't two dozen practitioners in all of Rigus capable of such intricate work, and I don't imagine any of them would resort to so vile an undertaking.'

'Power is no guarantee of decency, more often the opposite – but I'll grant you a mage of such ability would have easier means of satisfying his desires should they incline in that direction.' I could feel the old muscles working again, stretching off their torpor after years of neglect. It had been a long time since I'd investigated anything. 'Apart from magic, what else would work against your scrying?'

He took a decanter of vile-looking green liquid from above the mantel, then poured it into the tumbler that sat next to it. 'Medicine, for my throat,' he explained, before downing the fluid in one quick gulp. 'If her body had been cleaned very thoroughly, or sanitized with some kind of chemical. If the clothing she was wearing had only been in contact with her a short time, that might do it as well. It's not my specialty – I'm not really certain.'

The odor I had smelled on the girl's body could have been a cleaning agent. It could have been a dozen other things as well, but this gave me something to go on.

'That's a start at least.' Having gathered the nerve to return I found myself reluctant to leave. Part of me wanted to sit down in his soft blue chair and let it envelop me, to share a cup of tea with my old mentor and speak of days past. 'I appreciate your help. And I appreciate you receiving me. I'll let you know if I find anything.'

'I hope you find the person who did this, and I hope this isn't the last time you visit. I've missed you, and the trouble you track to my door – like a stray cat with a dead pigeon.'

I returned his smile and made a move for the exit, but his voice stopped me, suddenly stern. 'Celia wants to see you before you leave.' I tried not to flinch at her name but suspect I failed. 'She's in the conservatory. You still remember the way.' It was not a question.

'How is she?'

'She's up to be commissioned to First Rank in a few weeks. It's quite an honor.'

Sorcerer First Rank was the highest grade a practitioner could receive, held by perhaps twenty artists in the realm, all of whom had performed noble services in the interests of the country – or had done the right favors for the right people. The Crane was entirely correct, it was quite an honor, especially at Celia's age. It was also not at all what I had been asking. 'And how is she?'

The Crane's eyes fluttered away and I had the only answer I needed. 'Fine,' he said. 'She's . . . fine.'

I made my way back down the steps, stopping in front of a clouded glass door a level beneath the summit. I resisted the temptation to reach into my coat for a sniff of breath. Better to do this quick, and sober.

The conservatory was beautiful, like everything in the Aerie. Cultivated plants from across the Thirteen Lands thrived in its sultry environs, flowering in a spectrum of colors that complemented the blue stone of the walls. Bright violet strands of Queen's Fingers jutted out against vines of orange Drake's Skin, fierce blossoms of Daeva's Posies cast their scent throughout the room and stranger things still thrived in the damp hothouse heat.

She heard me come in but didn't stop what she was doing, tending to a small fern in the corner with a decanter of filigreed silver. A blue dress pulled tight across the bottom of her back and stopped just below the thigh, though as she stood straight it eased its way down to her knee. She turned to meet me and I caught a first glimpse of her face, familiar despite the time apart,

41

soft brown hair above dark almond eyes. Hugging the curves of her honey-colored neck was a cheap necklace, a lacquered wooden medallion with a strand of twine running through it, Kiren characters emblazoned on the front.

'You're returned.' I wasn't sure from her tone how she felt about it. 'Let me look at you.' She brought her hands up near my face, as if to caress or slap me. Either would have been appropriate. 'You've aged,' she said finally, opting for the former, running her fingers over my callused hide.

'They say time does that,' though whereas the passing of the years had withered my features and scored my face, for her the effects had been nothing but positive.

'That's what they say.' As she smiled I saw something of the girl she had been, in the open and friendly way she looked at me, in the speed with which she forgave my absence, in the light she radiated instinctively and without deliberation. 'I visited the Earl every day for a month after you left Black House. Adolphus said you were out. He kept saying it. After a while I stopped coming.'

I didn't respond, either to amend her belief as to how I'd left the Crown's service or to explain my absence.

'You leave us for five years, disappear completely, without a message, without a word.' She didn't seem angry, or sad even, the wound no longer tender but still visible. 'And now you can't even offer an explanation?'

'I had my reasons.'

'They were bad ones.'

'They might have been. I make a lot of bad decisions.'

'I won't argue that.' It wasn't much of a joke, but it was enough. 'It's very good to see you,' she said then, laboring over each word as if she wanted to say more.

I stared at my boots. They didn't tell me anything I hadn't already known. 'I hear you're to be commissioned Sorcerer First Rank. Congratulations.'

'It is an honor I'm not sure that I deserve. Certainly the Master's word went far in smoothing my ascension.'

'This means you get free rein to destroy any stray bit of architecture you find objectionable, and turn misbehaving servants into rodents?'

Her face assumed the strained pose I'd often seen her adopt as a child when she didn't get a joke. 'I have trained myself to follow in the footsteps of the Master, and thus studied the specialties he has perfected – alchemy, spells of warding and healing. The Master never saw fit to learn the patterns by which a practitioner does evil to his fellows, and I would not think to pursue avenues that he has determined to ignore. It requires a certain kind of person even to practice the darker shades of the Art – neither of us is capable of it.'

Anyone is capable of anything, I thought, but didn't say it.

'He's extraordinary. I don't think we ever quite realized it as children. To be given the honor of learning at his feet . . .' She held her tiny hands to her chest and shook her head. 'Do you understand what his spell of warding meant to this city? To this country? How many died from the plague? How many would have died if his safeguards didn't still protect us to this day? Before his working they needed to run the crematorium twenty-four hours a day in the summer just to keep up – and that was when the plague was at its ebb. When the Red Fever hit, there wasn't even anyone left to dispose of the bodies.'

A memory crept to my mind, a child of six or seven walking gingerly over the corpses of his neighbors, careful not to step on their outstretched limbs, screaming for help that would never come. 'I know what his working meant.'

'You don't know. I don't think anyone does, really. We don't have any idea of the numbers killed in Low Town, among the Islanders and the dock workers. With sanitation like it was, it could have been a third, half, even higher. He's the reason we won the War. Without him there wouldn't have been enough men alive to fight.' Her eyes trailed reverentially upwards. 'We can never repay him for what he did. Never.'

When I didn't respond she blushed a little, suddenly self-conscious. 'But you've got me started again.' Her loose smile revealed a thin cobweb of lines stretching across her skin, lines that contrasted sorely with my memories of her as a youth, images I knew to be defunct but couldn't discount. 'I'm sure you didn't return to us to hear my tired bromides to the Master.'

'Not specifically.'

Too late I realized my half-answer allowed her to conjure her own explanation for my arrival. 'Is this a forced interrogation? Am I to tie you down and tease it out of you?'

I hadn't planned on telling her – but then I hadn't planned on running into Celia at all. And it was better to let her know my real motivation, rather than stoke whatever fantasies she had been clinging to. 'You heard about Little Tara?'

She blanched white, and her sultry grin dripped away. 'We aren't so far removed from the city as you seem to think.'

'I found her body yesterday,' I said. 'And I stopped by to see if the Master knew anything about it.'

Celia gnawed at her bottom lip – the tic, at least, one thing that had held over from our time as children. 'I'll light a candle that Prachetas might bring comfort to her family, and one to Lizben, that the girl's soul will find her way home. But frankly I'm not sure what business it is of yours. Let the Crown handle it.'

'Why, Celia – that sounds like something I would say.'

She blushed again, faintly ashamed.

I took a few steps towards a towering plant in full bloom, stripped from some distant corner of the globe. Its odor was cloying and heavy. 'You're happy here, following in his footsteps?'

'I'll never have his skill, nor be capable of his mastery of the Art. But it is an honor to be the Crane's heir. I study day and night to be worthy of the privilege.'

'You aim to replace him?'

'Not replace of course, no one could ever replace the Master. But he won't be here forever. Someone will need to ensure his work continues. The Master understands that, it's part of why I'm being raised in rank.' She lifted her chin, confident bordering on imperious. 'When the time comes I'll be ready to safeguard the people of Low Town.'

'Alone in the tower? Seems like a lonely pursuit. The Crane was past middle age when he retired here.'

'Sacrifice is part of the responsibility.'

'What happened to your clerkship at the Bureau of Magical Affairs?' I asked, recalling the position she had occupied the last time we had spoken. 'You seemed to be enjoying it, last I remember.'

'I realized I had ambitions beyond spending the rest of my life shuffling papers across a desk, and arguing with functionaries and bureaucrats.' Her eyes iced over, unhappy contrast to the sweetness she had heretofore offered me. 'It's an aim you would be more familiar with, had you bothered to speak to me in the last five years.'

Hard to argue that one. I turned back towards the greenery.

The anger leaked out of Celia, and after a moment she was her jovial self. 'Enough of this – we've years and years to catch up on! What are you doing with yourself these days? How is Adolphus?'

There was no good to be found in prolonging this, not for either of us. 'It's been good seeing you. It's a comfort to know you're still looking after the Master.' And that he's still looking after you.

Her smile flickered. 'You'll return tomorrow then? Come by for dinner – we'll set a plate for you, like old times.'

I tapped at one petal of the flower I had been staring at, sending grains of pollen wandering through the air. 'Goodbye, Celia. Be as well as you possibly can.' I walked out before she could respond. By the time I reached the bottom of the stair-well I was practically sprinting, pushing open the tower door and fleeing into the early evening.

A half block past the Square of Exultation I leaned against an alley wall and fumbled in my pouch for some breath. My hands were unsteady and I found I could barely open the top, finally forcing out the cork and shoving the vial to my nose. I took a slow, deep draw – then another.

It was a shaky walk back to the Earl, and I would have been an easy mark for any thug who cared to make prey of me, if there had been any around. But there weren't. It was just me.

7

The boy was sitting at a table across from Adolphus, whose wide smile and broad gestures told me he was in the middle of some exaggerated anecdote before I could actually hear him speak.

'And the lieutenant says, "What makes you think that way is east?" And he says, "'Cause that's the morning sun in my eyes or I'm blinded by your brilliance, and if it was the latter you'd know how to work a compass."' Adolphus laughed uproariously, his huge face wagging. 'Can you imagine that? Out there in front of the entire battalion! The lieutenant didn't know whether to shit his pants or court-martial him!'

'Boy,' I interrupted. Wren slunk slowly from his chair, perhaps wanting to make clear that Adolphus's description of our martial careers hadn't instilled in him anything of a military bearing. 'How well do you know Kirentown?'

'I'll find whatever you need me to,' he said.

'Follow Broad Street past the Fountain of the Traveler and

you'll see a bar on your right beneath the sign of a blue dragon. At the counter will be a fat man with a face like a beaten mutt. Tell him to tell Ling Chi I sent you. Tell him to tell Ling Chi that I'm going to be snooping around his territory tomorrow. Tell him it isn't related to business. Tell him I'll consider it a favor. He won't say anything to you – they're a cagey bunch – but he won't need to. Just deliver the message and return here.'

Wren nodded and slipped out the exit.

'And get me something to eat on the way back!' I yelled, unsure if he'd heard me.

I turned on the giant. 'Quit telling the boy war stories. He doesn't need his head filled with nonsense.'

'Nonsense! Every word of that story is true! I can still remember you smirking as he walked away.'

'What happened to that lieutenant?'

Adolphus lost his smile. 'He slit his wrists, the night after he forced that charge at Reaves.'

'We found him bled out when he didn't show to reveille – so no more about the good old days. They weren't any fucking good.'

Adolphus rolled his eye at me and stood. 'By the Firstborn, you're in a mood.'

He wasn't wrong. 'It's been a rough day.'

'Come on, I'll pour you a beer.' We adjourned to the bar and he drew me a tall flagon of ale. I sipped at it while we waited for the evening rush to arrive.

'I like the boy,' Adolphus said, as if he had just realized it. 'He doesn't miss much, for all that he keeps quiet about what he sees. Any idea where he's sleeping?'

'In the street, I assume. That's where street urchins tend to live.'

'Don't be so sentimental – you'll get tear stains on the counter.'

'You have any idea how many lost children there are in Low Town? There's nothing special about this one – he's no kin of mine. I didn't know he existed until yesterday evening.'

'You really think you believe that?'

The day wore heavy on my shoulders. 'I'm too tired to argue

with you, Adolphus. Quit beating about and tell me what you want.'

'I was going to invite him to sleep in the back. Adeline has taken a liking to him as well.'

'It's your bar, Adolphus, you can do whatever the hell you want. But an ochre says he makes off with your bedroll.'

'Deal. Tell him when he comes back – I've got work to do.'

Customers were trickling in and Adolphus returned to his trade. I sat drinking my beer and thinking maudlin thoughts. After a short while the boy returned, holding a small cup of beef with chili sauce. He had sharp ears – I'd remember that. I took the crock and began eating. 'Adolphus feed you?'

The boy nodded.

'You still hungry? When I was your age I was always hungry.'

'I'm fine. I lifted something from off a fish-cart on the way back,' he said, as if this was something to be proud of.

'I gave you money this morning, didn't I?'

'Yeah.'

'You spend it already?'

'Not a copper.'

'Then you don't need to be stealing food. Degenerates steal when they don't have to – you want to go that route you can get the hell away from me. I don't need to give errands to some freak who snatches purses because it gives him a thrill.'

To judge by his grimace, he didn't much care for my comparison – but he didn't say anything in response.

'Where you bedding?'

'Different places. I was sleeping under the quay when it was warm. Lately I've been bunking in an abandoned factory near Brennock. There's a watchman, but he only checks once after dark and once before dawn.'

'Adolphus says you can sleep in the back. Adeline will likely make up a bed for you.'

His eyes contorted into little blips of fury, domestication the ultimate insult to a feral youth. 'I asked for a job, nothing else – I don't need your charity.'

'One thing you ought to know about me, kid, if you're too dumb to figure it out – I don't do charity. And I don't give a shit where you sleep – go nap in the Andel if you feel like it. I'm passing on an offer from the giant. You want to take it, go ahead. You don't, I won't remember we had this conversation tomorrow.' To prove it I went back to my drink, and after a moment he slipped off into the crowd.

I finished my meal and headed upstairs before the bar got busy. Somewhere on the walk home from the Aerie my bruised ankle had started to ache again, and the short climb was more unpleasant than it should have been.

I lay down on the bed and rolled a long twist of dreamvine. The evening wafted in through the open window, airing out the musk. I lit the joint and thought about tomorrow's work. What I had smelled on the body was strong, stronger than anything you'd use for cleaning a kitchen or bathroom. And a household cleaner wouldn't be enough to throw off a decent scryer. Maybe the soap plants, or one of the glue factories with their heavy solvents. The Kirens had a monopoly on that kind of work, which was why I'd sent the boy to clear my presence with their chief. Wouldn't do to make trouble for my real business while I was off pursuing this diversion.

I blew out the lamp and puffed ringlets of colored smoke into the air. This was a good blend, sweet to the tongue and strong against my chest, and it filled the room with threads of brass and burned sienna. Halfway through I stubbed the tab against the underside of my bed and fell asleep, the low-grade euphoria spreading through my body sufficient distraction to drown out the noise of our patrons below.

In my dreams I was a child again, lost and homeless, my mother and father taken by the plague, my little sister crushed during the grain riots that had destroyed all remnants of civil authority three weeks earlier. That was my first fall on the streets of Low Town. When I learned to scavenge for food, to appreciate filth for the heat it released around you while you slept. When I first saw the depths the average man will sink to, and learned what there was to win in wading deeper.

I was in the back corner of an alley, my legs pulled tightly against myself, when I was jolted awake by their approach.

'Faggot. Hey, faggot. What you doing in our territory?' There were three of them, older than me, only by a few years but those few years would be enough. Its tendency to spare children was one of the most curious of the Red Fever's effects – it was quite possible these were the oldest living human beings within ten square blocks.

I didn't have a single object of value – my clothes were rags that wouldn't have survived removal, and I'd lost my shoes at some point in the chaos of the last month. I hadn't eaten in a day and a half and I was sleeping in a dug-out I'd scraped against the walls of a side street. But they didn't want anything from me apart from an opportunity to practice violence, our surroundings sharpening the natural cruelty of children to a fever pitch.

I pulled myself off the ground, hunger making even this exercise exhausting. The three of them sauntered over – ragged youths, their attire and appearance not much improved from my own. The speaker was a fever survivor, the angry cankers discharging from his face attesting to a barely victorious battle with the plague. Apart from that there was little to recommend him from his fellows, famine and misery rendering them almost indistinguishable, gaunt scavengers, ghouls amid the rubble.

'You've got some nerve, you little cocksucker, coming into our neighborhood and not even having the common decency to ask permission.'

I stood mutely. Even as a child I found the inane exchanges that preface violence to be absurd. Just get to it already.

'You ain't got nothing to say to me?' The leader turned back towards the other two, as if shocked by my poor etiquette, then struck a blow to the side of my head that sent me spinning to the ground. I lay in wait for the beating I knew was coming, too inured to it to wonder at the fairness of it, too inured to it

51

to do anything but bleed. He kicked me in the temple and my vision went blurry. I didn't scream. I don't think I had the strength.

Something about my silence seemed to get to him, and suddenly he was on my chest, his knees pinning me to the ground and his forearm pushed against my neck. 'Faggot! Fucking faggot!'

From somewhere distant I heard my assailant's comrades trying to call him off, but their protestations proved ineffective. I struggled briefly, but he struck me again across the face, terminating my half-hearted attempts at self-defense.

I lay on the ground with his elbow on my throat, the world swirling around me, blood thick on my tongue and I thought – so this is death. It took a long enough time coming. But then She Who Waits Behind All Things must have been busy in Low Town that year, and I was a small boy. She could be forgiven for such a minor oversight, especially now that she had come to rectify her mistake.

The light started to fade.

A great rushing sound filled my ears, like the roar of falling water.

Then my hand closed around something firm and heavy, and I brought a rock up against the side of the boy's head, and the weight on my neck lessened and I brought my fist up again and then again until his grip was slack and I was on top of him now and the sound I was hearing were his screams and my own and still I kept at it and then I was the only one screaming.

Then silence and I was standing over the boy's body and his friends weren't laughing any more but instead looking at me like no one had ever looked at me, and even though there were two of them and they were bigger than I was they backed off warily, then broke into a run. And as I watched them retreat I realized I liked the look I had seen in their eyes, liked not being the one to wear it. And if that meant I needed to get my hands slick with little pieces of the boy's brain then so be it, that wasn't much of a price to pay, not much of a price at all.

A wild spurt of laughter bubbled up from my gut, and I vomited it forth at the world.

When I awoke my chest was heavy and my breath short. I propped myself up and forced my heart into rhythm, counting the beats, one-two, one-two. It was nearly dawn. I slipped my clothes on and headed downstairs.

The bar was quiet – our patrons gone home to beat their wives or sleep off their buzz. I took a chair at a side table and sat in the dark for a few minutes, then headed towards the back.

The fire had died to its embers, and the room was cold. On the ground next to the furnace lay a wad of unused bedding. There was no trace of the boy.

I walked out the front door of the Earl and leaned against a wall, rolling a tab and shivering. Morning was still a few minutes off, and in the twilight the city was the color of smoke. My hacking cough, spurred on by the autumn chill, echoed loudly through the abandoned streets. I lit a cigarette to ease it. In the distance a cock announced the dawn.

When I found the motherfucker who did for that girl I'd make what happened to Harelip look like the caress of a newfound lover. By everything holy, he'd be a slow time dying.

8

Eight hours and six ochres later and I was no closer to my goal. I'd been to every operation making or using a heavy solvent from Broad to Light Street, without so much as a bite. A few coppers were usually enough to get me information – if that didn't work I'd flash a paper that said I was a member of the guard and ask less affably. It was easy enough getting answers – it's always easy to find answers that don't lead anywhere.

Wren had caught up with me shortly after I'd set out from the Earl, not offering an explanation for his disappearance, not saying anything at all, just falling in line behind me. He was getting restless, presumably not anticipating that working for me would prove to be so boring. I wasn't enjoying our business any more than he was. The longer the search continued the more absurd it seemed to have trusted the outcome of the investigation to my olfactory senses, and I was starting to remember that one of the virtues of my adopted trade was that people came looking for me and not the other way around. But the memory of a dead girl and my innate obstinance drove me onward, hoping against the better dictates of reason that I'd get a lucky break.

At a worn counter sat an equally worn grandmother, her gray face not changing a fraction of an inch throughout the entire interview. No, none of her workers was absent the last three days. There were only two of them, they were both women, and they worked six days a week between sun-up and midnight. It was not a story sufficiently interesting to warrant the three coppers I gave her.

I stepped out of the tiny shop and into the late afternoon light, thinking it was time to call it off, head back to the Earl to regroup, when the wind changed direction and brought with it a familiar scent. A smile stretched the corners of my mouth. Wren saw it and cocked his head curiously. 'What is it?' he asked, but I ignored him and set myself against the breeze.

Two blocks further on and the acrid scent had grown stronger. A few more steps and it was almost overpowering, and a few steps past that I realized why. In front of us stood a massive glue factory, a stone gatehouse leading to a wide work yard where a small army of Kirens submerged bone and marrow in boiling vats. I was close. I opened the door and headed inside, Wren a half-step behind me.

A quick flash of my fake papers and the manager was the very picture of amicable obsequiousness. I spoke in worse Kiren than I was capable of. 'Workers, all here last three day? Any no?' I put an argent on the table and his eyes lit up. 'Important info, big price.'

A half second for his conscience to justify selling out a member of his race to a foreigner, and the coin disappeared and he pointed discreetly to a man in the work yard.

He was bigger than me, bigger than almost any Kiren I'd ever seen, the heretics tending towards short and wiry. He carried a huge sack of powder towards one of the tanks in the courtyard, and there was a dull, plodding quality to his movements. The right side of his face bore some light bruising, the kind that could have been made by a young girl frantically defending herself against a man bent on her despoliation. Of course it could have been made by any one of a thousand other things.

But it hadn't been.

And I felt that old thrill buzzing up from my groin, filtering out through my chest and into my extremities. This was the one – dead eyes only vaguely reminiscent of his fellows, the set of his face betraying his crimes even at this distance. A peculiar grin crept across my face, one I hadn't worn since before I had been stripped of the Crown's authority. I breathed deep of the poisoned air and bit back a chuckle.

'Boy, go back to the Earl. You're done for the night.'

Having spent so much time on the pursuit, Wren understandably wanted to be in on the payoff. 'I'll stay.'

The Kiren was looking back at me now, and I spoke without taking my eyes off him. 'This ain't an equal partnership, you're my lackey. If I tell you to swallow a hot coal, you'll sprint to the nearest fire, and if I tell you to head out, you'll disappear. Now . . . disappear.'

Wren held his ground for a moment before turning away. I wondered if he'd head back to the bar or fade off into the streets to repay my insult. I figured the latter but wasn't much concerned either way.

The Kiren was trying to decipher the origins of my interest. Now his crimes were running through his memory unbidden, his mind trying to convince his nerves that my attentions were innocent, that they had to be, that there was no way I could know.

I put another argent down on the table and said to the owner in pidgin, 'I wasn't here.'

The manager bowed slavishly and the argent went into the folds of his robe, a vacant grin plastered across his face.

I returned it but my gaze never left the target. A few seconds' pause to work his nerves, then I turned and walked out of the building.

This sort of operation would be better done with at least three more people, one to watch each exit and an extra just to be safe, but I wasn't worried. It seemed unlikely my man would run the risk of quitting work early. I could picture him inside the dusty pen trying to convince himself his fears were unwarranted, that I was just some ignorant *guai lo*, and after all he had been diligent, careful with the body, had even gone so far as to clean it with the acid he had stolen from work. No one had seen. He would finish out his shift.

I sat on a barrel in an alley across from the main entrance and waited for the shadows to lengthen. Back when I was an agent I had once crouched outside a whorehouse for eighteen hours dressed as a beggar until my quarry stumbled out and I had the chance to smack him in the head with a crutch. But that was when I was in fighting trim – patience is a skill that withers quickly when not used. I resisted the urge to roll a cigarette.

An hour passed, then another.

I was grateful when the bell above the door clanged, announcing the workday's end, and the Kiren filtered rapidly out of the mill. I pushed my aching body up from its perch, and took up a spot in the back of the crowd. My target towered over his fellows, an advantage in shadowing him that I didn't need but would take. The horde headed south, filtering into a drinking house marked by Kiren characters unfamiliar to me. I sat outside and rolled a tab. A few minutes trailed away with the smoke. I stubbed out the butt and headed inside.

The bar was the kind common to heretics, wide and dimly lit, filled with rows of long wood tables. A surly, inattentive staff brought bowls of bitter green *kisvas* to anyone with the money to pay. I took a chair against a back wall, conscious of being the only non-Kiren in the place but not letting it nettle me. A server with a face that had been hit with an oak branch walked by, and I ordered a draft of what passes for liquor among the foreign-born. It came with surprising speed, and I sipped from it while searching the room.

He sat alone, unsurprisingly. His kind of depravity tends to mark a man, and in my experience people can practically smell it. The other workers wouldn't describe it that way, of course.

They would say he was odd, or quiet, or that he had rotting teeth and didn't shower – but what they meant was there was something *wrong* with him, something you could feel though not quite name. The really dangerous ones learn to hide it, to camouflage their madness amid the sea of banal immorality surrounding them. But this one wasn't smart enough for that, and so he sat alone on the long bench, a solitary figure among the clumps of laughing workmen.

He pretended not to notice my attention but downed his liquor with a speed that belied his ease. Frankly, I was impressed with his composure – I was surprised he even had the presence of mind to follow through with his normal after-work routine. I checked my bag for the straight razor I kept attached to the canvas. It wouldn't be much use as a weapon, but it would come in handy for what I planned after. I gave him a wave. He blanched and his eyes flickered away from mine.

It was time to step this up a notch. I drained the remnants of my *kisvas*, grimacing at the sour aftertaste, and moved from the back table to join my prey. As he realized what I was doing his mouth shriveled up and he stared down into his drink. The men around him glared up at me anxiously, dislike of their compatriot contending against the instinctive antagonism of similarly colored folk towards an intruder of a different pallor. I disarmed them with a wide smile, half laughing, feigning drunkenness. '*Kisvas, hao chi!*' – kisvas, good – I bellowed, and rubbed my stomach.

Their suspicions assuaged, they returned my grin, happy to see a white man play the jester. They chattered back and forth, too rapidly for me to decipher.

My target didn't share their amusement, or fall for my ploy. I didn't want him to. I dropped myself onto a spot on the bench across from him and repeated my mantra. '*Kisvas, hao chi!*' I continued, broadening my smile to the point of imbecility. '*Nu ren*' – young girl – '*hao chi ma?*' I asked. Desperation sweated through his sallow skin. I spoke louder. '*Kisvas, hao chi! Nu ren, hao hao chi!*'

The giant Kiren stood abruptly, sliding through a narrow

opening in the long row of tables. I rose and blocked his path, getting in close enough to smell the sour stink of his unwashed body, close enough that he could hear me drop the drunkard act and condemn him in my awkward but decipherable Kiren. '*I know what you did to the girl. You'll be dead within the hour.*'

He shoved his paw against my chest and I stumbled backwards onto the table. The crowd laughed and I joined them, chortling uproariously, enjoying my theatrics, enjoying the entire enterprise. I remained supine, listening to the ridicule of the heretics, watching through the broad windows that flanked the door as he ran off. Once he was out of sight I slid myself off the table and moved quickly out the back exit, stumbling through a dirty kitchen and muttering something about the evils of drink. I pushed my way outside and started at a dead sprint, hoping to cut him off where the side street met the main thoroughfare.

I made it to the intersection and slumped against the alley wall casually, like I'd been there all day. The Kiren rounded the corner with his head turned over his shoulder, and when he saw me his skin went so white he could have passed for a Rouender. I bit my tongue to keep from laughing, his fear potent as a stiff drink. Śakra's cock, I had missed this – there are pleasures the life of a criminal cannot provide.

I bowed as he went past me, then peeled myself off the stone. He was almost broken now, guilt and terror overpowering him. Unsure whether to walk or run, he adopted a method of locomotion that was at once lacking in speed and subtlety. I followed at an even pace, gliding past the occasional pedestrian but not making an effort to catch up.

After a few blocks he twisted down an alley and I had him. He had taken one of those curious thoroughfares common to Kirentown that terminates within the center of the block, and provides no egress save backtracking to the entrance. A smile crept across my face. With days to plan, and all the resources of the Crown at my disposal I couldn't have run it any better. I slowed my pace and thought about how I would take him.

He was big, as tall as Adolphus though nowhere as broad.

But like a lot of big men I bet he never really learned to fight, to anticipate an opponent's reaction, to recognize a weakness and seize on it, which parts of a man's body hold firm and which parts the Creator botched in forming. Still, his lack of technique wouldn't matter if he got those monstrous hands near my throat. I'd need to put him down fast. He had favored his right leg – I'd work with that.

When I turned the last corner the Kiren was looking around frantically for a means of escape. Like most folk with his inclinations he was terrified of danger, despite his size only inclined to enter combat when all other options had been exhausted. He swiveled back towards me and I could see his fingerhold on sanity slipping. Beads of spittle pitched from his lips as he shouted something vicious and beat one thick fist against his chest. I felt a sense of certainty wash over me, the bloom of warmth that came whenever I bowed to the inevitability of coming violence. There was no retreat now for either of us. I set my guard in front of my face and came towards him, circling left to throw off his balance.

Suddenly from behind me came a fierce chill accompanied by the stench of feces and decomposing flesh. My stones shriveled up into my body and I lurched sideways, covering my nose with my arm as I took shelter against the worn brick wall.

It was eight or maybe nine feet tall, although determining its exact height was difficult because it didn't walk but hovered a few feet from the ground. Its shape was a blasphemous imitation of a biped, though sufficiently altered to make confusion with a member of the human race impossible. Lolling, obscene arms stretched down past the length of its body, each tipped by a pair of fanlike hands wider than my head. It was tough to make out more than that, as most of its body was covered by something that looked like a thick black cloak, but upon closer examination seemed more a strange carapace. I caught glimpses of the frame beneath the casing, hard and white as bone.

I hadn't ever thought I would see one again – another plea to Śakra unanswered.

Its face was a contorted parody of my own, a husk wrapped

tightly across ossein, eyes rabid and cruel. I felt a pain in my chest and collapsed to the ground, the agony coursing through me so terrible that my long history of injury seemed as nothing before it. A scream died stillborn on my lips. For an awful moment I thought of everyone I would betray, every humiliation I would endure and evil I would perpetrate to ease the torment. Then the thing turned its head away from me and floated onward, and the torture ended as abruptly as it had begun. I remained on the ground, my strength utterly spent.

It stopped a few paces before the giant. The lower hinge of its jaw seemed to dislocate, stretching down a half-foot to reveal an open and amaranthine void. 'The child was not to be mistreated.' Its voice was shattered porcelain and bruises on a woman. 'As she suffered, so now shall you.' The Kiren looked on with terror undiluted by conscious thought. With a speed that belied its earlier deliberateness the thing struck, locking a clawed hand around the man's throat. Without apparent effort it lifted his body off the ground and held him there, motionless.

Between the half-decade I had served in the trenches, and my long hours spent breaking criminals in the prisons beneath Black House, I had grown confident that there was no utterance of pain with which I was not familiar – but I had never heard anything to compare with the Kiren's screams. He let loose a noise that spread into the depths of my skull like rusted screws, and I pressed my hands to my head so hard I thought I might burst my eardrums. Gore poured forth from his nostrils, less a nosebleed than an open wound in his sinuses, and he whipped his head back and forth, struggling against the grip of the abortion. So furious were the Kiren's attempts to free himself that he crippled his hand raw against the unyielding substance of his foe, his fingers snapping as he clawed at the rough black covering. Some internal pressure erupted and his right eye burst in his socket, and his screams redoubled against the inside of my head.

Then they stopped, the muted sputtering and the fat swelling in his throat indicating he had bitten straight through the root of his tongue and was now struggling unsuccessfully to swallow it.

For all the many evils that stained my memory, I had no analog for this horror.

Finally the thing shook what was left of the body, like a terrier with a rat. There was a sharp crack and the corpse dropped to the ground, a tattered mass of ripped orifices and torn flesh. Its errand finished, the abomination twisted like a leaf on the wind and glided beyond my field of vision, the aftermath of the pain so intense I lacked the strength even to follow its movements with my eyes.

Lying there against the wall, staring at the shredded body of the man I had been tracking for the last half day, I thought that at the very least the Kiren hadn't made a liar out of me – in all my years I had never seen a death so horrible. Whatever torment he now suffered was a release from that which had sent him there.

9

W hat with all the excitement I figured that was a good time to pass out, so I never learned who called the guard or when they brought the small cadre of agents surrounding me when I awoke. I suppose the brutal murder of a child rapist by a demonic force managed to break through even the aversion to governmental authority ingrained in the heretics.

Of course I wasn't thinking about any of that as I was roughly shaken from my repose, my attention taken up with more immediate issues. The first of these was the unfriendly mug of a former colleague from Black House. The second was his fist balled up in front of my face.

And then my jaw hurt and the men in ice gray were shrieking questions at me, any memory of our shared past buried beneath the violent inclinations universal to law enforcement officials across the Thirteen Lands, or at least every one I've visited. Happily, my position against the wall and the exaggerated number of participants – I've hit enough men in shackles to know that more than three people is just showing off – rendered their enthusiasm less effective than it might have been. Still, it was no great addition to an evening already marked by unpleasantness.

Crispin managed to pull my attackers off long enough to drag me to my feet and lean me up against the morgue cart. The Kiren's shattered carcass lay over the dray, conspicuously uncovered. Despite the blood draining from my mouth, the madness of the evening had left me manic and strangely jubilant. 'Hey, partner! Miss me?'

Crispin was not amused. For a moment I thought he was going to indulge the darker shades of his character upon my bruised face, but he kept his rage under control like a good little soldier. 'What in the name of the Oathkeeper happened here?'

'I'd say divine justice but I don't have such a grim view of the Daevas.' I leaned in close enough that no one else could hear me. 'The thing next to us is the shell of the man responsible for the last corpse we had a conversation over. As to what killed him, if it has a name I don't know it. But if I was responsible you wouldn't have found his remains, nor would I have passed out next to the corpse.' I noted with a petty sort of joy that our contact had smeared a swath of sanguinary fluid on his duster.

A crowd of heretics had gathered at the mouth of the cul-de-sac, chittering loudly, fear and anger in their eyes. The frost needed to cover up the body, and they needed to set up a decent perimeter, and they needed to do it quick. What the hell had happened to Black House since I'd left? It's all well and good to engage in a little bit of casual violence against a suspect, but not at the expense of professionalism. Who did they think they were, the hoax?

The years we had spent tracking the lowest scum of humanity through the general detritus of civilization were enough to convince Crispin of my reliability as a witness, but the guarantees of a disgraced ex-agent-cum-criminal wouldn't be sufficient for the brass. 'You have any proof?'

'None whatsoever. But if you get his name and residence you'll find a memento he kept, maybe a piece of her clothing. You'll probably find a few of them.'

'You don't even know his name?'

'I don't have time for these trivialities, Crispin – I work in the private sector now.'

The crowd was getting boisterous, shouting past the loose cordon of troops blocking off the alley, although about what I still couldn't tell. Did they want my head for killing one of their kind? Had word somehow spread of the man's crimes? Maybe it was just the contempt for police countenanced by all reasonable people. Regardless, this whole thing was starting to get ugly. I saw one of the guardsmen get into it with a member of the mob, stiff-arming him back into his fellows and shouting ethnic slurs.

Crispin noticed what I had. 'Agent Eingers, take Marat and stop those assholes from making this situation any worse. Tenneson, you're in charge. Guiscard and I are taking the suspect back to headquarters.' He turned back to me. 'I'm putting you in irons,' he stated flatly. Not a shocking development, but I wasn't thrilled with it either. I stood up straight and Crispin chained my hands, firmly but without unnecessary cruelty. Guiscard took his place in front of me without comment. His characteristically unpleasant personality was mellowed, and I noted with some surprise that he hadn't taken part in his comrades' abuse.

The pair of them frogmarched me to the mouth of the alley, where two of the agents were trying without success to placate the crowd. Guiscard, acting as point, made an attempt to clear a path for us, but the heretics, normally a docile race, were unresponsive. A standoff seemed imminent, and not one that would redound to my advantage. Not in handcuffs anyway.

Crispin's hand rested on the hilt of his blade, dangerous but not immediately threatening. 'By the authority bequeathed to me as Agent of the Crown, I order you to disperse or be considered outside the protections of the Throne.'

The crowd was having none of it, the brutality of the hoax and the indignity shown to the corpse sufficient to drive them to uncharacteristic defiance. Though the heretics' natural inclination towards obedience was sufficient to stop them from surging on us, they made no move to follow Crispin's commands.

Crispin closed his hand around the gem hanging loose at his throat. He closed his eyes briefly, and the jewel glowed with a soft blue light that leaked out through his fist. This time his words allowed no challenge. 'By the authority bequeathed to me as Agent of the Crown, I order you to disperse or be considered outside the protections of the Throne. *Make way or consider yourself an enemy of the Crown.*' And although he hadn't raised the volume at which he spoke, his voice echoed through the assemblage, and the crowd of Kirens broke, quieting respectfully and swamping against the walls.

The Crown's Eye was another thing I really missed about being an agent.

Crispin nodded to a pair of guardsmen, who took up flanking positions as we continued back to the main street. Halfway around the block, out of sight of the Kirens, Crispin put his hand against the wall and broke down. 'A moment,' he gasped, his mouth open, his lungs working desperately to intake air. The Eye draws its strength from its owner, and even an experienced agent like Crispin couldn't use its power without exhausting himself.

We waited nervously for Crispin to regain his wind. I was getting antsy – it would go ill if the crowd regrouped and fell on us in the narrow confines of the alley. Guiscard rested his hand on his superior's shoulder. 'We need to keep moving,' he said, and his eyes were hard. Crispin took one last breath and fell into line.

They escorted me across half the city, like a dignitary with an honor guard, although in the past I'd never gotten the impression they were bound. It was the second time I had been brought to Black House in chains. It wasn't nearly as unpleasant as the first.

Black House is, frankly, less imposing than it probably should be. A squat, unattractive edifice, more like an oversize merchant house than the headquarters of the most dreaded police force on the face of the planet, it sits obtrusively but without grandeur at a busy intersection straddling the boundary between the Old City and Wormington's Shingle. Three floors of a city block and a maze of warrens beneath the ground remind the populace that the unwavering gaze of the Crown is always upon them. There is little ornamentation, and from the outside the structure fails to inspire or intimidate.

It is, however, mostly colored black. So there's that.

When we reached the grim ebony entranceway Crispin sent the guardsmen back to the crime scene, then he and Guiscard walked me inside. We moved deeper into the building, past the unmarked door that led to the underground rooms where the real interrogations take place, and I breathed a quick sigh of relief. That was one experience I wasn't eager to repeat, neither as participant nor victim. When we reached the main hallway Crispin broke off, presumably to report to the higher-ups, leaving Guiscard to continue my escort. I braced myself for further abuse but the Rouender showed no desire to rekindle our conflict.

He opened the door to the holding area, a featureless stone room, empty save for a cheap wood table and a trio of uncomfortable chairs. He set me down in one of them. 'Crispin will be back soon,' he said.

Dried blood was caked below my nose. 'Not interested in taking your turn?'

'The dead man – he was responsible for the girl?'

I nodded.

'How did you know?'

'Everybody knew,' I said. 'We just weren't telling you about it.'

He rolled his eyes and stomped out.

I spent about an hour and a half in the chair, wincing from the pain in my skull and trying to figure out how many of my ribs were broken. Three was my best guess, but without the use of my hands it was tough to be sure. I thought about slipping my chains as a fuck you to Crispin and the rest of his crew, but it seemed a petty sort of revenge, and one likely to earn another beating.

Eventually the door opened and Crispin entered, a dark look on his face. He took the seat opposite me.

69

'They won't touch it,' he said.

If I was a little slow on the uptake, it was understandable given the circumstances. 'What the hell does that mean?'

'It means that as far as Black House is concerned this matter is closed. Zhange Jue, mill worker and occasional hired thug, was the murderer of Tara Potgieter and several other girls, identities to be determined. He was killed by person or persons unknown in a manner that has yet to be established. You came across the person or persons engaged in the murder but were knocked unconscious before you could ascertain their identity or identities.'

'Person or persons unknown? Are you out of your fucking mind? You think the Kiren was stabbed to death? You know as well as I do this reeks of the Art.'

'I know.'

'Even the brass can't be so stupid as to think otherwise.'

'They aren't.'

'Then what are you talking about, the matter is closed?'

Crispin rubbed at his temples as if to alleviate some hidden pain. 'You worked here long enough, do I have to spell it out for you? No one's looking to get themselves involved in something this ugly, not on the say-so of a drug dealer. The Kiren killed Tara, and now he's dead. End of story.'

It had been a long time since I'd come across an outrage I was insufficiently jaded to accept. 'I get it, no one cares about the dead child – why would they, she's just another slum kid. But there's something loose in Low Town that was spat out from the heart of the void. People need to know.'

'No one's ever going to know. They'll burn the body and you'll keep your mouth shut, and after a while it'll disappear.'

'If you think this thing is done then you're as stupid as your superiors.'

'You know so much?'

'I knew enough to find Tara's murderer while the rest of you were up here holding your dicks.'

'And why don't you tell me how exactly that happened – or

am I to believe you were wandering through the back alleys of Kirentown and bumped into the man responsible for the body you found two days ago?'

'No, Crispin, obviously I was tracking him down. I assumed that being a member of an elite investigative organization, you wouldn't need the situation spelled out to you like a damn child.'

His upper lip twitched below his beaked nose. 'I told you not to go looking for him.'

'I chose to ignore your suggestion.'

'It wasn't a suggestion, it was the command of a legally empowered representative of the Crown.'

'Your orders didn't mean much to me when I was an agent, and a half-decade out of the service hasn't led me to rate them any higher.'

Crispin reached over the table and rapped me on the chin, almost casually but with enough force that I struggled to maintain balance on the chair. Damn, but the man was still quick.

I rubbed at a loose tooth with my tongue, nursing the pain and hoping it wouldn't fall out. 'Fuck you. I don't owe you a thing.'

'I spent the last forty-five minutes convincing the captain to keep you out of the hands of Special Ops. If it wasn't for me they'd be taking you apart with a scalpel right now.' The sneer sat awkwardly on his face. Crispin was not by nature disposed to reveling in the misfortune of others. 'You know how much those animals want you back under their care?'

Quite badly, I imagined. I had been working for Special Operations towards the end of my time as an agent, the unit tasked with fixing issues that fell outside the normal purview of law enforcement. Their retirement package generally consisted of a violent death and an unmarked grave, and avoiding that unhappy fate had taken a good bit more luck than a wise man ought to count on twice. I owed Crispin for averting a reunion, and even my well-honed sense of ingratitude wasn't sufficient to deny that.

From inside his duster Crispin pulled out a document and sent it spinning across the table. 'Here's your statement. The illegal goods found in the alley are assumed to be Zhange Jue's, and will be destroyed according to official policy.' That was right, they must have found my satchel – I guess I owed Crispin for that too; ten ochre worth of breath will get you five years in a labor camp, three more than the average inmate survives. 'Sign at the bottom,' he said, then leaned across the table and unlocked my cuffs.

I spent a moment rubbing circulation back into my wrists. 'Good to see the case wrapped up, justice pursued, righteousness restored and all that.'

'I don't like this any more than you do. If I had my way we'd be tearing apart the Kiren's house, and have half the force looking into your story. This . . .' He shook his head bitterly, and I saw the same young man I'd met ten years earlier, who fancied his service to the Crown was just that, service, and that what evil existed in the world could be defeated by the strong right arm of a virtuous man. 'This isn't justice.'

For all his intellect and physical prowess, at the end of the day Crispin wasn't very good at his job. His fantasies of what it should be blinded him to what it was, and that had doomed him to the middle ranks even though his family was one of the oldest in Rigus, and his service to the Crown noble and distinguished. Justice? I almost laughed. An agent doesn't pursue justice, he maintains order.

Justice – by the Lost One, what can you say to that?

I didn't have the energy to give him another civics lesson, and anyway this was a long-standing argument. Growing up surrounded by tapestries depicting his ancestors leading doomed charges against invincible odds had made him a sucker for words that didn't mean anything. I signed my name at the bottom of the document with a flourish.

'The Kiren got his, and I leave justice to the Firstborn. At the moment I'm more concerned with what happens when the thing that killed him comes back.'

'If I were you, I'd hope it doesn't – as of right now, you're the only link. So long as it stays gone, no one gives a shit about you, not any more. But if it starts popping up again Special Ops will set you a spot in the basement, and there won't be anything I can do about it.'

That was as pleasant a note as any to leave on. 'Until that happy day comes,' I said, giving him a final nod of farewell.

He didn't return it, his eyes downcast, fixed without purpose on the center of the table.

I left Black House with all possible speed, hoping to avoid both the pull of memory and any former comrades intent on displaying dissatisfaction with my career path via physical assault. I was more successful with the second than the first, and by the time I hit the streets my mood had plunged into something approaching outright despair. I walked home wishing I still had my stash, and could take a quick dip into it.

10

When I got back to the Earl I drank a flagon of ale and slept for about a day and a half, waking only to give Adolphus a quick blow-by-blow over a plate of eggs. I kept vague on what exactly had done the Kiren – the less anyone knew the better for everyone. He was suitably impressed.

For the next week I went about my business with a tight watch, backtracking and setting false trails in case anyone was shadowing me, but best as I could tell I was on my own. No ethereal spirits, no dark apparitions hovering out of the corners of my eye – just the boil on the ass of Rigus that is Low Town, stewing in all its fetid glory.

So for a while I assumed that would be pretty much it. I had some long nights thinking about the monstrosity, but even had I been interested in tracking it down, I had nothing to work from. And truth be told I'd had my fill of playing detective – pretending I was an agent had turned out to be even less satisfying than actually being one.

Then the Shattered Dagger Mob went to war with a clique of Islanders from near the docks, and I didn't have time to think about anything other than the day-to-day survival of my enterprise. Spending my afternoons explaining to stone-faced heretics why I owed them no tax on my operations, and my evenings convincing a crew of drug-addled rude boys that I was too crazy to muscle didn't leave much room for extracurricular activities.

As far as the rest of Rigus was concerned, the important people considered the matter forgotten, and the unimportant people didn't count. The ice kept a pretty tight lid on the whole thing. There were rumors of black magic and demons hiding in the shadows, and for a while there was a boom in the sale of defensive charms of dubious effectiveness, especially among the Kiren, by nature a superstitious people. But Low Town is a busy place, and as autumn gave way to early winter, the murder of Tara Potgieter sank into the realm of dim memory.

I thought about heading back to the Aerie to clue the Crane in on what had happened. I figured I owed him that much. But then I figured I owed him a hell of a lot more, and since I'd never be able to repay the full amount I decided to write off this last debt as well. He'd understand, even if Celia wouldn't. Scratch a scab long enough and it'll start to run. That part of my life was over – as far as I was concerned our reunion was an isolated incident.

Despite the best efforts of Adeline, Wren refused to spend a full night within the walls of the Earl. Like a half-trained version of his namesake, he'd flit in to snatch a few crumbs of food, then fly out again without a word. Once I caught him swiping something from a neighborhood stall, and he disappeared for a full week, leaving Adeline sick with worry and furious at me – but then he showed up again one evening, slipping through the back door like nothing had happened.

Though reticent to take to settled life, he was there when I needed him, and became an aid if not an asset to my operations. I kept him out of anything serious and never let him hold any weight, but his fresh legs were useful when I needed a message carried, and I found myself acclimatizing to his laconic presence, one of those few individuals unencumbered by the need to fill the air with rhetoric.

Adolphus offered to teach the boy to box, and much as it galled him to admit there might be a skill he'd yet to master, he had the good sense to take the giant up on his offer. He showed a talent for it, and I enjoyed wasting the occasional hour watching the two spar, burning a twist of dreamvine while Adolphus demonstrated basic footwork with his gargantuan frame. It was this idle enterprise I was engaged in late one afternoon when Adeline unknowingly set my feet upon the path of ruin.

'You can take five blows to the chest easier than one to your head,' Adolphus was saying, his fat face thick with sweat as his wife entered the courtyard. 'Always keep your hands up,' he continued, Wren aping his actions in miniature beside him.

So soft is Adeline's voice that on those rare occasions when she magnifies it beyond a whisper it has the effect of a shriek. 'Another girl's gone missing.'

I reminded myself to exhale a chest full of smoke. Adolphus dropped his hands to his sides, his voice low and guttural. 'When? Who?'

'Last night. Anne from the bakery told me. They've got guardsmen out looking now. I don't know the girl. Anne said her father is a tailor near the canal.'

Adolphus shot me a grim look, then turned to Wren. 'Training is over. Wash up and help Adeline.'

I could see the boy was unhappy to be excluded, but Adolphus can be a heavy character, and he kept his tongue resting in its cavity.

We waited until they were both inside before continuing. 'What do you think?' Adolphus asked.

'Maybe she got lost playing Rat-in-a-Hole. Maybe she caught the eye of a slaver and is stuffed in a barrel on her way east. Maybe her father beat her to death and hid her body somewhere. It could be a lot of things.'

His one eye flickered across my face, performing double duty as always. 'It could be a lot of things, fine. Is it them?'

It's usually best to assume the worst and work from there. 'Probably.'

'What will you do?'

'I'll keep my nose clean and stay out of it.' Though I doubted I'd have that option. If this was the work of the same crew that got the last girl, there'd be trouble – the Crown would make sure of that. They might not care about the dead child of a Low Town dock worker but they sure as shit would want to know who was summoning up otherworldly entities. Only the Crown gets to dabble in the dark arts – it's a privilege they preserve with great rigor. As of right now I was the only connection to whatever had killed the Kiren, and that alone was enough to merit me a session below Black House.

'Will the ones that killed the girl come after you?' Adolphus asked.

'I'm done playing lawman.'

'And will your former comrades let you off so easily?'

I said nothing. Adolphus knew the answer.

'I'm sorry that I pushed you to do this.'

I found myself very conscious of the gray hairs that speckled his beard, and of the sparse patches in his mane.

'I'm going to head over to the Aerie, see if I can't get a better handle on the situation. It's time I talked to the Crane.' I left Adolphus in the courtyard and went upstairs to grab my satchel. I considered taking a blade, but thought better of it. If the girl turned up floating in the canal I was sure to get a visit from the law, and if that happened I'd never see anything I was carrying again. Besides, from what I could tell steel wouldn't do much against the abomination I had seen. I exited the bar and set out on a brisk walk, my mind drawn back to what I had long assumed would be my first and only encounter with the thing that had killed the Kiren.

II

The War was almost over – we hovered at the precipice of victory. Everywhere the Dren whore was on her back, her defenses breached, her castles defended by old men with bent pikes and boys too young to shave. Of the seventeen territories that had once made up the United Provinces, only four remained in Dren possession, and once we took Donknacht these remaining holdouts were sure to fold as well. My five long years of service, killing and bleeding and pushing for a hundred yards a day, were almost over. We'd all be spending Midwinter at home, drinking hot toddies by a roaring fire. At that very moment, Wilhelm van Agt, Chief Steadholder of the Dren Republic, was considering an armistice as prelude to complete capitulation.

Unfortunately it seemed the news of our conflict's resolution had not yet reached the Dren themselves, who stood outside their capital city like lions, roaring defiance in the face of Allied might. A half-decade of preparation and a mastery of siege tactics had enabled them to create what was likely the most perfect defensive perimeter in mankind's long history of violence. It seemed they hadn't heard of the famine and disease afflicting their forces, of the terrible losses they'd suffered at Karsk and Lauvengod, of the generally hopeless nature of their cause – or if they had it had done nothing to weaken their resolve.

It was this collective intransigence, intransigence that bordered on outright foolishness, that I blamed for forcing me out of bed in the middle of the night to go on a covert mission. It was the stupidity of our own brass, however, that I blamed for the logistical failure that was to leave me and my squad absent appropriate camouflage during the operation.

Inwardly, at least. Outwardly, officers don't grumble about these little administrative mishaps, even if they're of the sort likely to get them killed.

Private Carolinus had no such qualms. 'Lieutenant, how are we expected to go on a mission at night with no faceblack?' he asked angrily, as if I had an explanation or a vat of the stuff hidden beneath my sleep-roll. Carolinus was red-haired and ruddy-cheeked, a Northern Rouender, one of that peculiar breed of men whose ancestors had invaded Vaal three centuries prior and never left. As squat and hard as the coal he had grown up mining, he was nearly as quick to complain as he was to go over the top. He had become, frankly, a constant source of annoyance, but with Adolphus invalided home he was the only man I thought capable of taking over if I caught a stray bolt. 'Lieutenant, the Dren have eyes like owls. We'll be porcupined for sure if we aren't inked.'

I cinched tight the straps of my leather armor, making sure my weapons were in place and my trench blade hung loose at my side. 'They aren't expecting you to do anything, Private. I, however, am ordering you to shut that flapping cunt mouth of yours and gear up, because you're going over the wall in a quarter-hour whether you're butt-fucking naked or covered in soot. And don't worry about the enemy, from what I hear they only fire at men.'

The others laughed and even Carolinus smirked, but their

humor was forced and so was mine. It wasn't just the absence of faceblack – I hadn't even known we were on prior to forty minutes earlier, when an aide to the company commander had roughly woken me from the first decent night's sleep I'd had in a week, telling me to grab a crew of my finest and report to the major.

Truth was none of it felt right. Donknacht the Unbowed was the capital of the Dren States, and for a millennium and a half it had stood free of foreign yoke. When the rest of the Dren provinces had been swallowed up by their neighbors, Donknacht alone had remained a free city. And when the surge of Dren nationalism seventy years past had unified these disparate states into one mighty confederacy, Donknacht had been the pivot around which the commonwealth had formed.

I couldn't speak for the remaining provinces, but the soldiers facing us across a half-mile of no-man's-land died on suicide missions cursing our mothers. Their defenses wouldn't be carried without a full-scale assault preceded by artillery and sorcery, and even then it was likely to cost us half a division of men. This assumed the bastards didn't fall back into the city and fight us for each house and street. Like everyone else I was hoping the rumors of the armistice were true, and we would stop our long advance here, on the plains outside the capital. Either way I was hard pressed to see what five lone grunts were going to do to alter the situation, with or without faceblack.

I turned to Saavedra, our pointman since a stray artillery shell had taken off the top of poor Donnely's skull. His dark eyes and the stern set of his face betrayed his Asher ancestry, though why he had signed up as a member of our mixed unit instead of among the regiments of his own people none of us could say. Saavedra refused to discuss it, or much else for that matter, and the men of the First Capital Infantry were not the sort to look closely at a man's papers, so long as he took his turn over the top. Despite his exile among us heathens, Saavedra hewed close to the standards of his race, taciturn and unreadable, the best card player in the regiment and a terror with a short sword besides. He'd have enough faceblack stashed somewhere to darken his own features, but sure as the single god of his people was a grim one, he wouldn't have enough for two.

'Get the rest of them ready. I'm to see the major.'

Saavedra nodded, silent as usual. I headed back towards the center of camp.

Our major, Cirellus Grenwald, was a fool and a coward, but not an outright lunatic and that alone placed him distinctly in the top half of the officer corps. If his primary talent consisted of being born at the top of a ladder, it was something at least that he'd yet to fall from it. He was talking to a man in a leather coat offset with silver trim, whom I took for a civilian at first glance.

The major offered me an ingenuous smile that, more than any actual competence, had hastened his ascent through the ranks. 'Lieutenant, I was just telling Third Sorcerer Adelweid here about you. Head of the fiercest platoon in the division. He'll provide an impregnable defense for your . . . undertaking.'

Sorcerer Adelweid was pale-faced, thin but with a wormy film of excess flesh. He had found the time to slip his raven-black, shoulder-length hair into a jeweled clasp, an adornment which, along with his gilded belt buckle and silver cufflinks, seemed singularly inappropriate to the situation at hand. I didn't like him, and I liked less the discovery that my mission involved his protection. The Crane aside, I hated sorcerers – every grunt in the force did and not just because they were showy and whiny and got their requisitions for arcane items filled in a hot minute while we scavenged for boot leather and millet. No, every grunt in the force hated sorcerers because, to a man and with vituperative language, each could tell of losing comrades when some spell-slinger got careless directing battle hexes and annihilated half a unit in a spray of blood and bone. The brass thought them great fun of course, certain that each new scheme they proposed would be the secret weapon that won us the War.

But it wouldn't do to let this animus play across my face. I saluted the man crisply, an obeisance he returned apathetically and without comment. Major Grenwald continued. 'Welcome to Operation Ingress, Lieutenant. Your orders are as follows. You and your men are to take Sorcerer Adelweid four hundred yards into no-man's-land, halting at a place of his choosing, at which point the sorcerer will perform a working. You are to detail one man to protect him, then you and the remainder are to travel another two hundred yards towards Dren lines, where you will place this talisman' – he handed me a small black jewel – 'on an overlook within sight of the enemy defenses. You are to hold that position until Sorcerer Adelweid has completed his part of the mission.'

Adding up the distances I came to the unfortunate sum of six hundred yards, closer to the Dren's territory than ours and well within the range of even short-distance patrols. Nor did it escape my notice that Grenwald had offered no estimate as to how long Adelweid would need to complete his task. Was it ten minutes? Twenty? An hour? For that matter, why did we all assume this slippery piece of black glass would even work? From what I had seen of the Art, it was just as likely to blow up in my hands.

I didn't imagine I'd get answers, even if I was foolish enough to ask the questions. Instead I snapped a hand at Grenwald, praying it wouldn't be the last time I'd salute the vainglorious motherfucker, then turned to Adelweid. 'Sir, our unit is grouped at the front trench. If you'll follow me.'

He nodded vaguely towards the major, then fell in line behind me without further comment. I took the opportunity to make one. 'Sir, now might be a good time to remove any reflective gear you have. That hair clasp in particular will give away our position to any Dren sniper we run into.'

'Thank you for the suggestion, Lieutenant, but my garments remain as they are.' His voice was every drop as oily as I expected, and he rubbed at the gleaming bangle possessively. 'Our mission would be quite impossible to complete without it. Besides, I have no wish to return to camp victorious only to discover that some grunt has made off with the cufflinks given to me by the head of the Order of the Twisted Oak.'

Better than not coming back at all, I thought, and better than sacrificing me and my men to your bloated sense of vanity. Although he was right, someone would have stolen them.

By the time we reached the outskirts of camp the men were in position, weapons at the ready, armor pulled tight. The six of us stood in a circle and I repeated our orders. It was clear they weren't happy, not with the job and not with Adelweid, but they were professionals and kept quiet on it. When I was finished I ordered a last equipment check and then we were up the ladders and alone in the wasteland between our camp and the Dren.

'From here on out full light and noise restrictions are in effect.' I nodded to Saavedra, his face predictably soot-colored. He shifted into a practiced stalk and fifteen seconds later I could barely make him out. Carolinus fell in behind him, and I followed with Adelweid a few steps ahead of me.

Behind me was our missilist, Milligan, a bright, decent-natured Tarasaihgn who could prick the Queen's face on an ochre coin at a hundred paces. I wasn't sure what good he would do us – it was pretty dark to be sending off bolts. He was calm in a mêlée at least, nothing special but steady and reliable.

Taking rear was Cilliers, a dour-faced Vaalan giant who smiled little and spoke less. He was about the only man in the company who hadn't switched exclusively to a trench blade, still carrying a double-edged flamberge across his back, the weapon passed down from son to son since before his ancestors had sworn fealty to the Rigun Throne. His frame was too broad to make him much use for covert operations, but we'd be happy to have his two-hander if we needed to make a stand on open ground.

Years of fighting had turned the once lush landscape into a barren desert. Bombardments, artillery and magical, had destroyed most of the vegetation and all fauna of the non-rodent variety. Even the topography of the terrain had been altered, explosives leveling hills and thrusting up piles of debris to replace them. Beyond any aesthetic concern, the devastation meant there was little cover to be found. Without faceblack, on a moonlit night, we were easy prey for any patrol that came within fifty yards.

We needed to move quick and we needed to move quiet. Unsurprisingly, the practitioner was having difficulty with both of these, his gait more appropriate to a morning stroll than our clandestine mission. I winced every time the light caught on his silver and noticed Milligan doing the same. If one of us got bled because this idiot wouldn't take off his jewelry, I didn't think I could stop the men from friendly-firing him. I didn't think I'd try.

After a quarter-mile I leaned in close to Adelweid and whispered, 'Four hundred yards. Let us know where to set up.'

He pointed to a low hill and responded in a voice that did little to maintain our stealth. 'That knoll will do nicely. Take me there, then deploy the talisman.'

I signaled to Saavedra and we swung our line towards the peak. I'll give this much for Adelweid, the bastard knew his craft. No sooner had we reached the top than he pulled a pack of arcane materials out of his bag and began drawing intricate symbols into the dirt with a short branch of black oak. His movements were sharp and natural, and I knew enough of the Art to appreciate that it wasn't such an easy thing to draw a pentacle in the pitch black, not when a mistake meant opening yourself up to forces that would fry your brain. In the midst of his work he turned to me. 'Continue the mission, Lieutenant. I'll take care of my end.'

'Private Carolinus, you're on guard. If we aren't back in three-quarters of an hour, take the sorcerer and return to base.' Carolinus drew his trench blade with his off hand and saluted. Saavedra went back to point and the remaining four of us pushed onward into Dren territory.

Two hundred yards and we crested a small incline, its geometry too sharp to be anything but the result of an artillery shell. In the distance I could see the first line of the enemy trenches, and the lights of their campfires out beyond that. Signaling to the men to form on me, I pulled the talisman from a pouch on my armor and dropped it in the dirt, feeling a bit foolish as I did so.

'That's it?' whispered Milligan. 'Just stand on a hill and leave a pebble in the middle of it?'

'Private, shut your mouth and keep your eyes open.' Milligan's nerves were understandable – this was the part of the mission I had liked least, and I hadn't been particularly crazy about any of it. On top of this ridge we were easy targets for any Dren patrol that wandered by, and they were a lot closer to reinforcements than we were.

In the dark, in those circumstances, every shadow hides a sniper and every glint of light reflects off steel, so I wasn't certain I saw anything until Milligan signaled down the line. We grabbed dust, hunkering beneath what little cover we could find. Twenty yards out from the base of our hill one of them noticed us and let out a cry of warning and I knew we were fucked.

Milligan sent off a bolt at the front man but it went spinning off into the night, and then they were sprinting up the dune and we prepared to meet their charge. Saavedra took the first one and I took the second, and after that it was hard to concentrate on the general arc of the battle, my attention occupied by the particulars.

Mine was young, barely old enough to pleasure a woman, and I winced at his lack of skill. Five years of killing anyone in a gray uniform had overridden any natural aversion towards murdering a virtual child, and my only thought was to finish him quickly. A feint to his side and a counter of his awkward defense and he was down, blood spurting from a killing strike through his abdomen.

It was a good thing I dropped him because it wasn't going all our way. Cilliers was showing one of the enemy the reason he had never abandoned his ancestral weapon and Saavedra was his usual self, holding down a pair of Dren with a display of coldly efficient sword work. But Milligan was on his last legs, a squat Dren with a trench blade in one hand and a hatchet in the other steadily pushing him back towards the slope of the hill. I unstrapped a throwing knife from my armor and sent it sailing into the back of Milligan's attacker, hoping it would be enough to even the odds.

I didn't have time to do more as one of the men facing Saavedra disengaged and came towards me. I hefted my trench blade and drew the battle club that was swinging from my belt.

This one was better, good in fact, and I didn't need to see the scar that separated his nose into two uneven masses of flesh to place him as a veteran of our conflict. He understood how to kill with a short blade, wary circling interrupted by the rapid exchange of blows, off hand poised to settle the business firmly. But this wasn't my first tumble either, and my own weapon stayed close on his, and the spiked rod in my left hand waited for an opening.

It came when he overextended trying for a thrust, and I lashed my club against his wrist. He let out an angry scream but didn't drop his sword. This fucker was tough as pig iron, but his stoicism, while impressive, wasn't sufficient to save his life. His hand crippled, he couldn't maintain our pace and a half-minute later he was down from a pair of fatal wounds.

For a moment I thought we might even pull it off, until I heard the twang of a bowstring and watched Cilliers's massive frame topple backwards, a bolt feather-deep in his breast. Now that it was too late I spotted the assassin cresting the top of the ridge, reloading his crossbow, while his partner, a hulking Dren nearly Adolphus's size, flanked him with a wicked-looking spiked hammer. Dropping my mace, I took a running start and dived into the bowman, knocking the weapon from his grip and sending the two of us hurtling down the embankment. We struggled as we fell, but by the time we stopped rolling I was on top, and I drove the pommel of my trench blade against his skull, till his hold on me slackened and I was able to reverse my grip and pull the edge sharp across his throat.

I caught my breath, then sprinted back up the hill. When I reached the summit Saavedra was the only one of us still standing, and barely at that. The Dren giant had him on the outs, the Asher's intricate style a poor match for the savagery of his opponent. Saavedra's defenses did, however, provide sufficient distraction for me to close in and hamstring the ogre, nor did my comrade stutter when I provided him an opening, dispatching our remaining enemy with a quick thrust beneath his chin.

The two of us stood staring at each other, then Saavedra slumped to the ground and I realized he had been tagged, a pool of blood seeping through his leather armor. Flinty bastard hadn't shown it until the combat was over. 'How bad is it?' I asked.

'Bad,' he responded, with the same unreadable demeanor that had won him half the unit's wages.

I gingerly removed his armor. He winced but didn't speak.

Saavedra was right – it was bad. The spiked end of the war hammer had penetrated his leather shell and into his intestines. He had a chance if I could get him back to camp. I settled him up against an incline and checked on the rest of my men.

Dead – no surprises. That bolt had done for Cilliers, an inglorious end for such a valiant soldier. I wanted to bring his flamberge back to base, try to get it to his family somehow – he would have liked that, but it was heavy and I would already be half-carrying Saavedra.

Milligan's head had been caved in while I was dealing with the enemy bowman. He was never more than average close in. I was glad at least that we had taken care of the bastard with the hammer. I had always liked the friendly little runt. I had always liked both of them, truth be told.

Saavedra was praying in the dissonant tones of his foreign tongue, the most I had ever heard him speak. It was disquieting, and I wished he would stop but didn't say anything, unwilling to begrudge a dying man the chance to get right with his god.

I crouched down beside the ridge and scanned the horizon. If another patrol showed we were fucked. I thought about grabbing Milligan's crossbow, but it was dark and I was never any good with those things. I wished I had some black powder. I wished that jewel would start working.

Minutes passed. Saavedra continued his alien monologue. I started to wonder if a passing Dren unit hadn't greased Carolinus and the sorcerer, leaving me waiting for a climax that wasn't coming. Then from behind me I heard a sound for which I had no context, followed by a startled gasp from Saavedra. I turned on my heel.

A wound was forming in the air above the gem, a hole through the universe that bled strange ichor around the edge. I had seen magic before, from the playful chicanery of the Crane to the platoon-killing firepower of a battle hex, but I had never seen anything like this. The rent let loose a high-pitched whistling, almost a cry, and against myself I peered into its depths.

Things strange and terrible gazed back at me, vast membranes of eyes swirling in apoplectic frenzy, gaping maws gnashing endlessly in an infinite black void, orifices pulsating erotically, tendrils coiling and uncoiling in the eternal night. The obscene whine babbled to me in a half-intelligible tongue, promising hideous gifts and demanding still more terrible sacrifices.

As abruptly as it began the noise ended, and a black goo leached through the rift. It dripped from the entrance into reality, bringing with it a smell so foul I had to choke back vomit, a rot deeper than conception and older than stone. Gradually the slime coalesced, shadowy black robes forming around a bone-white outline. Saavedra made a sound somewhere between a shriek and a sigh and I knew he was dead. I caught a glimpse of the thing's face, broken-glass eyes above rows and rows of sharp teeth.

Then it was gone, floating east towards the Dren line. It moved without visible signs of effort, as if propelled by a force external to its body. The stench remained.

My mind scrambled to regain footing amid the formerly rigid laws of existence. It was touch and go. The knowledge that more Dren patrols lingered in the area, and the suspicion that their sympathy for my mental state as I stood atop the corpses of their comrades was likely to be limited, ultimately proved sufficient inducement to get me moving.

A half-second of inspection confirmed that Saavedra was no longer living. He was a grim cur, but he had died like a man and in the end I had no complaint of his conduct or character.

The Ashers believe death in battle is their only path to redemption – on that account his forbidding deity had been well served.

There wasn't time for lamentation, there rarely is. Nine men lay dead, and there would be a tenth to add to the tally if I stayed around much longer. I hooked my trench blade through my belt and headed back to check on the sorcerer.

Adelweid stood at the peak of the small dune, his hands planted firmly across his hips, proud as a gamebird and twice as pretty. 'Did you see it? You must have – you were so near the epicenter. You have been allowed a glimpse into the realms that lie beyond ours, seen the tissue-thin walls between this world and the next separate before your very eyes. Do you realize how lucky you are?'

Slumped against a small gray boulder was Carolinus. He had been dead for at least a few minutes. A pair of Dren soldiers were sprawled a few feet in front of him, joining their enemy in repose. 'What happened to him?' I asked, knowing I wouldn't receive much of an answer.

Adelweid's reverie broke momentarily. 'Who? Oh, my guardian. He's dead.' The sorcerer turned flush towards me now, excitement in his voice, the closest to human I'd yet seen him. 'But his sacrifice was not in vain! My mission was successful, and across this shattered plain I can feel my comrades were as well! You are doubly blessed, Lieutenant, for you are privileged to stand watch at the collapse of the Dren Commonwealth!'

When I didn't say anything he turned back in the general direction of his creations, watching as the occasional burst of lightning illuminated the landscape. In the distance I could see waves of the things move steadily eastward. Adelweid was right – from far out there was something ethereal and even somehow beautiful about the things. But the memory of that horrible stench, and the sound Saavedra made as his heart went out, were still fresh, and I didn't share Adelweid's conceit that what I had seen was anything less than an abomination before the Oathkeeper and all the Daevas.

Then the screams started – a chorus of them erupting from across the Dren line. In combat the sounds of death are mixed with that of battle, the shrieks of the wounded merging with the clash of steel and the eruption of cannon fire. But the final sounds of the Dren were undiluted by any other noise, and a thousand times more terrible for that fact. Adelweid's smile widened.

I knelt down beside Carolinus. He had done his duty, then bled out while the sorcerer performed horrors in the darkness nearby. His trench blade lay broken at his side and his eyes were open. I closed them and took his damaged weapon in my hand. 'Once you've summoned these things your job is finished?'

Adelweid was still staring east, at the terrible devastation his creature and its brethren were spreading, something between lust and pride on his face. 'Once called, the creatures will complete their missions and then fade back to their world.'

He was so engrossed in the carnage that he paid no attention as I took up a spot beside him, and scarcely more when I put Carolinus's shattered weapon through his exquisitely tailored coat. His scream was subsumed by the sounds echoing off the Dren lines. I withdrew the blade and tossed it aside. Adelweid's corpse rolled awkwardly down the hill.

I figured somebody was owed for Saavedra and the rest, and if I couldn't get any higher up the chain, Adelweid would do. And I figured the world would be better off without him in it.

I slipped back to our lines and reported a successful mission, albeit one with a high casualty rate. The major was not concerned with our losses, neither my men nor the sorcerer. It was a big night, the eve before the final charge that would break the back of the Dren Republic, and there was much to prepare. At dawn I formed up my platoon as part of an all-out attack, the kind that should have taken us ten thousand men to pull off. But their defense was piecemeal, whole sectors of the enemy trenches containing nothing but dead men, bodies contorted horribly, the source of their demise uncertain in the full light of morning. The remaining Dren were too scattered and disheartened to muster much resistance.

That afternoon General Bors accepted the capitulation of the capital city, and the day after he received the unconditional surrender of Wilhelm van Agt, last and greatest Steadholder of the United Dren Commonwealth.

It ain't the way they tell it on Remembrance Day, and I don't imagine it'll ever make the story books, but I was there and that was the way the War ended. I got a medal for it – the whole company did for being the first men into Donknacht, beaten gold with a pikeman standing over a Dren eagle. I sold it for a top-shelf bottle of rye and a night with a Nestriann whore. I still think I got the better end of the deal.

12

When I finished relaying those parts of the story appropriate for public consumption the Crane poured himself a glass of his noxious medicine and sipped from it slowly, shivering. I'd never seen the Crane frightened. It did not bode well for my immediate future. 'You're sure Adelweid's monster was the same thing that killed the Kiren?'

'It left a vivid impression.'

'A creature from the outer emptiness, let loose on the streets of Low Town.' He threw the rest of the drink down his throat, then wiped at his lips with a bony arm. 'By the Oathkeeper.'

'What can you tell me about it?'

'I've heard legends. It is said that Atrum Noctal, the false monk of Narcassi, could peer into the nothingness between the worlds, and that the things he saw there would answer when he called. Sixty years ago, my master, Roan the Grim, led the sorcerers of the realm against the Order of the Squared Circle, whose violations of the High Laws were so egregious that all records of their activities were destroyed. But as for direct experience . . .' He shrugged his narrow shoulders. 'I have none. The study of the Art is a twisting path, and one with many branches. Before the creation of the Academy for the Furtherance of the Magical Arts, practitioners learned what their masters had to teach them and studied where their inclinations led. Roan would have no truck with the dark, and though I left his service I have stayed true to his precepts.'

He smiled then, and I realized with some surprise that it was his first since I'd entered. By the Oathkeeper, he was going fast. 'For me the Art was never a path to power, or a way to delve into the secrets hidden where nothing living dwells.' His hands began to shimmer with a soft blue light, the glow gradually forming into a scintillating ball that swooped around his arms. He had performed this trick often for me and Celia when we were children, sending the sphere dashing under tables and over chairs, always just out of our reach. 'My gifts were for healing and for protection, to shelter the weak and provide respite for the weary. I never wished to be capable of anything else.'

Two sharp knocks rang out on the outer door and Celia entered. The illusions diminished, then disappeared.

The Crane turned his eyes quickly towards her. 'Celia, my dear – look who's returned!' There was a strange note in his voice.

Celia crossed the floor, her pale green dress swaying slightly with her movements. I leaned in and she kissed my cheek, her hands trailing against my face. Coiled around her index finger was a silver ring with a fat sapphire, the symbol of her ascension to Sorcerer First Rank.

'What a pleasant surprise. The Master suspected that we wouldn't see you again, that your last visit was a fluke. But I knew better.'

'Yes, you were right, my dear! Right completely!' His grin was taut across his aged features. 'And now we are all together again, as we used to be.' He spread his hands, one resting lightly on each of us. 'As we were meant to be.'

I was grateful when Celia broke away, allowing me to shrug off the Master's grip. There was a slight arc to her mouth that looked like a smile. 'Much as I would love to think this call is purely social, I can't help but wonder about the hushed conversation the two of you were having before I entered the room.'

I shot a look towards the Crane, hoping to keep the content of our discussion secret, but he either missed my signal or ignored it. 'Our friend wants to know more about the creature that attacked him. He says he saw one in the War. I think he has notions of becoming another Guy the Pure, hunting down the enemies of Śakra with a sword of holy flame!' His forced laughter sputtered into a choking cough.

Celia took the empty cup from his hands and refilled it from the green decanter before handing it back. 'I would have thought you'd have had enough of playing hero. Few indeed survive an encounter with the void, and those that do are seldom anxious to repeat the experience.'

'I've survived a few things. Firstborn willing, I'll survive a few more.'

'Your bravery is inspiring. We'll make sure to commission an epic poem when your body lies mangled in a coffin.'

'See if you can't have it set to music. I've always felt I merited an ode.'

I thought that would at least get a chuckle, but Celia was having none of it and the Crane seemed not to be listening. 'It might not be up to me,' I said. 'Another girl has disappeared.'

This broke the Crane out of his repose, and his anemic eyes darted across my face before resting against Celia's. 'I hadn't heard. I had thought that . . .' He stuttered his way into silence, then drank the remainder of his tumbler. Whatever was in that concoction, he'd be sleeping it off tomorrow.

Celia's put one hand on the Master's back and escorted him into a chair. He flinched at her touch but allowed himself to be led, sinking down into the leather and staring off into space.

She bent over and patted his head, her wooden necklace hanging over the low cut of her dress, tightening against her skin as she stood erect. 'That is ill news, but I don't understand what it has to do with you.'

'The Crown knows I was there for the last one. It's only a matter of time before they come calling, and if I don't have something to give them . . . it might go badly.'

'But you have no skill with the Art! They have to understand that. You used to be an agent! They'll have to listen to you!'

'I didn't retire from the Crown's service with an honorable discharge – I was stripped of my rank. They'll be happy to have something to pin on me just to wrap up a loose end.' What a strange conception the upper classes have of law enforcement. 'These aren't kind men.'

When next Celia spoke it was with a firm seriousness. 'All right then. If you're in it, we're in it. What's the next step?'

'We?'

'Much as it suits your vanity to play the lone wolf, you aren't in fact the only one concerned with what happens to Low Town. And difficult as it may be to believe, time has passed inside the Aerie as well as out of it.' She held her hand up to the light, drawing attention to her ring. 'Given the nature of your investigation, perhaps it isn't altogether illogical to rely on the assistance of a First Mage of the Realm.'

'Perhaps it isn't,' I conceded.

She pursed her lips in thought. I tried not to notice their ripeness, nor that her lipstick brought out the color of her eyes. 'Wait here. I have something that can help you.'

I watched her leave, then turned to the Crane. 'Your charge assumes her new responsibilities ably.'

He answered without looking up. 'She's not the girl she was.'

I was set to continue but as I caught his face in the dying light, so frail that it seemed it might well fade into dust, I thought better of it, and waited quietly until Celia returned.

'Take off your shirt,' she told me.

'I'm well aware of my overpowering allure, but I hardly think this is the time to succumb to it.' She rolled her eyes and made a hurrying gesture with her hand, and I tossed my coat on a nearby chair and pulled my tunic over my head. Unclothed, I noticed the room had a draft. I hoped Celia's purpose wouldn't be a waste of my time.

She reached into a pocket of her dress and drew forth a sapphire, perfect blue and about the size of my thumbnail. 'I have ensorcelled this – if it feels warm, or if it causes you pain, it means you are in the presence of dark magic, either the practitioner himself or a close associate.' She pressed the stone against my breast, below the shoulder. I felt a burning sensation, and when she withdrew her digit the jewel was affixed to my body.

I gave a quick yelp and rubbed the skin around the gem. 'Why didn't you warn me you were going to do that?'

'I thought you'd take it better as a surprise.'

'That was foolish,' I said.

'I've just given you a powerful gift, one that might well save your life, and you complain over the bee sting required to implant it?'

'You're right. Thanks.' I felt like I ought to have said something more, but gratitude is an emotion I'm rarely called upon to display, and the reversal of our traditional positions left me unsteady. 'Thanks,' I said again lamely.

'You don't need to say that. You know I'd do anything for you.' Her eyes fluttered down my naked chest. 'Anything.'

I pulled my shirt over my head and reached for my coat, the better to mask my inability to muster speech.

'What's next?' Celia asked, all business.

'I've got a few ideas. I'll come by in a day or two and let you know if anything's panned out.'

'Do that. I'll ring out some people I know at the Bureau of Magical Affairs, see if they've got anything they can tell me.'

The Crane broke his silence with another fit, and I decided it was time to take my leave. I thanked the Master, who threw me a quick wave between barks.

Celia walked me to the door. 'Pay attention to the jewel,' she said, very gravely. 'It'll lead you to the culprit.'

I took a look back as I descended the stairs. The Crane's coughing echoed down the blue stone, and Celia watched me from the landing, her face worried, her eyes dark.

13

Recent misadventures aside, I earn my meager living selling drugs, and it wouldn't do much good to dodge the Crown if I lost my business in the process. Besides, after the day's chaos a simple spot of trafficking seemed just the thing to settle my mind. Yancey had asked me to show at the mansion of one of the nobles he spit for, said there was money in it. I stopped at an Islander cart near the docks and grabbed a quick plate of spiced chicken before beginning my trek.

Head straight north from downtown and you'll come to Kor's Heights, where the old families and the nouveau riche have erected a paradise out of sight of the masses. Clean air replaces the stench of the iron foundries and the rot of the harbor, while constricted alleyways and compact buildings give way to wide thoroughfares and beautifully maintained manors. I never liked going there, any hoax worth his bribe knew I didn't belong, but then I couldn't very well ask whatever patrician wanted ten ochres worth of brain loss to meet me outside the Earl. I shoved my hands into my pockets and doubled my pace, trying not to look like I was engaged in an errand of dubious legality.

I stopped at the address Yancey had provided. Through a wrought-iron gate I could make out acres of manicured lawn, even the dim light of the evening sufficient to mark the dormant flower beds and groomed topiary. I followed the brick wall towards the back of the estate – gentlemen in my profession rarely go in through the front door. After a few hundred yards I came to the much smaller, much uglier servants' entrance.

The guard next to it was a ruddy-looking Tarasaihgn with shocks of flame-red hair, uncommon among the swamp dwellers, extending in a roughly even circle from scalp to chin. His uniform was worn but well-kept, and so was the man beneath it, pushing fifty but with little more to show for it than a modest protuberance above his belt. 'I'm a friend of Yancey the Rhymer,' I said. 'I don't have an invitation.'

To my surprise he held out his hand in greeting. 'Dunkan Ballantine, and I don't have an invitation either.'

I took his palm. 'I guess it's not a prerequisite to stand guard.'

'It isn't one to enter either, least not for someone Yancey's vouched for.'

'He inside already?'

'Wouldn't be a party without the Rhymer on hand to entertain the highborn.' He looked around with an exaggerated suggestion of secrecy. 'Course between me and you he saves his best stuff for between sets! You'll probably find him outside, adding to the kitchen smoke.' He winked at me and I laughed.

'Thanks, Dunkan.'

'No problem, no problem. Maybe you'll see me on the way out.'

I followed a pebble-lined path through the verdant lawn towards the back of the mansion. I could make out the sound of music, and the familiar scent of dreamvine on the chill evening breeze. The first I assumed came from the party, but the second I attributed to the small, dark-skinned figure leaning against the shadow of the three-story brick estate and mumbling rhythmically.

100

Yancey passed me the twist he had been working on without interrupting his perfectly syncopated flow. The Rhymer's vine was good, as always, a sticky blend but not unduly harsh, and I spiraled silvery indigo into the night.

His final bar hammered home. 'Safe living.'

'And you, brother. Glad to see you made it out here. You've been a little shaky lately.'

'I've been taking a lot of naps. Did I miss your set?'

'First one, got the band on now. Ma says hey. She wants to know why you haven't been coming round lately. I told her it's because she keeps trying to catch you a wife.'

'Astute as always,' I said. 'Who am I walking in on?'

His eyes narrowed and he took the joint from my outstretched hand. 'You don't know?'

'Your message just gave the address.'

'This the king ape himself, brother. Duke Rojar Calabbra the Third, the Lord Beaconfield.' He grinned, white teeth sharp against his skin and the night behind it. 'The Smiling Blade.'

I let out a low whistle, wishing now I hadn't gotten high. The Smiling Blade — famed courtier, celebrated duelist and *enfant terrible*. He was supposed to be strong with the Crown Prince, and he was supposed to be the deadliest swordsman since Caravollo the Untouched opened a vein after his boy lover died of the Red Fever thirty summers past. Mostly Yancey played for the younger sons of minor nobles and mid-level aristos slumming. He really was moving up in the world. 'How'd you meet him?'

'You know my skills. The man saw me rhyme something somewhere, made himself an opening for me to fill.' Yancey was not given to undue humility. He exhaled a stream of smoke through his nostrils, and it pooled about his face, wreathing his skull in a spectral sterling aurora. 'The question is, why does he want to meet you?'

'I had assumed he wanted to buy some drugs, and you let him know I was the man to speak with. If he brought me up here for dancing lessons I imagine he'll be pissed with the both of us.'

'I dropped you the line, but I didn't put you into play — they

101

asked for you in particular. Tell truth, if I didn't know I was a genius, I might suspect I'd been hired for just that purpose.'

This last revelation was enough to put paid to any good humor generated by the dreamvine. I didn't know why the duke wanted to see me, didn't know how he had even learned who I was – but if there was one thing thirty-five-odd years gripping the underbelly of Rigun society had taught me, it was never to draw the attention of the highborn. Best to remain another amid the uniform army of folk Śakra had birthed to serve their whims, a half-forgotten name supplied by another member of their anonymous coterie.

'Go wary on this one, brother,' said Yancey as he flicked out the end of the joint.

'Dangerous?'

He spoke with remarkable solemnity given our last five minutes' recreation. 'And not just the sword.'

The Rhymer led me through the back door and into a wide kitchen, a small army of cooks moving about frantically, each attending to an array of edibles as appetizing as they were delicate. I regretted filling up on spiced chicken, though on the other hand I probably wasn't going to be offered a seat at the feast. Yancey and I waited for a gap in the traffic, then threaded our way into the main room.

I'd been to a lot of these little soirées courtesy of Yancey's connections, and this was definitely one of the nicer ones. The guests were the sort of people who looked like they deserved to be out somewhere – that's not always the case.

Although a lot of it was probably the architecture. The drawing room was three times as wide as the Earl, but apart from general scale there was little else to compare with Adolphus's modest establishment. Intricately carved wooden walls led up above elaborate Kiren carpets. A dozen grand glass chandeliers, each cupping a hundred wax candles, descended from a gilded ceiling. In the center of it all a circle of nobles amused themselves in the intricate patterns of a contra dance, moving in time to the band that had picked up after Yancey had stepped off. Radiating out from this core were small knots of courtiers laughing and chatting. Around them, at once ever-present and innocuous, swarmed the servants, carrying finger food and drinks of all kinds.

Yancey leaned towards me. 'I'll let the big man know you've arrived,' he said, moving off into the crowd.

I snatched a flute of champagne from a passing waiter who harrumphed with disdain. The degree of contempt underlings are willing to muster on behalf of their employers is a source of continual amusement to me. I sipped my bubbly and tried to remember the reasons I hated these people. It was hard going – they were beautiful and seemed to be having a great deal of fun, and I struggled to maintain class resentment amid the laughter and bright colors. The vine I had just burned wasn't helping either, its pleasant haze dulling my well-sharpened bitterness.

Among all the gild and glitter, the figure in the corner stuck out like a broken thumb on a manicured hand. He was short and stocky, runtlike, and what body he possessed he'd done little enough to care for. Rolls of fat sprayed over his belt buckle, and the broken red veins swelling his nose suggested more than a passing familiarity with drink. His clothing added another wrinkle to the mystery, for while I doubted very much the duke would employ an individual whose physique so clearly betrayed the poverty of his upbringing, I was certain he wouldn't allow him to wear such an odd costume. It had been expensive once, though never fashionable, a black dress shirt and pants of the same hue, the cut and cloth the product of a master tailor. But their maker's care had been betrayed by ill-use, a sheen of mud on his leather boots that ran up the cuff of his leg, the tunic in little better shape.

If I hadn't been invited to fulfill the function I might have taken him as a member of my competition, combining as he did a seedy affluence with a hint of violence. Had I ran into him in Low Town I'd have assumed him a con man, or some low-level fixer, and never given him a second look – but here, surrounded by the cream of Rigun society, he demanded notice.

Also, he had been openly staring at me since I'd come through the door, a mocking little smile on his lips, like he knew some shameful secret of mine, and was enjoying holding it over my head.

Whoever he was, I had no interest in responding to his scrutiny, so all these observations were made out of the corner of my eye. But still I kept enough focus to see him amble towards me with an awkward sideways sidle.

'Come here often?' he asked, and broke out into a chortle. His voice was a thick brogue, and he had an ugly laugh, in keeping with everything else about him.

I gave him the half-smile one adopts when refusing a vagrant's request for coin.

'What's the matter? I ain't high-class enough to have a conversation with?'

'It's not you personally. I'm a deaf-mute.'

He laughed again. In most people jocularity is at least an innocuous quality, if not a pleasant one. But the stranger was of that kind whose cackling dug into your ears like rough canvas against a sore. 'You're a funny one. A real joker.'

'Always here to lighten up a party.'

He was younger than I'd initially thought him, younger than I was – though bad living had aged him prematurely, graying his skin and sending lines out through his face and hands. These last were covered by an odd assortment of rings, sterling silver interspersed with jewelry so bright and gaudy I knew them immediately to be fake, frippery that once again spoke of wealth spent without the benefit of taste. He kept his mouth unfastened, filtering air through a row of crooked teeth, stained yellow where they hadn't been replaced with dull gold. His breath carried with it an unsavory combination of salted meat and vodka.

'I know what you're thinking,' he said.

'Then I hope you don't take offense easily.'

'You're thinking, how am I gonna get at any of the fine trim swimming around with this ugly bastard yelling in my ear?'

This was not, in fact, what I was thinking. I was here on

business, and even if I hadn't been I doubted I'd find much amorous success, being what I was and looking like I did. That said, if I had hoped to find a companion, the tumor standing next to me probably wouldn't have helped.

'But see, these cunts' – he wagged his index finger in front of my face like a disapproving school teacher – 'they ain't interested in folk like us. We ain't good enough for them.'

Even by my standards, this was a whole mess of hideousness. The stranger and I were getting to the end of our conversation, one way or the other. 'We got so much in common, you and me?'

'When it comes to women, we got a lot in common,' he said, speaking each word with a slow seriousness.

'This has been riveting,' I answered. 'But if it's all the same on your end, how about you do me a favor and step off.'

'Ain't no cause to be disrespectful. I come over here and talk to you like a man, and you give me the brush-off. You ain't no different than any of these pampered little bastards with their noses in the air. And here I was, thinking we might even get to be friends.'

We were reaching the point of being a spectacle, something one tries to avoid when one has entered another man's home for the purposes of selling him drugs. 'I'm all up on friends – stocked full with associates, and met my quota of acquaintances. The only openings I got left are for strangers, and enemies. Make yourself the first, before you find yourself the second.'

Up until that point I had taken the man for harmless if offensive, and I figured he'd be easy enough to frighten off. But my words had little effect on him, except to draw a glint of menace to his bloodshot eyes.

'That's the way you want it? That's fine by me. I been plenty of men's enemies – though never for very long.'

I found myself wishing that I could run through the play again, but having thrown down the gauntlet there wasn't much for it but to continue in the same vein. 'You talk like a man that ain't been smacked yet today,' I said, my eyes turned back on

Yancey, who was now waving me over. 'But now's not the time to rectify the situation.'

'You'll get yourself another chance!' he exclaimed to my back, loud enough to draw the attention of the surrounding guests. 'Don't you worry on that score!'

It was a disagreeable interlude, and one I had the sense presaged future unpleasantness – but I pushed it out of my mind as I slipped towards the duke, careful not to intrude on the groups of flirting patricians.

If the human race has ever invented an institution more effective in the propagation of intellectual and ethical cripples than the nobility, I have yet to stumble across it. Take the progeny of a half-millennium of inbred mongoloids, first cousins and hemophiliacs. Raise them via a series of bloated wet-nurses, drink-addled confessors and failed academics, because Śakra knows Mommy and Daddy are too busy diddling themselves at court to take a hand in the upbringing of a child. Ensure any youthful training they receive extends to nothing more practical than swordsmanship and the study of languages no longer spoken, grant them a fortune upon the attainment of their majority, place them outside the bounds of any legal system more developed than the *code duello*, add the general human instinct towards sloth, avarice and bigotry, stir thoroughly and *voilà* – you have the aristocracy.

At first glance Lord Beaconfield looked every inch the product of this infernal social engine. His hair was coiffed in what I took for the newest fashion at court, and he smelled strongly of honey and rosewater. His rouged cheeks led to a goatee so perfectly manicured you would swear it had been painted on, and he was clothed in a brightly colored ensemble that was frilly to the point of being vaguely nauseating.

But there was something that wouldn't allow me to dismiss him completely, a sharpness in his eyes that made me think the costume was half a put-on. Maybe it was the way his hand hovered about the hilt of his rapier, well-used and surprisingly plain compared with the rest of his costume. Maybe it was the fact that beneath his lace there was a hard leanness that spoke of long hours bathed in sweat rather than perfume. Or maybe it was just the knowledge that the man in front of me had likely killed more men than the Crown's executioner.

His entourage by contrast were such definitive examples of their type as to be barely worthy of notice, each attired similarly to their chief, each narcotized a few shades short of oblivion.

Yancey shot me a look meant to remind me of his earlier warning, and broke into the exaggerated patois he affected for the rich and white. 'This my partner, the one I was speaking on to you.'

'A pleasure it is to make your acquaintance, my lord,' I said, executing a bow that would prove acceptable in any court in the land. 'And truly may I say it is an honor to be allowed entrance to an affair of such elegance. Surely the Daevas on Chinvat fête no better.'

'One of my lesser affairs, little more than a warm-up for next week's gala.' He smiled, wide and winning, oddly natural even through the whore's paint.

'Men of my caliber would find even the meanest of your diversions fit for the divine.' That was laying it on thick, but then I was speaking to a man wearing pancake make-up.

'I was told you were a man of many resources, but no mention was made of your charm.'

'Had I the arrogance to contradict my lord I would deny such unwarranted praise – but being a timid soul, I can only thank my lord for his kindness.'

'Were you a teacher of court etiquette before you adopted your current profession?'

'I did many things before I adopted my current profession, good lord.' This was going on longer than it needed to – no doubt the guests were starting to wonder why their host was giving audience to an ugly man in a dirty coat. 'And I do a great many things even now. Perhaps his excellency might indicate to me which of them he finds it pleasing to command?'

There was a pause of substantial length while the Blade's bright

107

eyes rested on mine. I began to wonder if I had overrated the duke's sobriety. 'Perhaps one day we'll discuss in more detail the range of assistance you might render me. But in the meantime Tuckett here will fill you in on the details.' He gestured at a tight-lipped gentleman in a fine dark coat standing off to the side. 'Do return shortly. A man of such wit and use is welcome in my demesne regardless of the occasion.'

I bowed, once towards him and once towards his assemblage. Neither returned the gesture, though Yancey shot me a quick nod as I backed away. The Blade's servant led me out of the main room and into a small corridor beyond.

Up close Tuckett smelled like ink and the civil service. Clucking his tongue unpleasantly, he took out a sheet of paper from his breast pocket, unfolded it and handed it to me. 'This details the items the master wishes to procure.'

I tried not to look surprised at the volume and variety. 'The dreamvine and pixie's breath I can do now. The rest of it I can get in a day or two. Except this last one. I don't truck wyrm. You'll need to find someone else for that.'

'I didn't realize men in your line of work could afford to be so particular.'

'I'm happy to have helped further your education.'

He bristled and tried to think of something smart to say. I waited a few seconds to provide him with an opportunity. When it was clear he wasn't going to take it I spoke up again. 'I assume you've been provided with payment?'

He passed over a fat purse, handing it to me with an awfully high-toned manner, given that we were completing a narcotics transaction. There was more than there needed to be. A lot more.

'The duke is very kind.'

'The lord is buying your silence, and your loyalty.'

'Tell him the first is free, but the second isn't for sale.' I put the purse into my satchel and handed him most of my remaining stash.

He took it with an impressively choreographed air of disdain. 'Follow this hallway to the garden. A path will take you to the side gate.'

'The gentleman I was talking to earlier,' I interrupted, 'who was he?'

'Believe it or not, sir' – he laid on the last syllable thick enough to let me know he didn't think me entitled to it – 'I hadn't made a point of following your every movement.'

'You know who I'm talking about. He was out of place.'

'Not that it's any of your business, but I assume you're speaking of Sorcerer Brightfellow.'

If there was one thing I hadn't taken tubby for, it was the Queen of Ostarrichi – but if there was a second it was an artist. I let that piece fall into place while I found my way out into the night air.

All in all the evening was not much different from a hundred others, a gathering of bored blue-bloods happy to exchange inherited wealth for alchemical happiness, and I equally happy to be the agent of their deliverance. Business as usual really, par for the course – save for one detail, one minor particular that I'd barely had time to consider till I was walking back to the Earl.

From the moment I had begun speaking to Beaconfield till I had left his sight, the sapphire in my chest had burned like the sting of a wasp. I rubbed at it as I headed home, thinking that I might just be seeing the Blade sooner than he expected.

14

I awoke to Adolphus's fat face leering over mine, huge hands shaking me roughly from my repose. 'They found the girl.'

It was clear he didn't mean alive. I brushed him off and sat up. 'Are the chill here?'

'Not yet.'

We didn't have long. I grabbed my satchel from off the chair and handed it to him. 'Tell Wren to run this over to Kid Mac. And give him something to do that'll get him out of the bar for a few hours.'

'Anything else?'

'Just don't make trouble when they come in. Let them up and don't get hot. I'll handle it.'

He swallowed hard and left.

I pulled on my clothes and boots, then lay back down on the bed. At least I wouldn't be naked when they came for me; that was about all the preparation I could manage. Adolphus was right to be nervous – Crispin was one thing, whatever was between us he knew I wasn't out there killing children. But they wouldn't be sending Crispin after me, because Crispin went after murderers and criminals, and no one important cared about the dead girl. They cared about the practitioner who had likely killed her, and that meant Special Operations, and Special Operations was a whole new kettle of worms.

The Empire is a great machine, a massive engine, millions of gears churning, and nothing that complex operates perfectly. When it breaks down, when a speck of dust dirties a lens or a cog refuses to turn, someone needs to be in place to repair it. This is the purpose of Special Operations – to keep the wheels spinning swiftly and smoothly, and to make sure anyone caught between them gets ground fine enough that they aren't noticed.

I sighed ruefully. I had been the shining star of that outfit at one point. Life is strange, sometimes.

When they came they came hard. I could hear the door downstairs kicked open and obscene threats being shouted. I hoped Adolphus wouldn't do anything foolish – all that fat and good humor hid a man capable of extraordinary violence. If things went bad they'd need to kill him to get him down, and at the end the blood on the floor wouldn't be his alone.

But I didn't hear the sounds of shattered glass and broken furniture that would accompany the loss of my friend's temper, so I assumed he was following my orders. Footsteps echoed up the stairs and then the door flew open and I was staring down the wrong end of a crossbow at a young agent yelling at me to get on the ground. Following close on his heels was a pair of apish looking gentlemen who made sure I followed through on the first's command.

I was face down on the floor, my hands chained and a knee in my back when I heard a half-forgotten voice. 'I always knew if I stuck around long enough I'd get another crack at you. I just didn't think it would be such a good one.'

The pressure eased off my spine and rough hands pulled me

to my feet. Greeting me was a blunt face set atop a thick tun of gristle, broad muscle and scarred flesh.

'Hello, Crowley. Good to see stupidity is no barrier to a lasting career in the service of the Crown.'

'Still quick with that tongue, aren't we, boy?' He laughed, dull, beady eyes set above a pug nose flaring in anticipation. His fist shot forward and I was back on my knees, trying not to vomit and wishing I had the last ten seconds to do over. Crowley laughed and leaned in close to me. 'I've got you, boy. I've got you by the balls.'

I wheezed out a response. 'You always were fascinated with my junk.' It was a juvenile attempt at humor, and I regretted it even before Crowley sank another fat paw into my chin.

'You can take a beating, I'll give you that,' he said, rubbing his knuckles. 'You're the heavyweight champ of getting your ass whipped. But I ain't dumb enough to scrape any more skin on that stone jaw of yours. We've got specialists for that.'

I spat a stream of blood onto the dirty floor and tried to look brave.

Crowley hauled me up once more. 'Cochrane, you and Talloway are with me. The rest of you head over to the crime scene – make sure they've got enough men.' He turned back towards me. 'I'll admit, as much as it burned me up to see you get away, it was worth it to have the chance to break you all over again.'

This time I was smart enough to keep my mouth shut.

Adeline was downstairs by the fireplace, scowling with all the ferocity of a wounded matriarch, the moment of crisis revealing her bedrock core. Adolphus was seated at a table, an agent with a crossbow covering him. They were both being very brave for me. I appreciated it.

The walk seemed very long. They hadn't given me a chance to grab a coat and I shivered from the cold. Occasionally Crowley would say something ugly and unoriginal but mostly it was lost in the wind. Around us the crowds melted away – the citizens of Low Town were in no hurry to share the fate they saw I was heading towards.

By the time we had reached Black House it had started to drizzle. Crowley paused for a second, just to grind it into my gut. I looked up at the gray sky, watching beads of ice-water tumble from the clouds. A drop broke against my forehead. Then they pulled me inside and I worked to keep my face steady, even when we took the unmarked entrance into the underbelly of Black House, even when they opened the door to my cell.

The room was deliberately featureless, empty except for a prisoner's steel chair and the table beside it. In the center, small but impossible to miss, was a cast-iron drain leading down into the sewers. I had always hated this place when I was an agent, and I didn't like it any better on the other end.

Standing in the corner was a Questioner, wearing the traditional burgundy outfit, wrist-length robes beneath a tapered hood. A black bag containing the instruments of his trade dangled from his hand. This one was heavy, fat really, rolls of flesh stretching his red uniform. But then torture isn't particularly physically demanding, at least not for the one doing the carving. And the guild held to quite rigorous standards – I was sure he'd be up to his task.

'Enjoying the scenery?' Crowley asked. A kick to the back sent me tumbling. I struggled to stand but before I could Crowley's men grabbed me and forced me onto the seat, unchaining my hands from behind my back and strapping them to two leather restraints built into the arms of the chair.

'I knew we'd get you back in here one day. The Old Man thought you might sour on us, thought you might slip out of Low Town one night. I said no way. That boy loves us too much to ever leave. He'll be back. But even I didn't think you'd be this desperate – dark magic?' He wagged one stubby finger in my face. 'We've got you deep.'

Crowley pulled a cigar from a pocket. He bit off the end with his square gray teeth and lit it, pink-slug lips puffing until he had a good draw, thick trails of smoke escaping from his fractured leer. 'Who do you think we're waiting on now?'

As if on cue the door opened, and a grandfatherly man in a crisp uniform entered, and I knew I was well and truly fucked.

The most powerful person in Rigus might be the Queen, or it might be the High Chancellor – or it might be an open-faced little man who works from a windowless office in the center of Black House and has a recess where his soul should be. The Old Man, Custodian of Special Operations, an innocuous title for the Empire's chief spymaster. The eyes at the window are his, and the ear at the door. If there's dirt to be had on you he has it, and if there isn't and he needs it he'll make it. More men have died from a wag of his finger than of the plague. For a quarter-century he's stood at the helm of the largest organization ever constructed by the hands of man for the purposes of usurping and maintaining control of his fellows.

And if you passed him on the street, he'd tip his hat, and you'd tip yours right back. Evil is like that sometimes.

The Old Man's soft grin creased his face, eyes twinkling with merriment. 'What a grand thing it is to see one of my children return after such a long absence. How we've missed you here at your old home.'

The sight of him was enough to stoke a little fire in my belly. 'I figured I'd come by and see how the place was holding up. Y'all seem busy though, maybe I'll stop in another time.'

He held to his smile, then nodded to the Questioner, who promptly and without fuss began to unpack his bag onto the table.

'We're gonna put it to you,' Crowley said. 'We're gonna put it to you hard. By the time we're done with you we'll know every sin that stains your soul.'

I forced a laugh, no easy thing with the straps taut against my wrists. 'Better clear your dinner plans.' If it was only Crowley I wouldn't have gone through the bother of talking – he's an ape, useful only for his savagery. But the Old Man was sharp as a dagger and twice as cold. That grandfatherly visage hid the mind of a master strategist and an utter madman to boot. He'd like to see me in the ground, no doubt, but that wouldn't influence him – only humans base decisions on emotion. 'Apart from giving the Questioner here some unneeded practice, what exactly do you think you're going to accomplish with all this fuss?'

115

Crowley ground his cigar between the jagged line of his ivories. 'You know something about the child, and the demon, something that'll help get us closer. And if you don't' – his smile was rabid – 'I'll still get to watch the walls be painted red with your insides.'

'You see, Crowley, this is why you used to report to me. This is why you'll never take over for the Old Man. You can't see past your next victim. You're a blunt instrument, useless without someone ahead of you to mark a trail.'

Beside me the Questioner continued to unravel his tools, sharp silver things on a blanket of black velvet.

'When you finish today and tomorrow a child goes missing, what will you do then? There are issues here beyond indulging your sadism.'

Crowley had managed to hold his temper, though his flyspeck eyes had swelled up to near the size of egg-yolks. 'We'll get whoever's killing the kids – don't you worry about that.'

'Horseshit.' I focused on the Old Man. 'You don't have anyone here as good as me, and you know it. Whoever did this learned it from the Crown – you can't rely on your own people. I can rely on support outside the Throne, I've got contacts riddled through Low Town, and I know what these things look like.' I swallowed hard – time to play my trump. 'And I've got a lead.'

'Then we'll get it from you with the knife, and follow it where it goes,' Crowley said.

'You won't. No one will talk to you, and you wouldn't be able to put the pieces together even if they did.'

For only the second time thus far the Old Man spoke. 'Are you so desperate to return to my employ? From what I've heard you've become little better than a dog, an addict waiting for a knife in an alley.'

'I was sharp enough to find the first one. Either you throw in with me or you leave it to the ape. And we both know it's too important to let him foul it up.'

The Old Man's smile grew broader, and I knew his next words were to decide my fate – freedom in his service, or a session with the Questioner and an unmarked grave. It was a long moment. In retrospect I think I handled myself admirably, which is to say I didn't leak piss down the leg of my pants.

He set one gnarled hand on my shoulder and squeezed it with surprising firmness. 'You won't disappoint me, my boy. You'll find whoever is hurting these poor girls, and together we'll make sure to bring them to justice.' Crowley began to sputter a protest, but a glance from the chief shut his mouth. The Old Man undid one restraint with the care of a mother tending to a scraped knee. He made a move for the other, then stopped. 'A week ought to be sufficient, I would think, for a man of your intellect to determine who is responsible for these monstrosities.' He shook his head sadly, his gentle nature offended by the cruelty of a senseless world.

'Two,' I said. 'I don't have your resources – I'll need time to work my contacts.'

For a single tick of a second his eyes shifted and the façade gave way to the monster beneath, and I almost flinched – but his face was turned towards me and his voice remained friendly.

'We'll see you in seven days.' The illusion of humanity snapped back and he released the second cuff. He turned to Crowley. 'See our dear friend off then, won't you?' Flashing one last smile, he walked out the iron door, taking the other agents with him.

Crowley watched it close, his cigar clenched so tightly in his mouth I thought he might choke on it. He spent a while trying to think of something he could say or do to offset the humiliation he had suffered. When nothing came he turned and left.

The Questioner was repacking his tools with a vague air of disappointment. Deciding my legs were steady enough to carry me, I propped myself to my feet, then turned towards my would-be torturer. 'You got a cigarette?' I asked.

He shook his head, the burned red crown of his hood bobbing. 'I don't smoke,' he said without taking his eyes off his work. 'That stuff will kill you.'

'The Firstborn willing.'

Outside the rain had stopped but it was cold as ever. I massaged my wrists and wondered how much of it the Old Man had planned. The whole thing had the feel of theater – not for Crowley of course, he wasn't in on the gag – but this was an awfully blunt play for someone as knotted as the Old Man.

It didn't matter really. If this had all been a ploy to retain my services, I had no illusions that the deadline was anything other than deathly serious. I headed back home, to tool up, and to plan.

15

When I stepped into the Earl Adolphus was moping at the counter, his face wide and blubbery. I guess he'd figured I was dead. It wasn't an unreasonable assumption, though I was glad to prove him wrong. He turned when he heard the door open and before it had closed Adolphus had me wrapped in his massive limbs, pressing his weeping face against the top of my head and calling for Adeline and Wren.

It was all a bit much, particularly as in all likelihood I had only delayed the inevitable, and Adolphus's melodrama would be replayed in another week. But he seemed happy and I didn't have the heart to say anything, until his affection started to prove a danger to the integrity of my ribcage.

Adeline had come in from the back and set her round frame against me. Over her head I could see Wren descending the staircase, his usual neutral demeanor on his face. 'Not excited to see me? Just another day at the Earl, your benefactor getting arrested by the Crown and released before lunch?'

Adolphus responded elatedly. 'He said he wasn't worried! Said he knew you'd be back so there was no point in getting upset.'

'Nice to see you've got such confidence in me,' I said. 'Remember, though – just 'cause your horse came in doesn't mean you made a smart bet.'

If it were up to Adolphus I would have spent the rest of the day wrapped in a blanket like a fever victim, and much as the notion of a long nap appealed to me, the trail was growing cold. Brushing off his mothering, I headed to my room and removed a long black box from beneath my bed.

I don't pack a weapon regularly, hadn't for nearly half a decade, not since I first left the Crown's service and had to carve out my business from the ruins of the last big syndicate war. Carrying a blade means someone's going to make you use it, and corpses are bad for business. Better to be friendly to everyone, pay off who you need to, and keep a grin on your face until it's time to stop smiling.

And truth be told I don't trust myself with one. If things get heated and you start to lose the thread, so long as you aren't carrying, things are apt to end all right. Maybe someone walks away with a bruised jaw or a split nose but they walk away. With a sword at your side – well, I have enough on my soul without adding the blood of some poor bastard who looked at me sideways while I was hopped up on pixie's breath.

So under normal circumstances I don't strap a blade on except when I know I'm going to need to use it. But then circumstances ain't always normal, and although the thing that killed the Kiren hadn't shown any indication of being susceptible to cold steel, whoever sent it might be. I undid the latch and swung open the trunk.

I've seen a lot of weapons in my time, from the sickle-swords of the Asher priesthood to the bejeweled pig-stickers the nobility so love to play with, but for my money there was never an instrument of murder as perfectly built for its purpose as the trench blade. Two feet of steel wedged into a sandalwood hilt, single-edged for a stronger cut, widening towards the end but tapering off sharply at the tip – it had been my weapon of choice since the War. I wouldn't wear it on the parade ground, but with my back against the wall there was nothing I'd rather have filling my grip.

I had taken this one off a Dren commando my third month in Gallia. The Dren were always ahead of us with that sort of thing – they took to trench warfare like they were built for it, got rid of all their glittery armor and started sending soot-stained berserkers over the walls late at night with hand axes and black-powder bombs. The brass on our side were still passing out sabers and cavalry lances to us officers six months before the armistice, even though I hardly saw a horse in the five years I spent ducking artillery fire and trying to find water that hadn't been fouled by my comrades' waste.

I grabbed the hilt and hefted the blade in my right hand. It still felt good, natural. I pulled a whetstone from inside the box and sharpened the edge until it was cruel enough to shave with. The steel caught my reflection, vivid purple swelling merging comfortably with my previously acquired scars. It was an old face – I hoped it was up for what was coming.

Reaching back into the trunk I pulled out a pair of flat-handled daggers, too small to be used in a mêlée but balanced for throwing. I strapped the first against my shoulder and slipped the second into my boot. One final armament, a bronze knuckle with three cruel-looking spikes on the business end, went into my duster pocket for easy access.

The box was empty now, save for a thick square parcel that I had been saving since the War. I inspected it, making sure each item inside was in good condition, then put it back in the box and slid the whole thing under the bed. Feeling a bit self-conscious, I pulled my coat tight over the hilt of my sword and headed downstairs.

'Where was the girl found?' I asked Adolphus.

'South of Light Street. Over by the canal. You planning a visit?'

There was no point in explaining to Adolphus the bargain I had struck with Special Operations, not while I still had some chance to make good on it, so I ignored him and turned to Wren.

'Get your coat. I'm going to need you for a while.'

Assuming this would involve something more interesting than carrying messages and getting me dinner, Wren complied with uncharacteristic enthusiasm. Adolphus looked me over, recognizing the outline of metal beneath my clothing.

'What are you doing?'

'I'm going to visit an old friend of ours.'

Adolphus's one eye worked to read something from my pair. 'Why?'

'I haven't had enough excitement today.'

Wren came out wrapped in a hideous wool thing that Adeline had sewn together for him. 'Have I told you before how ugly that is?'

He nodded.

'So long as we're on the same page.' I turned back to Adolphus. 'The boy'll be back before sundown. Hold anything that comes for me.'

Adolphus nodded, sufficiently familiar with my customs at this point to know I wouldn't volunteer anything else. Wren and I left the Earl and started west.

16

When Grenwald finally entered I had been sitting in the dark for twenty minutes, reclining in the visitor's chair, my feet perched on the stained oak desk that dominated the room. I'd been worrying he had decided to skip whatever daily tasks required his attendance, and I'd be left waiting in his office like an asshole. But it was worth it to see his reaction as he swung open the door, his arrogant demeanor converting to one of abject horror in the span of a half-second.

A decade had done much to raise my old superior's position, although sadly damn little to improve his character, or to stiffen the rodent-like set of his jaw. His coat was expensive but ill-fitting, and his once firm body was running to fat at a somewhat greater speed than middle age strictly demanded. I lit a match off the wood and held it to my cigarette. 'Howdy, Colonel. What's the good news?'

He shut the door, slammed it really, hoping to hide this interview from his staff. 'How the hell did you get in here?'

I shook the match out with two fingers and imitated the motion with my head. 'Colonel, Colonel. I confess I'm hurt. To be addressed in such a fashion by so dear a friend?' I clicked my tongue in disapproval. 'Is this how two old comrades reminisce, united by the bonds of our noble crusade?'

'No, no. Of course not,' he said. 'I was just surprised to see you. I'm sorry.' That was one of the fun things about Grenwald – he broke so damn easy.

'A drop of water beneath a bridge,' I said.

He set his coat and hat on a rack by the door, playing for time, trying to figure out why I had come and what he needed to do to see me leave. 'Whiskey?' he asked as he moved towards a wet bar in the corner, pouring himself a tumbler-full.

'I try not to imbibe hard liquor before noon, part of my new life as a burgeoning teetotaler. Knock yourself out though.'

He did, throwing back his glass in one quick motion, then giving himself another few fingers and sliding past me to assume his chair behind the desk. 'I thought, after last time,' he swallowed hard. 'I thought we were through.'

'Did you?'

'I thought that you said we were even.'

'Did I?'

'Not, of course, that I'm unhappy to see you.'

I repulsed this concern with a theatrical wave of my hand.

'What is this about?'

'Maybe I just wanted to pop in and give a quick salute to my old commander,' I said. 'Don't you ever feel like reliving old times with your brother officers?'

'Of course I do, of course,' he said, willing to agree to anything I put in front of him.

'Then how come you never return the courtesy? Have you risen so high you've forgotten your old subordinate?'

He sputtered something halfway between an apology and an excuse before lapsing into silence.

I let that hang awkwardly between us for about fifteen seconds, trying hard not to laugh. 'As it happens though, and since you've so kindly offered, there is something you might be able to help me with – though I hesitate to ask, given that you've done so much already.'

'Think nothing of it,' he said coldly.

'Remember that operation outside Donknacht, the day before the armistice?'

'Vaguely.'

'Yes, I'm sure it was only of trifling interest to one so far up the chain of command. Dealing with key strategic and logistical issues, it might be easy to forget the skirmishes that fill the memories of the lower ranks.'

He didn't respond.

'I need to know the name of every sorcerer involved in that project – everyone who carried it out, and anyone who might have trained them. The Ministry of War will have kept a record.'

'They wouldn't have kept records for something like that,' he answered, immediately and without thinking. 'It was off the books.'

'They have it.'

He scrambled for some excuse to avoid acting the pawn. 'I'm not sure I'll be able to access them. They wouldn't be held in the general library with the rest of the documents from the War. If they're anywhere, they'd be under lock and key in the restricted section.'

'That shouldn't be a problem for an Undersecretary of the Army.'

'They've changed protocol,' he insisted. 'It isn't like the old days. I can't just walk into the archives and walk out with the documents under my arm.'

'It'll be as easy as it'll be. Or as difficult. But either way, it'll get done.'

'I . . . can't guarantee anything.'

'There aren't any guarantees in life,' I responded. 'But you'll try, won't you, Colonel? You'll try very, very hard.'

He drained the rest of the glass and set it on the table, then pushed his weasel face towards mine. The liquor was kicking in, flooding him with courage he could never muster sober. 'I'll do what I can,' he said, and the tone of his voice did not fill me with confidence in the outcome of his errand. 'And then we're square. No more of these surprise visits. We're done.'

'Funny – you said the same thing the last time I was here.' I stubbed my cigarette into his desk, grinding the ash into the finish, than stood and grabbed my coat. 'Be seeing you soon, Colonel.'

The door shut on a man barely deserving of the title.

His secretary, a pretty, stupid young thing who had allowed me to talk my way into Grenwald's office with a lie about the War, smiled up at me sweetly. 'Was the colonel able to help with your pension problem?'

'It won't be easy, but he'll come through for me. You know the colonel, nothing's more important than his men. He ever tell you about the time he carried me three miles across enemy lines, after I took a bolt in the thigh? Saved my life that night.'

'Really?' she asked, wide-eyed and bubbly.

'No, of course not – none of that was true,' I replied, leaving her more than usually befuddled as I walked out.

17

I left Grenwald's office and the boy fell in alongside me without speaking. The meeting had been a waste – Grenwald was a spineless fool, and I couldn't trust him to come through, not with something this important, not with the consequences I would suffer if it didn't pan out. That meant I had to move on to Plan B, and as far as Plan B went, there was a reason it hadn't taken priority of place.

Because Plan B meant Crispin, the only contact I had left high enough to get the information and who I thought might have a chance in hell of saying yes. After our last meeting the thought of asking him for help was faintly nauseating, but pride comes second to survival, so I swallowed mine and started walking to where Adolphus told me the child's body had been found.

My reverie was broken by a voice that I only belatedly realized was Wren's. I think it was the first time I had heard him speak without prompting.

'What happened when they took you to Black House?'

I thought about how to answer that question for a quarter of a block. 'I rejoined the Crown's service.'

'Why?'

'They made an appeal to my patriotism. I'd do anything for Queen and country.'

He swallowed this soberly, then spat out a response. 'I don't really care about the Queen.'

'Honesty is an overrated virtue. And we all love the Queen.'

Wren nodded sagely as we crossed the canal, the crime scene a bustle of motion a few dozen yards to the west.

The area was swarming with lawmen, and in contrast to their general tradition of incompetence, they seemed to be taking this one seriously. Crispin stood in the center of the chaos next to the child's body, taking down observations and issuing instructions. Our eyes met, but he returned to his duties without giving any indication he had noticed me. I could see Guiscard canvassing witnesses at an intersection in the distance, and some of the boys who had given me a working over last time were milling about as well, more comfortable causing violence than investigating it.

'Stay here.'

Wren took a seat on the railing. I crossed into the maelstrom, ducking beneath the cordon and approaching my old partner.

''Lo, Agent.'

He responded without looking up, jotting down notes in a black, leather-bound journal. 'Why are you here?'

'Ain't you up on the news? I missed you so damn much that I went to the Old Man and begged for my old job.'

'Yeah, I heard. Crowley sent a runner over an hour ago. I figured you'd use whatever time your bullshit bought you with Special Operations to get the hell out of town.'

'You never had enough faith in me.'

Suddenly the notebook was on the ground and Crispin had my lapel in his grip, the loss of temper striking in someone normally so self-possessed. 'I don't care what twisted agreement you made with the Old Man. This is my case, and I'm not letting your hatreds get dragged into it.'

My hand shot up and tore his paw off my shoulder. 'I've had enough of being manhandled by law enforcement officials for one day. And as gratifying as it is to watch the Crown discover they have a population south of the River Andel, in our last go-round your assistance proved less than efficacious. Far as I can tell, most of your job is to stand around corpses and look distraught.'

It seemed unfair after I said it, but it eased him back down a notch. 'What do you want from me?' he asked.

'For starters, why don't you go ahead and run down the scene.'

'There's little enough to run down. The body was found by a fish seller on his way to the docks. He reported it to the guard, they reported it to us. Judging by the state of the body, the girl was killed last night and dumped here early this morning.'

I knelt down beside the child and removed her wrapping. She was young, younger than the first one had been. Her hair looked very dark spread over her skin.

'Was the body . . . abused?'

'Clean, not like the last one. The only injury is the one that killed her, a straight line across the throat.'

I hid her corpse beneath the covering and stood back to my full height. 'What does your scryer say?'

'Nothing yet. She wants some time to work with the body.'

'I'd like to speak with her.'

He mulled this over unhappily, but his permission was a formality and both of us knew it. The Old Man wanted me in on this, and the Old Man's word is natural law. 'Guiscard is supposed to stop by the Box later in the afternoon. I suppose you could join him.'

'That's number one,' I said, 'here's number two. I need you to get your hands on a list of every sorcerer detailed to take part in Operation Ingress, in Donknacht just before the end of the War. They'll be buried deep but they'll be around.' I shook my head ruefully. 'The army can't stand to throw anything out.'

He stared at me, then down at the ground. 'Those are military records. As an Agent of the Crown I don't have access to them.'

'Maybe not directly. But you've got ten years of contacts and all the draw the blue blood pumping through your veins provides. Don't tell me you can't figure something out.'

When he looked back up at me his eyes were clear as glass. 'Why are you here?'

'What do you mean?'

'Why are you here? Why are you at this crime scene, right now, trying to find the killer of this girl?' The moment of anger was gone, and now he just seemed weary. 'You aren't an agent, you have no legal status of any kind. What business is this of yours?'

'You think I'm a volunteer? The Old Man was getting ready to bleed me – this was my only out.'

'Run. Get out of Low Town. If it's the Old Man you're afraid of, run, run and don't look back. I'll make sure there are no reprisals against your people. Just . . . disappear.'

I dug at a loose stone with my boot.

'What? Nothing clever? No witty retort?'

'What's your point?'

'Is this just to show how much smarter you are than the rest of us? Is there some scheme of yours I'm not seeing? Get out of here. You aren't an agent. So far as I can tell you're the furthest thing from it. In case you've missed the last five years, let me condense them – you're a junkie and a crime lord, you string out fathers and mothers, and you cut up anyone who gets in the way. You've become everything you ever hated, and I don't need you fucking up my investigation.'

'I was the best detective the service ever had, and I'd still be thinking circles around you and everyone else if I hadn't pissed off the brass.'

'Don't pretend your failure was a choice. Everyone else might buy your bullshit, but I know why you aren't an agent, and it isn't because you weren't willing to toe the line.'

I thought about how much fun it would be to scuff up that spotless gray uniform. 'I haven't forgotten, don't worry. I remember you standing in judgment with the rest of them, when they struck my name from the record and shattered my Eye.'

'There was nothing for it. I warned you not to join Special Operations, and I warned you double not to get involved with that woman.'

'Cautious, responsible Crispin. Don't make any waves, don't see anything you aren't supposed to. You're worse than Crowley – at least he's honest about what he is.'

'It was easier to run off. You never needed to put in the work, never needed to make any hard decisions. I stuck it out – it isn't perfect, but I've done more good as a cogwheel than you have selling poison.'

I could feel my fists clench at my sides and had to resist the urge to go for Crispin's face, and to judge from the black look in his eyes he was thinking the same. 'Fifteen years cleaning up shit,' I said. 'They oughta strike you a medal.'

We eyeballed each other, waiting to see if our dialogue wasn't about to end in violence. He broke first. 'Enough – I'll get you the list and then we're through. I don't owe you anything. You ever see me on the street you act like you would with any other agent.'

'Spit on the ground?'

He rubbed his forehead but didn't answer.

'Send the list to the Earl when you get it.' I walked back to the bridge and ripped Wren off the rail. 'Let's go.'

We were halfway over when the boy displayed another example of his recent loquaciousness. 'Who was that?'

'My old partner.'

'Why was he yelling at you?'

'Because he's kind of an asshole.'

Wren had to double-time it but his legs kept pace with mine. 'Why were you yelling at him?'

'Because I'm kind of an asshole too.'

'Is he going to help us?'

'Yeah.'

'Why?'

'You were better company when you didn't talk as much,' I said.

I took a last look at Crispin, now bent over the body, puzzling out some detail. I figured I had said some things I regretted. I figured I'd have the opportunity to apologize, out of practice at it though I was. I was wrong about that. I've been wrong about a lot of things, but that's one that hurts.

18

I'd been on the streets about four years the night I found Celia. I would have been ten or so, maybe a little older – birthdays tend to fall by the wayside without a family to celebrate them. This was after the Crane enacted his wards, so the bodies of the fever victims weren't piled like cordwood in the streets, but no one could rightly place Low Town too many steps above unadulterated anarchy. At night the guard retreated to the boundaries and didn't return except in force. Even the syndicates didn't much trouble with us, likely because there wasn't much worth taking.

Back then the borough had a haunted, lonely quality to it. It took almost a decade for the population to recover to what it had been before the fever, and for years after there were still parts of the neighborhood where you could walk for half an hour and never see a living soul. It made finding a place to sleep easy – just stumble down an empty block, throw a stone through a window and crawl inside. If you were lucky the owners had run off or died somewhere outside their residence. If you weren't you had to share a room with a corpse. Either possibility beat a night in the cold.

I would never again live my life with such mad abandon as I did during those early years on the streets. I needed nothing – Low Town provided. Food I stole, my other small needs I satisfied by force or cunning. I grew hard as a kettle and dog wild. At night I ranged the streets, watching the city's detritus scuttle about in the dark. That was how I found her, heard her first really, her frightened cries drawing me from my back alley wanderings.

There were two of them, wyrm addicts, thick with it. The first was ancient, a stutter step from the abyss, rotting gums attesting to the frequency of his habit, worn rags thick with urban fauna. His protégé was a few years older than me but preternaturally thin, sparse red hair spurting out over uncomfortably wide eyes. Both were fixated on the small child between them, her shallow weeping quieter now, fear stealing her voice.

Years sharing territory had initiated me in the secrets of the cockroach and the rat, and I moved in a fashion more closely resembling their scurry than the saunter of most children my age. Between that and the darkness I was practically invisible, though the pair ahead of me were so focused on the girl that nothing short of a marching band could have drawn their attention. I hugged tight against the alley wall and slunk towards them, more out of curiosity than anything else, careful to stay outside the arc of the moonlight.

'Three or four stems at least we'll get for her, three or four stems at least!' the old one said, running his gnarled fingers through the child's hair. 'Just give her straight to the chief heretic and tell him to send on over a pipe of his rawest choke.' The target of his glee stood mute, his sallow idiot features betraying little evidence of comprehension.

'I'll buy her from you.' It was out before I could take it back. I did things like that a lot in those days – no sooner did a stray thought flicker across my mind than its consequences echoed at me from the firmament.

The younger one turned, his awkward frame and clouded senses robbing his movement of grace or much speed. The older one was quicker, snatching the girl across the shoulder, his grip almost protective. For a moment her whimpering was the only thing to be heard. Then the elder laughed, the sound rolling over a thick veneer of rheum.

'Have we intruded upon your hunting grounds, gentle sir? Worry not, we won't be here long.' He was one of those junkies who had been something of substance before the wyrm had hollowed him out, a professor or a lawyer, and though his mind had long been reduced to its basest urges, still he retained a certain incongruous ability for fine speech.

I reached down to my boot and pulled out my stash, three argents I'd found or thieved and an ochre Rob One-Eye had given me for serving as lookout when he'd knocked off the old Light Street bank. 'There's yellow in here. It's a fair trade.' I didn't know what the price of a child was exactly, but there were too damn many wandering the streets of the city for it to be worth much more than that.

The two stared at each other, numbly, their slow reptile minds trying to process this new development. Given enough time one of them was going to realize that it was easier to kill me and take what I had than meet my demands – better not to allow them the opportunity.

I held the small packet of coins in my off hand, and with the other opened the straight razor I had pulled out with it. 'I'm taking the girl,' I said. 'You have your choice of payment – gold or steel.'

The younger one moved forward threateningly but I caught his eyes and he stopped short. The purse jangled.

'Gold or steel. Take your pick.'

Another sharp laugh from the one holding the child. That sound was grating on me, and I had the urge to throw in the towel on this negotiation business and see what the insides of this lice-ridden degenerate looked like.

'We'll take it,' he said. 'Saves us the trouble of bringing her to the docks.'

The other one seemed less certain, so I threw the pouch on the ground in front of him. He reached down to grab it and I thought about going for his face with my blade, a few quick swipes then on to his senior partner – but the old one still held the girl firmly, and I had no doubt he'd do her without blinking an eye. Better to play it straight and hope they'd do the same. The loss of my coin stung though. I wouldn't see another ochre for a long time, not with poor Rob doing twenty in Old Farrow for cutting up a priest in a bar fight.

'Walk out the other end of the alley,' I said as the youth stood up straight, my hard-won loot in his hands. 'And don't think yourself any sharp ideas.'

The one holding the girl stared at me. Then he smiled, checkerboard patterns of black and green. 'You make sure to keep your preserve well-tended now, young warden.'

'If I see you again I'll sever your balls from their stalk, and leave you to bleed out in the street.'

He laughed his ugly laugh and backed away, the boy following close after him. I watched them off until I was certain they weren't planning on rushing me, then closed my razor and walked over to the child.

Her almond eyes and dusky hue showed Kiren blood, and her tattered clothes and bruised skin spoke to at least a few nights on the streets. Around her neck was a wooden necklace, the kind you could buy two for a copper in Kirentown, back before the plague shut down their market. I wondered where she'd gotten it. A gift, probably, from her mother or father or a score of other relatives now in the ground.

The retreat of her abductors had done little to calm her nerves, and she still sobbed uncontrollably. I knelt down on one knee and slapped her across the face.

'Stop crying – no one is listening.'

She blinked twice, then wiped at her nose. The tears stopped, but I waited for her breathing to return to normal before I continued.

'What's your name?'

The thin stretch of her throat expanded as if to answer, but she couldn't force her lips to form the words.

'Your name, child,' I said again, trying to put some tenderness into my voice, for all that it was an emotion with which I had only passing relations.

'Celia.'

'Celia,' I repeated. 'That's the last time I'll ever hurt you, do you understand? You don't need to worry about me. I'm looking out for you, OK? I'm on your side.'

She looked at me, unsure how to answer. The time she'd spent on the street hadn't left her overflowing with trust for her fellow man.

I stood and took her hand in mine. 'Come on. Let's find you somewhere warm.'

It started to drizzle, then it started to rain. My thin coat was soon soaked to my body, so the girl had to make do in her ragged dress. For some time we walked in silence – though the storm pounded her tiny frame, Celia didn't weep.

The Aerie had been completed, its azure edifice jutting out into the ether, but the maze surrounding it was still being constructed. We had to struggle through a hundred yards of overturned mud, no easy task for the tiny legs of a small child, though she barely noticed. As soon as we had come within view her eyes had locked on the tower in awe and excitement.

Five weeks prior the entire population of Low Town, swelled by crowds of outsiders and shepherded by a flock of guardsmen, had celebrated the installment of the Blue Crane in his new surroundings. I'd watched from the back as the High Chancellor honored a lofty figure in extravagant robes. No one from the area had since shown courage enough to introduce themselves. Now seemed as good a time as ever to welcome the wizard to our neighborhood.

The little one by my side, I strode up to the tower with what arrogance I could muster.

A dozen feet above the ground a monstrous statue sat on a small ridge, jutting out from the building proper and marring the smooth perfection of the exterior. Beneath it I could see the outline of a door. I banged on its center and yelled into the night.

'Open up! Open up now!'

The movement of the gargoyle was no small shock, and Celia let out a shriek. I bit my lip trying not to do the same. The thing above the door twisted its heavy features with an ease that was unnatural, and its voice was inhuman if not directly threatening.

'Who is this that disturbs the repose of the evening? The Master is sleeping, young friends.'

I hadn't lost the savings of a childhood ill-spent to retreat at this gentle remonstration, and there seemed to be no reason to show this construction any more deference than I would have his fleshly equivalent. 'Then you'll need to wake him.'

'Sadly, child, I do not arrest the Master's slumber at the will of a pair of ragamuffins. Come back tomorrow and he might be willing to see you.'

A flash of lightning illuminated the landscape, the spire standing out uncannily against the barren ground surrounding it.

'Will the Blue Crane sleep warm in his bed and awake to the corpses of two children on his doorstep?'

Concrete eyebrows curled inward and the strange creature grew less friendly.

'Do not speak such of the Master – my patience is not infinite.'

Things had gone too far to back away, and even then I understood that advance is often the only alternative to retreat. I shouted louder, my voice cracking with the strain. 'Does the First Wizard care nothing for the people of his city? Will he rest in his castle while the children of Low Town drown in this storm? Call him down! Call him down, I say!'

The gargoyle's face glowed in the moonlight, and I was conscious of the danger I was courting. The thing hadn't shown itself capable of movement beyond its perch, but there was no knowing what forces it might martial in defense of the tower. 'Your abuse grows tiring. Leave, else the consequences . . .' It quieted mid-sentence, its visage frozen, all signs of intelligence absent.

Just as unexpectedly sentience returned. 'Wait here – the Master approaches.' It was not lost on me that this offered no guarantee of our safety. The wind screamed its hatred through the night. Celia squeezed my hand.

The stone shifted to reveal a tall, thin man with a long beard and eyes that glimmered even as they shook off the haze of slumber. I had only seen the Crane that once, from a distance, and he had looked more imposing in the midst of a vast crowd of people. I watched an inclination towards geniality combat the appropriate response to being woken late in the evening by a pair of vagrants. Somehow I wasn't shocked to discover the first winning out.

'I am not used to company after midnight, particularly company I've yet to meet. Still, the Daevas bid us show kindness to all our visitors, and I shall do no less. What is it you wish of me?'

'You're the Blue Crane?' I asked.

'I am.'

'The one they call the savior of Low Town?'

'If that's what they call me.'

I pushed Celia towards him. 'Then save her – she needs help, she's got nowhere to go.'

The Crane looked down at her, then back at me. 'And you? What do you need?'

Water ran down my sneer. 'Not a damn thing.'

He nodded and dropped to one knee, lowering himself with an extraordinary lack of pretension for one of the most powerful men in the Empire. 'Hello, child. People call me the Blue Crane. It's a funny name, I know. Do you have a name you'd like to share with me?'

The girl stared up at me, as if asking for permission. I patted her lightly on the back. 'Celia,' she barked out finally.

The Crane's eyes lit up in mock-wonder. 'That's my favorite name in the world! My whole life I've been hoping to meet someone with that name, and now you show up on my doorstep in the dead of night!' Celia looked like she wanted to giggle but didn't remember quite how. The Crane held out his hand. 'Let's get a cup of tea and you can tell me all about what it's like being born a Celia. I'm sure it's very exciting.'

This elicited a slight smile, the first I had seen from her all night. She took the Crane's palm, and he stood carefully, leading her into the tower. He turned as he headed into the doorway, his eyes offering entry.

'I'll be back to check on her soon,' I said.

Celia twisted herself around to face me, realizing now that I wasn't coming. She didn't speak but her eyes were trembling. My chest was full of fire and I felt a lightness untie itself from my bowels and rise up through my stomach. I sprinted off in the night, leaving the two of them standing there, together, illuminated by the soft light drifting out from the entrance.

19

I was thinking about the last time I had brought an orphan to the Crane's while I tried to catch the guardian's attention. It wasn't working. I punctuated a string of choice epithets by tossing a pebble against the gargoyle, but it bounced off without garnering a reaction.

'Why are you doing that?' Wren asked, perched on the innermost wall of the maze.

'Normally he responds.'

'Who?'

'The magic talking monster perched above the doorway, of course.'

Wren had the good sense not to antagonize me further. I sat down beside him, then pulled my tobacco pouch out of my satchel and started rolling a smoke. 'Fucking magic. We'd all be better off without it.'

'That's bullshit,' Wren said, oddly passionate.

'Is it now? Name one good thing that ever came from the Art.'

'The Crane's ward.'

I lit my cigarette beneath a shielded hand. 'Now name another.'

'I've heard Frater Hallowell has the touch, and heals people at the Church of Prachetas the Matriarch.'

'Frater Hallowell ever heal you?' I asked, breathing low-grade poison into my lungs.

'No.'

'He ever heal anyone you know?'

Wren shook his head.

'Doesn't really count then, does it?'

'No,' he responded, as usual quick to grasp the point. 'Not really.'

'Don't twist it up in your mind – the two in the Aerie are anomalies, exceptions that prove the rule. Start thinking otherwise and you'll get yourself into trouble.'

The boy considered that while I finished off my smoke. 'How long have you known the Blue Crane?'

'For twenty-five years.'

'Then why won't he let you into the tower?'

Why indeed? Even on those rare occasions when the Crane hadn't granted me an audience, his doorman had always animated to reject my plea. If the Aerie's defenses had fallen into disrepair, it meant the Crane's health was worse than I thought. I picked up another stone, larger this time, and flung it at the guardian. It had no more effect than the first, and I sat back down.

I poured ice water on my temper. There was still work that needed doing. Wren flipped his legs over the white stone. I did the same and we looked out towards the city.

'I like this labyrinth,' Wren said.

'It's a maze.'

'What's the difference?'

'A labyrinth only has one path and ends in the center. A maze has many different paths, and ends where you find a way out.'

I rose to greet Celia. Her dress looked soft in the afternoon light and she was smiling.

'I'm sorry that you had to wait. I've taken over running the

Aerie, but I haven't quite figured out how to operate the guardian yet.' She took my hand softly.

'Who is this here?' she asked.

I looked down to see Wren had pulled a snarl across his face. I chalked it up to the perverse instinct common among adolescents when presented with a member of the preferred sex, the root impulse that drives young men to rub mud in the hair of their future betrothed. There were few women walking the streets of Low Town to compare with Celia.

'Wren, this is Celia. Celia, this is Wren. Don't mind the face – he stepped on a bit of rusty metal yesterday. I think he's coming down with lockjaw.'

'Well, I'm glad he brought you over then. We'll have the Master take a look at it.' Celia's attempt to win over the boy from his opening offering of irrational dislike proved unsuccessful – if anything his grimace deepened a tic. With a graceful lift of her shoulders Celia turned her attention back towards me. 'Still picking up wastrels, I see?'

'He's more of an apprentice. Are we to continue this discussion in the street, or were you planning on inviting us inside?'

She laughed a little. I could always make her laugh. We climbed to the top of the tower and Celia walked us into the Crane's drawing room. 'The Master should be here shortly, I alerted him to your arrival before I went to let you in.'

We watched the afternoon sun fade through the south window. Wren stood close, his eyes scanning the Crane's treasures with the intensity of someone whose collected possessions could fit comfortably in a rucksack.

The bedroom door opened and the Crane entered, cheerily but with a stiffness that no good humor could hide. 'Back for some clandestine purpose no doubt,' he began, before noticing the child at my hip.

Then his eyes lit up like they used to, and the years seemed to shed off him, and I was glad that I had bothered to rustle Wren out of the Earl. 'I see you've brought a guest. Come over here, child. I'm old, and my sight isn't what it once was.'

Contra the unfriendliness he'd shown Celia, Wren moved forward without further prompting, and again I was struck by the easy grace the Crane possessed with children. 'You're thinner than a boy your age should be, but then so was your master. Chest like a mop-handle. What's your name?'

'Wren.'

'Wren?' The Crane's laughter echoed through the room, for once not trailed by a hacking cough. 'Wren and Crane! We might as well be brothers! Of course, my namesake is a creature of dignity and poise – while yours is a silly fowl, notable only for its rather aggravating song.'

This wasn't quite enough to bring a smile to the boy's face, but it was close, awful close for Wren.

'Well then, Wren. Will you grace us with a tune?'

The boy shook his head.

'Then it seems I shall provide the entertainment.' With a youthful burst of speed he moved to a shelf over the fire and pulled down an old creation of his, a strange-looking instrument halfway between a trumpet and a hunting horn, curling bands of burnished copper capped by pale ivory. 'You are certain you will not indulge your musical talents, young Wren?'

Wren shook his head again furiously.

The Crane shrugged in mock disappointment, then put the thing to his lips and let forth with a full-throated blast. It made a sound like the bellow of a bull, and a kaleidoscope of red and orange sparks erupted from the end, eddying about in the firmament.

Wren brushed at the glittering light that swirled through the air. I had loved that thing as a child – strange that I hadn't thought about it for so long.

Celia interrupted. 'Master, if you'd be so kind as to entertain our new friend, I need to have a few words with our old one.'

I thought he would object, but instead he flashed me a quick smile before turning back to the boy. 'Each note releases a different color, see?' He blew another tone on the trumpet, and a spray of blue-green shot out, like the foam of the sea.

144

We descended to the conservatory without speaking. The glass door was fogged from the heat, and Celia opened it and ushered me inside. Before I had time to appreciate the new suite of flowers that had taken bloom, Celia jumped into it. 'Well? What of our investigation?'

'Shouldn't we include the Master in this?'

'If you want to tear a dying man away from one of the few pleasures left to him, it's on your head.'

Having seen the man it didn't come as a complete shock. But still, I didn't like hearing my suspicions confirmed. 'He's dying?'

Celia sat on a stool beside a pink orchid and nodded sadly.

'What's wrong with him?'

'He's old. He won't tell me exactly, but he's seventy-five if he's a day.'

'I'm sorry.'

'So am I,' she said, but moved on quickly. 'It upsets him, this business with the children. He's always been . . . soft-hearted.'

'I'm not sure you need to be overly sensitive to find child murder distasteful,' I said, brushing a grain of pollen out of my eye and trying not to sneeze.

'I didn't mean that. What's happened to the children is terrible. But there isn't much the Master can do. He isn't what he was.' Her eyes were firm. 'The Crane has served the people of this city for half a century. He deserves peace in his final days. Surely you owe him that much, at least?'

'I owe the Master more than I could ever repay.' A memory came to my mind of the Crane as he had been, his eyes sparkling with wit and mischief, his back neither bent nor bowed. 'But that isn't the point. This thing needs to be stopped, and my resources are not such that I can afford to lose an ally.' I laughed caustically. 'In a week it won't matter one way or the other.'

'What does that mean?'

'Forget it, a poor attempt at humor.'

She was unconvinced, but didn't pursue it further. 'I'm not cutting you off. If you need help . . . I'll never be the Crane's equal in ability, nor in wisdom. But I am a Sorcerer First Rank.'

She nodded modestly at the ring that testified to this last fact. 'The Master has watched over Low Town long enough – having taken over the Aerie, perhaps it's time to adopt the rest of his mantle.'

The years since we had seen each other had aged Celia. She was no longer the child I had brought to the Aerie decades ago. Though she still spoke like it sometimes – adopt his mantle, the Daevas save us.

Celia took my silence as agreement. 'You have any leads?'

'I have suspicions. I always have suspicions.'

'Don't let me hurry you – if there's some other matter pressing on your shoulders, feel free to take care of that first.'

'I visited a party thrown by Lord Beaconfield, the Smiling Blade. Your gem throbbed against my chest while we talked.'

'And that didn't seem to you to be information that might benefit from being shared?'

'It doesn't mean as much as you'd think; as far as the law is concerned, it doesn't mean anything. If it were just some Low Town bum it might be enough, probably would be – I could point to him and the Old Man would drag him back to Black House and probe him for stains. But for a noble? Basic jurisprudence needs to be upheld, and that means you can't snatch a fellow from his house and carve him up on the say-so of an ex-agent's illegally acquired magical talisman.'

'No,' she said, deflating. 'I suppose you can't.'

'Besides, I'm not sure the amulet is right. I spoke to Beaconfield. He seemed like a violent flake, the sort bred in droves by the upper classes. But murdering children, summoning demons . . . It's out of character. The aristocracy tend to be too lazy to really commit to malevolence. Easier to spend their inheritance on costume galas and expensive whores.'

'Is it possible you overestimate him?'

'That's not a mistake I'm prone to. But say I did, say it is the duke. He's not an artist – I'd be surprised to discover he's mastered his sums. How would he go about contacting the void?'

'There are practitioners who see fit to sell their skills to anyone with sufficient coin. Did this Beaconfield character have anyone around him who might fit that description?'

'Yeah,' I said. 'He did.'

Celia crossed one leg over the other, the pink of her thighs barely visible beneath her dress. 'That might be something you'd want to look into.'

'It just might.' I mulled that over, then started up again. 'Actually there was something else I wanted to ask you about, something even the Master himself couldn't help me with.'

'As I said, I'm here to help.'

'I'd like to hear about your time at the Academy.'

'Why?'

'Abject boredom. I have absolutely nothing to occupy my mind, and hoped your tales of youthful revelry might give me something to gnaw on.'

She snickered, a giggle really, so light it barely escaped her mouth. There was a short pause while she weighed her words. 'It was a long time ago. I was young. We were all very young. The Master, the other practitioners of his ilk, they weren't interested in signing on, so it was just us apprentices, the weak and inexperienced, whoever they could corral in. The instructors, if you could call them that, were barely older than we were, and rarely as competent. There was no curriculum really, not then, not after it first started. They just . . . dumped us in a room, and let us loose. Still, it was the first time anything like that had ever happened, the first time we'd been encouraged to share what we knew, rather than hiding it in ciphered spell books and double-trapped grimoires.'

'Did you know a man named Adelweid?'

Her eyes narrowed, and she pursed her lips. 'We weren't a large group. Everybody knew everybody, more or less.' Celia was the sort of person who would happily spend the rest of her life locked away from the remainder of the species but had trouble mustering up the ill-will to badmouth any particular member of it. 'Sorcerer Adelweid was . . . very talented.' I thought she was going to continue, but then she closed her mouth and shook her head, and that was that.

So I figured I'd best volunteer something. 'Adelweid was part of a military project during the closing days of the War – Operation Ingress.'

'The Master told me your story.'

'You know anything about it?'

'As I said, we were left free to pursue whatever avenues of studies interested us. Adelweid and I had differing proclivities. I heard rumors, ugly things, but no specifics. If I knew anything I thought would help, I'd have told you already.' She shrugged, anxious to bury the subject. 'Adelweid is dead – he's been dead a long time.'

He was indeed. 'But Adelweid wasn't the only one involved. Whoever killed the Kiren must have been part of it. And something like that, a military project . . . they'll have kept records.'

Her head shot up from its perch on her shoulder. 'They'd be secret,' she said, almost insistent. 'They'd be hidden. You'd never get a look at them.'

'They would be hidden, and I don't imagine whomever is in charge of the army's classified files would be in a great hurry to share them with me. Happily I have other avenues of inquiry.'

'Other avenues?'

'Crispin, my old partner. I've got him looking into it.'

'Crispin,' she repeated. 'Is he still reliable? Will he come through for you, after all your . . . time apart?'

'I don't imagine he's happy to be doing me a favor, but he won't let that stop him. Crispin . . . Crispin's golden. It doesn't matter what's between us. This could help stop the killings, it's the right thing to do. He'll do it.'

She nodded slowly, her face turned away from mine. 'Crispin it is then.'

Around us legions of stiff-eyed drones buzzed about happily, fluttering from petal to stalk to stipule, the lullaby of their steady buzzing a mild soporific.

Celia stood up from the stool, her eyes dark against honey-colored skin. 'I'm glad . . .' She shook her head, as if to refresh her prose, and her long dark hair arched back and forth, the charm around her neck twisting in unison. 'It's been good to see

148

you again, even under these circumstances. In a way I'm grateful you've been entangled in this mess.' She took my hand lightly in hers, and stared into my eyes without blinking.

Her pulse was very rapid beneath her skin, and my own rose to meet it. I thought of all the reasons this was a bad idea, thought about everything that was rotten and spoiled and cheap about it. Then I thought about them again. This had been a lot easier ten years earlier. 'You and the Master always had a place in my thoughts,' I said quietly.

'That's all you'll say, then? That I hadn't completely deserted your memory?'

'I need to see how Wren is doing.' It was a weak excuse, for all that it was in fact true.

She nodded and walked me to the door, dejection marring her heart-shaped face.

Up in the main room, the Crane was sitting on an old chair, his back towards us, laughing and clapping his hands in rhythm. Each time he did so the collection of sparks that swirled about the antechamber would change color and shift direction, swooping up to the ceiling then diving towards the window. Wren hadn't quite joined the master in his jocularity, but to my surprise he wore an honest smile, a low thing that was mostly in his eyes, as if he was afraid someone would notice. It ended abruptly when he saw Celia and me return.

The Crane must have read our entry on the boy's face because he stopped clapping and the sparks dropped slowly to the ground, then disappeared into the ether. I put my hand on the Crane's back. The blade of his shoulder was sharp beneath his robes. 'I always loved that toy.'

The Crane laughed again, a bright thing, like his fireworks. I would miss it very much when he was gone. Then it faded and he elevated his head up towards me. 'That business we spoke of last time—'

Celia interrupted him. 'It turned out fine, Master. That's what he stopped by to tell us. Everything's taken care of – you don't need to think about it any more.'

149

The Crane's eyes flashed across Celia's face, then searched mine for confirmation. I did something that might have been a shrug or a nod. He was old, and tired, and he took it as the latter. A smile spread back over his face, or at least something close enough to mimic it, and he turned back to Wren. 'You're a fine boy. Not like this 'en,' he said with a glance in my direction.

But Wren was having none of it. As if to make up for his moment of lightness he had stamped a sullen growl on his face, and gave the barest hint of a farewell nod to the Master.

The Crane had long years of experience dealing with the ingratitude of over-proud youths, and he handled the snub with grace. 'It was a pleasure to have had the opportunity to entertain, Master Wren.' He continued with the same mock stiffness. 'And you, sir, as always, are welcome any time you wish.'

Tell that to the gargoyle outside, I thought, but he seemed happy and hale and I kept my mouth shut.

Celia stood by the stairs and leaned down to meet Wren as he approached. 'It was lovely meeting you. Perhaps when you return we'll have more of a chance to chat.'

Wren didn't respond. Celia kept her face friendly and waved the two of us past.

We left the Aerie and began our walk north. A few blocks went by as I ran over what I had learned, sifting through the noise for something valuable, something that would click with the rest of it.

Wren interrupted my contemplations. 'I liked the tower.'

I nodded.

'And I liked the Crane.'

I waited for him to continue but he didn't, and we walked on in silence.

20

I met Guiscard an hour or so later outside a small warehouse a few blocks from Black House. Having already availed myself once that day of the hospitality of my former employers, I wasn't altogether keen on returning to the neighborhood – but I consoled myself with the thought that if the Old Man wanted me dead, proximity wouldn't be an issue. It wasn't exactly the sort of comfort that keeps you sleeping soundly at night, but it was all I had.

The building itself was the sort of structure that seemed to have been deliberately built so as to give no hint to the activities that took place inside. Storage space, you might have guessed if pushed, but only because you couldn't think of anything more vague. Unlike Black House, the Box's value was not enhanced by having its purpose widely advertised. It wasn't a secret, though most of Rigus were happy to pretend themselves ignorant. Because inside the Box the scryers made their nest, and to draw attention from them was to have your secrets made known – and what man alive doesn't have a few things he'd rather keep quiet?

The kid towed himself behind me, silent since we had left the Aerie, shifty even by his standards. I didn't bother to draw him out. I had other things on my mind.

My favorite agent, after Crowley, sulked next to the doorway, smoking a cigarette like it was an affectation and not an addiction. He saw us from a hundred yards off but pretended otherwise, buying time for his histrionics to ripen. He was unhappy to be accompanied on this little side-errand, and he wanted me to know it.

When we were too close to keep up the pretense he flicked his half-smoked tab into the muck and looked me up and down with his usual tenderness, then trailed his eyes across Wren. 'Who's this?' he asked, almost decent, before catching himself and returning his thin lips to their practiced sneer.

'Can't you see the resemblance?' I shoved Wren lightly forward. 'The genteel nose, the grace and carriage which bespeaks of noble blood. You were fourteen, shallow and insipid – she was a chambermaid with a clubfoot and an overly developed jaw. When your parents learned of the affair they packed her off to a nunnery and sent the issue of your affair abroad.' I tussled the boy's hair. 'But he's back now. I imagine you two have a lot to talk about.'

Wren smirked a little. Guiscard shook his head, disdainful of any theatrics that weren't his own. 'It's good to see you've kept your sense of humor – I would think with all that's going on you wouldn't have time for these childish jibes.'

'Don't remind me, I've already changed pants twice today.'

That was about as much banter as he was capable of without outside assistance, and realizing it he headed inside.

'I'll be out in a few minutes,' I told the boy. 'Try and avoid doing anything that might lead Adolphus to beat me to death.'

'Don't take shit from the snowman,' he said.

I laughed, shocked at his outburst and vaguely flattered to see the child take my feuds as his own. 'I don't take shit from anyone,' I said, though in fact most of my life lately seemed to consist of doing just that.

He blushed and looked down at his feet, and I followed Guiscard into the building.

Scryers are a strange breed, strange enough that they have their own headquarters away from Black House, and not just because part of their duties includes the inspection and anatomization of dead bodies. They come in on big cases, murders and assaults, the occasional rape. Sometimes they get impressions, images or sense memories, bits of data, rarely entirely coherent but occasionally helpful. They aren't artists, leastways not as I understand it – they have no ability to affect the physical world, but rather a sort of passive receptiveness to it, an extra sense the rest of us lack.

Are blessed to lack, I should say. The world is an ugly place, and we ought to be grateful for any blinders that limit our comprehension – better to scuttle along the surface than dive in the noxious waters beneath. Their 'gift' is the sort that makes a normal life impossible, the undercurrents of existence bubbling up at inopportune moments. Those born with it are inevitably drafted into the service of the government, simply because any other kind of work is more or less impossible – imagine trying to sell a man shoes and flashing that he beats his children, or has his wife sewn up in a sack. It's an unpleasant sort of existence, and most investigators are hardened drunks or borderline lunatics. I've had a few as customers – ouroboros root mostly, though once they move on to the hard stuff it's not long before the brass come calling, or they decide to circumvent the authorities by falling into a river or huffing up a half-pint of breath. It's a common enough fate among their kind – few indeed die of natural causes.

Anyway, they're useful enough as part of an investigation, so long as you don't get too reliant on them. It's a touchy thing, their second sight, and for every decent lead you're liable to get two brick walls and a false trail. Once I spent a month digging through every hole in the Islander half of Low Town, only to

153

discover that the man I was working with had never seen a Mirad before, and had mistaken the cinnamon tan of the murderer in his vision for the dark chocolate of a seafarer. After that I stopped spending too much time in the Box, not that my presence was much in demand after I put the aforementioned scryer through a first-floor window.

I stepped into an antechamber manned by an aging Islander, who slipped off the wooden seat he had been napping on and moved to unlock the interior doorway. There were a lot of locks, and the gatekeeper was straddling the line between venerable and antediluvian, so we had opportunity for conversation.

'Who are we going to see?' I asked.

Knowing something I didn't perked Guiscard up a little. 'Crispin wanted the best on this one, angled for Marieke. You remember her? She would have been just starting out when they gave you the ax.'

'Not really.'

'They call her the Ice Bitch.'

It was the sort of jibe I could see making the rounds among the wits at Black House, misogynistic and unoriginal. That I didn't laugh seemed to offend Guiscard slightly, and he switched subjects.

'How did it happen, by the way?'

'How did what happen?'

'Your dismissal.'

The Islander reached the last bolt and dragged the door open, struggling against the heavy iron. 'I poisoned the Prince Consort.'

'The Prince Consort isn't dead.'

'Really? Then who the hell did I murder?'

It took him a moment to puzzle that out. 'You ought not speak so lightly of the royal court,' he sniffed, like he'd gotten the better of the exchange, then turned at a brisk pace and headed down the dank stone hallway. The further we got the heavier the place started to stink, an unpleasant mixture of mildew and human flesh. Guiscard passed a dozen-odd doorways before choosing one to open.

The room displayed that obsessive organization that suggests an unwound mind as surely as does chaos – rows and rows of cataloged boxes atop dusted shelves, and a floor clean enough to eat off, if for some reason you were inclined to take your supper against the ground. Apart from its spotlessness, there was nothing to give the impression that anyone worked there: the worn desk set against the back wall was absent of memento, absent even the usual detritus – pens and ink, paper and text-books – that signify a workspace. You might well have assumed it to be nothing more than a well-kept storage room, except for the dead body resting on a slab in the center of the room, and the woman who stood over it.

She would never be called beautiful, there was too much bone where one hoped to find flesh – but she might have sneaked into handsome without the scowl that defaced her finish. To judge by her height and skin, so pale you could trace the blue web of veins up her neck, she was a Vaalan. And not city-born either, if I had to guess. I wondered what series of events had brought her down from the frigid North and the stony islands her people inhabited. Taken bit by bit, there was much of her that was alluring – a graceful carriage, limbs long and fine, strands of strawberry-blonde hair falling down past her shoulders – a surfeit of physical blessings, all submerged by the raptor thinness of her frame. She looked up as the door opened, an arresting scan with eyes that custom would label blue, but that were, truthfully, virtually achromatic, then her focus returned to the corpse atop her table.

I did not find it altogether impossible to discern the origin of her nickname.

Guiscard elbowed me and I noticed that his smirk had returned, like we were sharing some sort of a joke, but I didn't like him and even if I did I wouldn't have had the time for antics. Finally he spoke up. 'Scryer Uys?'

She grunted and continued taking notes. We waited to see whether she was capable of upholding the social courtesies developed to paper over the untrustworthy nature of the human species. When it became obvious she wasn't, Guiscard cleared his throat and continued. In contrast to the scryer, I couldn't help but find myself impressed by the gentility with which he hocked up a gram of phlegm. I wondered how many years of finishing school it took him to master that trick.

'This is—'

'I recognize your guest, Agent.' She scraped her pen against the page like she was taking revenge for some past act of cruelty. Then, having made it clear that she ranked us well below the completion of routine paperwork, she deigned to offer her attention. 'I've seen him grace our premises before, some years back.'

That was a surprise – I'm good with faces, very good; it's one of the relatively few job requirements that remained constant despite my change in employment. Of course those last six months in Special Operations had been . . . hectic. Šakra knew I'd missed more pressing things.

'So the introduction is unnecessary. While you're here though, perhaps you might enlighten me as to what the fuck he's doing in the Box, since, to judge by the number of times I've heard his name reviled by members of your organization, he's no longer in the good graces of Black House?'

I gave a quick little laugh, half because it was funny and half because I wanted to trip her up. And indeed she seemed shocked at my reaction, her ability to cause offense for once falling short of the mark.

Crispin stroked the peach-fuzz below his nose, considering how to answer. He wasn't himself sure why I was there, who had decided to incorporate me into the investigation – though, obviously, decorum and his own unflappable sense of self-importance stopped him from saying so. 'Orders from the top.'

She narrowed her eyes in controlled fury, preparing to give full vent to her spleen. Then she froze, blinking as if lost and settling her hand against the table for support. Slowly she pulled herself upright, and stared at me with a disturbing intensity.

I'd seen enough of these fits to know she'd flashed on something. 'If you've got tomorrow's racket numbers, I'll go half.'

She kept right on staring at me, seeming not to notice the joke. 'All right,' she said finally, and turned back to the meat on the table. 'The girl's name was Caristiona Ogilvy, age thirteen, of Tarasaighn descent. She was taken two days ago, from an alleyway near her father's shop. There's no signs of struggle on her body, nor any evidence that she was restrained.'

'Someone drugged her?' Guiscard asked.

She didn't like being interrupted, even as part of the normal back and forth of a conversation. 'I didn't say that.'

'I assume she wouldn't have let herself be slaughtered without some sort of protest.'

'Maybe she trusted whoever took her,' I said. 'But I'm going to guess you've got a theory you're waiting to share.'

'I'm getting to it. The wound to the throat was the cause of her death—'

'Are you sure?' Guiscard asked. He was kidding, intimidated by her and trying to leaven the mood, but she couldn't see it, conditioned to take whatever she possibly could as an insult. Her upper lip, which had joined its twin in a placid if not particularly affable dash, curved back up to reveal her canines, and her eyes sparked in anticipation of the coming conflict.

Much as I liked the idea of watching Guiscard get himself knocked down a peg or two, it had been a long day, and I really didn't have the time for it. 'What else can you tell us?'

She snapped her head back at me, in her brittle gauntness and sharp movements resembling nothing so much as a kestrel scanning for prey – but I ain't Guiscard and after a few seconds she seemed to realize it. Sparing a quick glance for the agent, who, if his head wasn't lodged completely up his ass, was grateful for the reprieve, she continued. 'As I said, the wound to the jugular is what killed her. There were no other injuries on the body, nor any signs of sexual trauma. She was bled out, then dumped earlier this morning.'

I rolled that over. 'We're caught up on the physical evidence. You get anything off the body?'

'Not much. The echo of the void is so heavy over her it drowns out almost everything else. And even if I push that aside I can't get anything. Whoever did this erased their tracks.'

'The Kiren, the one who took Tara, he worked at a glue factory. I had assumed he had scrubbed her body with lye, or some other chemical that hampered your work. Could that have happened again?'

'I don't see how. I wasn't on the Potgieter case, and didn't get the chance to scan the scene fresh. That trick with the acid might have worked for some of my less talented colleagues, but I would have been able to find my way through it. But I was at the scene of the man who killed her, and the . . . thing that killed him had the same resonance I hear on Caristiona.'

I'd figured as much. There wasn't one chance in a thousand the deaths were unconnected, though it was good to have official confirmation.

'You pick up any other connections to Tara?' Guiscard piped in belatedly.

'No, the sample I had from her was too decayed.' She shook her head, angry again. 'I might have had more luck if you'd had the balls to pick up a piece of her, instead of leaving it to rot in the ground.'

We don't make a big deal out of it but the best thing for a scryer isn't hair, it's flesh – doesn't have to be a lot, just a taste. The good ones insist on it, and back when I wore the ice I made sure to deliver whenever possible. The little finger, sometimes an ear if we don't expect the newly deceased to get an open casket. I had no doubt if I searched the scryer's meticulously cataloged shelves I'd find jar after jar of pickled meat, short sprouts of sinew floating in brine.

This last insult managed to nerve Guiscard into a response. 'What was I to do, Marieke – slip in with a pair of garden shears before the public funeral?'

The Ice Bitch's eyes narrowed down to dark slits, and she ripped the sheet off the corpse, letting it flutter to the ground. Below it the child lay in stiff repose, her mouth and eyes shut, her body white as salt save for the dark tufts of her private hair.

'I'm sure she appreciates your willingness to uphold decorum,' Marieke said, ferocious without being animated. 'As will the next one, I don't doubt.'

Guiscard looked away. It was hard to do otherwise.

'You said you didn't have much to tell us,' I asked after I thought enough time had passed. 'What were you leaving out?'

It was a thoroughly innocuous statement, but she took a moment to work it around in her head, examine it from all angles, making sure there was nothing she could take offense over, no unintended insults to catch on and toss back. 'Like I said, I didn't flash anything off the body, and the scryings I've performed have come up useless. But there is something odd, something I haven't seen before.'

She fell silent, and I figured it was best to let her take her time rather than risk a tongue-lashing by speeding her along.

'There's a . . .' She paused again, trying to fit her thoughts into a language that hadn't developed terms to accommodate the full range of her senses. 'An aura, a sort of glow, which animates the body. We can read it, follow it sometimes, track it backwards from the spot of death, see it on things the deceased lived around or cared for.'

'You mean a soul?' Guiscard asked, skeptical.

'I'm not a fucking priest,' she snapped back at him – though frankly the profanity had already pretty much given that away. 'I don't know what the hell it is, but I know that's it's not here now, and it should be. Whoever is responsible for this took more than her life.'

'You're saying she was sacrificed?'

'I can't say for sure. This sort of thing is rare, I've never seen it. In theory, the ritual murder of an individual, especially a child, would generate a pool of energy – the sort of energy that could be used to initiate a working of immense power.'

'What sort of working?'

'There's no way to tell. Or if there is, I don't know it. Ask an artist, they might be able to give you more on it than I can.'

I'd do just that, as soon as I had the chance. Guiscard looked up at me, making sure there was nothing else. I shook my head and he began his retreat.

'Your assistance is appreciated, Scryer, as always.' Guiscard was smart enough to know the value of maintaining a working relationship with someone as competent as the Ice Bitch, for all that her idiosyncrasies left something to be desired.

Marieke waved away his gratitude. 'I'm going to run a few more rituals, see if I can't shake anything out before they bury her tomorrow. But I wouldn't hold my breath. Whoever wiped her clean was good, and thorough.'

I nodded a goodbye that she ignored, and Guiscard and I headed for the door. I was already thinking about next steps when she called me back.

'You, stop,' she ordered, and it was clear enough to which of us the command referred. I gave Guiscard the go-ahead, and he stepped out.

Marieke gave me a long, piercing look, like she was trying to see my soul through my ribcage. Whatever she made out through my aging mass of bone and muscle seemed to be enough, because after a moment she reached over the body. 'Do you know what this is?' she asked, drawing my attention to the child's inner thigh, and the small array of red bumps that defaced it.

I tried to speak but nothing came.

'Figure out what the fuck is going on,' she said, her constant bitterness replaced by fear. 'And figure it out quick.'

I turned and stumbled out.

'What was that about?' Guiscard asked, but I brushed past him without answering.

Wren was standing next to him and he set himself to say something but I put one hand on his shoulder and skirted him along, and he was smart enough to take the hint and keep his mouth shut.

Which was good, because at that moment I was no more capable of conversation than flight. The thought banging around my head was too big to allow anything else air to breathe, and had upended what remained of my equilibrium, already battered by the events of the day.

I had seen that rash before. Seen it on my father one evening when he came home from the mill, seen it on my mother a few days after. Seen it cover their flesh like a second skin, lines of pustules that crusted shut their eyes and swelled their tongues till they went mad with thirst. Seen it put so many men in the ground that after a while there wasn't anyone left to do the burying. Seen those little red bumps upend civilization. Seen them destroy the world.

The plague had returned to Rigus. On the walk home I muttered every prayer to the Firstborn I could remember, for all that they hadn't done a damn bit of good the last time around.

21

Marieke's news kept my mind working at half speed, and it was a while before I puzzled out why Wren couldn't stop fidgeting with his ugly woolen coat. When it did click we were almost back to Low Town, and I slowed my step to a halt. After a moment the boy did the same.

'When did you take it?' I asked.

He thought about lying to me, but he knew I had him. 'When you went to say goodbye.'

'Let me see it.'

He pulled out the horn, then passed it over with a shrug.

'Why'd you steal it?'

'I wanted it.' His eyes conceded nothing. This wasn't the first time he'd been caught pilfering, nor the first time he'd find himself whipped. It was part of the game, and he'd play it to the end.

So I decided to go another way. 'I guess that's a reason,' I said.

'He's got plenty of shit. He doesn't need it.'

'No, I suppose he doesn't.'

'You gonna hit me?'

'You're not worth the trouble. I've got too much on my mind to worry about teaching ethics to a stray dog. It's too late for you anyway – you'll never be anything more than what you are.'

His mouth curdled up furiously, face so poisoned with hate that I thought he'd take a shot at me. But he didn't, instead he spat on my shoe and sprinted off into the distance.

I waited till he disappeared before inspecting his loot. It was a smart pull – small enough to stash comfortably, and though only an artist would be capable of sparking its magic, it was well crafted. It might fetch an ochre from the right pawnbroker. My first time inside the Aerie I'd made a much more foolish choice, picked up a quartz ball the size of my head, so heavy it nearly dragged me double, and so clearly the product of magic that no fence would touch it. It spent two years hidden in a junkyard near the docks before I manned up the courage to give it back.

I put the horn into my satchel, and came out with a vial of breath. The vapor pushed out everything that had happened in the last hour, Wren's petty betrayal and Marieke's revelations. I needed to concentrate on the next task in line, otherwise I'd end up stumbling over my feet.

I had to see Beaconfield. If Celia's talisman was right, and he was involved in this business with the children, then I needed to try to suss out his purpose. And if he wasn't then I still owed a shipment to my new favorite client. I took another hit, then headed west to see the Kiren.

A mile and a half later I stepped into the Blue Dragon. The bartender, morbidly obese and yet to offer me his name in three years of patronizing the establishment, stood watch at the counter. Beyond him the room was mostly empty, its usual clientele finishing out their shifts at the factories that dotted the area.

I grabbed a seat at the bar. Up close the proprietor's flesh undulated in a singularly unappealing fashion, a hillock of fat rising and falling with each haggard breath. Apart from his labored panting he was motionless, apathy wearing a groove in his face.

'What's the good word?' I opened, knowing my pleasantry

wouldn't earn a response. It didn't. Sometimes it gets boring being right all the time. 'I need to make a pick-up.' One of the high points of dealing with the Kiren is you don't need to talk in code – no heretics work for the hoax, and a white man inside the pub stuck out like, well, a white man in a pub full of Kirens.

The bartender's eyes fluttered once, like the beat of a humming-bird's wing.

I took that for acknowledgment. 'I need half a pint of daeva's honey and six stalks of ouroboros root.'

There was a long pause, during which the man's face betrayed no hint of comprehension. This was followed by the barest shifting of his pupils towards the back door.

The Blue Dragons and I did a lot of business together; there shouldn't be any need to see the boss just to grab a few ochres worth of narcotics. 'Not now. I have somewhere to be. Tell Ling Chi I'll swing back around later.'

Another interminable intermission, and another sideways glance.

It seemed I was going to see Ling Chi after all.

Behind the back door was a small room occupied by a pair of Kirens holding half-moon axes and looking equal parts menacing and bored. They guarded a second door, as non-descript as the first. The one on the left bowed politely as I entered. 'Please put your weapons on the table. They will be returned after your meeting.' He spoke with a slight accent, but his grammar and diction were perfect. His associate yawned and scratched at the inner wall of a nostril. I tossed my armaments on a bench in the corner, then moved towards the next room.

The guard on the right dropped his hand from his face and raised his ax threateningly. I shot a look at his partner, appar-ently the brains of the outfit. 'We must regretfully insist on a search of your person,' he said, without discernible regret.

This was unexpected, and like any unexpected event in a crim-inal transaction, ominous. The Blue Dragon Clan had been supplying me with product for three years, ever since taking over the Dead Rat's territory. In that time we had developed a mutually beneficial relationship, founded like any relationship on trust and constancy. Nothing positive could come from altering the routine.

I allowed no trace of worry to flicker across my face – heretics are like dogs, any sign of fear and you're as good as lost. I held out my arms and the guard who had been picking his nose gave me a quick but thorough search. The other opened the second door and waved me through. 'We thank our esteemed guest for accepting indignity with grace.'

In stark contrast to the bar that surrounded his court, every inch of Ling Chi's inner sanctum was enveloped in the oppressively opulent fashion that is the height of taste among the heretics. Lanterns of red lacquered wood provided dim light while casting strange and grotesque shadows across the walls. The floor was covered with intricately woven Kiren rugs, man-sized figures consisting of thousands of colored strands spreading out to the back of the room. In the corners, braziers shaped like strange half-animal demigods puffed at yard-long sticks of joss, filling the interior with their heavy musk.

Ling Chi sat in the midst of it, lounging on a silk divan, a striking beauty carefully massaging his bare feet. A man in his early middle age, slight even for a Kiren, but projecting a presence the envy of someone twice his size. His face was a mask of white powder, interrupted only by a pair of false beauty marks, and his hair was elaborately styled, a black mane stretched across a gold wire that rose above his scalp like a halo. He watched me with the faintest hint of a smile, hands clasped, the artificial tips of his elongated nails clacking rhythmically.

For all that he played the part of the degenerate despot, there was something about the man that made me wonder how much was pretense. I could never quite shake the feeling that as soon as I was gone he'd kick away the maidservant for a pair of slippers, and replace the mad contrivance on his head with a decent hat.

Then again, maybe not. No foreigner can ever understand a heretic, not really.

But if his image was fabricated, his position was very much

earned – Ling Chi, the Death that Comes by a Thousand Cuts, whose word is law from Kirentown to the city walls. Rumor placed him as either the bastard son of the Celestial Emperor or the child of an immigrant prostitute who died in childbirth. Personally I'd put my money on the latter – nobility tend to lack the drive necessary to maintain control over such a vast enterprise.

In less than a decade he had turned a neighborhood gang into one of the most powerful criminal entities in Rigus, and done so in the face of the entrenched underworld interests. His leadership during the Third Syndicate War had made his coterie one of the rare few who left that bloody business stronger than they had entered it, unifying the smaller Kiren crews into a single horde vital enough to stand toe-to-toe with the Tarasaihgn and Rouender mobs. These days he ran half the docks, and had his fingers in most any illicit enterprise run by his countrymen within the city proper.

He was also an utter madman, completely lacking in any of those qualities like empathy or conscience which might prove a hindrance to the expansion and consolidation of a criminal organization. The story went that the year after his rise to power was the best for shallow water fishing in fifty years, made so by the supply of human flesh Ling Chi had seen fit to dump in the harbor.

He smiled at me, his teeth inked black in the Kiren fashion. 'My dearest comrade has returned, after too long away.'

I bowed very slightly. 'My most intimate confidant does me honor in marking my absence.'

'A small recognition of the many fine services my beloved ally has provided.' The slave took up an emery stone and brought it smoothly across his toenails, elevating his bare foot slightly as she did so. Ling Chi's face betrayed no sign that he had noticed. 'Much has happened to my closest of friends since last we spoke.'

I waited to hear where he went.

'Some weeks ago my brother asked for permission to enter my territory. I was grateful to be able to render so dear an associate service. My brother entered, my brother asked questions. A man, a Kiren man, died. Later, agents searched his house –

they said the dead man was a killer of children, they said that he killed a little white girl. Now my people speak of dark things that hide in the shadows and prey on the children of the Venerable Lands, and they speak of the constables of their new home, who are happy to let this happen.' His golden fingernails continued their drumbeat, *click, click, click.*

'Glory be to the Celestial Emperor, whose ways are subtle but certain, and who repays all evil in kind. Blessed are we who hold firm to the Empyreal Path, whose steps are watched by the Highest of his Ministers. May our words be uttered without deceit, and our actions redound to the glory of his Eternal Majesty.' Beat that, you stone-faced bastard.

Ling Chi laughed, a brittle sound like the roar of a locust, and gestured to the corner. A young boy approached the throne with a three-foot-long pipe, crafted to resemble an uncoiled dragon, and held it to his master's mouth. Ling Chi took a drag and blew a foul concoction of tobacco and opiates into the air. He offered it to me with one crook of his long fingernails, but I shook my head and he waved the boy back into the shadows.

'The piety of my associate is a source of perpetual inspiration. And yet . . .' His eyes grew doleful, tiny dark pupils ringed by black rouge. 'Many are the demons of iniquity that wait on the road to enlightenment, and crooked is the trail. Nothing more pleases the Lords of Vice than to twist the workings of a righteous man to their own dark purposes.'

'The words of my compatriot are dulcet to my ears, and ennobling to my spirit,' I said.

His talons kept even time. 'We are but a poor and benighted community, struggling to survive on alien soil. This foul business, the terrible doings of a dim and twisted mind . . . It threatens to disturb the delicate equilibrium between our tiny school and the sea of sharks in which we swim.'

I didn't respond, and after a moment he continued.

'I am but an aged grandfather whose fellow countrymen, lost amid the chaos of your country, look to for guidance and protection. The small esteem I have gained would evaporate as dew on a summer morning, were I unable to defend against the unwarranted attacks of their tormentors.'

'Grateful we are that the murderer's actions were discovered, and the threat to the children of the Emperor is over.'

His nails ceased their tattoo. 'It is not over,' he hissed, and I feared our interview was about to erupt into violence. But his break in composure was momentary, and so swift that I could barely be certain it had even happened. His claws resumed their cadence, and for a time all that could be heard was their echo against the shadowy fastness of the chamber. 'Another child has been found. A terrible development. Already your fellows call for vengeance against the heretics. Already they call for reprisals.'

I focused on looking inscrutable. The heretics are a useful target for the round eyes, but the threat of their abuse is part of what keeps Ling Chi's people in line. What was he moaning about?

Ling Chi beckoned to his attendant, who brought the pipe over a second time. He put his lips to the stem, then spewed out an impressive cloud of the dank vapor. 'I was terribly concerned for my intimate's safety today.'

'It flatters me that one so exalted would consider my well-being worthy of notice.'

'This morning I was informed by a wandering eye that my friend was arrested by Agents of the Crown.' He clicked his tongue in a fashion meant to be taken as sorrowful – it was grotesque and unnatural, like a she-wolf suckling a newborn. 'Terrible was the despair in my household. I ordered my servants to dress themselves in white, and to begin the forty days of mourning prescribed for the death of an esteemed companion.' He hung his head between his shoulders in feigned bereavement, observing a theoretical moment of silence.

'Then something extraordinary happened!' A smile appeared on his lips, though it didn't reach his eyes. 'I received another message. My ally had exited the house of justice! Great was the joy with which the news of my brother's survival was received! I ordered strings of burning chrysanthemums to be set off, and a black rooster slaughtered in his honor.' He cocked his head

169

contemplatively. 'But in the midst of my unadulterated happiness, I could not divest myself of the pangs of curiosity. For though I have heard tell of many men being taken into the rooms beneath Black House, word has never reached my ears of one being allowed to leave.'

'The visit from my former employers was a surprise, as was my release. Terrible are the workings of a government out of harmony with the heavens.'

'Former employers . . .'

'The delicacy of my associate's hearing is matched only by the perfection of his understanding.'

'Cunning are the servants of your Queen, unknowable their objectives. Great must be the concern of any who find themselves tangled in the intrigues of Black House.'

The pieces clicked together and I finally realized the purpose of this interminable interrogation. He thought the Old Man moved against him, that the dead Kiren was his opening gambit, that I had been drafted into it and my arrest a cover for a meeting. The impossibility of such a scheme would provide little defense against the blades of Ling Chi's underlings should he decide to act on his suspicions. 'What concern could honest citizens have for the doings of the lawful authorities, clouded though their sight may be?'

'I am certain my brother has the truth of it. And yet . . . I am a simple man,' he said, pausing to give the absurdity time to diffuse amid the smoke. 'So I speak to my revered brethren plainly. I do not know what trouble afflicts Low Town – but I cannot help but observe that since my associate's intrusion the round eyes howl for the blood of my kinsmen, and Black House sniffs about my home.'

There was no point in arguing further. 'The words of my honorable ally are water on parched earth.'

He closed his eyes and put his hand to his brow, his skills sufficient to carry the theatrics. 'Truly, the concerns of parentage weigh heavy on my brow. Many are the days when I wonder how I shall carry on. Many are the nights that I wish for the Emperor to call me to his side. I take solace only in the knowledge that my ally offers aid to my feeble body, and comfort to my senescent mind.'

'I watch after my mentor with vision that never clouds.'

'And I would expect nothing less from so stalwart a friend. The goods are at the bar, and I will provide a quarter discount in exchange for the precious moments my brother has given me. As for the other matters . . .' He leaned his body forward in such a fashion as to allow the girl below to continue massaging his foot. 'Remember what I said. I have no wish to antagonize Black House, but they cannot operate in my territory. I will be forced to meet any interference in a fashion . . .' He smiled, an ugly thing, black teeth sharp even in the gloom. 'Most unfriendly.'

I left Ling Chi's den as rapidly as decorum would allow. The whole thing was too much, the smoke so thick in my lungs I thought I might vomit. At the bar the fat man handed me my package without a shift of his dead eyes. I headed out the door without looking back.

22

By the time I made it back to the Earl the dinner rush was in full swing. I took a free spot at the bar and managed to break Adolphus away from his role as host long enough to call for a plate of food and something dark to sit on top of it. It was warm, and the press of bodies and the loud hum of vitality were having a lethargic effect. I rubbed my forehead and tried to keep myself awake.

Adeline came in from the back, a dish of meat and potatoes in one hand and a pull of good strong stout in the other.

'Thanks,' I said.

She nodded pleasantly. 'Where's Wren?'

'He took off. Said he had something he wanted to take care of.'

For all that I could trade half-truths and outright fabrications with the most dangerous Kiren in Rigus, I seemed utterly incapable of sliding a falsehood past Adeline's plump face. 'You chased him off, didn't you?'

'We had a disagreement about the relative merits of property rights. He'll be back eventually.'

She puffed herself up to something substantially larger than her diminutive span. 'Eventually,' she repeated, not a question so much as a condemnation.

'Lay off it, Adeline. He's been sleeping on the street for most of his life. Another night won't matter.'

'And the child that was killed this morning?'

'Wren ain't my kid, Adeline, and he ain't yours neither. Better you don't get too attached – he's likely to bite your hand in the end.'

'You unbelievable little shit,' she said, then whirled and headed back to the kitchen, as if she didn't trust herself to be around me any longer.

'Yeah,' I said to no one in particular. 'Probably.'

I tore through my chop steak and tried to force the pieces floating around my skull into a coherent picture. It wasn't working. I could see Beaconfield as corrupt, venal and sadistic – hell, I had settled on those three before I had even met him. But this didn't fit. There weren't many crimes that could disturb the position of a noble of the blood, but summoning a creature from the void, and using it to sacrifice children – that was one of them. If the Blade was caught, his name wouldn't be enough to save him. He'd swing, or swallow a draft of arsenic while awaiting trial. No doubt the duke had spent most of his life swimming in the noisome waters of the court, trying to one up his rivals with cheap intrigue and the occasional act of violence, but these were the common hobbies of the upper class, like adolescents and dry humping. The aristocracy are too comfortable with what they have to put it all in the pot – that's what makes them easy to play. What could he be aiming for that warranted running such terrible risks?

And if Beaconfield wasn't involved, why had Celia's talisman singed a hole halfway through my breast during our conversation? Was the duke damning his soul in some endeavor entirely unrelated to the one I was investigating?

Maybe Ling Chi was right, and this was all an elaborate set-up by the Old Man to try to break a potential threat to his power. But that didn't add up either. I had no illusions about my former boss, but unleashing this abomination on the people of Low Town was an awful lot of trouble to go through just to crush a mid-level clique, even one run by someone as vicious as my revered brother. And if he had needed a life to snuff he wouldn't have had to go through all the trouble of snatching a child – he'd just walk into the dungeons and pick a mother-fucker to disappear. Besides, the Old Man wouldn't have been so foolish as to involve me in his operation – if he had set this ball of twine rolling, he wouldn't want me following its trail. No, if the Old Man was behind all this I never would have walked out of Black House.

Would I?

Maybe Ling Chi was pulling the strings, and the interview had been a ruse to throw me off his scent. The only person I could say for sure was involved in this whole thing had been a Kiren, and I'd heard plenty of rumors about the dark arts of the heretics, though in the past I'd chalked this up to general racial antipathy. Maybe it was another syndicate, or a player at court – hell, maybe it was some fiendish retaliation by the Dren.

I downed the dregs of my beer and tried to get my head right. There was too much chaff in the air, and I couldn't get a clear picture of the game, let alone the players. I'd been better at this, once, but I was long out of practice – being a successful crim-inal doesn't require quite the same skill set as catching one. Nor did I suppose a half-decade of dipping into my stock had done wonders for my powers of deduction. Maybe Crispin was right, and I was too far gone even to be playing at any of this, my desperate gamble with the Old Man a fool's bet, a raincheck on the inevitable.

I was seeping myself pretty thick in self-contempt when I was interrupted by two quick taps at my shoulder. Wren stood behind me, his face red from humiliation, or the cold. I was surprised, and a little impressed. I'd figured it would take him a good day to work up the nerve to come back and take his medicine.

Still, it wouldn't do to let him off the hook quite yet. 'Back to pick Adeline's good china? It's in the kitchen, you might get a few argents for it.'

'You steal.'

'Not 'cause I'm bored. Not 'cause I see something shiny and wish it was mine. Thievery's a tactic, not a hobby. Not something I do because I've got a few spare minutes and feel like filling them. And never from a friend – never from anyone who did right by me.' His eyes slid away from mine. 'Besides, it ain't that you stole. It's that you were stupid. Malfeasance I can accept, foolishness is reprehensible.'

Like most people, Wren was happier to be thought immoral than incompetent. 'Didn't get caught.'

'By which you mean you managed to get out the front door – so what? He's noticed now, and you've burned a bridge with one of the most powerful men in Rigus for pocket change. Stop thinking like a street kid – if you can't learn to see past your next meal, you'll wake up one morning with a full belly and a knife in it.'

'I am a street kid.'

'That's something else we need to speak on. I'm going to start having more for you, and I can't worry tracking you down every time I need something handled. You're to sleep in the bar from now on.'

'What if I don't want to?'

'You ain't a slave. You prefer a gutter over a bedroll, that's your choice – but you make it and you get yourself unemployed as well. I've no use for an associate I gotta spend half the day hunting for.'

There was a long pause. 'All right,' he said finally.

That should get Adeline off my back for a few hours. By the Firstborn, she was near as bad as the Old Man. 'Fine. Now run over to the Lord Beaconfield's estate.' I rattled off directions. 'Tell the guard at the gate that I want to come by tonight to deliver the rest of what I promised.'

He slipped out. I returned to my drink, wishing I could solve the rest of my problems as easily as I had these domestic concerns.

I thought back to my first days as an agent, before I had gotten mired with Special Operations, when it was just me and Crispin kicking down doors and following up leads. We were pretty good at it for a while – Crispin was sharp, very sharp, but I was better. I learned something back then, something about the nature of crime, and of the things people do that are meant to remain hidden. Solving a mystery isn't about finding clues, or getting lucky with a suspect – it's about deciding what to look for, framing the narrative in your mind. If you can puzzle out the questions, the answers will come.

Most crimes are the ill-borne fruits of passion, and committed by an intimate of the victim. A husband comes home drunk and beats his wife with a claw hammer, a lifetime of discord between two brothers breaks out into open violence. It's terrible and tawdry but easy enough to investigate. If that wasn't the case, if there wasn't a clear suspect, then you already had your first question.

Who benefited by the committing of this crime?

But that wouldn't help me here. The first child had been murdered by a monster, and there was no mystery about his motivations. Sexual satisfaction, the silencing of whatever mad voices echoed through his skull in the stillness of the night. As for this second one, if Marieke's suspicions were right and the girl had been sacrificed, then the motive could be virtually anything.

But that was something then, wasn't it? This was a monstrous crime, demanding savage reprisal. Whoever was responsible must be in desperate straits to take such a chance.

I didn't know why they'd done it but at least I was forming an image of my quarry. If you can't figure out motive, then you have to move on to opportunity – who is capable of committing the crime?

Here I had a little more to work through. We weren't dealing with a snatched purse or a slit throat, the kind of thing any sufficiently depraved soul could engineer. The abomination was big magic, heavy juju – summoning it was the act of a skilled artist. Better still, there was a limited pool of people capable of this particular working. Operation Ingress was a secret military project, and they wouldn't have publicized its techniques.

It all depended on Crispin. If he could get me a list of the participants I could start making inquiries. If he didn't I'd be stuck stirring trouble and hoping that something I did shook out a decent lead. I started to wish I hadn't worked so hard to antagonize my old partner.

I lingered over each possibility rather than deal with the news that shaded the rest of my thoughts. The Old Man's deadline – the thought of spending my final hours, long hours no doubt, days maybe, with a red-robed man poking about in my insides and Crowley standing over me laughing – was no small concern. But I can say without bravado that I've spent a good deal of my life with imminent demise a distinct possibility, and learned how to function despite it. But what Marieke had showed me – that was something that opened up doors in the back of my mind that I'd jammed shut and barred, the sort of fear that wakes you up in the middle of the night with your throat dry and your sheets wet. If the Red Fever had returned to Low Town, all the rest of this was no more than a sideshow, a sprinkle of rain to introduce the deluge that was coming.

Were the Crane's wards slipping? Was his fading health weakening the spells he had put in place to protect us? I thought that over, then dismissed it. Even if it was true, what were the odds of the dead child being the only one infected? I hadn't heard about anyone else falling sick, and I knew I would have – all of Low Town lived in constant fear of the fever. The plague spread like, well, the fucking plague – if it was out among the population, the whole city would be in an uproar. No, I didn't imagine the fever had returned to the general public, nor that Caristiona's death was unrelated to her catching it. It was no coincidence, but for the life of me I couldn't figure out the connection.

I signaled Adolphus for another pint of ale and thought about running upstairs to grab a quick nap, but Wren would be back soon and I'd be moving out not long after that. Adolphus topped me off and I nursed my brew and sucked over each nugget of information like a child with a piece of hard candy.

A few minutes passed and I noticed that Wren had slipped into the Earl and was standing by my arm. By the Oathkeeper, the boy was quiet. Either that or my mind was further out of tune than I had thought. I decided to believe the first. 'By the Oathkeeper, you're quiet.'

He smirked but didn't say anything.

'Well? What have you got for me?'

'The butler says that the Lord Beaconfield is indisposed, but that he wants you to come speak to him around ten.'

'He said he wanted to speak to me personally?'

Wren nodded.

I had hoped I might get a chance to talk to the Blade, see if I couldn't suss something out, but had figured I'd at least have to con my way past his second. Why did Beaconfield want to talk to me? Was it simply idle curiosity, the lurid fascination of the well-fed for those of us struggling through the seedy underbelly of the city we all inhabit? Somehow I doubted this was the first time that walking vice den had met a drug dealer.

From behind the bar I grabbed some pen and parchment, then scratched a short note into the vellum:

Don't deal with the Blade or his people until you hear otherwise. Avoid anyone he sends for you. Will come round tomorrow, noon.

I folded the paper lengthwise, then turned it and folded it lengthwise again. 'Take this to Yancey's house and leave it with his mother,' I said, handing the message to Wren. 'He probably won't be in but tell her to make sure he gets it once he shows. After that you're done for the night – do whatever Adolphus tells you.'

Wren scampered off.

'And don't read the letter!' I yelled after him, probably unnecessarily.

Adolphus's voice was low amid the background chatter. 'What's the trouble?'

'How much time you got?' I grabbed my coat. 'If I'm not back tonight, tell Crispin to take a hard look at the Lord Beaconfield, and especially any ex-military men in his employ.' Not waiting for a response, I turned and headed out of the Earl, away from the boisterous crowd and into the still quiet of the evening.

23

My demeanor eased as I approached the back entrance to Beaconfield's manor and saw Dunkan waving me down with a wide smile. 'And here I was thinking I wouldn't see you, what with your boy not sure when you'd make it out here, and my shift almost over.'

'Hello, Dunkan,' I said, taking his outstretched hand with an unfeigned grin. 'Keeping warm?'

He laughed good-naturedly, his face nearly as red as his hair. 'Colder than the nipples on a hag, as my father used to say! Course, strictly between us as gentlemen, I've armed myself with a secret weapon against the onslaught of winter.' He took an unlabeled bottle from his waistcoat and shook it invitingly. 'Don't suppose I can interest you in a taste?'

I knocked back a shot and my stomach filled with liquid fire.

'Good stuff, ain't it?' he asked.

I nodded and took another. It was good, strong as the kick of a mule but with a sweet aftertaste.

'Brewed over a peat fire – that's the only way to do it. My cousin's got a still in his backyard, sends me a monthly shipment. One day I'll have enough saved to move back home and start a real brewery – Ballantine Distillery Co. That's the plan, anyways. Course, I might change my mind and blow it all on loose women!'

I laughed along with him. He was that kind of fellow. 'If you go the first route, make sure to send me along a pony keg of your first batch.'

'Will do. Enough jawing with the help – I'm sure you've got more important things to discuss. I signaled inside that you were here – Old Man Sawdust should be waiting for you. If I'm still on guard when you leave, give me a shout and we'll share another drop.'

'Looking forward to it,' I said and headed through the entrance.

He was as good as his word, and before I could rap on the off-white door it had swung open and Tuckett, Old Man Sawdust as Dunkan had termed him, stared down at me, shriveled eyes over a pointed nose. 'You've arrived,' he said.

'It would seem that way.' The chill blew in and the servant was without hat or coat. I enjoyed watching him try to maintain his staid composure.

'Will you enter?' he asked, his fastidious mannerisms tarnished somewhat by the chattering of his teeth.

This courtesy extended, I ducked inside. He clapped his hands and a boy appeared to take my outerwear. As I tossed him my heavy wool coat I realized I'd forgotten to disarm before leaving the Earl. Tuckett rested his gaze long enough on my weapon to let me know he had seen it, but not so long as to make it an issue.

Then he took a house-lantern from off the wall and shone the light down the hallway before us. 'The master is in his study. I'll take you to him.' As usual his speech was halfway between a command and a plea, incorporating the worst aspects of both.

I followed him down the corridor, taking mental notes of the layout. There was nothing about the line of rooms we passed that suggested inside were cells built for children, or altars stained with their blood, but then in a house this size you could hide almost anything. Tuckett noticed my fascination with the architecture, and to keep him from thinking too long on it I decided to needle him some.

'Does the master often entertain drug peddlers in his private chambers?' I asked as we ascended the main staircase.

'To whom the master grants an interview is no concern of yours.'

'Well, it's sort of my concern, as I'm about to be interviewed by him.'

We reached the top and turned right, then continued a while longer in silence. I couldn't help but think his maddeningly slow movements were less a factor of his age than a way to abrade me, for in truth he was only a few years past forty, though his tedious nature made him seem older. It was a petty retaliation, but not entirely ineffective – by the time we had reached the Blade's study I was as desperate to leave Tuckett's presence as he was mine.

I held my breath through another interminable pause while he mustered the energy to rap on the entrance. From inside I heard the shuffle of footsteps, and the door swung open.

Beaconfield had toned down his appearance since last I had seen him, which is to say he was no longer dressed like a whore. A dark coat covered his chest, and a sober if well-trimmed pair of pants made do for the lower half of his body. His face was shorn of make-up or other affectation, and his throat and long fingers seemed almost naked without their earlier ornamentation. Indeed the only aspect of his wardrobe unchanged from the party was the rapier that hung at his side. Was he wearing it for my benefit, I wondered, or did he regularly go armed within the walls of his home?

'Thank you, Tuckett. That will be all.'

The butler shot me a snide look and cleared his throat obtrusively. 'May I remind my lord that Sorcerer Brightfellow is expected?'

Beaconfield nodded seriously. 'Of course. Let me know when he arrives.'

Tuckett disappeared with the felicity of a natural servant. Beaconfield beckoned entrance.

The Blade's study was surprisingly somber given what I had seen of his proclivities – no tapestries memorializing mad bacchanals, or bloody trophies from murdered enemies. Instead I saw a well-appointed parlor, luxurious but tasteful, the walls ringed with bookshelves holding volumes of ancient tomes, Kiren rugs covering the ground between them. Beaconfield moved to stand behind an ebony table, the sort of ancient, massive thing that suggested the remainder of the structure was built to accommodate it. He eyed my weapon. 'Expecting trouble?'

'Your butler's a heavy customer.'

He had a decent laugh, robust and almost honest – not the forced nasal chuckle common to his class, closer to an expulsion of waste than an expression of levity. 'Yes, indeed.' He noticed me looking over his décor and offered the grin that had won him half his nickname. 'Not quite what you expected?'

'It seems a bit out of character.'

'One of the downsides of owning an ancestral estate – there's nothing in this room that wasn't here when I was born. See that one?' He pointed to a portrait on the wall of a man who loosely resembled Beaconfield. The protagonist was clad in full plate and standing atop an impressive pile of corpses, staring off into space with an expression meant to indicate the gravity of the situation – though what the hell he was doing contemplating the horizon while in the midst of a mêlée was beyond me.

'Yeah.'

'What do you think of it?'

'It's a painting.'

'Quite hideous, isn't it? The old King gave it to my great-uncle, to commemorate his famous stand at . . .' He waved his hand apathetically. 'Somewhere. It's part of the package – I can't so much as redecorate without betraying the blood.'

'That's not an issue I find myself plagued by.'

'No, I suppose not,' he said. 'Normally I'm good with faces, but I can't mark yours. Too tall for a Tarasaihgn, too broad for an Asher. Your eyes say Rouender but you're too dark, near as dark as an Islander. Where do you come from?'

'A womb.'

He laughed again and motioned me into a chair. I took it, setting my weary body into its environs with a barely audible sigh. Beaconfield followed my lead, planting himself firmly into the high-backed throne behind his desk.

'Long day?'

I opened my satchel and set two items on the table. The first was a pint of amber goo in an unmarked jar, the second a bundle of intertwined brown roots. 'Be careful with that honey, it's uncut. Don't take more than a lip-full unless you feel like getting real intimate with the bottom of your chamberpot.'

'Excellent. I'm hosting a Midwinter ball next week. It wouldn't do to be without party favors for my guests.' He picked up the dried stems and inspected them casually. 'How's the root? I've never tried it.'

'A good excuse to stare at your boots for three or four hours.'

'Sounds riveting.'

A chuckle slipped out before I could grab it.

He set the ouroboros root back on the table and looked me over. He was trying to work up the nerve to ask me something, but before he had the chance I cut in. 'So Brightfellow's up next? You line up your unsavory interviews so you can burn the upholstery afterwards?'

'Is that how you'd describe yourself? Unsavory?'

'That's how I'd describe Brightfellow.'

'I wouldn't introduce him to the Queen. But he's useful, and clever. Damn clever.'

'How'd you meet the man? I don't imagine the two of you run in the same circles.'

Beaconfield leaned back in his chair and thought this over, his hand resting affectionately on the pommel of his weapon. I got the impression this wasn't meant to be intimidating, that the duke was simply the sort of person who liked to stroke his chosen instrument of murder. 'Do you believe in fate, Warden?'

'I doubt the Daevas have any hand in the mess we've made of their creation.'

'Normally I'm inclined to agree with you. But in the case of Brightfellow that seems the best way to describe it. I've had some . . . bad runs lately. He's going to help turn my luck around.'

'I knew a priest once who liked to say that the Oathkeeper prefers to work through imperfect vassals.' I suspected it had been the Frater's favorite aphorism because he couldn't go an hour without a half vial of breath, but that was neither here nor there. 'And has the sorcerer has made good on his promises?'

'Not yet. But I'm confident in the eventual success of our enterprise.'

Did this enterprise include the murder of two children, and opening a door to the abyss? I wouldn't put it past either of them, but then suspicion isn't the same as certainty, let alone evidence. I'd pushed the duke as far as he'd go, so I went quiet. He'd called me here for a reason; if I waited long enough I figured he'd get to it.

'It wouldn't surprise you to hear that I made inquiries into your past, into your conduct and character, before deciding to do business with you.'

'My life's an open book.' With the pages torn out, but someone with the Blade's draw wouldn't have had trouble getting the outline. 'And I'm not that easily surprised.'

'They say you're a modest criminal presence, not attached to any of the bigger players. They say you're reliable, quiet.'

'Do they?'

'They say something else too – they say you used to play on the other side of the fence, that you wore the gray before taking up your current occupation.'

'They'll say I was a babe in swaddling clothes if you go back far enough.'

'Yes, I suppose they would, wouldn't they? What incited it? Your fall from grace?'

'Things happen.'

'True, exactly as you say. Things happen.' His eyes traced

patterns on the wall behind me, and the fire crackled in the corner. His face took on a wistful quality that tends to augur monologue, and sure enough the pregnant pause gave birth to soliloquy.

'It's strange, the paths a man finds himself on. In the story-books everyone's granted some critical moment, when the road forks and your options are laid out clear in front of you, heroism or villainy. But it's not like that, is it? Decisions follow decisions, each minor in and of themselves, made in the heat of the moment or on the dregs of instinct. Then one day you look up and realize that you're stuck, that every muttered answer is a bar in the cage you've built, and the momentum of each choice moves you forward as inexorably as the will of the Firstborn.'

'Eloquent, but untrue. I made a decision, once. If the consequences were worse than I had anticipated . . . that's because it was a bad decision.'

'But that's my point, you see. How can you know which choices matter and which choices don't? There are decisions I have made that I regret, that were – that were not who I am. There are decisions I would unmake, were it possible to do so.'

By the Lost One, he was worse than the heretics. What was he admitting to? The children were dead – there was no do-over coming on that. Or was I reading subtlety where none existed? Was Beaconfield the sort of patrician who likes to reminisce with us low folk about the difficult and forlorn nature of human existence? 'One way or the other, we pay what we owe.'

'Then there is no hope for any of us?'

'None.'

'You're a cold man.'

'It's a cold world. I've adjusted to the temperature.'

His jaw tightened, and the moment of openness ended. 'Quite right, quite right. We play our hands out to the end.'

Beaconfield began radiating something that might have been threatening, or might have been just general aristocratic disdain – it was tough to tell. I was relieved when a knock signaled the end of our meeting.

We both rose and moved towards the exit. The Blade opened

the door and Tuckett ducked his head in, muttering a few words to his master before disappearing.

'Thank you for your services,' Beaconfield began. 'It occurs to me I may need to make use of them in the future, perhaps before Midwinter. You're still at the Staggering Earl, then, with your comrade from the War, and his wife?' he asked, the threat obvious and unanticipated.

'A man's home is his castle.'

He smiled. 'Indeed.'

It had been a long day, as long a day as I could remember, and as I headed back the way I'd come part of me hoped that I'd be able to make the exit without running into the duke's next appointment. But the rest figured that he was worth taking another run at, and this latter portion was gratified when I reached the top of the steps and saw Brightfellow seated on a bench below, looking every bit as prepossessing as he had during our first meeting. He pushed himself up to his feet and broke into a broad grin, and so numerous were Beaconfield's parlor steps that I got to spend a good fifteen seconds staring at it as I descended.

I hadn't expected Brightfellow to have transformed himself into a respectable member of the human race in the day since we'd seen each other, and he'd been kind enough not to refute my assumption. If he wasn't wearing the same soiled black suit as when we'd met, he was in a close enough cousin to make my confusion reasonable.

But there was something that struck me, something that I'd noticed earlier but hadn't been able to square with the rest of him. A lot of men affect hardness, fortifying themselves with dreams of their potential menace like it was sack wine. It's something of a local pastime in Low Town, rent boys and bumblefucks leaning against crumbling brick walls, convincing each other that they were deadlier than an untreated wound, that their reputation kept passersby on the other side of the street. After a while they become part of the scenery. There are some things a man can't fake, and lethality is one of them – a lapdog might learn to howl, even bare its teeth on occasion, but that don't make it a wolf.

The real ones don't put on airs; you can feel what they are in the bottom of your stomach. Brightfellow was a killer. Not like the Kiren who'd taken Tara, not a maniac – just a murderer, an everyday sort of fellow who'd put a few members of his species in the ground and not felt any particular way about it. I set that thought squarely in my mind as I went to meet him – that the buffoonish exterior was only part of who he was, and maybe not a big part either, a sliver he'd ballooned up to cover the rest.

I pulled out my tobacco pouch, rolling up the cigarette I'd wanted to light from the moment I'd stepped inside the Blade's mansion, figuring the smoke might do something to cover up Brightfellow's unwashed meat. He held his cap in hand, and his uneven teeth formed a false smile.

'Well, if it ain't the funny man himself. How you doing, funny man?'

'Tell me something, Brightfellow – do you make a point of eating liver before you see me, or is it such a regular part of your schedule as to make the coincidence unavoidable?'

He laughed nastily, grinding his yellowed ivories against one another. 'Caught my name, did you, funny man? Nice to see I've gained a little renown – sometimes I think all my hard work goes unappreciated.'

'And what exactly is it you do?'

'What do you think I do?'

'I figure that most of the people around here are employed to clean off whatever shit the duke finds himself stepping in. And since you smell distinctly of a latrine, I figured you for being in that same general line.'

Brightfellow barked out another ugly chuckle. That laugh was a real weapon – it let him slip blows and keep coming. 'I have the honor of being the Lord Beaconfield's court mage, and I strive daily to be worthy of it,' he said, doing a pretty good impression of the butler, though with enough of his toothy smile to make clear it wasn't more than that.

'And what exactly does a court magician do, other than occupy the lowest rung to which an artist can descend, short of selling love potions at traveling fairs?'

'I guess it must not seem like much – but then we can't all sell drugs for a living.'

'I'm going to cut you off there, because I wouldn't want your attempts at banter to get in the way of a last shot at saving your ass. I know you and the duke are up to something. You give me your side now and I might be able to swing it so you don't catch all the weight – it doesn't take a candle to see you aren't running the show.' The tip of a match flared to life against the wood of the banister, and I brought it to my cigarette. 'But if you put me to the trouble of sniffing it all out, you'll get nothing, hear? The chips will fall where they fall.' I took a quick huff of smoke. 'Think it over, but do it quick; the clock is running, and if you suppose the blue-blood is going to have your back when shit crumbles, you're dumber than you look – and you don't look like no genius.'

I hadn't expected him to crack, but I'd hoped for some sort of a reaction beyond a repeat of that grating laugh he was always giving me. That was what I got though, and for the second time I had the unpleasant impression that I'd misplayed it, that as far as Brightfellow and I were concerned, he was up two nil.

I could hear Tuckett making his way down the stairs, and figured that was as good a time as any to make my exit, out the servants' entrance and through the back gate. Dunkan was gone, replaced by a grim-faced counterpart who discharged his duties without comment. It was just as well – I wasn't in the mood to deal with the Tarasaihgn's exuberance. I rubbed the skin around the Crane's talisman, its heat only now beginning to diminish, and headed back to the Earl, hoping to make it to bed before I passed out.

24

I spent half the night tossing and turning through the haze of dreamvine I'd immolated before going to bed, and woke the next morning later than I'd meant to. Later than I should have, given that, as things stood, I'd only have six more opportunities to sleep in. The sun peering in through the window was halfway to its zenith by the time I pulled on my pants.

The bar was empty, usual for this time of day, and Adolphus was sitting at the counter, his jowls dragged down in sorrow. Adeline was dusting under a table and nodded when she saw me.

I took a seat next to Adolphus. 'What's wrong?'

He made an attempt to cover his grimace with an unconvincing smile. 'Nothing – why would you ask that?'

'Fifteen years and you still operate under the misconception that you can lie to me?'

For a moment his smile was real, if slight. Then it went away. 'Another child is missing,' he said. Adeline stopped sweeping.

Another one, Śakra. I hadn't expected it to stop but I had

hoped for more time between this one and the last. I tried not to think about how this would affect the Old Man's deadline, or if the neighborhood toughs would take the opportunity to make trouble in Ling Chi's territory. 'Who is it?'

For an unhappy second I was afraid he would start to blubber outright. 'It's Meskie's son, Avraham.'

A bad day got worse. Meskie was our washing woman, a sweet-natured Islander who raised a brood of children with methods equal parts loving and severe. I didn't know Avraham particularly, except as one of the mass of amiable youths that surrounded their matriarch.

Adeline ventured a question. 'Do you think he might still be . . .' She trailed off, not wanting to form the thought in its entirety.

'There's always a chance,' I said.

There was no chance. Black House wasn't going to find him – it was me or no one. And I couldn't move on the Blade, not with what I had, hell, he might not even have done it. Maybe something would break open soon, maybe I'd get lucky, but these were hopes, not expectations, and I'm not an optimist. The child was as good as dead. It was ten thirty and already I needed a hit of breath.

Adeline nodded, her round face looking very old. 'I'll bring you breakfast,' she said.

Adolphus and I sat there for a while, neither bothering to fill the air with conversation. 'Where's Wren?' I asked eventually.

'He's off at the market – Adeline needed some things for supper.' He reached into his back pocket and pulled out a slip of paper. 'This came for you before you woke.'

I took it and opened it. Five words scrawled in black ink, the letters sharply drawn against the parchment:

> *Herm Bridge, six thirty.*
> *Crispin*

He was quicker than I had expected, although it didn't figure him wanting to set a meeting when he could have just sent over the list. Maybe he wanted to apologize for our earlier exchange, though I thought it more likely he expected me to grovel a bit before he coughed up his information. I lit a match off the bar and held it to the paper, letting the ashes drop to the ground.

'Adeline will have to clean that,' Adolphus said.

'We're all cleaning up somebody's shit.'

Halfway through breakfast, Wren returned with a sack of goods. Adolphus's face perked up a bit. 'How much did you save me?'

'Two argents and six copper,' he said spilling the change on the counter.

Adolphus slapped his leg. 'He don't say much, but you're looking at the best damn haggler in Low Town! You sure there ain't no Islander blood in you, boy?'

'Dunno. Maybe.'

'Doesn't miss a trick, this one! Sees everything, everything there is to see.'

'You hear about Meskie's son?' I asked, interrupting Adolphus's praise.

Wren looked down at his feet.

'Head over and make sure the ice are finished with whatever perfunctory investigation they managed to pull together.'

'What does perfunctory mean?'

I drained my cup of coffee. 'Not serious.'

I went upstairs to grab my armaments and snatch a hit of pixie's breath. A boy this time. What was the connection? Three children, different sexes, different races – all from Low Town but that didn't tell me anything except that it's a lot easier to grab a street urchin than a noble. I thought back on my interview last night with Beaconfield. Had that sick son of a bitch finished our meeting, then turned around and snatched up a kid? Was Avraham hidden in some corner of the Blade's mansion, tied to a chair weeping, waiting for the torment that was to come?

I took another snort and tried to clear my head. I didn't have anything on the Blade yet, and if I tipped my hand and was wrong, I didn't imagine the Old Man would have much sympathy. Better to follow the trail than ruin the scent by trying to jump ahead.

I took one last bump and put the rest of the vial into the bag. I had always liked Meskie, to the limited extent we had interacted. I wasn't wild about the idea of intruding on her grief, even for the purpose of making sure she was the last weeping mother.

The breath shook me out of my morning torpor. My mind felt clean again – it was time to get it dirty. I grabbed my coat and headed downstairs.

Wren waited at the foot of the steps, tense as a muscle. 'She's alone. The law came and went.'

I nodded and he followed me out.

Low Town in winter is mostly miserable. Not quite as bad as summer, when the air is stale with soot and whatever doesn't rot bakes in the hot sun, but pretty miserable just the same. Most days the smog from the factories congeals into a miasma that hovers at about throat level, and between that and the cold your lungs have to work double just to keep up.

But once in a while a strong southern wind comes off the hills and sweeps the city clear of the haze enshrouding it. The sun radiates that particularly perfect blend of light it offers sometimes in place of heat, and it seems like you can see all the way down to the docks, and it even seems like you might want to. I'd been a child on days like that, and every wall had stood to be climbed, and every vacant structure demanded exploration.

'Did you know him?' Wren asked.

That was right, we weren't out on a morning stroll, were we? 'Not really. Meskie has a clutch of children,' I said by way of explanation.

'I guess there are a lot of kids in Low Town, huh?'

'I guess.'

'Why him?'

'Why indeed?'

I had been to Meskie's house once or twice, dropping off things for Adeline. She'd always invited me in for a cup of coffee, insisted really. Her home was small but well kept, and her children were unflaggingly polite. I tried to conjure up an image of Avraham in my mind, but nothing would come. I might have passed him the day before and not known it, one more offering to She Who Waits Behind All Things from her most devout congregation.

If Avraham had been dead his home would be packed with mourners, weeping women and mounds of fresh-cooked food. As he was only missing the neighborhood didn't know how to respond, the usual gestures of sympathy premature. The only people outside Meskie's were her five daughters standing clumped together. They looked up at me in dumb silence.

'Hi, girls. Is your mother inside?'

The eldest nodded, her jet-black hair bobbing up and down. 'She's in the kitchen.'

'Boy, wait out here with Mrs Mayana's girls. I'll be back in a moment.'

Wren looked uncomfortable. Domesticated children were a separate species to him, their trivial games unfathomable, their friendly chatter foreign to his ears. The trials of his childhood had marked him as other, and the status quo has no more rigorous champion than the adolescent.

But he'd have to endure it for a few minutes. This business was subtle enough without a teen at my side.

I knocked lightly but didn't get a response, so I let myself in. It was dark, the wall sconces unlit and the front shades drawn. A short hallway led into the kitchen, and I saw Meskie leaning over her wide table, dark flesh spread like an ink spot over the sanded wood. I cleared my throat loudly, but she either didn't hear or chose not to respond.

'Hi, Meskie.'

She inclined her head slightly. 'It's nice to see you again,' she said, her tone suggesting the contrary. 'But I'm afraid I can't do any washing today.' Despair wore heavy on her face, but her eyes were clear, and her voice steady.

I mustered up the courage to continue. 'I've been looking into

195

some of the things going on in the neighborhood the last few weeks.' She didn't answer. Fair enough. I was the interloper – it was time to put some cards on the table. 'I was the one who found Tara. Did you know that?'

She shook her head.

I tried to think of an explanation for why I was banging on her door before noon, a virtual stranger violating the bounds of intimacy to pimp her for information about a child likely dead. 'We've got to look out for our own as best we can.' It sounded more puerile out loud than it had echoing in my skull.

Slowly she slid her eyes up to mine, not saying anything. Then she turned away and muttered, 'They sent an agent around. He asked me about Avraham. He took my statement.'

'The ice will do what they can. But they don't hear everything that I hear, and they aren't always listening.' That was about as much as I could say for Black House. 'I'm trying to find out if there was some common thread connecting Avraham and the other children, something about him that stood out, something unique . . .' I trailed off feebly.

'He's quiet,' she answered. 'He doesn't talk much, not like the girls. Some days he wakes up early and helps me with the wash. He likes being up before the rest of the city, says it helps him hear things better.' She shook her head, the colored beads set in her hair trailing back and forth. 'He's my son, what do you want me to say?'

That was a fair enough answer, I supposed. Only a fool would ask a mother what made her child special. Every freckle on his face as far as she was concerned, but that wouldn't do me much good. 'I'm sorry, that was tactless. But I need to understand why Avraham . . .' It was hard to gauge how imprecise a euphemism I should insert here. 'Why Avraham might have gone missing.'

She choked an answer back down in her throat.

I followed up with what finesse I could muster. 'You were going to say something. What was it?'

'It doesn't matter. It doesn't have anything to do with it.'

'Sometimes we know more than we think. Why don't you tell me what you were going to say?'

Her body seemed to expand and contract with every breath, like the only thing keeping her upright was the air in her lungs. 'Sometimes he'd know things that he couldn't have known about, things about his daddy, other things, things I had never told him, things nobody could have. I'd ask him how he found out, but he'd just smile that queer smile of his and . . . and . . .' Her composure, firm as stone up to this point, broke, utterly. She buried her face in her hands and wept with all the full force of her matronly body. I tried to think of some way to calm her but failed – empathy was never my stock-in-trade.

'You'll save him, won't you? The guard can't do anything, but you'll bring him back to me, won't you?' She took me by the wrist, and her grip was strong. 'I'll give you whatever you want, I'll pay you anything, whatever I have, please – just find my boy!'

I pried her fingers off as delicately as I could. It was beyond me to tell a mother she wouldn't see her child alive again – but I wouldn't lie either, put my name in hock to a promise I'd never redeem. 'I'll do what I can.'

Meskie was not a fool – she knew what that meant. She set her hands in her lap, ending her despondency by sheer force of will. 'Of course,' she said, 'I understand.' Her face had that terrible calm that comes when hope lies buried. 'He's in Śakra's hands now.'

'We all are,' I said, though I doubted it would help poor Avraham any more than it did the rest of us. I thought about leaving her some coin but didn't want to insult her. Adeline would come around later with some food, though Meskie wouldn't need it. The Islanders were a tight community – she'd be provided for.

Wren was waiting for me outside, clumped with Meskie's daughters, but easy enough to pick out. Contra their mother's description they were very quiet. 'It's time to go.'

Wren turned towards the girls. 'I'm sorry,' he said. It was probably the first thing he'd said since I'd left him.

The youngest burst into tears and ran inside.

Wren blushed and started to apologize, but I put my hand on his shoulder and he shut his mouth. We walked back to the Earl in our customary silence, though somehow it seemed quieter.

25

I dropped the kid off and headed out to see Yancey. The more I mulled over last night's conversation with Beaconfield the less I liked it. He knew where I slept – there was nothing I could do there. But if the Blade decided to move on me he'd go through the Rhymer first, and that was a possibility that I might have a hand in affecting.

I knocked lightly on the door. After a moment it opened, revealing Yancey's mother, an Islander in her mid-fifties, aging but handsome, her brown eyes smiling and vital. 'Good morning, Mrs Dukes. A pleasure to see you again after such a protracted absence.' There was something about Ma Dukes that brought out the courtier in me.

She waved off my compliment and embraced me. Then she pushed me away lightly, holding my wrists with her long-fingered hands.

'Why haven't you been round to see me lately? You found yourself a girl?'

'Busy with work, you know how it is.'

'I know all about your kind of work. And why are you so formal all of a sudden?'

'No more deference than is due so revered a matriarch.'

She laughed and ushered me inside.

Yancey's home was warm and bright, regardless of the season. The Islanders were renowned as the greatest sailors of the Thirteen Lands, and they served more than their quota in the Imperial Navy. True to form, her eldest took the Queen's copper and was at sea nine months of the year, but even an occupant short the house still seemed crowded, overflowing with bric-à-brac acquired from foreign ports and Yancey's collection of drums and curious, hand-carved instruments. Ma Dukes led me into her kitchen and motioned towards a stool at the table.

'You eat already?' she asked, spooning me a plate from the steaming mass of bubbling pots and pans on the stove.

I hadn't actually, not that it mattered. Lunch was fried fish and vegetables, and I tore into it with relish.

Her duties as a host fulfilled, Ma Dukes eased herself into the chair across from mine. 'Good, huh?'

I mumbled something affirmative through a mouthful of onions and peppers.

'It's a new recipe. I got it from a friend of mine, Esti Ibrahim.'

I shoveled another piece of cod into my maw. It never failed – somewhere along the line Ma Dukes had become convinced that all my troubles stemmed from the absence of an Island woman to share my bed and cook my meals, and was determined to make good this lack. It made my visits a bit exhausting.

'Widowed, lovely hair. You could do a lot worse.'

'I'm not sure if I'm the most stable bet right now. Remind me next time you see me.'

She shook her head with something approaching disappointment. 'You in trouble again? Always gotta stir the pot, by the Firstborn. Smirk all you want, you aren't a child. Closer my age than Yancey's, am I wrong?'

I hoped that wasn't true, though it might have been.

'He's on the roof.' She slapped my arm with a damp dishrag. 'Tell him lunch is ready when he wants it.' Her eyes turned steely. 'He stays out of anything you're into – don't forget you're a guest in my home.'

I kissed her lightly on the cheek and made my way upstairs.

Yancey's house buttresses the Beggar's Ramparts, a steep canyon that acts as de facto divide between the Islanders and the white citizens of the docks. At ground level the crevasse was filled with trash, and the sight of it would belie the suggestion that the divide was a positive addition to the landscape – but from on high the break from the skyline it offered was actually quite soothing. When I came up the Rhymer was lighting a banana leaf stuffed with dreamvine. We shared the blunt and the view for a few quiet moments.

'I need two favors,' I began.

Yancey had one of the best laughs I'd ever heard, rich and full. His whole body shook with mirth. 'You've got a way of beginning a conversation.'

'I'm quite the charmer,' I acknowledged. 'First, I need someone who can give me the word on Beaconfield.'

'Ain't me, man, I only met him twice now.' He smiled conspiratorially and his voice dipped an octave. 'Besides, it ain't wise for the help to pay too much attention to the master of the house, you hear true?' He breathed out a trail of smoke rings, verdant greens and bright oranges. The wind carried them south towards the harbor, the bustle of the docks vaguely discernible even at this distance. 'I might know somebody though. You ever hear of Mairi the Dark-eyed, runs a place north of downtown called the Velvet Hutch?'

'A house of worship, no doubt.'

'You bet your life on that, brother. Praise the Firstborn!' He chuckled and slapped me on the back. 'Nah, man, she's an old friend. Word is she used to be the Crown Prince's mistress, back in the day. Now she sells high-class tail to nobles and rich bankers, and, – he winked at me – 'she's on first-names with every skeleton in every closet from here to Miradin.'

'Quite the necromancer.'

'She's multi-talented,' he confirmed. 'I'll send word that you're coming by to see her.'

'That's the first favor – you won't like the second one. I need you to disappear for a little while.'

He slumped against the railing, the hogleg dangling from his lips. 'Come on now, don't tell me that.'

'Take a trip to the coast for a few days, or if you want to stay in the city go visit your Asher friends. Just keep away from your usual hangouts, and don't perform.'

'I ain't in the mood for taking no trip, man.'

'If it's about money . . .' I began.

'Ain't about money, man, I got enough money, I don't need to beg coin.' His eyes cut through the haze of smoke with dull ferocity. 'It's you – you fuck shit up, it's all you ever do. You a poison – everyone you meet is worse for it, you know that? Every single person. I ain't got no problems with nobody, then I do you a kindness and what happens?' His tone had switched from condemnation to regret. 'I'm an exile in my own fucking city.' He sighed and took another hit, spewing multicolored fog into the air. 'This about the Blade?'

'Yes.'

'I told you he was dangerous. Don't you listen to anyone?'

'Probably not enough.'

'Why he after you?'

'I'm pretty sure—'

Yancey cut me off with a chop of his hand. 'Never mind, man. I don't want to know.'

That was probably for the best. 'I'll make it up to you.'

'I ain't holding my breath.'

We leaned against the barrier for a long time afterward, passing the blunt back and forth until it was down to the roach. Finally Yancey broke the silence. 'Mom try and hook you up again?'

'Esti Ibrahim, I believe her name was.'

He sucked his teeth in contemplation. 'Makes the best fried fish in Rigus, but she's got an ass like the stove you'd fry it on.'

'That was some damn good fish,' I acknowledged.

He snickered at that, and I should have joined in, as a courtesy if nothing else. But the talk with Meskie had me out of sorts, and I was finding it tough to be a cheery companion. 'So you'll talk to Mairi for me?'

The Rhymer's glimmer of humor died quick, and he turned moodily back towards the rail. 'I told you I would, didn't I? I look out for my people, when I say I'm gonna do something it ends up getting done. I'll send someone by after lunch, you can go see her whenever the hell you want.' He took one last puff of vine and belched out a cloud of vermillion. 'If there ain't nothing else I can do for you, how about you get the fuck off my roof. I gotta figure out where I'm gonna be sleeping tonight.'

Yancey's profession demanded a certain skill with his tongue, and I suppose I'd earned the rough edge of it. To punctuate his dismissal he flicked the end of the butt over the edge and into the expanse below. I wondered if we'd ever smoke another. With nothing left to do I cut downstairs and out the front, making sure not to catch Ma Dukes on the way out. After today she probably wouldn't be so keen to find me a mate.

Another bridge burned, I supposed.

26

I headed back to the Earl and killed the rest of the afternoon catching up on lost sleep. Around six I slipped out, first sending Wren on a bullshit errand to make sure he couldn't follow. My last interaction with Crispin was at that boundary of antagonistic and intimate that didn't require a spectator, and it seemed likely this one would go in the same direction, particularly as Crispin would probably make me shine his shoes in exchange for the information he had discovered. The Oathkeeper knew I would have.

The walk to Herm Bridge was a rare moment of silence, a brief half-hour in the dimming light of the evening. It was the time of year when it pays to be conscious of every last ray of sunshine and gust of warm air, the fading heat soon to be submerged beneath winter's implacable thrall. For a few minutes the events of the last two days lay half forgotten in the recesses of my mind.

I suppose it's the nature of reverie to end.

A body doesn't look like anything else, and even with the spread of night blurring the landscape I was certain the one lying at the foot of the crossing was Crispin's. I broke into a quick jog, knowing it was useless, that what had come for Crispin hadn't left him injured.

He'd been terribly mutilated, his fine face bruised and battered, his aquiline nose caked with blood and pus. One eye had burst in the socket, white ooze leaking, the gleam of his iris offset inside. His face was frozen in a hideous grimace, and at some point during his torment he had bitten through most of the flesh of his cheek.

It was dark but not that dark, and Herm Bridge isn't a back alley but a minor thoroughfare. Someone else would stumble on the body soon. I knelt beside his corpse and tried not to think about the time he had invited me to his family's house for Midwinter, his eccentric mother and spinster sister playing the grand piano, all of us drinking rum punch till I passed out by the fire. I slipped my hand into his coat pocket. Nothing. A quick search of the rest of his clothing revealed the same. I told myself that the stench was hallucinatory, that he hadn't been dead long enough to rot, and the cold would keep him whole for a while longer anyway, that I needed to concentrate on my task. It's what he would have done – by the book.

Finally I hit on the bright idea of checking his hands, and after a moment of frustration in opening their vice-clench, found a half-torn sheet of paper Crispin had been holding – whether to keep it from his attacker or as some sort of a talisman I would never know.

It was a government form. At the top was some sort of bureaucratic code, followed by a warning against unauthorized viewing. Below, under the title *Practitioners, Operation Ingress*, was a list of names and a one-word description of their status – *Active, Inactive, Deceased*. I was unsurprised to see a great many marked with the third. I scanned to the bottom and felt my heart stutter a beat – the last legible name on the list, just above the tear, read Johnathan Brightfellow.

So Beaconfield was behind it after all. It was a hell of a way to have my suspicions confirmed. A hell of a way.

I did one more thing then, something that I barely thought about even while I was doing it, something cheap and ugly and only partly justified by necessity. I reached up to Crispin's throat and ripped his Eye from off his neck, then stuffed the gem in my pocket. The ice would figure that whoever had killed him had taken it, and though I didn't know how yet, I had a feeling it would come in handy.

I forced myself to my feet and looked down at Crispin's shattered body. I felt like I ought to say something but wasn't sure what. After a moment I put the paper into my satchel and slipped off. Nostalgia is for saps, and vengeance doesn't send out heralds. Crispin would have his eulogy when I settled up with the Blade.

I cut back towards the main thoroughfare at a fast clip, stopping in front of a partially constructed townhouse bordering the river. After making sure no one was in sight, I wedged open a plank of nailed wood and snuck inside, slumping against a wall in the darkness.

After a short wait a group of workmen stumbled upon Crispin's body. They spent a few moments yelling things at each other I couldn't hear, then one sprinted off, returning shortly after with a pair of guardsmen who further degraded the crime scene before leaving to make contact with Black House. I took the opportunity to backtrack a block and buy a bottle of whiskey at a dive bar, then hustled back to my hiding spot.

I returned in time to sit aimlessly for twenty minutes while the freeze responded to the murder of one of their own with impressive alacrity. When they did show they rolled deep, a whole pack of them, ten or twelve with more coming and going throughout the next few hours. They swarmed around Crispin's body like ants, looking for evidence and canvassing witnesses, following procedures rendered irrelevant by the fact that Crispin's murder had few parallels in the city's history. At one point I thought I spotted Guiscard's patrician mug standing over his partner's body and talking animatedly with one of the other agents, but there was a lot of ice gray swirling around, and I might have been wrong.

I alternated pulls from my whiskey bottle with snorts from my rapidly diminishing supply of breath. It was almost eleven by the time they wrapped up their search and tossed Crispin's body on the mortician's cart. His mother and sister had died some years prior, and I wondered who would take care of the funeral, or that comically monstrous structure he had been raised in. It went hard to think of it shuttered, its antiques sold off at auction, its ancient title passed to whatever tax-farmer had the coin to afford it.

I crept out of the abandoned house, the street at this point empty of traffic, agent or otherwise, and began the long walk back to the Earl, despair bleeding through my best attempt at narcotization.

27

I woke the next morning to find my pillow soaked through with a liquid that I very much hoped was not vomit. Blinking myself out of sleep, I rubbed at my nose and found a crust of dried blood. Not bile at all, just the after-effects of a hard night of breath. I wasn't sure if that was better or worse.

A thick wad of phlegm landed in the chamberpot and I followed it with a selection of other waste, then opened the window and emptied it into the alley below, wincing at the freezing gust that came in as I did so. A dark cloud hovered over the cityscape, swallowing the light such that it was difficult even to determine the time. Down on the street I could see those few poor souls forced to travel holding tight to their outerwear and struggling through the gale.

I cleaned my face with water from the basin. It was cold and stale, there since yesterday or the day before. The reflection in my hand mirror revealed red-shot pupils, each individual vein swollen perversely.

I looked like shit and felt worse. I hoped it wasn't too late for coffee and some eggs.

Downstairs the front room was empty, the foul weather keeping out any patrons, Adolphus and his wife busy in the back. I sat down at the bar and pulled out the form I had taken from Crispin, running down the names of each practitioner listed and seeing if any of them triggered a flash of memory.

None did. With the exception of Brightfellow, whose name was not so common that I could reasonably expect him to have a double running around, I hadn't heard of any of them. I turned to the second column. Of the twelve others on the list, eight were deceased and three were active. The dead are difficult to dig up information from, and I couldn't imagine anyone still in the service of the Crown would be excited to talk to me about the classified experiment they had set loose on the world a decade past. That left only one entry – Afonso Cadamost, a Mirad transplant to judge by his name.

Celia's help had been invaluable, critical even, but there were things she couldn't tell me. I needed to know exactly what it was I faced, the nature of Brightfellow's hideous creature and how to stop it. To do that I needed to speak to someone with dirty hands – and I had an idea this Cadamost's were as foul as they came.

Which was all very well, but of course I had no idea how to find him. I could ring out my contacts, but it probably wouldn't do much good. He wasn't necessarily in Rigus, or even alive – just 'cause the government doesn't know something happened doesn't mean it didn't happen; you can trust the continued solvency of my business on that one.

I was ruminating when Adolphus came in, his face ashen and trembling, preparing to unburden his soul of the terrible news. It was becoming a singularly unpleasant morning ritual.

'It's OK. I heard.'

'You heard about Crispin?'

I nodded.

He looked puzzled, then relieved, then apologetic. Adolphus

has an expressive face. 'I'm sorry,' he said simply, the fact that he honestly meant it worth more than any attempt at eloquence.

'You want to make it up to me, you could have Adeline fry some eggs.' I stopped him halfway to the kitchen. 'How did you find out?' I asked, the obvious question not so obvious after a night spent pounding my brain into submission.

'An agent stopped by while you were asleep. He said he'd come back around later.'

'The Crown came by, and they didn't roust me?'

'He wasn't on official business. He said he just came by as a courtesy.'

That supposed a degree of civility unlikely under the best of circumstances. 'What was his name?'

'Didn't give it, and I didn't much want it. Young fellow, platinum blond, bit of an ass.'

What business did Guiscard have with me? Revenge? I couldn't imagine Crispin was so foolish as to publicize the highly illegal search he had performed.

Adolphus recommenced his trip towards the kitchen. 'And make some coffee, while you're back there,' I yelled as the door swung shut.

I pondered the circumstances that enveloped me and tried to blink away my headache. The giant returned a few minutes later with breakfast. 'Did Adeline cook these?' I asked, chewing my way through a cut of burned bacon.

He shook his head. 'She took Wren to market. That's my work.'

I spat out a piece of egg shell. 'Shocking.'

'You don't like them, you can cook your own breakfast.'

'I don't imagine our friend is much of a chef,' a voice from behind me commented.

'Close the door,' I said.

Guiscard did just that, the baying of the wind rendered inaudible once again. Adolphus stared over my shoulder at the newcomer with an expression of undisguised dislike.

The agent took a seat on the stool next to mine. He looked

weary and haggard, his blond-white hair disheveled. There was even a small food stain on his right lapel, certain evidence of the turmoil our ex-partner's death was causing him. He tossed me a quick nod, then turned to Adolphus. 'Black coffee, thanks.'

'We ain't open,' Adolphus said, setting his rag on the bar and disappearing into the back.

I enjoyed my own cup of java quietly.

'He doesn't much care for me, does he?' Guiscard asked.

Actually Adolphus has a soft heart and an even softer entrance policy – he probably would've served the Steadholder of the Dren Republic, should his eminence have seen fit to make an appearance. I suspected the cruelties he had suffered the last time the Crown came through his establishment had left him less than enamored of law enforcement. 'I'm sure I'd get a similar reception at your favorite watering hole.'

'You probably would. Did he at least give you my message?'

'I heard the news.'

'I'm sorry.'

Everyone was so contrite all of a sudden. 'Don't apologize to me – I've barely spoken to him for half a decade. You were his partner.'

'An awfully junior partner, and that only for six months. I don't think he even liked me.'

'I know he didn't like me, and I'm still sorry he's gone. Any leads down at Black House?'

'Canvas didn't turn up anything. We've got the Ice Bitch going over the crime scene now. Some of the men wanted to question you, but we got pressure from the brass to stay off. I guess you still have a few friends on the upper floors.'

The Old Man wasn't a friend, however loosely one defined the term – but he wouldn't want my operations interfered with.

'What about you? You have any ideas?' Guiscard asked.

I stared into my drink, the liquid thick and black. 'I've got suspicions.'

'I don't suppose you feel like sharing?'

'Suppose all you want.'

For the first time in the conversation I caught a glimpse of the man I had met standing over the body of Little Tara. He worked to uncurl his snarl, and to his credit when he spoke his voice was empty of contempt. 'I'd like to help if I can.'

'I thought you said you didn't like him?'

'I said he didn't like me. I always liked him – but that's not really the point. He was my partner, and there is a code to these things. And if Black House can't find who killed him, then I suppose I'm for throwing my hand in with you.'

That last note smacked a bit too strongly of youthful sentimentality for my tastes. I scratched at my chin and wondered whether he was lying, and whether it mattered. 'Why should I trust you?'

'I didn't realize you were so awash in resources that you could afford to reject an offer of aid.'

'All right,' I said, handing him the slip of paper from my pocket. 'This is what Crispin was killed over. I picked it up off his corpse before you boys showed. It's a critical piece of information in an unsolved crime. By not immediately giving it to the agent in charge of the investigation you are violating your oath as an impartial arbiter of the Throne's Justice, and by not turning me in to Black House you are aiding a person of interest in a capital offense. The first will get you demoted, the second stripped of the gray.'

'Why are you showing this to me?'

'There's a man on that list I'd very much like to speak to, a man who might be able to shed some light on Crispin's end. I can't find him, but you could. And if you did, and if I were to hear it . . . That would be of use to me. Provided, of course, I wasn't in the gaol for violating a crime scene.'

We eyeballed each other, custom dictating one last round of challenge, then he nodded sharply. 'You won't be.'

'It's the Mirad, third from the bottom.'

He got up from the stool. 'I'll let you know what I find out.'

'Agent. You forgot something.'

'What's that?' he asked, with what might have been honest confusion.

'You've still got my form.'

'Right, sorry,' he said, pulling it from his coat and handing it back to me before dropping out the exit.

Maybe Guiscard wasn't as slow as I'd put him down for. I sipped at my coffee and plotted out the rest of the day.

Adolphus returned from the back. 'The blue-blood gone?'

'He ain't hiding under the tables.'

Snorting, Adolphus reached into his pocket and handed me a thin sheet of off-white parchment, stamped shut with a wax sigil. 'This came before you woke.'

I held it up to the light, taking notice of the seal, a lion quartered with a trio of matched diamonds. 'In the future, you can just inform me of anything I've missed when you first see me. You don't need to drip it out like an old man pissing.'

'I'm not a mail carrier.'

'You aren't a cook, you aren't a mail carrier – what the hell do you do here?'

Adolphus rolled his eyes and started cleaning the back tables. The afternoon drunks would be in soon, inclement weather or no. I tore through the wax seal with my thumbnail and read the missive.

> I find the supplies you tendered the night we first met have proved insufficient for my needs. Perhaps you could find your way to Seton Gardens tomorrow before nine with an equal amount, and we might speak after I complete some unrelated business.
>
> Your Trusted Friend,
> His Highness the Lord Beaconfield

In general My Trusted Friends did not send demands couched as requests, but allowances had to be made for the habits of the upper crust. I folded the note and put it into my bag.

'You open?' the slurred voice of a patron queried from behind me.

That seemed as good a cue as any, and it was about time to see what light the most expensive hooker in Rigus could shed on my situation. I grabbed my coat from upstairs and headed out into the storm.

28

I was standing in front of the entrance to a red-brick row house north of downtown, near Kor's Heights and the palatial estates of the nobility. Modest and unassuming, there was little besides Yancey's word to confirm it as one of the most expensive brothels in the city. Low Town whores ply their trade honestly, uncovered bosoms peeking through red curtains, propositions tossed from open windows. Here it was different. Next to the ash-colored door there was a bronze plate with the words THE VELVET HUTCH engraved on it.

I knocked firmly, and after a short pause it opened to reveal a fair-skinned woman in a comely but modest blue dress. She had dark hair and bright blue eyes, and offered a fetching smile, well-practiced this side of mercenary. 'Can I help you?' she asked, her voice sweet and clear.

'I'm here to see Mairi,' I said.

Her lips curved down in disappointment. I was impressed with her ability to convey warmth and condescension in equal measure.

'I'm afraid Mairi doesn't see many people, and those she does she's seen for a long time. In fact, no one in the house is interested in meeting new friends right now.'

I cut in before she could close the door in my face. 'Could you tell the mistress that Yancey's friend is outside? She should be expecting me.'

Her smile seemed a bit more natural after I mentioned the Rhymer. 'I'll see if she's available.'

I thought about rolling up a cigarette but decided it might show a lack of class. Instead I rubbed my hands together in a futile effort to keep warm. When the door swung back open a few minutes later the dark-haired girl had swapped genial disregard for sultry welcome.

'Mairi has a few moments to speak. Please, come in.'

I stepped into an elegant hallway, tiled marble floors leading to a staircase draped in red velvet and flanked by ebony banisters. A very large, very dim-looking man in a well-tailored suit sized me up discreetly from beside the entrance, unarmed save for fists the size of ham hocks. I had no doubt they'd do in a pinch.

The pretty greeter stood at the foot of the steps, hands clasped behind her back. 'If you'll follow me please, the mistress is just this way.'

I tried without success to avoid staring at her bottom as she climbed the stairs ahead of me. I wondered how old she was, and how she came about her employment. I supposed there were worse ways to make money – it beat working the line at a mill ten hours a day, or serving tables at some Low Town dive. Still, lying on your back is lying on your back, even if the sheets beneath you are made of silk.

We took a right at the top and followed a narrow hallway past a row of bedrooms, ending in front of an oak door, gilded slightly to distinguish it from the others. The girl knocked lightly. A throaty voice from inside beckoned us onward, and my guide opened the door ahead of me.

The room centered, perhaps not shockingly, on a sumptuous four-poster bed draped in white lace. Everything about the interior spoke of old money and refined taste, more the bedchamber of a duchess than a whore's boudoir. Seated at a make-up table in the corner was the woman I assumed to be Mairi the Dark-eyed.

Given the mental image engendered by Yancey's introduction, I have to say I found myself underwhelmed. She was a dark-haired Tarasaihgn, south of middle age but not by much. Quite handsome, even with the few added pounds she carried about her midsection – but not beautiful, certainly not exceptionally so. Between the two of them I would have preferred the greeter, younger and firmer as she was.

But then Mairi turned towards me and I saw her eyes, dark pools of sable that held my attention longer than etiquette strictly allowed, and suddenly I couldn't understand what had possessed me to compare the woman before me to the girl who had led me to her. My mouth was dry. I tried not to lick my lips.

In one smooth motion Mairi rose from her throne and narrowed the distance between us, offering her hand with a casual air. 'Thank you, Rajel, that'll be all,' Mairi said in unaccented Nestriann.

Rajel curtsied and left, closing the door behind her. Mairi stood silently, letting me inspect the wares before beginning her pitch.

'Do you speak Nestriann?' she began.

'Never had an ear for it.'

'Really?' She stared into my eyes, then broke out into a full-throated laugh, like the song of a bullfrog. 'I think you're lying.'

She was right – I spoke Nestriann, not like a native but well enough to avoid getting mugged on the way to the Cathédrale Daeva Maletus. The first year and a half of the War my sector of the trenches had run into Nestriann lines. They were a decent bunch of fellows, for mud-rutting serfs. Their captain had broken down and wept when he found out his generals had signed a separate armistice – but then, odium and incompetence on the part of the higher-ups was pretty universal during our unfortunate conflict.

She fluttered her lashes and smiled. 'You realize you've told me more by lying than you would by answering truthfully.'

'And what did I tell you?'

'That deceit comes more naturally to you than honesty.'

'Maybe I'm just trying to fit in with my surroundings – or was every moan that ever echoed off these walls authentic?'

'Every. Single. One.' She held each word for a long beat. A wet bar sat in the corner, and from a decanter on top of it she poured smoky liquid into two glasses, then handed one to me. 'What shall we drink to?' she asked in a tone just short of lewd.

'To the health of the Queen, and the prosperity of her subjects.'

The old blessing was an awkward transition, but she was enough of a professional to roll with it. 'To the health of the Queen and the fertility of her land.'

I took a taste. It was good, very good.

Mairi perched herself on a red leather couch and motioned me towards the divan across from it. I followed her direction and we sat facing each other, our legs nearly touching. 'How do you know Yancey?' she asked.

'How does anyone know anyone? You meet people, in my business.'

'And what business is that exactly?'

'I solicit funds for war widows and orphans. On off days I nurse abandoned puppies.'

'What an astonishing coincidence! That's the very same line of work we pursue.'

'I suppose your kennels are in the basement.'

'Where do you keep your orphans?'

I chuckled and sipped at my drink.

Her mouth curled upward and she caressed me with soot-black eyes. 'I know who you are, of course. I made inquiries after I heard from the Rhymer.'

'Did you now?'

'I had no idea, when Yancey spoke of you, that I'd be given the opportunity to meet such a famed underworld figure.'

I let that one hang in the air between us. She missed the hint and pressed onward, confident I was enjoying her build-up.

'I always wondered what had happened to Mad Edward and

the rest of his people. Imagine my surprise to discover that the man who ended syndicate presence in Low Town was coming to pay me an afternoon visit.'

Mairi's sources were good. There were only a half-dozen people who'd ever known the truth of what had happened to Mad Edward's Mob, and two of them were dead. I'd have to figure out which of the remaining four were running off at the mouth.

The tip of her tongue scanned the lower half of her lip. 'Imagine my excitement.'

It is one of the relatively few advantages of being quite physically misshapen that you can generally dismiss honest arousal as a reason for a woman's advances. In Mairi's case I'm not sure there was even a purpose – at bottom I suspect she just didn't remember how to turn it off. The whole thing felt sour, my witty banter and her clockwork response to it.

'Riveting.' I took another swallow of whiskey, trying to get the taste of being played out of my mouth. 'But I didn't come here for my history. I'm quite familiar with it – comprehensively so, you might say.'

She took the slight with less than absolute equanimity, the flushed heat of her face fading to match the weather. From a silver case on the table next to her she took a thin black cigarette and sank it between her blood-red lips, lighting it with one quick pass of a match. 'Then what are you here for, exactly?'

'Yancey didn't mention it?' I asked.

A quick stream of tobacco smoke escaped from her nostrils. 'I want you to ask me.'

I'd suffered more galling indignities. 'Yancey says you've got a sharp ear and a long memory. I'd like to hear what they offer on the Lord Beaconfield.'

'The Blade?' She did something that conveyed the intent of eye rolling without actually being so uncouth as to roll her eyes. 'Apart from the talent that earned his nickname he's your typical bored aristocrat, cold-blooded, amoral and cruel.'

'Those are more observations than secrets,' I said.

'And he's broke,' she finished.

'So the mansion, the parties, the money he paid me . . .'

'The first is in hock to pay for the second two. The Lord Beaconfield was blessed with an old name, a deadly arm and not much else. And like most nobles, his pecuniary abilities don't go beyond spending. He sank tens of thousands of ochre in the Ostarrichi national loan, and lost everything when they defaulted last fall. Word is the creditors are baying at the door, and his personal tailor won't accept his commission. I'd be surprised if he makes it through the season without declaring bankruptcy.'

'So those diamonds on his crest?'

'Let's just say the lion is the more pertinent half.'

The threat of poverty could drive a man towards terrible acts – I'd seen plenty of that. But did the thought of losing that gorgeous house of his really push the Smiling Blade to child murder and black magic? 'What about his connections to the Prince?'

'Exaggerated. They were chums at Aton, one of those dreary boarding schools choked with tradition and staffed by pedophiles. But dear Henry . . .' I wondered if this offhand reference to the Crown Prince indicated a grain of truth behind the rumors of their liaison, or if she just wanted me to think it did. 'Is a bit too buttoned-down for the Blade's wild ways.'

'Interesting,' I said, as if it wasn't. 'How about his hangers-on, you know anything there? He's got a cut-rate practitioner running errands for him, goes by the name of Brightfellow?'

She crinkled up her nose like I'd dropped a fresh turd on the floor. 'I know the man – though I hadn't heard he'd hooked up with your duke. Brightfellow's one of that unpleasant breed of artist who flits about the peripheries of court, pimping his talent to whatever nobles are bored or stupid enough to pay for his parlor tricks. I hadn't thought much of Beaconfield, but I thought enough of him not to expect he'd get mixed up with trash like that. He must really be desperate.'

'What would Brightfellow be doing for the Blade?'

'I really wouldn't know – but having met the two, I'd guess it doesn't involve philanthropy.'

I figured she was probably right.

After another moment she cleared her throat, a sound that made me think of sugar and smoke, and our interview was over. 'And that's it then – that's all the information I can provide you with as to the secret dealings of the Smiling Blade.' She uncrossed her legs, then crossed them again. 'Unless there's anything else you wanted.'

I stood up abruptly, setting my glass on the table next to my chair. 'No, nothing else. You've been a help – you've got a chit to cash in with me if you need it.'

She stood as well. 'I'm tempted to cash it in right now,' she said, her eyes tilting towards the bed.

'No you aren't. Not even a little.'

Her wanton leer faded, to be replaced with something more closely resembling a genuine smile. 'You're an interesting man. Come back again some time, I'd like to see you.' She moved close enough for me smell her perfume, intoxicating, like everything else about her. 'And that I do mean.'

I wasn't sure I believed that either. Rajel was nowhere to be seen on the way out, but the bouncer gave me a sullen nod as I approached the exit.

'Fun place to work?'

He shrugged his shoulders. 'Three weeks of the month.'

I nodded sympathetically and left.

29

I was heading south when I saw him, a bony runt shadowing me from the opposite side of the street, a half-block back in my wake. He could have picked me up any time after I left Mairi's – it would have been easy to slip out from a back alley in the thick fog.

I stopped at a corner stall run by an aged Kiren and inspected his wares. '*Duoshao qian?*' I asked, angling a chipped bracelet up to the dull light as a pretext for scanning behind me. The vendor quoted me a price ten or twelve times what the junk was worth, and I feigned disappointment and dropped the bauble into a bin. He snatched it up quickly and shoved it back into my face, streaming forth a broken monologue as to the exceptional merits of his goods. By this point my tail had drawn close enough to make out some detail. I couldn't see the Blade hiring the brand of cheap thug this hooligan epitomized, and he obviously wasn't a heretic, so Ling Chi was out. Of course, there were plenty of other people scattered about the city who wouldn't mind seeing me fall on something sharp, some dealer I'd wronged or slumlord who thought I threatened his business. We'd find out soon enough.

I hadn't tooled up before going to visit Mairi, seemed like a bad way to make an impression, but I wouldn't need a weapon to get the jump on this skinny little bastard. The only thing better than ambushing a motherfucker is ambushing the motherfucker who thinks he's ambushing you. I slipped past the merchant, heading down a side alley, cutting around the corner, accelerating slightly as I made the turn—

Then I was on the ground, the strange sensation of light and heat that accompanies a strong blow to the head distorting my vision, so much so that the figure standing above me was, for a moment, unrecognizable.

But only for a moment.

'Hey, Crowley.'

'Hey, faggot.'

I made a play for his ankles, but my movements were slow and clumsy, and Crowley shut down any hopes of escape with a booted toe to my ribs.

I slumped back against the wall, hoping that last shot hadn't broken a bone, the agony in my side suggesting such optimism was unfounded. My lungs worked to fill themselves properly, a pause during which Crowley was kind enough to resist beating on me, making do with an excessively unfriendly grin. I managed to cough out a few sentences. 'Having trouble with your arithmetic? I've got five days, Crowley. Five days. If big numbers confuse you, take your shoes off and count on your toes.'

'Didn't I tell you how funny he was?' Crowley said to someone behind him, and now I realized that Crowley hadn't come alone. He was backed by three men, not agents I didn't think, but hard folk, syndicate muscle maybe – regardless, unfriendly in the extreme. They stared at me with expressions that ran the gamut from outright boredom to sadistic glee.

I had been played like a rank amateur. The first one had let himself be seen, drawing my attention while Crowley and his crew lay in wait. By the Scarred One, how had I been so stupid?

'You see a uniform on me, punk?' Crowley asked. 'This ain't got nothing to do with the Crown, or the Old Man.' He accentuated this last point with another kick to my shoulder. I winced and bit my tongue. 'Today's my day off.'

'So running into me was just a quirk of fate?' My mouth was full of copper and I could feel blood dribbling down my chin.

'I wouldn't chalk it all up to chance. Might have something to do with me thinking you've long outlived your usefulness. Another body showed up earlier today – a boy this time.'

Poor Avraham Mayana. 'Don't pretend you give a shit about the victims.'

'You're right. This isn't about them.' He shoved his brutish face into mine, hot breath filtering rank across my nose. 'It's you. I fucking hate you. I've hated you for ten years, ever since you second-guessed me on the Speckled Band case. When the Old Man gave the orders to bring you in last week, I almost did a jig I was so happy. Then when we let you go . . .' He shook his head and spread his arms wide. 'Ten years waiting to close your book, and you get another pass because of that slick mouth of yours? I know they say you shouldn't bring work home with you, but . . . what can I say? Maybe I'm just too devoted a civil servant.'

'What do you think the Old Man will say when he finds out you aced me?'

He laughed, a guffaw that was no less threatening for being clownish. 'When I leave this alleyway you'll be alive and kicking.' He dabbed a fat finger in the gusher coming from my nose, bringing it back wet with a red sheen that he inspected carefully, almost tenderly. 'Course, I can't speak for these gentlemen. Untrained, you know, but full of enthusiasm. Besides, I wouldn't count too firm on your patron's good humor. Last I checked you ain't done much to curb violence in your little ghetto. We found that boy in the river today – and I assume you heard about your old partner's unfortunate demise.'

Something hot flared up in my stomach. 'Don't talk about Crispin, you sodomitic gorilla.'

The toe of his boot clipped my forehead, and my skull rang against the wall. 'You're pretty feisty for a man about to get a long look at his insides.'

One of his boys, a whip-thin Mirad with the ritualized facial scarring they use to mark criminals in that unfortunate theocracy, shook a poignard out of his oversize coat and said something I couldn't make out.

Crowley took his eyes off me to snarl at him, his face mad-dog with hate. 'Not yet, you fucking degenerate. I told you – he bleeds first.'

This was as good a chance as any. I cocked back my right foot and shot it at Crowley's kneecap. Something was still up with my vision though, and it went wide, catching his shin.

It was enough, barely. He howled and backed up a step and I leapt to my feet. I guess Crowley had figured that first knock would keep me down longer. Dumb motherfucker – he'd known me a decade and still hadn't learned to compensate for the thickness of my cranium.

I turned a corner and heard the distinct thunk of metal on stone indicating the Mirad's blade had missed its mark. Then I was putting one step ahead of another with as much alacrity as my battered frame could muster, making west for the canal with every drop of energy I had left.

The alleys in that part of Low Town ring the main thoroughfares like a cobweb spun by a drunken spider, weaving back and forth irregularly. Even I don't know them all that well, a fact reinforced when once or twice I stumbled back through previously traversed intersections. But if I was having trouble I could tell Crowley and his gang weren't doing any better – the gray walls echoed with the angry shouts of my pursuers, providing an unneeded impetus to my movements.

I broke cover through the warren of passageways and into the wide boulevard that skirts the canal. Here the channel broadens to its widest point, just south of the River Andel, Rupert's Trestle covering its shoulders. I broke into a dead sprint, reaching the foot of the bridge and ascending its limestone arch. On a normal day this area would be bustling with travelers hurtling towards their destinations and picnickers taking in the view, but with the weather I was the only one in sight. At first, anyway.

Coming across from the other side, a long, curved knife held backwards against his arm, was the man I first saw following me, and he looked a lot bigger than before. Behind me the scarred Mirad slipped from the mouth of the alley, his features dim in the heavy mist.

I stopped at the zenith of Rupert's, working desperately to figure an out. I debated making a break for it past the goon rapidly narrowing the distance between us, but unarmed as I was he'd hold me up long enough for the rest of his gang to cut me apart. From over my shoulder I heard Crowley cursing my lineage and promising gratuitous punishment. A quick look revealed him hot on the tail of the Mirad, who slowed up, waiting for his pack before coming against me.

Sometimes success is about complex stratagems – a sacrificed pawn, or a cornered bishop. More often, though, it's about speed and surprise. Crowley would never be mistaken for a genius, but I wasn't the first poor bastard he'd trailed through the streets of Rigus. With a few more seconds to think he would have known I'd rather take a bath than go toe-to-toe with his goons. But as he rounded the corner he hadn't yet processed the possibility, and was left flat-footed as I climbed the railing and took a swan dive into the canal below.

The ice wasn't as thin as it looked from the bridge and I bruised my shoulder pretty good going through. I didn't feel the injury for long, the cold water anesthetizing me straight through to the bone. Righting myself, I managed to shed my heavy coat and tear off my boots, my numb hands fumbling at the laces, fingers stupid and unresponsive.

Crowley would figure me to head downriver, but I ain't ever been much of a swimmer and didn't fancy my chances of outrunning him and his boys. Instead I kicked my feet and headed deeper into the depths. The canal was thick with the city's waste, too opaque to see through even had I been foolish enough to open my eyes, so I had to hope Crowley fell for it. I held my breath as long as I could then spurted up to the surface for air, lifting the top layer of ice half an inch above the water, then diving back to the bottom. I couldn't keep this up for long. Already my limbs felt languid and heavy, each movement increasing in difficulty, the willingness of my body to obey my commands diminishing with each passing second.

I came up for air twice more before the cold got to be too much, and then I swam to the west embankment and hauled myself over the side of the canal. For a few seconds I lay prostrate on the dirty cobblestones, willing myself to move, my injured body unsympathetic to my demands. The thought of what would happen if Crowley and his men found me, that is to say the looming threat of torture and death, provided sufficient energy for me to pull myself to my feet.

Another afternoon it wouldn't have worked – they'd have seen me climbing up out of the brine and run me down – but the fog was thick off the bay, walling off anyone unlucky enough to be caught in it and rendering pursuit almost impossible. Crowley had swallowed my deception – in the distance I could hear them yelling to each other, trying to figure out where they'd lost me.

I knew I'd never make it back to the Earl. I didn't even try, I just turned south down a side alley and moved as fast as I could. The wind whirled heavy about my face, and I could feel the peculiar sensation of my hair freezing to my scalp. If I didn't get out of these wet clothes and in front of a fire soon the cold would do what Crowley had been unable to, less painfully perhaps, but just as permanent.

The narrow streets twisted and turned, my vision blurring in and out of focus and a terrible ache rising up from my chest. I only had a few blocks to go – I figured it was even money if I'd make it.

My jog became a half-jog, then a slow walk, then a sort of awkward stumble.

Another step.

Another.

I climbed over the white stone hedges with an appalling lack of dignity, banging my knees as I did so, even those low walls proving difficult to negotiate with my frozen limbs. I tripped over the last one, landing headfirst in front of the tower. My hands fumbled inside my shirt for Crispin's Eye, belatedly thinking I might burst the Aerie's defenses, but my fingers wouldn't work, and anyway I knew I'd never be able to muster the concentration its powers required. Pulling myself to my feet, I banged futilely against the door, my pleas for entry lost amid the wind.

The gargoyle remained silent, mute witness as I slumped to the ground.

30

In high summer of my nineteenth year Rigus came down with war fever. The streets were abuzz with the failure of the Hemdell Conference, and the news that our continental allies, Miradin and Nestria, had mobilized to defend their borders against the Dren menace. High Chancellor Aspith had called for an initial commitment of twenty thousand men, then the largest collection of soldiers the Empire had ever assembled. Little did anyone appreciate that this first sacrifice would prove to be no more than kindling for the conflagration that would ravage the continent to its embers.

In the years since it ended I've heard a lot of different reasons as to why we went to war. When I first signed up I was told we were dying to uphold the treaties we had sworn with our comrades-in-arms – though what conceivable interest I had in ensuring the territorial integrity of the aging Mirad Empire and their degenerate Priest-King, or of helping the Nestrianns avenge the injuries the young Dren commonwealth had done them fifteen years prior, was beyond my understanding, then or now. Not that it mattered – the powers-that-be jettisoned that one pretty quick once our eternal allies capitulated two years into the conflict. After that I started to hear that my presence hundreds of miles from home was needed to protect the Throne's interests overseas, to stop the Dren from gaining a warm-water port that would allow them to threaten the scattered jewels of our Empire. A professor I knew, a client of mine, once tried to explain that the War was the inevitable byproduct of what he called the 'expanding role of the oligarchic financial interests'. We were pretty cooked on breath at the time, though, and I was having trouble following him. I've heard a lot of explanations – hell, half of Low Town still blames the whole thing on the Islander banking houses, and their preternatural influence at court.

But I remember the build-up before the War, and the packed lines at the recruitment centers. I remember the chants – *The Dren, the slaves, we'll lay them in their graves!* – you could hear bellowing out from every bar in the city, any time of the day or night. I remember the lightning in the air, and the lovers bidding goodbye to each other in the streets, and I can tell you what I think. We went to war because going to war is fun, because there's something in the human breast that trills at the thought, although perhaps not the reality, of murdering its fellows in vast numbers. Fighting a war ain't fun – fighting a war is pretty miserable. But starting a war? Hell, starting a war is better than a night floating on daeva's honey.

As for me – well, spending your childhood fighting the rats for fresh trash doesn't do much to inculcate the middle-class virtues of nationalism and xenophobia that make you leap at the thought of killing people you've never seen. But a stint in the army beat another day at the docks, or at least that was how I figured it. The recruiter said I'd be back in six months and gave me a sharp suit of leather armor and a kettle-cap that didn't quite fit my skull. There was little in the way of training – I didn't so much as see a pike till we had disembarked in Nestria.

I signed up with the first wave of recruits, the Lost Children they would euphemistically call us when our casualties during those first terrible months ran three-in-four and four-in-five. Most of the boys I went in with wouldn't live another twelve weeks. Most of them died screaming, a crossbow bolt in the gut or a sharp spray of shrapnel.

But that was all in the future. That summer I walked around Low Town in my crisp uniform, and old men shook my hand and tried to buy me ale, and pretty girls blushed in the street when I passed.

I was never the sociable sort, and I doubted the rest of the men at the docks would weep at my absence, so I didn't have much in the way of an elaborate farewell. But two days before I was required to take passage to the front, I went to see the only two people living that I figured might mourn my demise.

When I came in the Crane had his back to me, a fresh breeze filtering in through the open window. I knew the guardian had already alerted him to my arrival, but even so I was slow to greet him. 'Master,' I said.

His smile was broad but his eyes were sad. 'You look like a soldier.'

'One of our side, I hope. Wouldn't do to get knifed on the transport ship over there.'

He nodded with an unnecessary seriousness. The Crane was not generally concerned with politics, tending like many of his kind towards more esoteric interests. Despite the status conferred upon him as a Sorcerer of the First Rank, he rarely went to court and had little influence. But he was a man of great wisdom, and I think he understood what the rest of us didn't – that what was about to come wouldn't be over in time for Midwinter, that once unleashed this beast called war would not prove easy to again cage.

He didn't say any of this to me of course – I was going either way. But I could read the concern on his face. 'Celia will be off to the Academy in the fall. I have a feeling the Aerie will be very cold this winter, without her here. And without your visits, infrequent though they've lately become.'

'You've decided to send her?'

'The invitation was not styled as a request. The Crown aims to consolidate the nation's practitioners into its own sphere of influence. No more puttering about in towers on windswept moors. I'm not ecstatic about it but . . . there's little enough one old man can do against the future. It's for the greater good, or so I'm told. It seems a great many things these days are to be sacrificed to that nebulous ideal.' Perhaps realizing his condemnation could apply to my situation as well, he brightened his tone. 'Besides, she's excited about it. It will be a good thing for her to spend more time with people her age – she's been alone too long with her studies. There are times I worry . . .' He shook his head, as if wiping away ill thoughts. 'I never planned on being a father.'

'You've adapted well enough.'

'It isn't so easy, you know. I think perhaps I treated her too much as an adult. When I realized she had a talent for the Art . . . Sometimes I wonder if I didn't take her as an apprentice too early. I was twelve when I went to live with Roan, twice her age and a boy besides. There are things she learned, things she was exposed to . . .' He shrugged. 'It was the only way I knew to raise her.'

I had never heard the Crane so openly speak of his concerns – it was disturbing, and I had enough to worry about already. 'She turned out fine, Master. She's become a fine young woman.'

'Of course she is, of course,' he said, nodding with exaggerated vigor. A moment passed while he gnawed at his mustache. 'Has she ever told you what happened before you found her? What became of her family, how she lasted on the streets?'

'I never asked. A child that young, and a girl?' I left it at that, preferring not to answer the question, nor to consider the matter too closely.

He nodded, thinking the same grim thoughts. 'You'll see her before you leave?'

'I will.'

'Be kind. You know of her feelings for you.'

It was not a question, and I didn't answer it.

'I wish I could guarantee your safety with my Art, but I'm no battle-mage. I can't imagine my whirligig that spins unassisted would be of much use in a fight.'

'Can't imagine.'

'Then I suppose I have nothing to offer but my blessing.' Without practice, our embrace was awkward. 'Be careful,' he whispered. 'For the love of Śakra, be careful.'

I left without responding, not trusting myself to speak.

I headed down the stairs to Celia's bedroom, and stopped in front of the door. My knuckles rapped against the wood. A soft voice answered. 'Enter.'

She was sitting on the corner of her bed, a gigantic, mauve-colored monstrosity that sat incongruously with her small menagerie of stuffed animals. She had been crying but was doing her best not to show it. 'You did it then? You enlisted?'

'It was a precondition to getting the uniform.'

'Do you . . . do you have to go?'

'I signed a contract. It's Nestria or the gaol.'

Her eyes flooded, but she blinked twice and pressed on. 'Why?'

How to answer that question? How to compress a thousand wasted nights staring up at a slum-house ceiling, crowded three to a bed, elbows jabbing at your sides, sleep endlessly disturbed by the labored snoring of the half-idiot beside you? How to describe the realization that the world is quite happy to see you exhaust your strength in another man's service, kill your spirit building a fortune you'll never see? How to explain that the deck is stacked, that if you play straight you'll end up broke?

'This is my chance. War changes things – it shakes up the order. Here I'm nothing, trash washed away in the rain. Over there?' I shrugged. 'They'll have to raise enlisted men to officer – there won't be enough who can afford to buy their way in. I'll make lieutenant – you can double down on that. And afterward? There's room in the world for a man who can keep an eye open for his future.'

When I finished Celia's eyes were puppy-dog wide, and I wished I'd kept my mouth shut. It didn't do to feed her infatuation. 'I know you will. You'll be a general before the war is out.' She blushed, and leapt up from her bed. 'I've loved you since the moment I saw you, shining fierce in the dark.' I was very conscious of her nearness, and the thin gauze of cloth that separated her body from mine. 'I'll wait for you – I'll wait for you as long as I need to.' Her words broke through like water over a dam, syllables tumbling out one after another. 'Or, if you don't want to wait . . .' She wrapped her arms around me. 'You have no lady – I know you've been saving yourself.'

I patted her on the back awkwardly. Best to do this quickly, one sharp moment of misery. 'When I was thirteen I paid a dock whore two argents to take me behind an outhouse. That I've never brought a woman to meet you doesn't mean what you think.'

I could not have created a more pronounced effect if I had struck her. She took a long moment to collect herself, then threw her body against mine once again. 'But I love you. I've always loved you – we're the same, you and I, don't you see?'

Her face was buried in my chest and her slender arms were wrapped tight across my ribs. I put my finger beneath her chin and raised her eyes to meet mine. 'You aren't like me. You aren't anything like me.' Her skin was slick with tears. I combed her dark hair with my fingers. 'I gave you to the Crane that night to make sure of that.'

She pushed me away and ran weeping to her bed. It was better this way. She would hurt, for a time. But she was young, and it would fade, and in the years to come the memory would be nothing more than a faint embarrassment.

As quietly and swiftly as I could I withdrew, down the steps and out into the afternoon. Then it was back to my flophouse and two days of drinking and whoring, making sure to waste every copper of the meager bonus the Crown had distributed in recognition of my future service. When I stumbled to the docks forty-eight hours later I was piss broke and had a headache like a mule kick to the temple. It was an inauspicious beginning to an unprofitable enterprise.

As for Celia and the Crane, well, I sent letters and so did they.

But like everything else in that damned army, communication back home was terrible, so I didn't get most of theirs and they didn't get most of mine. It would be more than five years before I set eyes on either of them again. By that time much had changed for all of us – little of it I suspect for the better.

31

When I awoke I was lying on a bed, staring up at a gauzy overhang and the four carved posts that supported it. Someone had stripped me of my wet clothing and dressed me in a plain white robe. The agonizing cold and terrible sensation of exhaustion were gone, replaced by a warm glow that emanated out from my chest into each extremity.

'Am I dead?' I asked no one in particular.

Celia's voice answered from out of my field of vision. 'Yes. And this is Chinvat.'

'I wonder what I did to warrant an eternity surrounded by lace.'

'Something wonderful, I would imagine.'

That didn't sound much like me. 'How'd you get me up here?'

'Magic, obviously. A minor use of my Art.'

'I'm a little slow on the uptake. Hypothermia will do that. I assume you hocus-pocused that as well?'

I could see her now out of the corner of my eye, as she came to sit beside me. 'Just a touch – most of it was getting you out of those wet clothes and in front of a fire. You've been sleeping for the last hour or so.' She shifted my head onto her lap. 'I'm sorry I kept you waiting. I had an experiment going in the conservatory, and foolishly didn't foresee you coming to visit me half-naked and freezing.'

'The second-in-command of Special Operations was offended by my hygiene. I decided I'd improve our relationship with a quick bath in the canal.'

'I thought you got Black House off your back?' Her charm dangled from the soft of her neck. She smelled of sunshine, and fresh cinnamon.

'Apparently I evoke a level of hatred that renders the Old Man's protection inadequate. Besides, I haven't exactly held up my end of the bargain. Another child was killed.'

'I heard.'

'And Crispin too.'

'I'm sorry,' she said.

'How's the Crane?'

'Not well. He's in and out.'

'I should go up and see him. After I put on some pants.'

'It's best if you don't.'

'I always wear pants,' I said. 'I wouldn't know what to do without them.'

She laughed softly and shifted her body out from under me. 'You should rest now. I'll check on you in a little while. We'll talk more then.'

I waited till she left the room, then sat up in bed – too quickly, as it turned out. My vision swirled and my stomach clenched, and I thought I might boot all over Celia's pretty sheets. I laid my head back on the pillow and waited for my body to forgive me for this most recent round of bad decisions.

After a few minutes of penance I swung my feet to the floor and slowly pulled myself erect. My gut gave notice of its disapproval, but less forcefully than before. I grabbed my satchel from the foot of the bed, then slipped out the door and into the stairwell, ascending two flights to the top floor.

Inside the room was vacant, the windows shut tight, the fireplace filled with ash. I waited there for a while. The Crane was a man of boundless generosity and virtually infinite patience, but he was also very private. In the entirety of our relationship I'd never entered his personal quarters. But then I couldn't very well walk home in the cotton robes I wore.

Feeling very much like an intruder, I slipped into the Master's bedroom. His chambers were smaller than Celia's, little more than a bed and a night table, with a wardrobe in the corner. The wall sconces were unlit, and dark cloth had been stretched over the windows, blocking out what little illumination the gray day would have provided.

Celia had warned me of the Crane's decline, and seeing him I couldn't accuse her of exaggeration. He lay twisted on the bed, his body contorted in a fever pose. Most of his hair was gone, and what remained hung in loose tendrils down his neck. His eyes were glazed and unfocused, and his color was nearer to that of a corpse than the hale, if aging figure I had spoken to only a few days earlier.

I wished I was wearing pants.

He didn't react to my entrance, and when he did speak his voice was fractured and strained, in line with the decay the rest of his body had suffered. 'Celia'. . . Celia is that you? Honey, listen to me, please, there's still time . . .'

'No, Master. It's me.' I took a spot on a small stool by his bedside. He did not look better close up.

His eyes fluttered, then focused on me. 'Oh. I'm sorry, I . . . I haven't had any visitors lately. I'm not feeling very well.'

'Of course, Master, of course. Can I get you anything?' hoping as I asked that he wouldn't call for the decanter of green liquid that sat on the bed table. Every man has the right to choose the manner in which he meets death, but it was a difficult thing to be complicit in the erosion of the Crane's fertile and imaginative mind.

He shook his head, more of a shudder really. 'No, nothing. It's too late for anything.'

243

I sat at his bedside for five or ten minutes while he slipped into a fitful sleep. I was about to get up and leaf through his wardrobe when it occurred to me I owed the man something, and I reached inside my satchel and set the horn Wren had stolen onto a table next to the bed.

The Crane's hand shot out from beneath the covers and grabbed my wrist, and I had to restrain a yelp. 'Roan, you were right. I'm sorry I didn't listen to you.'

In his delirium it seemed he had mistaken me for his old teacher. 'It's me, Master. Roan the Grim has been dead for half a century.'

'I tried to keep it out, Roan, tried to ward it off. But it got in – it always gets in.'

'Your wards hold, Master,' I said. 'The people of Low Town remember, and are grateful.'

'There's nothing to keep out, Roan. That's what you knew. What you knew but what I couldn't understand. The rot's inside, it's already inside.'

I tried to think of something soothing to say but nothing came.

'It's always there. I understand that now. How do you build a wall to keep out what's always been there? It can't be done, it can't be done!' He was nearly shouting now. 'Erect a fence, dig a moat, toss up a barricade and mine the approaches – it'll do you no good! It's already here! At the bottom there's nothing but blood and shit!' He spat out the last words and I flinched back unconsciously. I had never heard the Master curse before, nor was he much given to displays of anger. I began to wonder how much of his abilities were left to him, and whether in his dementia he might not incinerate the Aerie and everything around it.

'Who can keep it out?' he asked, flecks of spittle catching in his tattered beard. 'Who can burn it out?'

I wanted to comfort my old mentor, and I spoke without thinking. 'I will. I'll take care of it – you can count on me.'

He laughed then, and I had the terrible certainty that his mania had broken and he'd recognized me, that his cackling was no mad reflex but an honest assessment of my character – and I wished I'd kept my mouth shut.

That was the end of it, though I waited a few minutes to make sure. The Crane returned to his shallow sleep and showed no signs of waking. I raided his closet, returning in an ill-fitting pair of breeches and a dress shirt that dragged down to my knees and was tight across the chest. I grabbed a pair of boots from a trunk in the hall and went down to the kitchen.

Celia was busying herself above the stove, setting a kettle to boil, her dark hair bobbing up and down.

'Remember that time you and I tried to make hot chocolate and almost set the Aerie on fire?' I asked.

'You shouldn't be up. If you'd gotten here five minutes later I'd be picking out a grave site rather than making dinner.'

'You didn't mention that earlier.'

'I was trying not to worry you with the extent of your injuries. Given your difficulty distinguishing foolishness from bravery, I ought probably to have exaggerated it.'

'Everything's always clearer in hindsight. If I had the day to do over again I would try to avoid getting my ass kicked.'

There's only so long one can maintain disapproval faced with the devastating and continuous onslaught of my humor. The kettle whistled, and Celia poured herself a cup, then added some loose leaves, knowing without asking I wouldn't want one.

'I spoke with the Master,' I said.

'I assumed that was how you got your pants.'

'He thought I was Roan the Grim.'

'As I said, he's fading in and out.' She sighed. 'Sometimes he calls me by his mother's name, sometimes by the names of women he's never mentioned before.'

It was strange to think of the Master as having had a past before he was the Crane, of his acne-ridden adolescence or the escapades of his youth. 'How long do you think he has?'

Celia blew softly over the tea. 'Not long,' she said, and that was enough.

We sat together silently. I reminded myself I had too much in my head to start spending energy on the Crane's impending demise. It was cruel, and the truth, like a lot of things. 'I've been digging,' I said finally.

'And?'

'You know anything about a practitioner named Brightfellow? He would have been around your class in the Academy.'

The brim of the cup masked her mouth, and the eyes above it were dark. After a moment she set the porcelain against the table. 'Vaguely,' she said. 'Not a lot. He was part of Adelweid's clique, always pushing into areas best left unexplored.'

'Seems like you remember more than you think.'

'Try to follow along,' she said. 'I told you, it was a small class. I didn't know him well . . . didn't want to. He came from one of the provinces, I don't remember which. His people were peasants, and he never seemed to get over the idea that the whole world was laughing at him for being raised in a barn. Walked around looking for someone to hit. He was close with Adelweid though, thick as thieves.'

I couldn't imagine the vainglorious prick I'd met during the siege of Donknacht having much to do with Brightfellow. But apart from that everything Celia had told me jibed with what I knew of the man.

'Do you think the Blade and Brightfellow are working together?' Celia asked.

'They're into something. I'm just not sure what it is yet.'

'And does the talisman still point to the duke?'

'Yeah.'

'Then what more do you need? Can't you just . . .' She made a motion with her hand meant to indicate either imprisonment or assassination.

I chose to assume the first. 'Based on what? A stolen scrap of evidence, hinting at the culpability of an individual loosely affiliated with a powerful noble? Crispin's information went a way towards confirming my suspicions, but as far as Black House is concerned . . .' I shook my head. 'I don't have anything.'

She chewed at the tip of her thumb. 'There might be something I can do to help you.'

'You know me. I'm too proud to ask for help, but not too proud to take it.'

'I could perform a divination on the duke's home – it might shed some light on his activities, or at least show you where to look to find more evidence.'

'Whatever you can do,' I said, wondering why she hadn't thought to try it earlier.

'It'll take a day or two. I'll send a runner over when I've got something.'

'Thanks,' I said, meaning it.

Celia nodded, then poured herself another cup of tea, spooning a pair of sugar cubes in after it.

'I had a meeting the other day with one of Black House's scryers,' I said.

She twirled a curl of hair around her index finger. 'I'm surprised to hear that Black House would allow you access to their resources.'

'You mean given that one of its operatives just tried to kill me? Funny thing about these clandestine organizations: one hand tends to be ignorant of its partner's activities, even when they include murder.'

'Were they able to pick up any signs from the body?'

'Nothing on the murderer. But the scryer saw signs that the girl had been sacrificed.'

'I suppose it's what we feared. We knew the duke was dabbling in the shade. It makes sense he would go the whole way.'

'Assuming it is the Blade.'

She waved dismissively. For her it was already a settled issue.

I'd rather have left it at that – Celia's was too kind a heart to involve in such a dirty business. But there were things I needed to know, and no one else to ask. 'What can you tell me about it?'

'About human sacrifice? I'm afraid I don't have much to tell – they didn't teach that sort of thing at the Academy.'

Why not? They'd taught Adelweid to summon fiends from the outer darkness, draw horrors into the world and set them upon his fellows. 'I'm not trying to recreate the mechanics of it, I'm just trying to suss out motive. What would be to gain from such an act?'

Celia paused before answering. 'Most workings are powered by the innate strength of the practitioner, filtered and directed by their will. For larger workings, energy can be tapped from places of power, or from items crafted for that purpose. In extreme cases, a practitioner might even cull the essence of a lower life form, and use that to form a spell. In theory the sacrifice of a human would offer the same opportunity, though on a much greater scale.'

I rolled that over in my head, trying to settle it into a coherent equilibrium. 'I can't work the sums. The Blade's broke, fine – for a man like Beaconfield that's a powerful motive, he loses his money and he loses everything, his status, his name even. Not like he can go out and get a real job. But still – he throws in with Brightfellow, starts summoning monsters from the ether and slaughtering children, for what? To refill his bank account? It's slim.'

'You're thinking too small,' she said. 'If they've sacrificed the children, the energy they have to draw on would be virtually limitless. He could turn a mountain of dirt into gold. He could rework the fundamental fabric of existence. Is that the sort of power you want in the hands of a man like the Blade?'

I rubbed my fingers in little circles against my temple. Whatever Celia had done to me was fading, and I could feel the beginnings of a headache brewing. 'There's something else the scryer showed me. Even if Caristiona hadn't been murdered she wasn't long for the world. She had the plague.'

'That's . . . unlikely,' Celia said.

'I saw the rash.'

'A rash can be a symptom of any number of things.'

'It was the plague,' I said, a bit too harshly, then continued in a softer tone. 'I saw it enough to be sure. Could the Crane's wards be weakening?'

'That's not possible.'

'How do you know?'

'Because I've taken over running them,' she said, raising her tea cup to her mouth as she dropped an artillery shell in my lap.

'You didn't tell me that,' I said.

'The city sleeps at night because they know the Master is watching over them. It's better not to do anything to shake that certainty. Only a few people at the top of the Bureau of Magical Affairs know of the switch. It's why I was raised to First Sorcerer, so I'd be ready when the Master can no longer perform his duties.' That was a hell of a euphemism for the death of a parent, but it was good to see Celia handling this so dispassionately, given that the future of Rigus apparently sat on her slim shoulders. 'I'd know if the wards were failing, and they aren't.'

'You're saying it's impossible that Caristiona could have had the plague?'

'No, I'm not saying that at all. There's no way the plague could occur naturally, but it could be spread deliberately. If someone were to introduce it into the population, spread it to enough people . . . the protections the Master created aren't impermeable. They could be broken by sheer weight of numbers.'

'You think the Blade is infecting children with the plague? To what end? What does he gain from it?'

'Who has any idea of the bargains the duke must have struck to receive assistance from the void? Somehow I don't imagine the creature you saw would act without compensation. Perhaps Beaconfield's part lies in spreading the fever.'

'You think this is some sort of a . . . diabolical exchange? How can you be sure?'

'I'm not fucking sure,' she snapped. The profanity sat uneasily on her tongue, evidence of how frightened she was. 'I can't read the man's mind, I don't know every detail of his sick plot. What I do know is that if he continues, it'll only be a matter of time before the wards fail. While you sniff around in circles, Low Town flirts with death.'

I could feel myself getting hot. 'I'll handle it.'

'How many more children are going to die before you take care of your responsibilities?'

'I'll handle it,' I said again, angry at being pushed but knowing deep down that Celia was right, that I shouldn't have let this sprawl on so long. The stakes were too high to delay – Beaconfield was my man. He'd find out what that meant soon enough.

'We can't let the Master's work have been in vain.'

'That won't happen,' I said. 'By the Firstborn, I'll make sure of it.'

That seemed to calm her down some. She set one soft hand atop mine, and we sat like that for a long moment.

It was getting late, and the walk home wasn't getting any shorter. 'There was something else I wanted to ask you. I spoke to the mother of the last child. She said that he knew secrets without being told them – it reminded me of some of the things that let the Crane know you could be trained to the Art.'

Celia answered without looking at me. 'I'm sure it's nothing. Every child is special, to a parent.'

True enough. I gave her a last farewell and slipped out. It was early evening, and the chill winds that had oppressed my earlier travels had faded, leaving behind the thick blanket of gray fog. There was more I had wanted to do, business I needed to take care of, leads to follow. But in my weakened state it was all I could do to make it back to the Earl, swallow some burned chuck and pass out in my bed – which, I noted sourly, was far less comfortable than Celia's.

32

I awoke the next morning with a bruise on my shoulder the size of an eggshell, but nothing else to show that I had come a fingernail from death not twenty-four hours prior. I had experienced curative magic before, but nothing that could compete with this. The Crane had taught Celia well.

Shaking off the last strands of sleep, I opened the bottom drawer of my bureau and sprang the hidden latch, revealing the niche below. I took a few dozen vials of pixie's breath out of my business stash, along with a handful of other chemicals, then sat down at my table and went to work. It was slow going, and forty-five minutes had passed before I could pull on my clothes and stow my weapons. I would need to hustle to make my meeting with the Blade.

Wren sat at a table below, listening to Adolphus bullshit about his youth. It was nice to walk downstairs without being subject to the news of some horrible tragedy, as a change.

'It's true – I once ate an entire side of ham in a single sitting.'

'He did, I was there. It was as impressive as it was grotesque. He reeked of pig for the next month and a half. The Dren took to calling him the *Varken van de duivel*, and fainted at the smell of cooked bacon.'

Adolphus bellowed a laugh and even Wren cracked a smile.

The devil pig stood and brushed off his pants. 'You want me to tell Adeline to cook up some breakfast?'

'Afraid not. I'm late as it is.'

'I'll get my coat,' Wren said.

'No need. It's plenty warm in here.'

His eyes slanted angrily. 'I'm coming along.'

'Interestingly, you aren't – you're staying here and keeping Adolphus company. Though it's nice to see you have such an active imagination.' The scowl he shot me was wasted effort – I had too many people trying to kill me to worry much over the fury of an adolescent.

The previous day's mist had evaporated, leaving in its wake the kind of crystal-clear morning that prefaces snowfall. I turned north up Pritt Street and headed towards the Old City. I'd be a few minutes late for my requested audience with Beaconfield, but I could live with that – a little rudeness is good when dealing with blue-bloods, reminds them you aren't as interested in them as they are. Halfway there it started to snow, the flurries signaling a storm soon to come. I picked up my pace and tried to plot out the next hour in my head.

Seton Gardens is a lovely little park towards the outskirts of the city, near the old walls and just north of the Asher enclave. Stone avenues lead through a wooded preserve, a dollop of verdant green in a gray landscape, far enough from the slums to keep out the riff-raff. In the center is a lovely granite fountain, and next to it a curiously tailored green – an awkward addition to the topography, and one that would have no meaning to the average picnicker. On most mornings it's virtually empty, too far from the interior to see much use.

But on rare occasions the peaceful solitude of the gardens is interrupted by the flash of blades and the piercing of silk shirts.

By long tradition the park had been designated the arena by which the city's upper crust thin out their herd, and the short stretch of manicured turf had soaked up near as much blood as the plains of Gallia. Dueling is technically illegal in the Empire, though in practice the Crown is generally happy enough to overlook the occasional murder – in this way at least, the law treats the very high and low equally.

That was the main reason I didn't want Wren following along. The Lord Beaconfield hadn't called me out for a morning stroll – he'd invited me to watch him kill someone. By my count it would be his fourth this week.

I entered the park and was soon engulfed by its beech trees. A few hundred yards along a smoothly cultivated path and the city's noise was lost in the stillness of the morning. Further in and that quiet was broken by the low commotion of a crowd. Apparently I wasn't to be the only audience to the proceedings.

A small group had gathered in front of the dueling grounds, twenty or thirty men – friends or acquaintances of the participants; these things aren't exactly advertised. I took shelter beneath an outlying tree and sucked at my teeth. I was in the presence of some old names. It had been a long time since I'd needed to be familiar with the court, but my tattered memory was sufficient to recognize two earls and a marquess who used to pass Black House information. Probably still did, come to think of it.

Opposite the audience were the combatants and their coteries, separated from each other by about twenty feet of lawn. Beaconfield sat on a small bench, lounging comfortably in a multi-hued tunic and a long black coat. He was surrounded by a half-dozen of his usual crowd, dressed less extravagantly than at the ball but, by my own aesthetic, still in attire inappropriate to the business before us. They were enjoying themselves thoroughly, cavorting for the benefit of their captain, who smirked but didn't laugh.

Across the way the atmosphere was quite different. The Blade's opponent was alone save for his second, and the pair showed little in the way of gaiety. The duelist sat on the bench, staring off into the distance, his eyes unfocused but hard. He was more middle-aged than young, not old but too old to be involved in this kind of nonsense. His man stood next to him, the bulge of his paunch stretching his overcoat, hands frittering nervously.

I never did find out what they were fighting over. Some fracture in etiquette, the kind of nebulous bullshit the upper classes love to spill red over. I suspected it was Beaconfield's fault – people like to display what makes them exceptional, and the Smiling Blade's forte rested on his hip.

The duke noticed me and gave a little half-wave. Did he do this so often that he could work it in as an exclamation point to our own engagement? Sick motherfucker.

Out of the corner of my eye I saw Beaconfield's butler detach himself from the crowd. 'Do you have the merchandise?' he asked, by way of greeting.

'I didn't walk this far for my health,' I said, handing him a nondescript package containing a few ochres worth of dream smoke and pixie's breath.

He slipped it into his waistband, then handed me a pouch that felt heavier than it ought to. Nobles love to throw money around, though if Mairi was right Beaconfield didn't have it to lose. Tuckett seemed to think I was going to say something further. When he realized I wasn't he said, 'I hope you appreciate what a privilege this is. You've been invited to witness an extraordinary spectacle.'

'I hate to break this to you, Tuckett – but death isn't that rare an occurrence. Nor murder, leastways not where I come from.'

He sniffed and walked back to the crowd. I rolled a smoke and watched snowflakes melt on my coat. A few minutes passed. The judge stepped to the center of the grounds and waved for the two seconds, who approached the battlegrounds.

'I speak for Mr Wilkes,' said the fat man, his voice steady enough not to embarrass him.

The Blade's adjunct was not as bad as he might have been. To the best of my knowledge the *code duello* doesn't require participants to curl their hair, but at least he walked out instead of sauntering. 'I speak for Duke Rojar Calabbra the Third, the Lord Beaconfield.'

Wilkes's second spoke again, sweating despite the cold. 'Can there be no resolution between the two gentlemen? My party, for his part, is willing to make an admission that his information was gained second-hand, and does not amount to an exact transcription of the conversation.'

I couldn't entirely decipher the legalese, but that seemed like a step towards reconciliation.

Beaconfield's second responded haughtily. 'My party is satisfied with nothing less than a complete retraction, and an apology presented in a public forum.'

Apparently it wasn't.

The fat man looked back at Wilkes, his eyes pleading and his face very pale. Wilkes didn't look at him but jerked his head once in the negative. The fat man closed his eyes and swallowed hard before speaking. 'Then the issue must proceed forward.'

The judge spoke again. 'Gentlemen are to approach me with their weapons drawn but lowered. Combat is to continue until forfeiture or first blood.'

The Blade managed to extract himself from his mass of brightly colored partisans and moved towards the field. Wilkes pushed himself up from the bench and did the same. They met a few yards from each other. Beaconfield smirked, as was his wont. Wilkes's face was impassive. Against my better judgment I found I was pulling for him.

'On my signal,' the judge said, stepping off the green. Wilkes snapped his blade to the ready. Beaconfield held the point of his weapon arrogantly off to the side.

'Begin.'

I learned early on that She Who Waits Behind All Things was an indiscriminate mistress, when the plague took broken old men and well-born youths without distinction. The War reinforced the lesson, years watching thick Dren pikemen and Asher sword-slaves die from well-placed artillery shells disabusing any lingering illusions as to the inviolability of flesh. No one is immortal. No one is so good that they can't lose it to a rank amateur if the light is wrong or their foot gets caught in a divot. A couple hundred pounds of meat, a frame of bone that isn't nearly so sturdy as it seems – we were not built for immortality.

That being said, I never saw anyone like Beaconfield. Not before and not since. He was faster than I thought a person could be, fast like a bolt from the ether. He fought with a heavy blade, something mid-way between a rapier and a long sword, but he wielded it like a razor. His technique and composure were astonishing. No movement was wasted, no drop of energy exhausted unnecessarily.

Wilkes was good, very good, and not just in the archaic and formalized style of the duel. He had killed men before, maybe in the War, maybe in one of these little tête-à-têtes the rich engage in rather than do any honest work, but he was no stranger to the spilling of blood. I wondered if I could take him and thought maybe, if I got a little lucky or if my style surprised him.

Regardless, he was absolutely outclassed, embarrassingly so. Watching the Blade play with him I wondered what in the name of Maletus could have convinced this poor bastard to draw steel with Beaconfield, what absurd point of honor could have necessitated so foolish a gesture.

In the midst of the mêlée the Blade's eyes flashed up and locked on mine, a flourish that would have seen anyone else dead. Sensing an opening, Wilkes threw everything into his attack, surging forward, the tip of his weapon searching for flesh. The Blade deflected his opponent's blows, parrying each thrust and cut by some preternatural instinct.

Then one eyelid winked shut and Beaconfield struck, a flash so quick that I couldn't follow it, and Wilkes had a hole in his chest, one he stared at awkwardly before dropping his weapon and sinking to the ground.

I will admit I'd wondered, in an off moment here and there since I'd met him, about the extent to which the Smiling Blade's reputation rested on rumor and hearsay. I wouldn't waste any more time. It's an important thing to know your limitations, not to be blinded by pride or optimism as to what you're capable of. I'd never be pretty. I'd never out-wrestle Adolphus, or beat a drum better than Yancey. I'd never get comeback on the Old Man, never be the kind of rich that lets you start your life over, never find a way out of Low Town.

And I would never, ever, be able to take the Lord Beaconfield in a fair fight. To draw a weapon against that man was suicide, as sure as swallowing widow's milk.

Wilkes had gotten what he'd asked for I supposed – it doesn't do to go around antagonizing people with 'blade' in their nick-names. Still, the small crowd seemed unenthusiastic about the outcome. Beaconfield's *coup de grâce* had been bad form. It's one thing for a combatant to die of septum from a gut wound, and another to be laid out deliberately with a killing stroke. There was a code of conduct about these things – first blood usually isn't last as well. The Blade's men offered the appropriate obeisance of course, ruffled cuffs clapping against each other, but the rest of the gathering was in no great hurry to laud the victor. A medic rushed onto the field, followed closely by Wilkes's second, but they couldn't have had much hope and if they did it was soon dashed. I could tell that wound was mortal at fifty paces.

The Blade had returned to his perch on the wooden bench, surrounded by his entourage of courtiers, fawning over themselves in congratulations at his ritualized slaughter. His shirt was unbuttoned below his neck and snowflakes were gathering in his dark hair. Apart from a lively flush there was little enough to show he'd been in an athletic contest of any kind – the bastard hadn't even broken a sweat. He was laughing at something I couldn't quite make out as I approached.

I greeted him with a bow. 'May I say it was a pleasure to see my lord demonstrate his skills in the service of such a noble endeavor.'

He sneered slightly, and I was struck by how different he was in front of his lackeys. 'I'm glad you had the opportunity to witness it. When you didn't respond to my invitation, I wasn't certain you'd be coming.'

'I remain my lord's servant, in this as in all things.'

The sycophants took that as the obsequiousness due their leader, but the duke knew me well enough to appreciate the sarcasm. He rose and brushed off the parasites surrounding him. 'Walk with me.'

I did as he directed, falling in beside him on a narrow stone path that radiated out from the fountain. The white sky shed light but no heat through the bare branches of the trees. The snow was coming down harder now, and would only get worse.

Beaconfield kept quiet until we were out of earshot of the rest of the assemblage, then pulled up in front of me. 'I've considered our last discussion.'

'It flatters me to know I have a place in my lord's thoughts.'

'Your words disturbed me.'

'Oh?'

'And more so your actions against me in the interim.'

'And what alterations to my behavior would satisfy my lord?'

'Cut the shit – I don't find it amusing,' he said, coming on strong, swaggering like a cock now that he had a homicide under his belt. 'Stop your investigation. Tell your superiors whatever they need to hear to get them off my back – I'll make it worth your while. I have influence throughout the court, and I have money.'

'No, you haven't.'

His face, bright red from his earlier exercise, blanched, and he answered awkwardly, less practiced with his tongue than his weapon. 'I've got other ways to settle my debts.'

'You waste a lot of vowels,' I said. 'For a man holding trumps.'

He smiled a little, and I was reminded that there was something about him that didn't quite fit the archetype he sometimes chose to embody. 'I responded in haste.' He swallowed hard, humility an unfamiliar taste in his mouth. 'I've made some poor decisions, but I won't let Black House use them to destroy me. It hasn't gone too far – it's not too late for forgiveness.'

I thought about Tara's fractured body, and Crispin lying in

the Low Town muck, and I disagreed. 'I told you last time, Beaconfield – there's no such thing.'

'That makes me unhappy,' he said, drawing himself up imperiously. 'And you've had ample evidence of what happens to those who earn my displeasure.'

As if I had forgotten the part of the morning where he'd murdered a man for my benefit. 'You're aptly named – but I won't dress up for it, nor set a convenient time to be slaughtered. I didn't make my reputation stabbing noblemen on shaped grass. I made it in the dark, in the streets, without a crew of courtiers clapping their support, or a rulebook to let me know procedure.' I bared my teeth in a bitter smile, happy to dispense with the dissimulation, happy to finally lay my simmering hatred of this monstrous fop on the table. 'You come at me you best start thinking crooked – and you best put your affairs in order.' I turned on my heel, not wanting to give him the chance for a last word.

He took it anyway. 'Greet Wilkes when you see him!'

You'll meet him first, you son of a bitch, I thought, heading east back to the city. You'll meet him first.

33

I was hustling through Alledtown when I caught the flicker of Wren's hideous woolen coat as he ducked behind an apple cart. I wondered if he'd been waiting for me outside the gardens, but dismissed it as unlikely. He must have been shadowing me since I'd left the Earl, all the way from Low Town, through the greenery and now back into the city. That wasn't an easy thing to do – I might have said impossible, if you'd asked me prior to him doing it.

After I was done swallowing my surprise I just got angry, real fucking pissed, the thought of that fool child dogging my footsteps with Crowley, Beaconfield, and Śakra only knew who else doing their concerted best to end my existence near enough to send me apoplectic.

I hooked down a side street, following it around the back exit of a dive bar. Then I faded behind some packing crates and put my back to the stone, pulling the lapels of my coat up over the bottom half of my face and letting the shadows cover the rest.

Wren must have figured me oblivious by that point, and he stalked around the turn with less care than he should have. Before he thought to check the alcove I'd jacked him up, pinning his arms against his head and lifting him above the ground.

He cursed a blue streak and flailed madly, fighting to gain some leverage, but he was still just a pup. I gave him a good shake and tightened my grip until he started to go limp. Then I dropped him ass-first into the mud.

He scrambled to his feet, apple-sized fists guarding his face, fire in his eyes. I'd have to tell Adolphus that his afternoons spent teaching the boy boxing hadn't gone to waste.

'This is how you make yourself useful? Ignoring my orders any time it suits you?'

'I'm tired of being your fucking errand boy!' he screamed at me. All I do is tend bar and run messages! So I came after you, what's the harm?'

'The harm?' I feinted to his gut, then sent the heel of my off hand against his brow. He stumbled backwards, trying to keep his balance. 'Yesterday afternoon some dangerous men made a credible effort to kill me. What if they'd come back and noticed you following me? You think you're too young to have a man open up your insides?'

'I've made it this long,' he said, all pride and steel.

My composure cracked, and my rage spilled out in a torrent. I battered aside his guard and threw him up against the alley wall, forcing my forearm into his sternum. 'You survived this long because you're garbage, lower than a fucking rat, not worth the effort to down. Raise your head up above the gutter and see how quick they come after you, knives sharpened for the pink of your throat!'

I realized I'd shouted these last words an inch from his face, and that my lesson was likely to do the boy permanent injury if I didn't cut it short. I let my elbow off his chest and he dropped to the ground, and this time he stayed there.

'You gotta be smarter than you are, do you understand? There are lines of smart Low Town boys lying in unmarked graves.

You've gotta be smarter than that, smart all the time, smart every minute of the day. If you were the son of a cotton merchant it wouldn't matter, you could afford your youth. But you aren't, you're ghetto trash, and don't ever forget it – because Śakra knows they won't.'

He was still angry but he was listening. I rubbed sleet out of my hair, water melting against my brow and running down my cheeks. Then I extended a hand and helped him back to his feet.

'What did you see?' I asked, surprised at how quickly my temper had cooled, surprised that it had run so warm a moment earlier.

He seemed as willing as I was to return to the calm back and forth we'd perfected. 'I saw one noble kill another, and I saw you walk off with him. That was the Blade, right?'

'Yeah.'

'What did he say to you?'

'He suggested it was unlikely I would die in my sleep.'

Wren sneered at that, still convinced I was invincible. 'What did you tell him?'

'I told him folk queue to put me down, and if he doesn't step up he might find himself late to the party.' He smiled, and despite what I'd said earlier I was glad I left him his illusions, maybe even a little proud that he thought so well of me. 'Where does Adolphus think you are?'

'I told him you sent me round to Yancey's, that you wanted to get something else on Beaconfield.'

'Try not to lie to them.'

'I'll try,' he said.

The snowfall was getting worse, and standing around like this I was starting to shiver. 'If I let you trail along for a while, you promise to head back to the Earl when I tell you?'

'I promise.'

'And is your word any good?'

He narrowed his eyes, then gave a quick up-and-down with his chin.

'All right then.' I set off down the alley, and after a moment he caught up with me.

'Where are we going?'

'I need to see the scryer.'

'Why?'

'Now would be the part of the morning where you walk next to me in silence.'

We reached the Box thirty minutes later, and when I told the boy to wait outside he nodded and stretched against the wall. Happily the Islander who let me in last time was manning the door, and despite his age he was sharp enough to recognize me, and decent enough to let me in unaccompanied.

Marieke was bent double at her desk when I entered, raking over a weathered, leather tome with an intensity that would have frightened a syndicate heavy. I slammed the door shut and she whirled her head around, preparing to excoriate whatever poor bastard was foolish enough to intrude upon her work. When she saw it was me she breathed out slowly, a little bit of her seemingly inexhaustible anger draining away with it.

'You're back,' she said, careful to make sure she didn't sound happy about it. 'Guiscard stopped by earlier. I figured you would have come with him.'

'We had a falling out. I needed my freedom, and he's a one man sort of gal.'

'Do you think that was funny?'

'Give me a few minutes and we can try again.' On the slab in the center of the room a shroud covered a body about the size of a child. Beneath it Avraham lay in permanent repose, soon to be set beneath the ground. For him there would be no grand funeral, no public outpouring of grief, and the weather being what it was I doubted the High Priest would manage the trip from his chapel to the plot of land near the sea where the Islanders buried their people. Low Town had enjoyed the autumnal pathos, a moment of communal mourning amid the vibrant foliage, but with the mercury falling no one was in any great hurry to leave their houses just to pay sympathy to the family of a little black boy. And anyway, at the rate children were disappearing from Low Town the whole thing had lost its novelty.

'I assume you didn't have any more luck reading this one than you did his predecessor?'

She shook her head. 'I've tried every trick in the book, worked through every ritual, meditated over every scrap of evidence, but—'

'Nothing,' I finished, and for once she didn't seem to mind being interrupted.

'You come up with anything solid on your end?'

'No.'

'You keep talking like this and I'm never gonna get a word in edgewise.'

'Yeah.' Thus far our conversation had been within a stone's throw of pleasant – I could almost fool myself into thinking the scryer had taken a shine to me.

'Does the Bureau of Magical Affairs know about the talisman you've got sewn into your shoulder?' she asked.

'Of course. I make a point of telling the government every time I do something illegal.'

The beginnings of a smile worked themselves through Marieke's growl, but she snapped its neck before it could mature. 'Who put it there?'

'I can't remember. I'm high a lot.'

She set her hands against the desk behind her and arched her spine backwards, a startlingly uninhibited display given her almost pathological self-consciousness, the rough equivalent in a normally functioning human of dropping her drawers and taking a shit on the floor. 'Fine, don't tell me.'

That was my preference anyway. 'If I slipped off this covering and checked the boy for spots,' I asked, 'would I find any?'

She gave a conspiratorial glance around, unnecessary, given that we were in an enclosed room, but understandable all the same. 'Yes,' she said. 'You would.'

It was what I expected, but that didn't make it any easier to swallow. The Blade had done another child, taken him from beneath my nose, hidden him somewhere in the catacombs beneath his mansion, drained his life and left him face down in the river. And as if somehow these blasphemies were insufficient, he'd infected the boy with the plague, weakened the wards that protected the city from its return – all because he couldn't stand the thought of honest labor, or forgoing a few exotic debaucheries.

'If you took off the sheet and saw the rash,' she responded, 'would you have any idea why it was there?'

'I'm looking,' I said, though my effort would mean little enough if the city again found itself awash in Red Fever.

Her eyes, normally as bright as the unclouded sky, fogged up. Uncertainty was a guise Marieke wore infrequently, and with more than her usual discomfort. 'Right now, you're the only one who knows. I don't trust Black House, and I didn't want to start a panic. But if there's another . . .'

'I understand,' I said. After a moment I asked the obvious question. 'Why tell me?'

'I flashed something off you the first time we met, who you are and where you're going. Something that told me I ought to let you in on it.'

That would explain the fit. That would explain, for that matter, why someone so congenitally incapable of kindness would even take the time to speak with me.

'Don't you want to know what I saw?' she asked. 'Everyone always wants to know what's ahead of them.'

'People are fools. You don't need a prophet to tell you the future. Look at yesterday, then look at today. Tomorrow is likely to be the same, and the day after that.'

It was time to leave. Wren was outside in the cold, and I had a ways left to go before I'd earn my day's rest. I took a long look at Avraham. He'd be the last, I told myself, one way or another.

Marieke interrupted my thoughts. 'Did you survive it, the first time?'

'No, it killed me. Can't you tell?'

She blushed a little, and rushed forward. 'I meant did you . . .'

'I know what you meant,' I said. 'And yeah, I survived it.'

'What was it like?'

People asked me that sometimes, if they knew I'd been in Low Town during the worst of it. 'Tell me about the plague', like it was some piece of neighborhood gossip, or the outcome of a prize fight. And what could you tell them, and what did they want to hear?

Tell them about the first days, when it didn't look to be any worse than every other summer – one or two from a block, the old and the very young. How the sick marks on the houses began to grow, to spawn and multiply till there was scarcely a shack or tenement that didn't have an 'X' scrawled on its front door. About the government men who came to burn them, that sometimes they weren't so careful to make sure everyone inside was dead, or to contain the flames.

Tell them about the second night after they put Momma and Papa on the wagons, when the neighbors ransacked our house, just walked in, not happy about it but not ashamed either, leaving with the few argents my father had managed to save, giving me a blow to the face when I tried to stop them. The same neighbors we borrowed sugar from, and sang hymns with at Midwinter. And who could blame them really, because nothing anyone did mattered any more.

Tell them about the cordons around Low Town, the fat-faced guards who gorged themselves on bribes but didn't let a single poor bastard out, 'cause as far as they were concerned we were scum, best kept from decent folk by the head of a pike. That I kept my eyes open for years and years afterward looking to even up the score, that I keep my eyes open today.

Tell them about Henni's face when I came back without food the third day in a row, not angry, not sad even, just resigned – my poor little sister putting her hand on my shoulder and telling me it would be all right, that I'd have better luck tomorrow, and her voice so sweet and her face so thin that it broke your heart, just broke your fucking heart.

I guess I could have told her a lot of things.

'It wasn't no big deal,' I said, and for once Marieke had the good sense to keep her damn-fool mouth shut.

And by that point it was time to leave, leave before I did something I shouldn't, and I gave Marieke a last quick nod, and I guess I looked hot because she tried to offer some sort of apology – a powerful show of contrition by her lights – but I ignored it and headed into the cold and sent Wren home with a curt dismissal. And even though I was too near downtown for it to be safe I jammed a vial of breath beneath my nose and pulled from it until my head was so filled with the buzz that there wasn't room for much else, and I leaned myself against a wall until I felt steady enough to start the long walk home.

34

I holed up at the Earl for a few hours, drinking coffee with cinnamon while the storm buried the city under a solid layer of white. Towards the end of the afternoon I smoked a joint of dreamvine and watched Adolphus and Wren build a snow fort based upon what was, in my estimation, a lack of sound architectural principles. My concerns proved valid when a portion of the east wall collapsed, offering a decisive avenue of entry for an invading force.

They were enjoying themselves. I was having more trouble getting into the spirit of the season. The way I figured it there was at least one group of people trying to kill me, and possibly as many as three. Beyond that, the certainty of the Old Man's deadline loomed omnipresent, a hum settled an inch behind my eyes. I couldn't stop running over the math – seven days minus three days is four days, seven minus three days is four days, four days, four days.

Worse came to worst I could flee the city. I had made contingencies in case of similar circumstances, lives I had set up in remote regions that I could wrap myself up in and never return. But with the Old Man involved I couldn't be certain any of them would last – nowhere in Rigus would be deep enough if he put his mind to smoking me out. I might have to flip, offer what I could to Nestria or the Free Cities and have them settle me in some distant province. I still knew where enough dirt was buried to be of interest to someone, I hoped. But that would mean I'd have to make provisions for Adolphus and Adeline – and Wren now too. I couldn't leave them to catch my heat.

Deal with that when it comes, I told myself and started going over it all again, hoping to catch something different this time. I laid out the pieces in my head, one at a time, running over how Beaconfield had gone from a dilettante to a mass murderer.

He wakes up one day and realizes he doesn't have enough ready coin to shortchange his tailor, and starts thinking of a way to rectify the situation. Probably Brightfellow wasn't his first option, probably he'd had a few false starts. At some point he gets in touch with the sorcerer, and the two start talking. He wasn't always a hack, doing chicanery for the upper crusts – he was a real practitioner, and he might have a way out, a happy ending on tap, so long as the duke isn't squeamish about the means. The duke is not. They contract out Tara to a Kiren, some acquaintance of Brightfellow's, but they pick wrong, their man botches the job and they have to kill him before he can be followed up the chain. They put the operation on pause for a few months and retool – no more freelance work, all the kidnappings are to be done in-house. First Caristiona goes, than Avraham, stolen and sacrificed, then dumped where their bodies couldn't be traced.

It was thin, damn thin. I had motive and means, but no more. What connected the children? Why had the last two been infected with the plague? Too many questions, and little in the way of concrete evidence. Brightfellow's name on a slip of paper that I didn't even have any more, lost during my tumble in the canal. A few threats during a conversation that the Blade would deny having. I knew Beaconfield was guilty, but a hunch wouldn't be good enough for the Old Man, and moving on the duke wouldn't do me any good if I couldn't square myself with Black House.

Now I wished I had taken the opportunity to pump more out of the Blade during our last conversation, rather than use it to score points. The Old Man used to give me shit about it, back during my stint under his tutelage – that I couldn't quite control my temper. He said that was why I'd never be as good as him, because I let the hatred get through my teeth. He was a sick motherfucker, but he was probably right.

I needed to speak to Guiscard, needed to find Afonso Cadamost, needed to figure out what I was up against. I wasn't too concerned about the men Beaconfield could muster, but what about Brightfellow and his blasphemous pet? Could it be targeted on me? From what distance? How could I defend myself against it, and, most critically, how the hell did I kill it?

These were all questions I wished I had answered before declaring open warfare on the Smiling Blade.

I was sitting in front of the fire, reading from Elliot's *History of the Third Isocrotan Campaign* when a messenger boy entered, dressed in a heavy coat and calling my name. I waved him over and he handed me his letter.

'Bad out there?' I asked.

'Getting worse.'

'It usually is.' I tossed him an argent as tip – I figured I probably wouldn't need it to buttress my retirement fund. He nearly pumped my arm out of my socket thanking me.

The envelope was made of fine pink parchment, with a stylized capital 'M' on the back flap.

> *I found our first conversation so captivating that I endeavored to undertake what actions I needed to tempt you to a second. Suffice to say, I have acquired further information that may be of interest to you. Shall you return to my abode, say, eleven?*
>
> *Impatiently awaiting your arrival,*
> *Mairi*

I read it over twice more, then consigned it to the flames, watching the rose-colored vellum curl up and dissipate with a quick pop. Apparently Mairi thought whatever she had to tell me would go better after hours. I returned to Elliot and the foolishness of great men.

The crowd at the Earl stayed small for most of the night, the storm heavy enough to keep out even the neighborhood traffic. I took my usual from Adolphus's tap, eating away the time, trying not to think of Mairi's tan flesh and dark eyes, my success mixed at best.

I headed out around ten, making sure Adeline and the boy were in the back room. Two minutes under the falling sleet and I was certain that this was a mistake. I was no youth to go tramping through the snow at the whiff of quim; whatever Mairi had to tell me could wait till morning. But having begun I was too stubborn to turn back, though the weather was so awful I resolved to cut straight through Brennock, rather than follow the canal north.

I was halfway there when I heard them, easy enough as they made no attempt at stealth. Probably they figured their numbers were sufficient advantage, though more experience might have taught them never to offer up succor to the enemy, however certain the contest may seem.

Apart from their childlike exuberance they had set the ambush quite professionally. By the time the pair behind me had drawn my attention their comrades had already circled around to my front. A quick glance was enough to let me know I wasn't being jumped by a gang of street toughs braving the cold – beneath their thick black cloaks I caught flashes of bright cashmere. Each of them wore a half-mask the same color as their capes, masquerade style, fashioned to cover the lower half of the face with that of a wild animal.

I hadn't been paying much attention because of the snow, thinking that and the irregularity of my hours would be sufficient protection. Was the invitation fake, I wondered now, ginned up by the Blade to lure me out of hiding? It hadn't looked like it, nor did it strain credulity to think of Mairi and her cool black eyes turning around and selling me off the moment her door had slammed shut.

I filed that in the growing stack of things I would think about if I survived the next five minutes and ducked into an alleyway, sprinting through the treacherous frost. Behind me I could hear them whooping, hounds running a quarry to ground. The buildings in the area were all garment factories in the new style, long rows of laborers at unforgiving machines, closed since last year's trade war with Nestria. Out of the corner of my eye I saw a side entrance to one of them and threw my shoulder into it, smashing through whatever rotted lock had been holding it shut.

I entered a cavernous structure a good hundred yards across, broken windows offering enough light to navigate the huge sewing contraptions decaying in the interior. Against the back wall I saw a steep metal staircase and above it a pair of long-abandoned offices, and I sprinted up the steps. The gangway led towards a second stairwell and another locked door, the latter proving no greater impediment than its brother below.

I scrambled forward onto a flat roof, the wood warped and treacherous. The cityscape spread out ahead of me, a panorama of civic rot broken up by the huge industrial smokestack that crowned the factory. My subterfuge had gained me only a few seconds, and I drew my blade to deal with the one coming up behind me.

His mask was carved into a narrow beak, like a finch's, and he was laughing, laughing and drawing his blade, a thin fencer's épée that looked more like a child's toy than the means to commit murder. He started to say something but I didn't have time for pleasantries and I closed quickly, hoping to put him down and continue my escape.

He was fast, and younger than me by a good ten years, but a lifetime of fencing was poor preparation for the business at hand. The powdery snow fouled up his footwork, and his style, honed in less lethal circumstances, bespoke the natural tendency towards offense one adopts when the worst a miscalculation promises is the loss of a match. I'd have him in a moment.

But I didn't have a moment. I could hear his compatriots on the stairwell and I knew if I didn't finish him quickly I'd learn how difficult breathing becomes with a foot of steel in your innards. After his next pass I feigned a stumble, dropping forward on one knee, hoping he'd take the bait.

The thought of tagging me proved irresistible, and he pushed forward for a killing stroke. I ducked lower, so low my face was nearly touching the roof and his rapier passed over my shoulder harmlessly. Bracing my left arm against the frozen wood I surged upward, swiping with my trench blade and cleaving his arm at mid-joint. He shrieked and I spent a quick quarter-second in astonishment at the high pitch of his voice before my follow-up severed his neck to the spine. Conscious of the men close behind, I sprinted over his corpse and made my way forward.

I climbed the cast-iron ladder ten feet to the top of the chimney. Reaching the summit, I sprang to my feet and looked down at my pursuers, the thought occurring to me that if any of them had brought a crossbow I was as good as dead. None had. Two stood staring back at me, swords clutched tightly in their hands, while the third checked on his dead friend. I laughed, filled with the exhilaration that accompanies violence. 'Blue blood spills like any other!' I shouted, my trench blade dripping ichor. 'Come get me if you've got the stones!'

I took three quick steps and leapt into the air, bracing myself as I smashed through the glass panes of the adjacent office building. I tumbled as I fell, awkwardly and not without injury. Stumbling to my feet, I rushed into the room beyond and took up position in the black interior, hoping my pursuers were foolish enough to follow the way I had come.

A half-minute went by, and then I heard a boyish yell and saw two of them hit the floor, their frocks apparently not proving a critical impediment to the maneuver. The jump didn't put either of my pursuers down for long. They charged after me, cognizant of the danger that hesitation posed.

I tossed a dagger at the first one through the door, aiming at his chest but throwing high, the blade burying itself in his throat – a rare dividend of incompetence. He dropped to the ground, his last few seconds painful. I wasted no time mourning his loss, and pressed on to the one behind him. Between the death of his comrade and the bad light he didn't last long. There was a moment of terror as I maneuvered him back towards the broken windows, and I put him down with a flurry of blows.

I stood at the edge and thought about going over, dropping the two stories and heading out into the night, but I wasn't sure if my ankle could take another fall. And truth be told, I wanted the last one, wanted to see his face as he realized I'd done for the other two, wanted to put my hands on someone after days of running around in the dark.

So I sprinted down the second-floor landing, just in time to see him break through the front door. Somewhere along the line he had dropped his cowl, but he retained the jet-black muzzle that obscured his identity. He was larger than his comrades, and in place of the thin dueling blades they had sported he held a long saber with a thick bronze hand-guard.

I reached into my boot for my second throwing dagger. Gone – it must have fallen out at some point during the scuffle. I hefted the trench blade backhanded, the blunt side against my forearm. We'd do this old-fashioned. The two of us circled warily, getting a sense of each other, then he feigned a blow to my chest and I lost myself in the clash of steel on steel.

He was good, and his weapon was well suited to dealing with the thick edge of my own. The pain in my ankle wasn't making things any easier, and I found myself struggling to maintain the pace. I needed to do something to alter the odds – when it comes to lethal engagements, three and one isn't much of a record.

We locked swords and I forced myself against him, then spat a thick wad of phlegm into his face. He had sufficient where-withal not to wipe it away but I could see it rattled him.

I moved back a few steps. 'Were those your friends I killed?'

He didn't answer, closing the distance I'd put between us and making me uncomfortably aware of how little space there was to maneuver. I made a quick play for his head but he deflected it without difficulty and launched a riposte that nearly took off my own. By the Firstborn he was fast. I couldn't keep this up much longer.

'I bet they were. Schoolyard chums, I bet.'

We engaged again, and again I came off the worse for it, a cut across my off arm indicating his advantage in speed. I continued my provocation, doing my best to seem unconcerned by the wound. 'Make sure you don't forget the first one's hand when you bury him, else he spends eternity a cripple.'

The smell of blood fired his temper and he came at me with a roar. I slipped my off hand into my pocket and gripped the spiked knuckles, barely parrying a wild, two-handed stroke that would have caved in my skull had it connected. While he was off balance I struck twice, landing a pair of hooks to his body, each blow leaving my fist wet with blood. One hand dropped to his side, and I gave him a firm shot across his jaw, the blow driving through his mask and into the flesh beneath. He screamed, the sound wheezing through shattered teeth and mutilated tissue, and I followed it up with a blow from my trench blade that sent a chunk of bone whistling from his chest. He screamed again and collapsed.

Their clothing and weapons were evidence enough, but if I needed more proof of Beaconfield's involvement I had it. With his face uncovered I recognized the man dying at my feet as the Blade's second from earlier that morning.

I crouched beside him, drops of his blood falling off my weapon. 'Why is the Blade killing children?'

He shook his head and coughed out a response. 'Fuck you.'

'Answer my questions and I'll see you get bandaged up. Otherwise I gotta go at you ugly.'

'Bullshit.' The word was four syllables, broken by his labored panting. 'I won't die a punk.'

He was right of course – there was no way I could get him to a doctor before his body lost the spirit. Couldn't cut him for the same reason – and anyway, I didn't think I had it in me to torture someone just then.

'I can make it quick for you.'

It was a struggle for him to nod his head. 'Do it.'

A trench blade isn't built for thrusting, but it would do. I slipped the point through his chest. He gasped and brought his hands up around it reflexively, cutting his palms on the metal. Then he was gone. I wrenched the weapon out of his ribcage and got to my feet.

I hadn't killed a man in three years. Hurt plenty, sure, but Harelip and his ilk were still above ground, or if they weren't it wasn't because of me.

Bad business all around.

I had underestimated the Blade – he had moved quickly and surely, and if his approach lacked subtlety it had very nearly made up for it with brutal efficacy. But then he'd underestimated me too, as the scattered corpses of his companions could attest. I doubted Beaconfield could muster another attack, but it still seemed imprudent to head back to the Earl. I'd stop by one of the apartments I kept scattered about the city and check back in tomorrow.

With the flush of combat fading my body began to remember its injuries, my ankle sore from where I had landed on it, and the wound on my arm starting to ache unpleasantly. I wiped my blade with a spare rag and moved to leave. Brennock was a manufacturing center, and I thought it unlikely anyone had heard the screams, but I didn't care to wait around to see my suspicions confirmed. Slipping through the broken front door out into the night, I discovered the snow had picked up again, heavier than before, and I headed into it, knowing whatever tracks I left would soon be covered by the storm.

35

I woke the next morning in a single-room apartment in the
shadier section of Offbend to discover that the cut running
across my bicep had turned into a nasty colored thing,
bright and livid. I put on my clothes and coat, trying to avoid
contact with the wound as I did so. Walking out, I banged my
shoulder against the wall of the flophouse and had to stop myself
from screaming.

I couldn't go back to the Earl like this – they'd be cutting off
my arm in half a day. And I didn't want to alarm Celia any
worse than I already had, so the Aerie was out too. Instead I
headed south towards the harbor and a street doctor I knew, an
aged Kiren woman who sewed up injuries in the back of a dress
shop. She couldn't speak a word of Rigun, and her dialect of
heretic was sufficiently unrelated to mine as to make dialogue
effectively impossible, but despite that and her irascible temper
she was as good a battle medic as you could ask for, quick,
practiced and discreet.

The evening's snowfall had ceased, although it seemed to have continued through most of the night and would likely pick up again in an hour or two. In the interlude, however, it felt like the whole city was out on the streets, the thoroughfares packed with lovers walking arm in arm, and children celebrating the approaching festivities. These manifestations of the season started to die off as I made it to Kirentown, whose inhabitants were uninterested in the upcoming holiday, assuming they were even aware of it.

I turned down a nondescript side street, hoping the ache in my chest didn't signal a fever. The alley was organized according to the commercial instincts of the heretics, a dozen shops sub-dividing the hundred-yard stretch of street, each announcing their wares with brightly colored signs covered with Kiren characters and pidgin Rigun. I stepped into one midway down the alley, distinguished only by its curiously bland bill, a small fading tablet that read simply 'DRESS'.

Inside sat a frowning grandmother, ancient as stone, the sort of antediluvian creature whose youth seemed even theor-etically impossible, as if she had sprung from the womb wizened and oak-tree old. She was surrounded on all sides by bolts of colored cloth and bright ribbons, strewn about without regard for organization or aesthetic. Anyone foolish enough to enter in the hopes of purchasing the advertised merchandise would find themselves quickly disabused by the state of disrepair, but then the old bitch made more than enough with her illicit dealings to forgo the troublesome sideline of legitimate mercantilism.

The proprietress waved me to the back room without comment. It was tiny and dirty, with a swivel stool in the center. The walls were occupied by shelves of medical supplies, poultices, drafts and alchemical ingredients of all kinds. Most of these were almost certainly useless, but then medicine is half illusion anyway, and two-thirds among the heretics.

I sat down on the chair and began to disrobe, the dowager looking on unhappily. Once my shirt was off she took hold of my arm, not roughly but with less tenderness than I'd have preferred given the agony shooting through my left side. She inspected my injury and chattered away in her foreign tongue, the words indecipherable but astringent.

'What do you want from me? You're right, I should have seen it coming – Beaconfield as much as warned me. I figured he'd need longer to man himself into it.'

She started pulling jars from her shelves, inspecting and re-inspecting the unlabeled bottles in a fashion that did not do wonders for my confidence. She settled on one and poured the contents into a strange-looking kettle, then set that on the iron furnace pumping heat from the corner of the room. We waited for it to boil, time the matron spent glowering at me and muttering incomprehensible pejoratives. She pulled out a small vial from a fold of her robes and shook it enticingly.

'I probably shouldn't – I have a pretty firm no opiates before brunch rule.'

She pushed it at me again, insisting in her sing-song.

I sighed and waved her forward. 'It's on your conscience.'

She pulled a tiny dropper out of the vial and placed a bead on my tongue. It tasted acrid and unpleasant. The drug went back into her pocket, replaced by a small blade which she cleaned with a length of cloth.

My vision was spinning and it was hard to concentrate. She pointed to my arm. I tried to think of something witty but couldn't come up with anything good. 'Do it,' I said.

With one firm hand she pushed my shoulder back against the chair and dragged her blade quickly against the abscess that had formed over where the Blade's man had tagged me. I bit my tongue till I tasted blood.

Grandma moved on to the next part of her work without offering much in the way of sympathy. While she was puttering about in the corner I made the poor decision to inspect the now reopened wound, with predictable effects on my digestive tract. Seeing me turn green she dashed over and smacked me once across the cheek, pointing her finger in my face and letting forth with a stream of invective. I twisted my head away from the laceration, and she returned to the stove and poured the contents of the now steaming kettle into a small clay cup.

She moved back towards the chair, and the look in her eyes was enough to let me know what was coming wasn't going to be fun. I gripped the underside of my seat as tightly as my body would allow and nodded once, quickly. She raised the tumbler.

Then I did scream, a bright exultation of torment as she dribbled the boiling oil into my wound, the fierce heat torture against my torn muscle. I took a few deep breaths while water drained from my eyes.

'Why don't you break that vial back out?'

She ignored me, waiting for the wax to harden. After a moment she pulled out a blunt iron tool and began to scrape away the excess resin.

'You're a fucking cunt,' I said. 'Śakra's swinging cock, I hate you.'

It was impossible to imagine she hadn't picked up a smattering of obscenities during her long years of providing medical attention to criminals, but if she understood me she gave no sign. The pain receded to a dull warmth, and I sat in silence as she pulled out a needle and began sewing up my arm. Whatever was in that bottle was absolutely amazing – I was barely aware she was even there. After a few minutes she cocked her head curiously and gibbered what sounded like a question.

'I told you. The Smiling Blade did this – you should be proud. I'm not some bully boy stumbling in here 'cause he lost a knife fight. Important people are trying to kill me.'

She smirked and drew her thumb across her throat, the universal symbol for murder, evil being man's mother tongue.

'I'd love to, believe me, but you can't just sneak into the bedroom of a noble and put a razor to his windpipe.'

By that point her interest had faded and she went back to sewing shut my wound. I enjoyed a comfortable few moments basking in a static narcotic glow, so deeply anesthetized that I didn't even notice she was done until she shook my shoulder roughly, threatening to undo the work she had just completed.

I brushed her hand off and looked at her craftsmanship. It was first rate, as always. 'Thanks,' I said. 'Hopefully I won't see you again for a while.'

She muttered something that suggested she held little faith in my prophetic abilities and held up five fingers.

'Are you out of your mind! I could get an arm reattached for that!'

She narrowed her eyes at me and lowered two digits.

'That's more like it.' I set three ochre on the table, and she scooped them up and tucked them quickly into her robes. I grabbed my shirt and coat, putting them on as I walked outside. 'As always, whatever language you speak, anyone hears about this visit and you'll need to find someone better with that scalpel than you are.'

She didn't answer, but then she wouldn't. By the time the painkiller she gave me wore off I was halfway to Low Town and it had started to snow again.

36

B ack at the Earl I got to watch Adolphus try to pretend he hadn't been worrying about me. His shoulders tensed up as I came in, but then he returned to wiping the counter with little more than a grunt. I took a seat at the bar.

'Everything OK?' he asked, feigning a lack of interest.

'Fine,' I responded. 'Just out late, didn't want to walk home with the weather.'

It was clear he didn't believe me. 'These came for you while you were out.' He handed me a pair of envelopes, and waited while I tore open the seal.

The first, tight script against cream-colored paper, was from Celia.

My workings have borne fruit. You will find evidence of the Blade's crimes in a hidden chamber in the desk in his study, beneath a false bottom. Good luck.
C

Short as it was, I had to read it twice to make sure I got it right. Then I set it aside, trying to keep the smile off my face. I'd all but forgotten about the working Celia had promised to perform – those things rarely go as advertised, and never quickly enough to be of help. But if she was right, then I had a line on something real I could take to Black House. I set my mind towards Beaconfield's mansion, and the machinations that would be required to again gain entrance to it.

Wren bolted his way in from the back room, so finely attuned to the mood of the place he could tell when I'd arrived. Which was good, because there was a man I needed to make contact with, and I didn't feel like walking. 'You need to run a message for me.'

His expression remained unchanged, but I'd had enough evidence of the bear-trap quality of his memory not to need any outward displays of attention.

'Take Pritt Street east past the docks, into Alledtown but before you hit the Asher enclave.' I rattled off a street name and house number. 'Tell the woman at the entrance you need to speak to Mort the Fish – she'll let you on up. Tell Mort I need to see the Doctor. Tell him it's urgent, and tell him the Doctor will be glad he made time.'

'Don't forget your coat!' Adolphus added, although the boy was heading towards it anyway. Wren pulled it over his shoulders and set out into the snow.

'He can tell the weather,' I said after the boy was gone.

'I didn't want him to get cold.'

'Just because you got him three months ago doesn't make him three months old.'

Adolphus shrugged and tapped his finger against the remaining letter. 'The aristocrat came by earlier this morning for you. Wanted me to give you this. You got any more business with that one, try and do it outside of my bar.'

'Guiscard's not so bad.'

'I wouldn't trust him.'

'I'm not. I'm using him.' I read through the note. 'And he seems to have been of service.'

Afonso Cadamost spends most of his waking hours at a wyrm den on Tolk Street beneath the sign of a gray lantern. You were right – we are still keeping tabs on him.

Guiscard was sapling-green if he didn't know Black House kept tabs on damn near everyone. I looked back up at Adolphus. 'Are you going to get me breakfast or not?'

He rolled his eyes, but stepped into the back room and called for Adeline.

I was massacring my plate of eggs when Wren returned, his hair slick with snow and his face flushed red with enthusiasm, or perhaps the cold.

'He says OK. He says the Doctor will meet you at the Daeva's Work Pub, off Beston, in two hours.'

I nodded and went back to finishing off my sausage.

'Who's the Doctor?' Wren asked.

'You'll find out in two hours,' I said. 'Take off your coat – it's warm in here.'

He looked at me, then shrugged and headed back to the rack.

37

There are two ways to meet the best second-story man in Rigus. The first is quick and easy. Catch a shiv anywhere from Kirentown to Offbend and, if you're lucky enough not to bleed out in the street, you'll be taken to Mercy of Prachetas Hospital. Inside this somber edifice, assuming you aren't forgotten by their massive and incompetent bureaucracy, you'll be taken to an overworked medical professional who will pronounce your wound untreatable and prescribe a few drops of attaraxium to speed your ascent into the afterlife. As the light goes from your eyes, you'd likely be shocked to discover that the short, affable-looking gentleman standing over you and easing your meeting with She Who Waits Behind All Things is responsible for three of the five most lucrative heists in the history of Rigus, including the legendary theft of the Amber Pagoda, the exact details of which have never been successfully recreated.

If the first option doesn't sound square you'll have to settle for the second – putting a word into the ear of his agent, a fat-faced, unpleasant Rouender, and hoping that his client decides your job is interesting enough to warrant an interruption of his schedule.

To that end I was sitting in a small neighborhood bar on the outskirts of the Old City. I'd left Wren at a corner table in the front, not wanting to spook my prospective envoy – although the Doctor would need to have awfully weak nerves to be overcome by the sight of a hundred-and-ten-pound prepubescent.

I'd been waiting about twenty minutes when he walked in. The single most talented larcenist since the execution of Fierce Jack Free was an open-faced little Tarasaihgn, somewhat fairer of skin than most swamp dwellers, but apart from that quite utterly average. We had met a few times, under the kind of predictably clandestine circumstances that didn't encourage intimacy.

'It's been a while,' he said.

'Doctor Kendrick, a pleasure.'

He hung his coat on the hook next to our booth and sat down across from me. 'Not at all. Actually I was surprised when Mort told me who'd contacted him. I always got the impression you didn't much care for me.'

His impression was correct – I didn't like Doctor Kendrick. He was friendly enough, and his skills were beyond question, but I'd never worked with him, and would have preferred to keep that streak unbroken.

The code of the criminal is clean if not honest, based on naked self-interest and the accumulation of capital. You don't need to respect a man to work with him, or even trust him. You just need to know you're giving him the best deal. But Kendrick didn't care about money. Doctors aren't paupers, and anyway he'd made enough through his various heists to retire rich a dozen times over. He was in it for the thrill – you could see that in his eyes.

At the end of the day I didn't care how many ochres he'd stolen, or that his street name was spoken in reverential tones throughout the underworld. I didn't care that he could scale the sheer face of a rock wall, or pick a triple-rated lock while tossing back shots of corn liquor. I learned quick growing up in Low

Town that the only excuse for crime is survival. Excitement and renown are concerns one busies one's mind with on a full stomach. The Doctor was a thrill-seeker, and this wasn't a business for him, it was a game. You can't trust a man like that. He's apt to go screwy at inopportune moments.

Of course, no self-respecting professional would have come within a hundred feet of a job this half-baked – I hadn't even bothered to ring out any of the rest of my contacts. The peculiar nature of the gig limited my options.

'I don't have much need for subcontractors. Normally I prefer to handle my own business. But I have a situation that requires your unique skill set.'

'Indeed,' he said, flagging down our homely waitress and ordering a beer. I waited till she was out of earshot before continuing.

'Nor do I refer to your renowned ability with a scalpel.'

'I didn't think you called to discuss my research into the ocular cavity.'

I took a sip of ale. 'You ever do a job on short notice, without much prep work?'

He nodded, unimpressed.

'You ever work in public? Like during a dinner party?'

'Once or twice. It's not my normal style, but . . .' He shrugged. 'I've done everything.'

'You ever do both on the same job?'

'Not yet.'

The waitress returned with Kendrick's drink and tried to catch his eye, but he was having none of it. She sulked as she walked off, and I took another swig to let the Doctor's anticipation build. 'I need you to break into the Lord Beaconfield's house tomorrow night and toss his study. It'll be during his Midwinter party, so half the nobility in Rigus will be there. And I only have a passing knowledge of the topography. I can give you a general layout but that's it.'

'You mean the Smiling Blade.' He chewed at his lip to keep from grinning. 'What am I trying to steal?'

'In the desk in his study, beneath a false bottom, you'll find a secret cache. I'd like to peruse the contents.' I could see his interest was flagging, so I tossed in a few crumbs. 'It'll be trapped, I'm sure. And of course, the lock will be the best money can buy.'

'How do you know there's anything there?'

'I'm well informed.'

'An inside job, huh? Why not have your source do it?'

'Because then I wouldn't have had the pleasure of this meeting.'

'If it's trapped like you say, there'll be no way to cover up my presence. He'll see someone's rifled through his stuff, and find what's missing soon after.'

'That's fine. I'd rather he knows it's gone.'

'One of those, huh?' He worried the tip of his thumb with his teeth. 'I don't usually go in for that sort of thing.'

'It would be a favor. You ask around, you'll hear I'm a good man to do favors for.'

'That's the word.' He bit a callus off the top of his finger and spat it on the ground. 'Why during the party?'

'It has to be done soon, and the party will be the best chance.'

'There'll be a lot of people around. I could use a distraction.'

'And as it so happens,' I said, 'I've arranged one.'

The germ of a grin spread contagion-like across his face as I explained what I had planned for the Blade's Midwinter soirée. When I was done he gave the answer I'd expected.

'Sounds like fun.'

I mimicked his amity, wishing I didn't have to place my survival in the hands of this dilettante. 'What's your fee?'

He was too much the artist to enjoy discussing money. 'Usually I get cut in on a percentage, but I assume this isn't for sale.' He scratched his chin thoughtfully. 'Twenty ochre?'

Absurdly low for the job at hand, but I wasn't about to complain. 'There's one more thing I ought to tell you,' I said. 'The man you're stealing from, the things you're stealing – if you're caught, the hoax will be the least of your worries.'

'Good thing I don't get caught.'

'Good thing,' I responded, hoping he was as skilled as he was confident.

He extended his hand and stood. 'I've got to get back to the hospital – my shift starts in twenty minutes. I'll take a look at the place later on this evening. You'll hear from me the day after tomorrow.'

'Contact me if you need anything.'

'I won't.' He slipped on his coat. 'Who's that kid you're here with?'

Kor's Bellows, he was sharp. I hadn't realized I'd made any sign. 'He's sort of my ward. I was hoping if I brought him by you could give him some career advice.'

'On which one?'

'Which do you prefer?'

'Thieving,' he answered confidently.

'Maybe we'd best skip the pep-talk then.'

He laughed and strutted out.

After a moment Wren came over. 'That all for the afternoon? Weather's getting worse.'

'Not quite. I've got someone to see, and you've got another message to run. I need you to pay a visit to the Blade. Tell the guard at the front gate that I'll be attending tomorrow's party.'

'I didn't know you'd been invited.'

'Neither does the Lord Beaconfield.'

Wren waited for a follow-up, but when it didn't come he headed out. I took his lead a minute or two thereafter.

38

I was halfway to Tolk Street when I made Crowley's scarred Mirad following about a block behind me. I didn't have time for this nonsense, I needed to look in on Cadamost, see what he could tell me about Brightfellow – but then I didn't imagine Crowley would be sensitive to the complexities of my situation. Slipping the tail wasn't an option either, my ex-colleague was a tenacious motherfucker and things were getting too busy to leave any loose ends floating around.

So I decided to do something I'd been thinking about since taking a dip in the canal two days prior. Stopping abruptly to let him know I'd seen him, I took a sharp turn down a side alley and headed south towards Kirentown. I moved fast but not too fast, making sure Crowley and his boys didn't lose me in the dark. They played along, sharp enough to stay on my trail but too blunt to run me down. Fifteen minutes later I was standing beneath the standard of the Blue Dragon, and another second after that I was through the door.

The bar was crowded, and I ignored the unfriendly stares that greeted me. At the front counter the whale was chatting to a customer, but when he saw me he stopped and assumed the vacant pose he adopted whenever we did business. There wasn't time to do this with any subtlety, so I forced my way to the front.

I leaned in close, conscious of the odor wafting from his excess flesh. 'I need to see Ling Chi. Immediately.' He gave no indication that he heard me, weighing his options, keenly aware of Ling Chi's policy on lenient doormen. 'In three years, have I ever wasted the man's time?'

He nodded, and I headed through the back door and into the antechamber beyond. If the two guards inside were surprised to see me they didn't show it – whatever set-up the fat man had going to alert them was apparently both silent and effective. I tossed my weapons on the table and went through a quick pat-down before being ushered inside to see the man himself.

I still had my suspicions about the authenticity of Ling Chi's costume, but if he was putting on a show he could set it up pretty damn quick. His attire was impeccable, from the silvery-white diadem atop his head to the beauty mark that accented his maquillage. He held his hands prayer-like before his chest, the yellow gold of his false fingernails replaced with a set of green jade. 'The joy that stirs in my breast at the unanticipated arrival of my companion is almost too much for my aged heart to bear.'

I bowed low, accepting the rebuke. 'It is a blot on my honor that I am forced to intrude upon the tranquility of my mentor, one that I will work tirelessly to expunge.'

He waved away my concern, happy to begin the discussion from a position of strength. 'The worries of my beloved friend do credit to his sense of principle. But what need have we of ceremony, we who are closer than brothers? Gleefully do I order the unbarring of any gate that separates us – with all haste I command the doors of my sanctum opened to the twin of my heart.'

'Happiness beyond measure is the lot of your servant, to know that I am granted consideration by one whose word is law, and whose hand shelters his children.'

He blinked twice, the shift in his placid countenance impossible to miss. 'Shelter . . .'

'Well does my protector know that innocence is no guard against the wolf, and actions born of amity are like to destroy us.'

'The Celestial Emperor sets upon no man's back more weight than he might carry.'

'Endless may he reign,' I intoned.

'Endless may he reign.'

'Great men stand before the ocean and command the very waves, while we small folk struggle to avoid the rocks.'

'All are bound by the will of the Emperor,' he said guardedly.

'Spoken truly – and yet where the wise find patterns in the Celestial Order, we lowly creatures struggle to discern the road set before us. I fear, in my haste to be of service to my companion, I have become a target for those who would work against him.'

'That is unfortunate,' he said, his sympathy less than palpable. 'And who are these men who seek the injury of my dearest cousin?'

'It saddens me to report the corruption of those tasked with upholding the laws of our land, and of their mistaken crusade against myself and my brother.'

His eyes grew cold as a late season frost, and I began to worry I'd made a mistake in coming. 'Great as my love is for my ally, I cannot interfere with the representatives of the Throne.'

'The men who follow me are on no sanctioned business of Black House, nor, save one, have been adopted officially into its service.'

'Save one?'

'A deputy of the head of Black House, whose iniquities are manifold and beyond dispute. Perhaps you are familiar with him, an Agent Crowley?'

A snarl played across his stony features. 'Our paths have crossed.'

I had hoped as much – Crowley had a particular talent for

engendering hatred. 'To the shame of my ancestors, there was once a time when the agent and I had dealings. Not knowing of our ties as brothers, Agent Crowley hoped to use my services to bring harm to the house of Ling Chi. Briefly, so briefly did I pretend to aid this duplicitous official, that I might gain his trust and knowledge of his movements. But the veneer of a traitor cannot gild the core of a righteous man, and my deception has been discovered.'

Ling Chi beat a steady pulse with his jade fingernails, sifting through the bullshit for nuggets of fact. Crowley's corruption was deep and long-standing – I could name a dozen criminal enterprises he made money from, and there were probably a hundred more of which I had no idea. The Old Man was aware of some of them, more than he let on to Crowley I'm sure, but the Old Man wasn't the sort to toss aside a good tool just because it occasionally worked without his direction.

Most importantly it fit into Ling Chi's overarching paranoia, a justified mania born from a lifetime of betrayal and deceit. He could well believe that I'd sell him out to Crowley, only to switch sides once things got too hot. It was the kind of thing he would have done – had done, and would do again.

'The cat is unaware of the workings of its paw?' he asked.

'Who can say what secrets are possessed by the master of Black House? He may know of his lieutenant's doings – he does not support them.'

The tapping slowed, then stopped altogether. 'So dear was my well-being to my brother that he jeopardized his safety and reputation in hopes of thwarting a plot against it. How could I, Ling Chi, be expected to do any less?' He smiled savagely, and I was grateful I was not the target of his anger. 'Harmony is to be prized above all other possessions – but should my associate discover that the men who plot our destruction have no ear for the words of reconciliation, he may rest comfortable knowing that what meager force I can offer is at his disposal.'

I bowed deeply, almost to the ground, and left. Rearming myself from the bench outside, I scurried into the bar and took an empty table in the corner. Four Kirens followed me in from the back room, hard men, as distinct from the other patrons as a wolf is from a dog. The workers at the table next to mine vacated their spot without comment, allowing the newcomers to take their place. One of the four, a thickset man with an elaborate dragon tattoo spiraling across his face, looked over and nodded at me. I nodded back. Then I flagged down a serving boy and told him to send over some *kisvas*.

After a few minutes the front door opened and Crowley walked in, backed by the three boys he'd introduced me to earlier. The bar fell silent and Crowley met the sea of heretic faces with a look of undisguised contempt. He saw me and whispered something to his men. They split off to the counter, and Crowley ambled towards my table.

He stopped behind the chair opposite mine, flush with petty glee. The tavern had returned to something that resembled normality, if you weren't paying much attention. Crowley wasn't. 'I thought maybe we'd lost you,' he said.

'Just having a drink.' I kicked the seat towards him. 'Take a load off, I know it's been a little bit of a walk.'

'We're here though, aren't we,' he responded, dropping his oversize frame onto the beat-up wooden chair.

'It might be more of a contest now that I'm armed.'

'If you thought anything of your chances, you wouldn't have run.'

'You always had trouble grasping the concept of a tactical retreat.'

'Yeah, I'm an ogre and you're a genius – but where's all your smarts gonna get you? Dead in a ditch on a winter night.' His thick bulk shifted back into his chair. 'Doesn't sound so fucking bright to me.'

'Not when you put it that way.'

'Course, if you were smart you wouldn't be here. If you were smart, you'd be head of Special Ops by now. That's why the Old Man hates you so much, you know – 'cause you disappointed him.'

'Daily do I lament my failure to live up to his expectations.'

'I tell you, he was shocked as hell when you did what you did. It was the only time I ever saw the bastard get hot.' He flashed his ugly grin, formed as a child when he first pulled the wing off a fly, perfected throughout the long years since by daily acts of cruelty. 'What was her name again?'

'Albertine.'

'Right, Albertine,' he said. 'Let me ask you, was she worth it? Because as far as I'm concerned, one piece of cunt's the same as another.'

I let that seep in through my pores, rubbed at it like a sore tooth, saving it up so I could pay it back.

The serving boy came by for an order but Crowley waved him away. 'Why the hell did you pick here to hide? Fucking Kirens.' He looked about disgustedly. 'They're like insects.'

'Ants,' I said. 'They're like ants.'

He pointed one thick finger at me. 'Every one of these motherfuckers that bows and calls you master would put their foot on your neck if you gave them half a chance.'

'Either they're playing at tyrants or cringing like slaves.'

'Exactly! Not like us. No sense of pride, that's the problem.'

'Not like us,' I agreed. Behind Crowley Ling Chi's men were getting restless, understanding enough to be insulted.

'And that monkey talk!' Crowley slapped his knee. 'Speak Rigun, you slant-eyed bastards!'

'It's not that hard, once you get the hang of it – here, we'll practice.' I drained the last of my *kisvas*. '*Shou zhe cao ni ma*,' I said.

'*Zou ze ca nee maa*,' he repeated, then chuckled at his own awkwardness. 'What does that mean?'

The tattooed Kiren said something in his native tongue. I nodded at him. 'It means, *End this motherfucker*.'

I swear Crowley was so dumb it took him three or four seconds to put that together. Realization finally dawned on his face and he tried to stand, but I caught him flush against the face and he stumbled backwards.

The bar erupted into violence. The men who first moved on

Crowley were in Ling Chi's employ, but it wasn't long till the crowd got in on the action, happy to provide the arrogant round eyes in their midst a permanent come-uppance. Crowley's boys went quick. The bartender, whose value I generally rated closer to lichen than mammal, pulled a cleaver from beneath the counter and took the head off a well-built Vaalan with a dispassion suggesting this was not the first time he'd decapitated a patron. The scarred Mirad managed to draw his knife before being swallowed, screaming as the press of men beat him senselessly to the ground with whatever makeshift weapons they could find.

After that I decided it was best to pull towards the back – we didn't want the heretics getting confused on whom they were supposed to be killing, and anyway the cuff I'd given Crowley had torn at the wound I'd gotten the night earlier. My ex-colleague put up what resistance he could, rocking one of Ling Chi's henchmen with a left hook before the tattooed Kiren sapped him to the ground. I stepped in then, waving off the heretic before he could draw a razor across Crowley's throat. I wanted him alive. His friends I didn't so much care about.

The Kiren were unprofessional and overzealous, but they were thorough. After five minutes there was nothing to reveal that three white men had just been murdered, the corpses removed to be disposed of in one of the myriad ways Ling Chi had devised to eliminate evidence of his frequent executions. Crowley lay on the ground, two of Ling Chi's men taking turns booting him when he squirmed. I nodded towards a side door and they dragged him outside by his arms.

There was a break in the storm, and the evening light reflected bright off the snow. Crowley's knees left a line in the fresh powder, the trail inset with red leaking down from his scalp. We stopped in a cul-de-sac behind the bar, the henchmen holding my old nemesis firmly, their support the only thing keeping him from collapsing. I pulled out my tobacco pouch and rolled a tab, waiting for him to come to.

It was no small joy watching him awake to my ugly mug square against his own. 'Back with us?'

He cursed something fierce and inventive.

I pulled a throwing knife from my shoulder holster and held it lightly in my left hand. One of the Kiren said something to his counterpart too rapidly for me to catch. 'Crowley, look at me.'

I laid the knife to his throat. To his credit, he neither flinched, nor pissed himself. 'I could do you right now, Crowley, and the heretics would make your body disappear, and there wouldn't be a single person in the Thirteen Lands who'd care.' His skin twitched against the cold metal.

I let the weapon fall to my side. 'But I'm not going to fade you, Crowley – I'm gonna let you walk. And I want you to remember, from now until the day I decide to kill you, this act of kindness. I am your benefactor, Agent – and every sunny afternoon, every fuck and full stomach, you owe to me.' He blinked twice, confused. I smiled broadly. 'But just in case you get forgetful.' My dagger opened a wound from the bottom of his forehead down through his cheek, and he screamed and went limp.

I watched him bleed for a moment, then nodded at the tattooed Kiren. He and the other exchanged quizzical looks – apparently there was no tradition of last-minute reprieves among the heretics. I nodded again and they released Crowley, who slumped to the ground, motionless except for the involuntary hemorrhaging.

The Kirens walked back inside the bar, laughing at the absurd customs of this alien country. As for me, I ducked down the alley and headed back to the Earl. It was too late to follow up with Cadamost – I'd have to hope this side-errand wouldn't end up costing me more than it had been worth. Still, walking home I had to struggle to keep a smile off my lips at the thought of the permanent one I'd given Crowley.

39

I woke up early, and snuck out of the bar. The address Guiscard had given me was deep in Kirentown, the part of the city where you could walk five blocks without seeing anyone who wasn't a faithful subject of the Celestial Emperor. Of course, three days into the storm of the century you could walk five blocks without seeing anyone period. By the time I arrived beneath the sign of the Gray Lantern my boots were soaked straight through, and I found myself wondering whether the Old Man might give me an extension on account of the weather.

Inside was a comically small storefront, maybe eight feet from the front door to the back. The shelves were stocked with a disparate variety of general goods – pots and pans, needles and spools of loose thread, consistent only in the layer of accumulated dust. Very little effort was being put forth to maintain the façade that this was a functioning enterprise, but then I supposed so far into Kiren territory the hoax didn't show up much and were easy to bribe when they did. A pinched-face heretic sat on a stool and stared at me with an expression that made me want to teach him the basics of customer relations with my fists. He nodded curtly and I slid past him, happy to have gotten through so easily but disturbed that I was apparently indistinguishable from a common junkie.

Against the back wall an iron fence had been erected, long stalks of wyrm hanging from the top of the cage, to be cut up and sold as needed. Inside a young Kiren girl sat ready to trade a few hours of oblivion for whatever coin one could muster. She watched me open-mouthed. I wasn't sure if she was high or just stupid. The rest of the room was occupied by all manner of tables and booths, acquired without the slavish desire for uniformity or cleanliness that tends to plague legitimate businesses. Wafting over everything was the unmistakable mélange of the drug itself, noxious and enticing, like baked goods and burned flesh.

It was early, and the weather discouraged casual errands, but just the same there were a dozen victims strewn about the place, puffing on their pipes or sunk back into oblivion. All but one was a heretic though, so it was easy enough to find my man. He was huddled in a back booth, his head lying awkwardly on the table in front of him, and he didn't react to my approach.

'Afonso Cadamost?'

He answered without lifting his skull off the counter. 'Fuck off.'

I set an argent on the wood beside him.

The clink of silver brought his face up, and I wished him still supine. The tawny color of his race had been altered to a sickly gray, and his skin hung heavy and sallow. Decayed teeth are the most common mark of a wyrm addict, but even expecting that the black-green rot of his smile was unsettling. More unsettling were his eyes, acetic, stygian things, angry dark dots centered amid an off-white iris.

I dropped myself into the chair across from him, careful not to think about whose ass has rested there before my own. 'I'd like to know some things,' I said.

He put the argent to his teeth, and I worried the weakened ivories might break against the metal. When they didn't he shrugged and dropped the coin into his pocket. 'Yeah?'

'I hear you were part of Operation Ingress.'

Fear is the last thing an addict loses – apparently Afonso still had enough on the ball for my reference to worry him. 'What do you know about it?' He licked his lips, trailing saliva across the chain of sores that disfigured the lower half of his face.

I thought about lying but decided against it – he wouldn't remember this conversation in twenty minutes, and no one would listen to such an obvious degenerate even if he did. 'My unit was outside Donknacht before the armistice. I provided protection for a counterpart of yours.' Not very well I might have added, but he didn't need to know that. 'Sorcerer Adelweid.'

'Adelweid,' he repeated slowly, like he was having trouble placing it.

'The two of you were classmates at the Academy.'

'I know who he was,' Cadamost snapped back. 'Who the hell do you think you're talking to?'

A junkie, obviously. Cadamost took a hit from his pipe to calm himself, doing little to alter my opinion.

'I remember Adelweid,' he began again. 'He was the start of it, you know, the start of everything. He found a journal one day in the archives . . . the Crown had tons of that shit, papers they'd confiscated over the years but never bothered to look at. It was nearly ruined from age, and written in a strange hand, but what was left . . .' His eyes darted about like a coursed hare. 'You say you were there at the end?'

'Lieutenant in the Capital Infantry. We were the first into Donknacht, although you boys had softened them up pretty good by the time we got there.'

'Yeah, I suppose we had. You . . . saw one?'

'I saw one.' It wasn't hard to figure out what he referred to. 'Where do you think it came from?'

'Another world? I don't know – metaphysics was never my strong suit.'

'Not another world, not a world at all. The absence between all of them. In the nothing between the universes, in the space where light doesn't reach – that's where she came from.'

'She?' I asked.

'She,' he confirmed. 'She was dancing in the darkness when I called her, waltzing endlessly in the center of forever. Waiting for a suitor.'

I clenched tight on my revulsion. 'How did you summon her?'

His breath reeked of carrion, fetid and unnatural. 'She wasn't some common whore to come at your beck and call! She was a lady, prim and proper, like one of those sweet-looking cunts you see out by the capital! She didn't just spread her legs for me 'cause I crooked my finger! I had to court her!' He took a hit, then coughed into my face.

'What does that mean, you had to court her?'

'What are you, some kind of faggot, down on your knees at the public bath house, sucking cock through a hole in the wall! Ain't you never had a woman? You speak soft words to her, you tell her she's beautiful. When the time is right, you give her something special – a token of your love.'

'What kind of token?'

'That's the catch, isn't it? She didn't see like we saw – one human was the same as another. She needed something of mine to remind her, something special, something that had some of me in it.'

'What was it?'

'A bracelet – my mother gave it to me when I left Miradin.' This seemed an unwelcome memory, and he offered no further explanation. 'I cast it into the void and when it came back to me it hummed with her song, hummed with it, morning through night. It's what bound us together. She was beautiful, and devoted – her love for me was as endless as the black sea she swam in. But she was a jealous mistress, and quick to anger. The token connected us.' He smiled grimly. 'Without it, she would have been very, very displeased.'

At the time I had thought Adelweid's refusal to part with his bauble was sheer vanity. That might also explain Brightfellow's penchant for jewelry, though bad taste would do the same. 'These . . . things,' I said, 'you can summon them, but they can't stay here?'

'She was too perfect, undiluted by the dross of our reality. It took the strength of my love for her to cross over.'

That jibed with what I had seen, Adelweid's creature dissipating after completing its task. 'There was another student in the Academy with you – Brightfellow, Johnathan Brightfellow.'

Cadamost ground a dirty fingernail against the cracked skin of his scalp. 'Yeah, I remember him. He was a few years older than the rest of us, came from some petty province up north.'

'What else you remember?'

'He had a temper. There was this little piece he used to follow, one of the boys said something about her and he lost it, cracked his head against a wall before anyone could think to do a working.' Cadamost strained to shake his mind out of its debasement, the simple act of recollection a marathon sprint. 'He didn't have much in the way of talent, maybe because he started learning so late – but he was sharp, sharper than you'd think, sharper than he let on.'

'And he was part of Operation Ingress.'

'Yeah, he was part of it. Most of us were, anyone with any sense and skill, you could tell what it would lead to, everything it promised. To see what came out when you cracked open the cage, to get a look at the bottom, way down at the bottom, the nothing that makes up everything. It wasn't about the War, we let them think it, but it wasn't about that at all – they were gods, and they wanted to look at us, talk to us and touch us, love us.'

'What happened to her?' I asked, though I already knew.

'The others were cowards. They didn't understand, they wouldn't let themselves understand. I knew what she wanted, knew what she wanted and wanted to give it to her. For that they feared me, and they took her away.' He stroked his wrist and gazed out past the walls, as if his obsession might reveal itself in the distance. 'I can feel it out there, somewhere. They have it and they keep it from me!' He coughed this out, along with something that looked very much like blood.

'And the rest of the practitioners? They still have their tokens?'

'I was singled out for my genius. The rest of them were allowed to keep theirs, I suppose. Or at least they still had them when I was stripped of my rank.' His eyes squinted to slits in his rotting face. 'Why? What's all this about anyway?'

'Thanks for your help,' I said, laying another argent on the table.

The sight of more silver was enough to make him forget his concerns. 'You're a good man, to help a fellow veteran. There's a spot in Chinvat for you, no doubt about that!' He laughed and reached for the bowl.

'Go careful on the next round,' I told him as I buttoned up my coat. 'I'd rather mine wasn't the coin that killed you.' Though on the way out I realized I didn't care much either way.

40

I picked Wren up and spent the rest of the morning at a tailor I used to frequent, getting my outfit ready for Brightfellow's party. The snow was not letting up. I had lived in Rigus for thirty of my thirty-five years, only leaving it to wage war on the Dren, and in all that time I'd never seen anything like this. The streets were deserted, the hum of city life dulled to an almost pastoral quiet, the season's festivities canceled.

By the time we got to the tower I wished I'd hired a coach, though the inclement weather at least eliminated the first barrier towards entering the Aerie, the snow spreading a low hummock over the maze. Wren stopped at the incline. 'I didn't know we were coming here,' he said.

'I'll only be a minute. I want to stop in and let Celia know what's going on.'

'Say hello to the Crane if you see him.'

'You aren't coming?'

'I'll wait here.'

Waves of shaved ice came down on us like curtains. I set my hand on his shoulder. 'Forget about the horn – I took care of it.'

He pulled away. 'I'll wait here.'

'Your pride's gonna leave you frozen to death. Swallow it and get in the fucking tower.'

'No,' he said, simply and evenly.

And that was the end of my willingness to debate the point. 'You lose a digit from frostbite, don't expect sympathy.' The Aerie's guardian opened without comment. It hadn't spoken since the Crane had first taken ill. I found myself vaguely nostalgic for its concrete quips.

Celia was waiting for me on the top floor, sipping tea by the fire, steam rising up around her bright face. 'I hadn't expected we'd see you today.'

'I thought I'd check in on the two of you. How's the Master?'

'Better. He was up and about for a while this morning. He ate breakfast and watched the snow.'

'That's nice to hear,' I said. 'I wanted to let you know I got your note. I'm going to pay the Lord Beaconfield a visit tonight, take a look at what your working turned up. All goes well I'll pass the information on to Black House some time tomorrow.'

She wrinkled up her face in confusion, or perhaps disappointment. 'I thought we agreed this is too important to let the law muck it up. I thought we agreed you'd handle it on your own.'

'Unfortunately it's still a crime to murder a noble. And anyway it wouldn't square me with the freeze, not if I can't show them why I did it. Besides, crossing out the Blade is something I'd just as soon leave to someone whose life isn't as valuable to me as my own. Black House will handle it. With what I'll give them they'll have enough to put the Question to him – after that it's just a matter of time.'

'And what if he moves on you first?'

'He's made his move. I'll make mine while he's recovering.'

She rubbed her necklace between two fingers and didn't respond.

'When this is over, I'll bring the boy around, and the four of us can build a snow fort, like when we were kids.'

Her attention snapped back to me. 'The boy?'

'Wren.'

There was another long pause, then the smile returned to her face. 'Wren,' she said. 'Yes of course.' She patted me lightly on the arm. 'I can't wait.'

I headed downstairs in half a hurry. Whatever whim he was indulging, I wouldn't let Wren wait long in the storm. Adeline would kill me if anything happened to him.

41

Four hours later I stepped out of a carriage and onto a roll of crushed red velvet. Two guards in speckled livery flanked the doors to Beaconfield's mansion, stiffly at attention despite the bitter frost. It was my first time entering through the front. I felt very important.

In the parlor a servant with a roll of parchment guarded access to the delights on offer in the main hall. He gave me a deferential nod, but my pose as a member of the upper crust didn't allow me to return it. I barked out my name and waited as he scanned for the corresponding entry.

It would intrigue the Blade that I'd asked for a spot on the guest list after he had sent men to murder me, and curiosity alone is often enough to get in with a noble, desperate as they are for anything that breaks up the monotony of profligate hedonism. If his instinct for melodrama wasn't enough, self-interest might be. Though he had pushed us into open warfare, I didn't figure he had the steel to play at it for long. He would hope that my message signaled a desire for reconciliation, and would leap at any hint of a truce.

That being said, it was one of the several potential hitches within my plan that I had not, in fact, been invited to the Lord Beaconfield's Midwinter party. It would be a chilly walk home if I'd played this wrong.

But I hadn't. The doorman waved me onward, and I brushed past him and headed down the hallway.

Whatever else you wanted to say about the Blade, he knew how to throw a soirée.

A cunningly wrought cage of filigreed silver hid the ceiling, giving the impression that we were carousing in the belly of some great beast. Baubles of glass and semi-precious stones trailed beneath it, drawing the eye with their cunning design. Closer inspection revealed every third of these was a tray of joints wrapped in brightly colored paper. The floor had been covered with glistening drifts of fake snow, ingeniously mimicking the genuine article. In the center of the room was a ten-foot-high ice sculpture of Śakra, his hand outstretched to bless the revelers below. The core of the sculpture had been filled with some sort of liquid light which permeated throughout the chamber, reflecting off the ornaments and bathing everyone in a scintillating iris of color.

If Beaconfield was broke, you couldn't tell it from the spread.

The décor was matched by the opulence of the guests, who filled the room with a low hum of festivity and amusement. Next to me a pudgy noble with bad skin and a brocade made of peacock feathers gestured flamboyantly to an anemic youth dressed in skin-tight, gold-threaded pants. To my left a middle-aged woman who might have been comely if she weren't so desperate to appear youthful was wearing a choker with an emerald the size of a baby's fist.

A server came by, shockingly beautiful in a silver costume that exaggerated more than it concealed. On her tray were flutes of champagne and the vials of the pixie's breath I had sold to Beaconfield the day of the duel. She accompanied these two with a look that suggested there was a third option on offer. I took a glass of bubbly and declined the rest, and the vixen cycled onward. The champagne was very good, as would be expected.

The woman with the choker slid over, inspecting me with all the subtlety of a dog in heat – it seemed she had no better taste in men than jewelry. Up close she looked like someone better seen from further away. 'I don't believe I've had the pleasure,' she began.

'Are you mad? I had you last year at Lord Addington's spring formal! We went behind his pagoda and I took you from the rear. You said I was the best you'd ever had!'

The color drained from her face – clearly she didn't find my scenario entirely implausible. Stammering an explanation, she hurried off, leaving me to watch the celebration solo. I grabbed another glass of bubbly the next time a waitress came by.

Beaconfield was standing across from the statue of Śakra, as befitted his status as host and general self-importance. He waved me over as if he'd just noticed my presence, though in fact he'd been watching me since I'd come in.

Up close the light was blinding, vivid orange-yellow washing away detail and nuance. The Blade had his arm tight around a perfect-looking Mirad, and smiled at me like we shared a joke. No reason to allow my slaughter of his associates to color our burgeoning friendship.

'Darling, this is the man I was telling you about.' He made no move to introduce us.

'Charmed,' I said, without taking my eyes off Beaconfield. 'This is quite a party. It must have set you back a copper or two.'

Beaconfield leaned towards me, champagne overrunning the lip of his glass. 'What's money?'

'Nothing, if you got it. Wake up broke and you'll start re-figuring your scales.'

He swallowed the rest of his drink. 'I have to admit, I was surprised to hear you'd be joining us. I didn't think you went in for this sort of tomfoolery.' His hand ran down the nape of the girl's neck, her pleasant docility unaltered.

'I couldn't let the evening slip by without paying you the compliments of the season.'

'I love Midwinter – the promise of rebirth and renewal, the past year forgotten, the new one yet ahead.'

'If that's how you look at it.'

'And how do you look at it?'

'As a distraction from the cold,' I said.

The Blade turned hard. 'The cold came early this year.'

'Yeah, it did.'

Beaconfield's woman broke the silence. 'Do you have a resolution?'

'I'm resolving to make it to next Midwinter,' I said.

'That doesn't sound too challenging.'

'Some of us will have trouble with it.'

I took the approach of another guest as an opportunity to make my exit. 'Far be it for me to monopolize the attentions of our host,' I said. 'And I'm afraid I need to find the powder room.' I bowed to Beaconfield and the slattern and made for an exit.

A guard slumped against the main stairway, clearly not ecstatic about manning a post four rooms away from a budding orgy. I built a roll into my gait. 'Say, brother, which way to the head? I'm about to drain down my pants.' While he decided whether household security took priority over service to the master's guests I brushed past him. He offered my back a belated grunt of agreement, and I took a side corridor and found my way to the servants' entrance.

Getting onto the mansion's grounds wouldn't be difficult for Kendrick, the defenses little more than a dozen acres of greenery protected by a tall hedge. Nor did I imagine he'd have much trouble with the lock, although it was new and well designed. But I'd been doing this too long to pass up an advantage, and I slid open the bolt and unfastened the bottom catch before heading back the way I'd come.

The party was in full swing, the jovial conviviality of the early evening giving way to an outright bacchanal. Multicolored clouds of smoke hovered above the congregation, and the once immaculate counterfeit snowdrifts had been scattered about haphazardly. The hanging trays of dreamvine were distinctly depleted, a far cry from the cornucopia of narcotic delights they had once offered. Off in the corner I could see a fat man doing something with one of the servers which I understood to be frowned upon in polite society. The magical light emanating from the statue of Śakra had faded from a bright orange to a duller violet, rendering the proceedings at once malefic and chimerical.

I'm not sure what it was that possessed me to speak to Brightfellow, our previous interactions not being so enjoyable as to warrant sequel. When I'd seen him slip in earlier in the evening I was worried he'd attach himself to me, and I'd be stuck trading barbs all night. Instead he'd taken a seat in the back and downed every glass of booze that came within reach, supplementing it with frequent sips from a pocket flask.

It made all the sense in the world to leave him alone. If Kendrick came through, and if Celia's working was right, there was no point in shaking him down, not that the sorcerer had shown himself easily susceptible to intimidation. Maybe it was my innate instinct towards making trouble. Maybe I just felt like killing time.

But in truth I think I relished the opportunity to give him a few solid kicks now that he was on the ground. He was an easy man to hate, indeed he almost seemed to cultivate it. It's better not to feel that way about whoever you're going up against, personal enmity clouds the mind – but then self-control was never my strong suit. I thought about the children, and Crispin, and then I was on my feet and heading over.

He looked up as my shadow dropped over him, struggling to make me out against the kaleidoscopic backdrop. During our brief acquaintance I had yet to see Brightfellow sober – but neither had I really seen him drunk. He'd struck me as the sort of person who needed a shot or two to get through the day, who isn't at peak condition until his blood reaches a few points proof.

He was well clear of that point, at the end result of an active effort to reach insensibility. His eyes were carmine dots surrounded by swelled flesh, thick beads of sweat trailing down the slant of his forehead and off his stubbed nose. At first he managed something of his usual bravado, sneering at me with a credible imitation of homicidal loathing. But it faded quickly, buried beneath the booze he'd been swilling, and his head sank back down to the ground.

'Long night?' I asked, taking the seat next to him. His rank press leaked through the perfume he'd doused himself with.

'The fuck you want?' he asked, forcing each syllable through an uncooperative maw.

'You looked so pretty, I thought I'd ask for a dance.'

He let that one pass. Indeed he seemed barely to register it.

I sipped at my glass of champagne. It was my fourth or fifth, and the fizz was playing havoc with my stomach. 'Really a bunch of hateful motherfuckers, aren't they? To think that half the nobles in Rigus are here defiling themselves. I'd say they need religion but I'm pretty certain that's the First Abbot over there, passed out in the punch bowl.' The First Abbot was not passed out in the punch bowl – he was passed out next to the punch bowl, but it sounded better the way I said it.

'I'd see every one of them rotting in the ground,' Brightfellow answered, and I nearly recoiled at the malice in his voice. 'I'd like to put them there.'

'Would the Blade get a pass?'

'Not if I'm handing them out.'

'Then what the hell was the point? When this thing falls it'll be the end of both of you.'

'You know why you do everything you do?'

'I can usually hazard a guess.'

There was a long pause, so long I thought maybe the sorcerer had slipped full-on into stupor. Finally, with a great deal of effort, Brightfellow swung his eyes up to meet mine. 'You were an agent,' he said. 'And now you aren't.'

'Yeah.'

'Was that your choice?'

'In a sense.'

'Why'd you make it?'

'A woman.'

'That's a pretty good answer,' he said, and turned back towards the blur of the crowd. 'I didn't think it would go this far. I didn't want it to.'

Something about Brightfellow's self-pity reignited my fury. 'Don't mistake me for a priest – I'm not interested in your confession, and I'm not selling redemption. You dug your hole, now lie in it,' I sneered, though since he wasn't looking the effect was wasted. 'I'll tip the Blade in after, so you don't get lonely.'

I thought that was a pretty good shot and I thought it'd rattle him.

But when he spoke his voice was level, and he didn't sound angry, just certain and sad. 'You're a fucking idiot,' he said.

I took a twist of colored dreamvine from a dish beside us. 'You might just be right about that one.'

He didn't say anything else, and I got up and faded into the background, and after I finished my glass of champagne I didn't grab another.

Up front the Blade and his entourage were drinking and smoking and occasionally laughing uproariously. I wondered where he was getting his supply of cronies – I'd done for four of them two nights earlier, but he wasn't having difficulty finding replacements, nor did the death of his previous coterie seem to weigh heavy on the duke's soul. Every so often he would toss me what he thought was a threatening glance, though having been tutored in intimidation by men the likes of Ling Chi I found myself unimpressed.

The Doctor was in the building by this point. The night was only getting later, and my initial awe had given way to the generalized contempt I felt for my betters, sybarites so degenerate even their base pleasures were synthetic and hollow. The prospect of pawing at one of the servers was less than enticing, so I just sat alone, worrying what would happen if I'd misjudged Kendrick, or if Celia's working had rung false, or if my alchemical skills hadn't been up to the task.

It happened without preamble. One of the servers dropped her tray and followed it soon after, huddled on the ground weeping – apparently she had dipped into the master's stash a bit early. By coincidence the next to go was a young fop standing over her, who fell to his knees and soured the air with bile. Like a wave it passed through the crowd, groups of people throughout the party overcome with nausea, clutching their bellies and scanning desperately for an appropriate place to boot.

Any fool can cut pixie's breath with something that will kill a man, spite's bloom or a few drops of widow's milk, but to mix in something non-lethal is more difficult. And of course it wouldn't have been possible if Beaconfield hadn't run through the first cache of breath I had given him and demanded more for the party. But I did, and he had, and here we were. Whatever the Blade thought, I hadn't come to negotiate, or to engage in another tête-à-tête. He wasn't much of a sparring partner all told, and it was a long trek up here to tell a man I hated that I hated him.

I'd come to make sure the hour I had spent dropping three grains of mother's bane into every vial of pixie's breath I'd sold Beaconfield that day in the gardens hadn't been wasted. I'd promised the Doctor a distraction, after all.

The duke hadn't yet made the connection between me and the illness sweeping his guests, and I decided to head out before that changed. At least I could rest comfortably knowing I had done my part to make what would likely be the Blade's final Midwinter party the most memorable one yet.

I slipped out through the main door and started back towards Low Town. If Kendrick couldn't find a way to break into Beaconfield's study while the entirety of the party was violently ill then his reputation was pretty damn far from earned. I took the joint from my pocket and put it to my lips, lighting it despite the snow. All in all it had been a fine evening, clean as clockwork.

So I couldn't understand why I spent the walk home in anxious silence, unable to shake the nagging feeling I'd fucked myself sideways.

42

The next morning I bundled up tight and headed out to meet the Doctor, and against the storm there was a bounce in my step I hadn't had for days. Unless my thief had completely blown his assignment, I'd be able to clear myself of the Old Man's sentence with a solid day to spare, and that was enough to make me forget the snow for a few minutes.

Once inside the Daeva's Work Pub I took a back booth and ordered a cup of coffee. A few minutes later the Doctor came in, brushing ice off his thick winter coat. He sat down and slipped me a packet of papers underneath the table. 'From a false bottom in his desk, and the dart trap was coated with fen-eel venom.'

'I hope it proved difficult enough to interest you,' I said.

He didn't answer, and I started to flip through the file he'd given me. Mairi might be a treacherous whore, but her sources weren't bad. The first half of the package consisted of the Blade's ledgers, and it didn't take an accountant to see that he was deeper in red than a virgin on her wedding night. I had motive.

But that wasn't the interesting part. Coupled with the ledger were a series of correspondences between Beaconfield and several men I knew to be the espionage agents of various foreign embassies. It seemed that before moving on to child murder, the Blade had studied treason. Miradin, Nestria, even the fucking Dren – there wasn't a country on the continent poor Beaconfield hadn't tried to sell his soul to. None of it had gone very far – like most amateurs in the field of spycraft, Beaconfield mistook gossip for intelligence. In fact the letters listed little more than the polite refusal of various low-ranking operatives to contract the Blade's services. His incompetence would be no defense at trial of course, and his status as a peer made any contact with a foreign emissary a hanging offense.

It was interesting, but it didn't relate directly to the murders, and I knew it wouldn't be enough for the Old Man, not with the hard-on he had for me. My heart beat double-time, and I worked to settle it. 'Was that everything?'

From the moment he had sat down in front of me I could see Kendrick had an edge to him that contrasted with the amiability he had displayed during our first conversation. Now it reached a crescendo, my casual question eliciting a scowl that sat incongruously on his face. 'No, that isn't everything. That isn't everything at all.' Underneath the table he passed me a parcel wrapped in butcher's paper.

I undid the tie and let the object inside fall into my hands.

If I saw it on a shelf or behind glass it wouldn't have meant anything, an open razor of the sort you could buy in any corner store in the city, a bit of sharpened steel folded back into a brass hilt. But holding it I could tell clear what it was, as soon as I touched the metal a line of bile retched itself up from my throat and my testicles held firm to the flesh of my thigh. Vile things had been done with this weapon, acts that had stained its very substance. Its contact with the void had leaked out into our reality and left behind a memory of its blasphemies. You didn't need to be a scryer to recognize it, needed no extra degree of perception – you felt it in your gut, in your soul. I wrapped the thing back in the paper and shoved it into my bag.

The Doctor had felt it and he was not happy to have done so. 'You didn't say anything about this.'

'I didn't know anything about it.'

He brought himself to his feet. 'Send my money to my agent, and don't contact me again. I don't like being in the dark.'

'It's a shit way to spend time,' I agreed.

I sat there as he walked out, and for a while after. The Doctor wasn't my favorite person, and I wouldn't have tossed him another gig even if he'd been up for taking it – but I couldn't fail to recognize that lately I'd been convincing a lot of people to stop speaking to me.

Still, I had what I needed. There was no way the Old Man could ignore the instrument of sacrifice with which Beaconfield had disposed of two children.

I was back in the Earl twenty minutes later – the whole errand had taken less than an hour. I yelled a greeting, crowing with success and expecting accolades from the gallery. I knew Adeline would be out for groceries, but still figured Wren and my partner would be around to commiserate my success.

But the boy was nowhere to be seen, and I found Adolphus sitting next to the fire, his face stone and a slip of paper open in his hand. He passed me the note without comment, and before I'd opened it I had a pretty good idea what it said.

I have the child.
You will do nothing until I contact you.

I crumbled it in my fist and cursed myself for a fool.

43

Adolphus and I were plotting in the corner when Adeline came in, plump and red-cheeked, anticipating the Midwinter feast she was about to prepare. If it was just me I could probably have carried the deception, but you don't share a man's bed for a decade without gaining some ability to appraise his mood. Besides, Adolphus ain't much for guile. 'What's wrong?'

Adolphus and I exchanged the kind of look that prefaces the arrival of bad news, but neither of us said anything.

She inspected me with a gaze that would be the envy of many a magistrate. 'Where's Wren?'

A hole opened up in the bottom of my stomach and I fell into it. I stumbled through a lie. 'I left him at the Aerie.'

'You never mentioned anything about visiting the Crane today.'

'I don't tell you every time I void my bowels, but the chamberpot still gets plenty of use.'

A burst of movement, faster than I would have credited

her for, and she stood in front of me. Her voice was louder than usual, but steady. 'Stop lying – I'm not a fool. Where is he?'

I swallowed hard and nodded at Adolphus. He slipped the paper out of his back pocket and handed it to her.

I'm not sure what I expected, how I thought she would react. For all her low voice and sweet nature, for all that she allowed Adolphus his delusions of tyranny, Adeline was no weakling. But then I couldn't imagine what the arrival of Wren to a woman long childless meant.

She read over the missive, the grim set of her face unaltered. Then she looked back at me, her eyes incredulous. 'How could this happen?' Not angry yet, just confused.

'He must have followed me out of the bar. He did it once before, but I thought I told him off. I'm not sure, I didn't see him.'

She struck me once across the face, closed palm. 'You stupid, stupid man.' She raised her hand again, then dropped it. 'You stupid man.'

I swallowed that.

'Swear to me you'll find him.'

'I'll do what I can.'

She shook her head and grabbed the lapel of my coat, her eyes wide and furious. 'No – swear to me, swear to me you'll bring him back safe.'

My throat was so dry I stumbled over the words. 'I swear.' As a rule I don't promise anything I can't deliver. I wished I could take it back as soon as I had said it.

She let go of me and collapsed into Adolphus, her composure broken. He patted her softly on the back.

I moved to leave. 'I'll be back in an hour.'

'You aren't . . .' Adolphus let the sentence trail off.

'Not yet. I've got something I need to do first.'

It wouldn't do to murder a member of the peerage without notifying the authorities. I needed to see the Old Man.

44

I pushed open the doors into Black House like I was still the top agent in the place, instead of a low-rent pusher. I must have done a decent enough impression because the guard on duty let me by without any trouble. From there I made my way deeper into the labyrinthine layout of the building, unsurprised to discover I hadn't forgotten my way.

The Old Man's office is located in the dead center of the building, at the heart of a web of dull offices and unattractive carpeting. I entered without knocking, but somehow he knew I was coming and sat comfortably in his chair, owning absolutely the space he inhabited. The wooden desk in front of him was clean of paper, book or bauble, the only adornment a small bowl of hard candy.

'A day early,' I said, taking the seat opposite his and tossing the packet onto the desk.

It landed with a thud. The Old Man looked up at me, then at the dossier, then back at me. He took hold of the folder and settled into his seat, flipping through it with agonizing slowness. Finally he set the papers back on his desk. 'This does make for interesting reading – unfortunately, it isn't the information I tasked you to find. For your sake, I certainly hope this isn't all you came here with.'

The razor sat in my satchel. All I needed to do was lay it down on the table and walk out, free and clear, at least until the next time they wanted something from me – the razor pulsed with the void, it was as good as a signed confession. But with the boy gone that was out; one street urchin didn't matter anything to the Old Man, didn't matter an eyelash or a clipped toenail.

The Blade drew too much water for him to disappear into Black House and never come out again. If they went after him they'd have to uphold a pretense of legality, weeks of subpoenas and judicial wrangling, and I didn't imagine Beaconfield would leave Wren alive through that. This of course assumed the Old Man would try to bring him down, which I doubted. More likely he'd use what I gave him to flip Beaconfield, put him back out on the street in Black House's employ – the duke was worth more in his pocket than swinging on a rope.

The only chance I had of getting the boy back safe was if I was holding the reins, and that meant I needed to play this tight, pass out enough to get sanction on the duke without tipping my hand so far that the Old Man decided to steal my play. I took a sweet from the dish, unwrapping the paper slowly and popping the confection into my mouth. 'That was just motive of course. I assume Guiscard already told you of the Blade's connection to Operation Ingress.' The agent's sudden willingness to help had never smelled right, but it wasn't until I was sitting in front of his boss that I decided to voice my suspicions. It was something of a shot in the dark, and I was gratified to see surprise hiccup across the Old Man's perfect composure. 'After he failed to find any takers for his illicit services, the Blade moved on to Plan B. Someone, probably Brightfellow, contracted out the abduction to the Kiren. When that didn't work they aced him and took the matter into their own hands. I can go on if you want – I know it's been a long time since you did actual police work.'

The Old Man's face returned to its friendly hollowness. Then he shook his head, saddened by the bad news he was about to relay. 'Not enough. Not nearly enough. Perhaps it's my fault – perhaps I've failed to motivate you sufficiently. Perhaps I should send someone down to that bar you own, pay your friends a nice visit.'

I let that slide past without grabbing at it. 'Not enough for a warrant maybe – but enough for the two of us to be sure.'

'What are you suggesting?'

'I'll take care of it. Off the books.'

He tut-tutted disapprovingly. 'So much blood, so much fuss. What will it look like?'

'You're Special Operations – it'll look like what you say it looks like. Don't pretend you don't relish the idea of taking out a noble, and an ally of the Crown Prince at that. I'm doing you a favor, and you know it.' I pushed across the desk, narrowing the air between us. 'Unless you feel like waiting around for the Blade and his pet sorcerer to complete their ritual.'

The Old Man's eyes were blue as a summer evening. 'Are you offering to return to the Crown's service?'

I knew he was baiting me but damn if I didn't want to take it. 'A singular proposition. The Lord Beaconfield and I have a discussion, and you wake up tomorrow with one less problem to deal with.'

'And why are you so keen to take responsibility for the good duke's demise?'

'I bore easily – what do you care? It'll get done.'

He clasped his hands in front of his face, giving the impression of serious contemplation. After fifteen seconds of uncomfortable silence he spread his palms face up and leaned back in his chair. 'Accidents happen,' he said.

I started to walk out, opening the door then turning back towards him. 'You ought to know there'll be some clean-up required. It'll be quick, but it'll be noisy.'

'As you said, we're Special Operations.'

'When I do you it'll be quiet as a chapel.'

He let out an embarrassed chuckle, chagrined at my misbehavior. 'Such a temper! You'll never make it to my age if you don't learn to enjoy life a little.'

I didn't respond, closing the door on the blank office and the evil man who lived there.

45

T hen it was back to the Earl, half jogging through the knee-high snow. The constant cold was wearing on me. I could remember a time when the sky was light and the clouds didn't spew ice, but only dimly.

I arrived to discover the bar had closed for the night – not that we'd see much business, the weather being what it was. The front room was deserted, Adolphus presumably in the back looking after his wife. I didn't have time to search for him. I wasn't planning to move on the Blade till nightfall, but I'd need every minute of the interim to ready the set-up.

Up in my room I noticed a small envelope on my dresser. Across it Adolphus had scrawled a quick note: *Grenwald's messenger came while you were out.* Under different circumstances this would have warranted a good laugh. To think for once in his useless fucking existence my old major actually came through for me, and it was too damn late to do any good. I ignored it and turned to more pressing duties.

I removed the brown-wrapped parcel from the trunk beneath my bed, then sat at my table and began to unpack it. Two hours were lost in the haze of critical but menial tasks required to bring the equipment into readiness. I grabbed a couple of throwing knives and a thin stretch of wire before slipping a tin of faceblack into my pocket and heading downstairs.

I was so fixed on my purpose that I nearly rebounded off Adolphus, who stood at the foot of the steps, rendered nearly invisible by the low light and his own uncanny stillness. Beneath his heavy overcoat a ragged suit of studded leather stretched taut against his chest, and he'd dug up his old kettle helmet, the steel dented by five years of close calls. Apart from his dress he was also festooned with weapons, two short blades hanging at his side and a battle-ax strapped to his back.

'What the hell are you wearing?' I asked, astounded.

The savagery in his eyes left me with no doubt that my comrade was quite serious in his choice of attire. 'You didn't think you were going alone? This isn't our first time over the top. I've got my eyes on your back, as always.'

Was he drunk? I sniffed at his breath – apparently not. 'I don't have time for this. Watch Adeline, I'll be back in a few hours.'

'Wren's my son,' he said, without affectation or aggrandizement. 'I'll not sit by the fire while his life is in danger.'

The Oathkeeper spare us from such pointless nobility. 'Your offer is appreciated, but unnecessary.'

I tried to squeeze by, but he put one hand against my collar and held me firm against the banister. 'It wasn't an offer.'

The streaks of gray outnumbered the black in his once charcoal hair. His pockmarked face was heavy. Was I that old? Did I look that foolish, my collar pulled up like a hoodlum, steel bulging from my pockets, a middle-aged man playing at the adventures of youth?

It didn't do to think like that. Wren needed me – I could go through an existential crisis if I was still alive in six hours.

I brushed off Adolphus's hand and took a step back up the stairs, giving myself enough room to maneuver. 'You're fat – you were always big, but you're fat now. You're slow and you can't sneak, and you don't have it in you to kill a man any more, not the way I'm going to do it. I'm not sure that you ever did. I've no time to flatter your vanity – every second you waste the boy gets closer to death. Get the fuck out of my way.'

For a moment I thought I had overplayed my hand and he would knock my head off my shoulders. But then he turned his face to the ground and all the energy seemed to slump out of him, like a hole at the bottom of a jug. He turned away from the staircase, his collection of cutlery jangling.

'Look after Adeline,' I said. 'I'll be back in an hour or two.' That was far from certain, but there was no point in saying so. I slipped out into the night.

46

I crouched by a bush twenty yards out from the back gate of Beaconfield's mansion. I'd darkened my skin with face-black, and the wire hanging from my hands shimmered in the moonlight. I was trying to think up a way that Dunkan didn't have to die. So far nothing was coming.

I couldn't knock him out. That doesn't work the way people think it does – one quick sock in the noggin and your mark wakes up an hour later with a dull headache. Half the time they move and you don't hit them right, and you're left standing there like a fool. If you do knock them out they'll probably be back up in time to cause trouble, and if they stay down it usually means their brains are scrambled and they're going to spend the rest of their lives shitting themselves, and for my money that's no great improvement on being dead.

And it was going to be a close thing, even if it went straight this would be as close a thing as I'd ever done.

And I'd made a promise to Adeline.

The night was getting on and every minute that passed was another for Beaconfield to decide the best way out of this was to feed Wren to Brightfellow's abomination. The ordnance in my satchel gave me a fighting chance, but not if someone saw me while I was setting up. I cursed the quirk of fate that had mandated the smiling watchman's presence here, instead of by a fire sipping his whiskey – but there was nothing for it.

I closed my eyes briefly.

Then I was up, a stone flung against the outer wall drawing the unsuspecting sentry, ten yards, five yards and I was behind him and the loop pulled tight.

The garrote is quiet but slow, and Dunkan took a long time to die. First he grabbed at the wire, fingers scratching savagely at his swollen throat. After a while his arms dropped to his side and he ceased struggling. I held on till his skin turned purple, and he kicked his legs in one final spasm. Then I lowered him to the ground, behind the wall where no one could see him.

I'm sorry, Dunkan. I wish it had gone another way.

I closed the lantern above the open gate. The guards would notice the absence of light soon – I hoped the murder of my friend had bought me enough time.

I crept about the perimeter, securing what I needed for the thing to work out. No one noticed – security was lax. Beaconfield might just be dumb enough not to realize I was coming. I hoped so at least.

After everything was set I returned to the back door and picked the lock, not as expertly as the Doctor perhaps but without any trouble. I started counting off the seconds in my head once I was inside, my back to the walls, stopping at every sound. The defenses were strangely delinquent, no patrols, not even anyone posted at the stairwell.

When I opened the door to the Blade's study he was standing in front of the broad windows behind his desk, drinking from a rocks glass and watching the falling snow. He whirled his head around with defined celerity. There was a moment of purest shock when he recognized me. Then a smile spread across his features,

336

and he downed the rest of his liquor and set the cup on the table. 'This is the second time you've come uninvited into my study.'

I closed the door behind me. 'Just the first. I sent a man around yesterday.'

'Is that how friends behave? Taking advantage of hospitality to steal intimate correspondence?'

'We aren't friends.'

He looked a little hurt. 'No, I suppose we're not – but that's just circumstance, really. I think if things had worked out differently you would have found me a very reasonable man. Affable, even.'

Two and a half minutes. 'I don't think so. You blue-bloods are a little too bent for my tastes. At heart I'm a simple creature.'

'Yes, forthright and candid, that's exactly how I would describe you.'

We were each waiting to see if the other would drop this pretense of amiability. Inside my skull the clock ticked away – three minutes.

The Blade lounged against his desk. 'I have to admit, I'm surprised at how you've decided to play this.'

'I'll admit this is a bit direct, but then I didn't have much of a choice.'

'The Old Man sent you, then? It shocks me the loyalty that madman instills. It won't be his life taken on your suicide mission.'

'Not loyalty – I practically had to twist his arm.' A flicker of surprise crossed his face. 'And what makes you so certain I'm the one who won't be walking out of here?'

He burst out laughing. 'No one's calling you an incompetent, but – let's not exaggerate your prowess.'

Three and a half minutes. 'You tell that to the men you sent to kill me?'

His eyes filmed over, a rare show of regret. 'That was Brightfellow's idea – he wanted me to go after you from the beginning, and once Mairi let us know you were sniffing around

. . . I had hoped we might be able to scare you, or buy you off. I suppose you were more frightened of the Old Man than me.'

'You're right about that,' I said. 'Where is the practitioner, anyway?'

'Your guess is as good as mine. I haven't seen him since the party. I suppose he scampered off. Not many have the stomach for the end game.'

'Not many do,' I agreed, figuring him for a liar, figuring the sorcerer was holed up in the basement with his hands around Wren's throat.

Beaconfield trailed his hand to the hilt of his sword. 'We're not so dissimilar as you pretend. We're both warriors, children birthed in the screams of men and the flow of blood. There can be no dishonesty between us, no prevarication in the perfection of the thrust or the candor of the riposte. And so I speak to you as a brother. The men you killed, my friends – they were not the palest shadows of myself. No one is. There has never been anyone as good as me, not in the long ages leading back to when the first man struck the second with a rock. I am the perfect engine of death, the apex predator, an artist in the oldest and noblest of man's activities.'

'Did you rehearse that in front of a mirror?'

'Watch your tone.'

'I've known your kind my whole life, punk boys who get a length of steel in their hand and decide it makes them men. You think you're special 'cause your hand is a touch faster? I pass a dozen of you on my way to breakfast every morning – only difference between them and you is the cost of your coat.'

'Why are you keeping up your end of the conversation, if I'm of such little interest?'

'Why indeed.' That had to have been five minutes already. Śakra's swinging cock, what the hell was taking so long? If Beaconfield wasn't such a desperate megalomaniac I'd be dead, I had no illusions on that score. 'Why did you do it?' I asked. 'I understand the events – I'm just trying to get some perspective.'

'What's there to say? I needed money, they had it, or I thought they did. I never burned with the desire to betray the country, but then, like you said – things happen.'

I was counting the seconds desperately now. 'I don't care about your pathetic attempts at espionage. How did you get involved with Brightfellow – when did you start with the children?'

He looked at me with an expression of curious astonishment, and to my dawning horror I realized it wasn't feigned. 'What children?'

The floor below us erupted, kicking me backwards into a wall.

I suspect the history of mass combat has never seen a more incompetent logistic corps than the one I suffered through during the War. For five years we struggled to make do without the most basic supplies – spare bandages, cob nails, faceblack. Two days in Donknacht and the flow of goods wouldn't stop. Saddles for dead horses, armor no one had any idea how to put on, crates of wool socks, as if the War had multiplied our supply of limbs rather than diminishing them. When I mustered out I had enough small goods to start a general store, and one other item less commonly found stocking the shelves of local merchants – twenty-five pounds of black powder, and the explosive components required to detonate it.

Part of it I had used while still wearing the gray. Part of it had gone to make my name after I left the Crown's service. The remainder I was using to introduce the Smiling Blade to the joys of modern warfare.

The blast flung the two of us to opposite ends of the room, but I was expecting it and managed to get up first. I pulled a dagger from my boot and moved on Beaconfield with what speed I could muster. He was slumped in the corner, groggy but conscious. That wasn't good – I'd hoped the discharge would put him out long enough for me to make sure he wasn't a threat. I reversed my grip on the knife and leapt at him. His eyes fluttered but he reacted with extraordinary speed, shifting out of the way of my blow and wrapping his fingers around my weapon hand.

He was stronger than I thought, and though I had assumed otherwise he was a fighter. Not just skilled with his sword – that

I had known of course – but a fighter, the kind of man who attacks when wounded, who doesn't back down from pain or shock. He had grit, though you couldn't tell it from his dress. I guess that deserves to be remembered, though it doesn't cancel out much else. I tried for a rabbit punch to his throat but he blocked it with his usual astonishing agility.

I don't know how it would have ended if we'd fought straight – but then I'm not that big on fair play. The second bomb went off, directly beneath us this time, and then I was looking up at the ceiling and there was a glare in my eyes so bright it seemed to stun as well as blind me. In time the light began to fade but not the terrible ringing in my ears. I put my hands against them – no blood, but that didn't mean anything; in the War I'd seen men go deaf who hadn't shown any sign of injury. I screamed out loud, my throat raw but the sound itself lost.

Pull it together, pull it together. The ringing will stop or it won't – if you lie here you'll be dead either way. I stood up, knowing I'd be useless in a fight, hoping to Meletus the Blade had gotten it worse than me.

He had. The floor of the study had blown out, leaving gaping holes in the wood and sending shrapnel everywhere. A jagged splinter the size of a man's arm had lodged itself in Beaconfield's stomach. He lay with his back arched over a fallen support beam, blood draining from his mouth. I stumbled towards him, my equilibrium utterly scrambled.

'Where is Wren?' I asked. 'The boy, where is he?'

The Blade had enough in him for one final smile, and he played it for everything he could, mouthing his words slow enough that I could make them out despite the clamor in my ears. 'You're a better killer than you are a detective.'

I couldn't argue with that one.

His last shot of energy expended, Beaconfield slumped down on the spear embedded through his torso. After a few seconds he was gone. I closed his eyes and pulled myself to my feet.

No man wastes his last breath on a lie. He had let forth the secret out of spite, a final blow thrown before meeting She Who

Waits Behind All Things. He didn't have Wren. I'd screwed something up – I'd screwed something up terribly, but I couldn't tell
where.

Time was passing, and it seemed likely someone had noticed
the detonation of the Lord Beaconfield's mansion. I headed downstairs, knowing if I ran into trouble I was good as dead.

The back wing of the house seemed to have collapsed in on
itself, tons of wood and brick burying the back hallway. In the
main parlor the once beautiful carpets were destroyed by soot,
shards of glass from the broken chandeliers coating everything.
One of the explosions had set off a fire in the kitchen, and the
blaze was rapidly moving to cover the rest of the house.

The Blade's butler lay prostrate beside the door, his head cocked
in a fashion no contortionist could have matched. Death seemed
an inequitable punishment for his arrogance and general unpleasantness, but then few enough of us get what we deserve. I stepped
over him and into the snow.

I was stumbling towards the outside gate when I realized the
ringing in my ears had died down, not much but enough to let
me know I wasn't deluding myself – I hadn't gone deaf, and I
wanted to sink down and weep, to thank the Firstborn for sparing
me. Instead I continued on through the frost, jumping the hedge
when I saw lights coming down the path ahead of me and sneaking
back to the Earl as quickly as a broken man is capable.

47

I slid into the bar as quietly as I could. I needed time to think, to figure out where my reasoning had gone awry. One way or another Wren was gone, and if the Blade hadn't taken him that didn't make the boy any safer. Once upstairs I ripped a vial of breath from my stash and put it to my nose. My hearing was returning slowly, and after the first hit I couldn't make out anything but the beating of my heart, accelerated by the drug.

On the dresser sat Grenwald's missive. I opened it with dull fingers, cutting my thumb in the haste to confirm my growing sense of dread, smearing red across the white parchment.

The top of the document was identical to the one I had taken off Crispin, but the bottom half was undamaged, the page listing every practitioner involved in Operation Ingress. I recognized Brightfellow, and Cadamost.

And I recognized one more name, at the very bottom, beneath the tear that had defaced my earlier version.

I pulled my shirt over my head, then took out the straight razor nestled in the bottom of my satchel and flicked it open. The full weight of my sins began to settle across my back, and for one self-indulgent moment I wondered where to put the edge of the blade for best effect. Then I cut a shallow incision below the sapphire in my shoulder, wincing at the pain as I did so.

Five minutes later I was double-timing it through Low Town, bleeding through the hastily tendered bandage I had torn from my undershirt.

By all the Daevas, I hoped there was still time to stop it.

48

The Blue Crane had been dead for about six hours. His body was slouched in the oak chair in his study, azure eyes lolled back in his head, the wounds on his arms and the blade resting on the ground confirming his demise was self-inflicted. On the desk in front of him sat a scroll of parchment, two words in his scrawling chicken scratch.

I'm sorry.

So was I. I closed his eyes and walked downstairs.

The door to her study was open, and I slipped inside. Celia and Brightfellow were turned away from me. Wren sat limply on a chair in the corner, unbound, his eyes glazed over insensibly.

'I say we do him now.' The last day had seen Brightfellow slip further towards collapse. He wore the same clothes as at the Blade's party, and gestured wildly. 'Let's do him and dump him, before anyone gets wise.'

Celia by contrast was steady as a block of quarried stone, her hands busy with the array of alchemical equipment on the table before her. 'You know as well as I do the fever takes a half-day to set, and we haven't even passed it to the boy yet. I'm not going to ruin everything we've accomplished because you're getting jumpy.' She poured the contents of a beaker into a smaller one, then jerked her head at Wren. 'Why don't you take a seat, keep an eye on him.'

'He's not going anywhere. My working will keep him down for the rest of the night.'

'He's got the gift, like the others, even if he doesn't know how to use it yet. You can't be sure how he'll react.'

Brightfellow peeled a dirty fingernail between his teeth. 'You said you can't feel the gem any longer.'

'Yes, Johnathan, that's what I said.'

'That means he's dead, right?'

'It means exactly what it means,' she said, but not angrily.

'He must be dead,' Brightfellow repeated.

Celia lifted her head up and sniffed at the air. 'I doubt that,' she said, setting aside an alembic and turning to face me. 'How long have you been here?'

'Long enough.'

When Brightfellow saw me what was left of his equilibrium departed completely. He turned corpse-white, and his eyes flickered back and forth between Celia and me, as if in the air between the two of us there was something that would salvage the situation.

'This would mean that Beaconfield...' Celia began, implacably calm, my arrival apparently not representing the slightest hiccup in her planning.

'Has thrown his last Midwinter's party,' I confirmed. 'Poor, dumb bastard. He never knew any of it, did he? I guess you brought him in after I started asking questions, to make sure you had a sucker to pin things on.'

'Johnathan had prior dealings with him. He fit the bill.'

'He was perfect. I hated him as soon as I saw him, wanted him to be behind it, was happy to latch onto what your stone gave me as proof. And of course you were always there with your advice, and to plant the occasional piece of evidence.' I pulled the razor from my satchel and tossed it on the ground. 'I take it you've got another prepared for Wren.'

Celia glanced at the instrument with which she had sacrificed a pair of children, then looked back up at me casually. 'How did you get into the Aerie?'

'The Crown's Eye has the ability to dispel minor workings. I used Crispin's to force my way in. You remember Crispin? Or do they all start to blend together?'

'I remember him.'

'Let's see now – there was Tara, and the Kiren you paid to kidnap her. And Carastiona, and Avraham. We've already mentioned my old partner. And upstairs the Master took the straight razor cure rather than face what you've become – though I'm not sure suicide adds to your tally.'

Brightfellow stiffened in surprise, but Celia only blinked. 'It saddens me very much to hear that.'

'You seem real broken up.'

'I was prepared for it.'

'I guess you were – that's what all this was for, wasn't it? Preparing for the Crane's death. You never took over powering the wards, that was a lie; you can't, and you knew once the Master died his working would go with him.'

'The Master was a genius,' she said, and a flicker of regret passed over her features. 'No one could do what he did. I was forced to seek out alternatives.'

'You mean murdering adolescents.'

'If you want to put it that way.'

'And giving them the plague?'

'An unfortunate requirement of the ritual. Necessary, though unpleasant.'

'For them especially.'

Brightfellow made his entrance into the conversation with gusto. 'Why are you telling him this? Kill him, before he ruins everything!'

'No one's going to do anything rash,' Celia commanded.

'How about you, Brightfellow? You in this for the good of the city? Somehow I hadn't pegged you for a humanitarian.'

'I don't care anything about this shithole. Let it burn to the ground.'

'A woman, then?'

He turned away, but I knew the answer.

'What did you think, you'd kill a couple of children and she'd fall madly in love with you?'

'I'm not a fool. I know I don't mean anything to her. I never meant anything to her, not back in the Academy, not ever. She said she needed my help. I couldn't let her do it alone.' He wasn't talking to me, but I was the only one listening.

'No one means anything to her. Something broke in her a long time ago; she didn't break it but it doesn't matter, it can't be fixed. She talks about Rigus, about Low Town but they aren't real to her. People aren't real to her.'

'You are,' he said. 'You're the only one – and you'll die for it.'

Celia snapped back to attention. 'Johnathan,' she started, but he'd already made his decision.

Four things happened then, more or less simultaneously. Brightfellow brought his arm up to perform some working, but before he could get it off there was the sound of meat sizzling, and the air was hot with burned flesh. That was the second thing. With the third I took shelter behind Celia, or seemed to.

The fourth happened very quickly, and Celia didn't notice.

Brightfellow looked at the red expanse that was now no longer covered by skin, an aperture deep enough to make out the cream of his ribcage. He swung his head back up to Celia, then pitched forward.

Celia's hand still glowed with the working that had killed Brightfellow. She began speaking immediately, the body in front of us forgotten as soon as she'd made it. 'Before you do anything, before you say anything, there are things you need to hear.' She strayed backwards, out of my effective range. 'What the Master did, the working he performed, it can't be duplicated. Do you understand? I didn't want to use the children, believe me, I didn't. I spent the last ten years in this damned tower, preparing for today, preparing for Father's death. I wish I was better.' Her eyes shut, then fluttered open. 'By the Firstborn I wish I was better. But I'm not. With the Master dead his ward no longer holds. It's winter now, but once the weather warms – you don't understand what it will be like if the plague comes back.'

'I remember what it was like. Don't say that again.'

She sighed in acknowledgment. 'Yes, I suppose you do.'

I thought she would continue. When she didn't I took over. 'Why do you need Wren?'

'We needed a child with potential in the Art. They aren't so easy to find.' Her voice carried the barest trace of apology, but it was so light I might have imagined it. 'We didn't have time to look further afield.'

'And you knew snatching him up would drive me after the Blade.'

'Yes.'

I tried to keep how I felt about what she was saying off my face but I must have failed because her lips closed tight and she snapped at me. 'Don't look at me like that. I could have killed you, you know. I could have set the thing on you at any time, or let you freeze in the snow.'

'You're a peach.' It felt like something had burrowed its way into my brain, a spiny creature that had taken root in the center of my skull and now was playing havoc with my tissue. The only thing keeping me on my feet was too much breath, and I had to strain to hear Celia, so fierce was the din echoing through my ears. 'What happened to you?'

'I appreciate what I've traded – I have no illusions. But I won't let the Master's work be in vain, I won't let it go back to the way it was. Ten thousand mothers, twenty thousand fathers, dead stacked like walls, more than you can count in a week's worth of counting. Summer after summer, year after year. I don't expect you to forgive me, I can't imagine anyone would – but come next summer the people of Low Town won't rot like carrion in the sun.'

'I guess this high up it gets hard to see faces. Dig a child out of the mud and you might do your sums different.'

'I didn't think you'd understand.'

'Maybe I'm not the altruist you are. I murdered men today – some of them didn't deserve it.'

'People die,' she said, and there was no arguing that. 'I did what I did – I had hoped you would never learn. But it's too far along to stop it. I won't let the sacrifices be in vain. I owe them that much. I won't let anyone stop me, not even you. And you will try, won't you?'

'Yes.'

'Do you remember that day before you left for the War?'

'Yes.'

'Do you remember what you said to me?'

'Yes.'

'I guess you were wrong. I'm more like you than you thought.'

'No, Celia,' I said, holding up her necklace, the one she'd worn since I'd first met her, the one she'd used to bind her abomination to her soul, the one I'd snatched while she was saving my life a moment earlier. 'You aren't anything like me.'

Her hands flew to her neck. 'How . . . how did you . . .'

'I'm taking Wren now,' I said, picking him up from the chair and throwing him over my shoulder. I kept the pendant between us. It seemed to squirm in my hand, and had an uncanny warmth.

'He's fine, he isn't infected, there's nothing wrong with him,' she stuttered, her eyes doe-wide and fixed on the bauble. 'You need to put that down, you don't understand what that is, you need to—'

I snapped the charm in half. 'Too much blood, Celia – too much blood.'

The color drained from her face. A low whistling filled the air, and a gust of wind kicked open the shuttered windows. We stood staring at each other. She looked like she wanted to say something, but didn't.

Thank the Oathkeeper for what blessings he provides.

I felt it coming and stepped into the stairwell, my stomach clenching up in terror. The thing congealed from the wall behind her, and she gave me one last look, her eyes mournful and condemning.

Not everything needs to be chronicled. Suffice to say after that things got pretty terrible.

49

I was sitting on the top of one of Kid Mac's houses a few days later, a block or so from the Aerie, watching Rigus mourn the Blue Crane. His body, carefully preserved and dressed in his finest robes – the kind I had never once seen him wear – lay on a golden pedestal atop a small stage. Seated on the podium were the cream of the city's business and aristocratic elite, a few dozen nobles the Master couldn't have picked out of a line-up. The stage was surrounded with security, not the hoax either – military men with halberds at the ready, scanning the crowd for any signs of disturbance. Around this core virtually the entirety of Low Town had come to pay their final respects.

It was still bitterly cold, but it hadn't snowed since that last night. What remained had turned to the unattractive mixture of sleet, dirt and shit that characterizes a city snowdrift. Mac and I passed a joint back and forth, adding graphite-colored smoke into the already gray sky. This last batch of dreamvine had been particularly dull – if things didn't improve I'd start looking for another wholesaler.

The Patriarch was praising the virtues of the deceased on the platform below – at least that was what I assumed was happening. My hearing hadn't fully recovered, and between that and the low murmur of the crowd I was having difficulty making out the speech. Mac didn't seem impressed. I doubted I was missing much of substance.

'You knew him, right?' Mac asked.

Behind us a couple of his whores were smoking cigarettes and sobbing quietly, happy for the opportunity to indulge their innate sense of melodrama.

'Yeah.'

'What was he like?'

'He was fairly tall,' I said.

Yancey was down there somewhere, surrounded by the sweaty assemblage that had filtered in for the ceremony. I called him back from hiding after it was all over. He said we were square but I didn't think he meant it. Regardless, he had been right about what he said that day on the roof – it would be a long time before I'd be invited back for lunch at Ma Dukes'.

In retrospect I didn't think the Blade would have gone so far as to hurt him. I had misread Beaconfield. I had misread a lot of people. The Old Man cleaned up the mess, and if he knew I'd gotten the wrong man he didn't care, filing it away to use against me should the situation warrant it. As far as he was concerned the whole thing had wrapped up neatly enough. The murders in Low Town stopped and a famed but irrelevant member of the peerage had an unfortunate accident with his furnace. Lord Beaconfield was the last of his line, and in contrast to the glittering soirée only a few days prior, his funeral was sparsely attended. For all his celebrity he was not well-loved, and outside of his creditors few mourned his loss.

Wren lounged against the railing. If it had been up to him he'd be down there with the rest of the city, but ever since his return Adeline had been wary about leaving him unattended. If he remembered anything about being taken, or his time spent under Brightfellow's spell, he never mentioned it to me. He was a tough little runt. He'd be all right.

I wasn't so sure about Low Town. There had been talk of turning the Aerie into a free clinic, but we'd see how that went. The Crane had no family, and with Celia gone there was no one left to look after his estate. It was hard to imagine the government would dispose of his property in a fashion advantageous to the general population. Either way, Low Town would miss its protector.

As far as the wards went – we'd have to wait till summer to see what would happen. Not every year had brought the plague, and the city's medical care and sanitation had improved since the epidemic that had orphaned me.

But some nights the dreamvine wasn't enough and I'd wake up in a sweat, thinking about the carts they'd sent to collect the dead, one-man traps piled high with rotting flesh. Nights like that I'd nip a bottle of whiskey from the cupboard, sit by the fire and drink until I couldn't remember why I started. There wasn't much else to do.

'I'm gonna head back,' I said. Mac nodded and turned to watch the proceedings. Wren looked up as I passed. 'If I let you out of my sight, do you promise not to get killed?'

He laughed and sprinted downstairs. He'd be all right. Later, when I thought he was old enough, I'd get him the training his talents required. But not at the Academy – he'd never have some government worm whispering counsel into his ear. There were still practitioners out there unaffiliated with the Crown. I'd find one.

The walk back seemed longer than usual, and not just because my boots were soaked through with slush. There wouldn't be much call for me to come back to the Aerie, not any more. My days of navigating that stone labyrinth were over. It would have been better for everyone if they hadn't started up again.

The Earl was slow when I came in, Adeline preparing for the dinner rush and Adolphus leaning against the bar, roots going down through the cellar, a tired smile on his face. He waved at me and I waved back. Neither of us said anything.

I took a seat at a back table, and Adolphus came over with a pint of stout. I waited for the bar to fill up, pulling from my drink until it was gone. It didn't help much, but I called for another one anyway.

ACKNOWLEDGEMENTS

A lot of people helped me finish the book, and a lot of people just generally help me. Some of these are:

Chris Kepner, who took a shot on me when (not exaggerated for effect) no one else was interested.

Robert Bloom, who was instrumental in turning the novel in your hands into something that actually made sense, instead of just kind of making sense.

Oliver Johnson, for advice and assistance, and obviously for publishing my book.

Sahtiya Logan, without whose early aid and encouragement I might still be working that 9-5 grind.

David Polansky, Michael Polansky, and Peter Backof, who were kind enough to give their feedback on an overwritten, poorly edited manuscript with an extremely gratuitous sex scene. And in all three cases, for a great deal more than that.

John Lingan, who was kind enough to sort of give feedback on an overwritten, poorly edited manuscript, and who also has a wife and child so gets a free pass.

Dan Stack, whose excellence as a photographer made up for my deficiencies as a subject, and whom I practically speaking owe a couple of thousand dollars to.

Marisa Polansky, my biggest fan and staunchest supporter, a princess with the heart of a lion.

The Boston Polanskys, even Ben, despite his inability to return a phone call.

The Mottolas broadly speaking, with apologies that I've missed two Thanksgivings – in particular my Uncle Frank and Aunt Marlene, who put me up for a week and whom I never properly thanked, and for my Aunt Connie, aka Mom #2.

Robert Ricketts, whose advice on medical matters was less critical than he supposes, but whose years of friendship have been an incomparable gift. And who really ought to be thanking me for working him into the text.

Michael Rubin, a kinder, sweeter gentleman I have yet to meet – with apologies for not being able to write a black-tongued Jewish dwarf into the manuscript. Maybe the sequel.

Will Crane, for generally being the man.

Alex Cameron, who is staunchly not the above, but an all right individual just the same, I guess, maybe.

Lisa Stockdale, heir to Edward the Black, 'Hindoo' Stuart and T.E. Lawrence – and a true and dear friend.

Alissa Piasetski, for advice.

John Grega, a paragon of virtue and wisdom, for sharing some of that stock with myself.

Kristen Kopranos, R.I.P.

Julie, Tim, and the rest of the Snaprag crew.

Envictus, whose assistance was as unwitting as it was instrumental.

Everyone who put me up during my various travels – hope to get you back some day.

Lots of other people, with apologies that I didn't get to you specifically.

Last, definitively not least, Martina.